TALES OF THE UNDYING EMPIRE

The Tower of Dust

ANDREW J. LUTHER

VANISHING GOBLIN

www.vanishing-goblin.com

The Tower of Dust

© 2012 by Andrew J. Luther

All rights reserved.

ISBN: 9780993650260

Vanishing Goblin Inc.
www.vanishing-goblin.com

For Pam

You've been with me all this way, and it never would have happened without you.

By Andrew J. Luther

Tales of the Undying Empire

Undying Empire: Rebellion

Acknowledgements: There are a few people I want to thank for helping me with this novel.

My wife, Pam, for helping me make time, for listening to my ideas, and for all the great feedback.

Dan and Bev for reviewing the text and pointing out inconsistencies and errors. The book is much stronger due to your feedback.

And I want to thank Dean Wesley Smith for his series of web articles Killing the Sacred Cows of Publishing (found at www.deanwesleysmith. com). These articles convinced me that I didn't need to write for the particular tastes of some hypothetical editor of a major publishing house. I just needed to tell a good story.

Prologue

I T WASN'T JUST THAT SOMEONE HAD TO DIE EVERY TIME A SHIP crossed the water of the bay. There are few adults in the Empire who are squeamish about taking a life. Few children, too, come to think of it.

It also wasn't the danger. Sea captains faced much the same every time they dared the Straits of Yadasuir. The crystal storms ripped up the ships just as well as those tentacles, and were far more unpredictable at that.

It certainly wasn't the cost. Crippled slaves seemed to be just as good to the beast under the waves as young virgins, at a substantial savings for those same captains. It cost little more than a round of drinks at a local dive.

No, it was none of those things. I sat with Captain Bakiah of the *Final Spirit* in some nameless hole on the edge of the wharf and listened as the big man, slabs of forearm muscle crossed above his belly, explained why he wasn't coming back until the creature in the bay was gone.

"Can't keep it up. My guts are like knotted ropes."

I nodded sagely, disturbed by the unlikely admission of weakness from a Sea Captain—a man who needed to be respected, always in command of himself and others.

"But there's little danger, now, isn't there? If you keep making the sacrifices, your ship comes and goes as you want."

He shook his head.

"Danger? Pah! Tis not my concern. I seen the beast open the belly of the *Windroarer* from bow to stern. I seen it eat them all up as they thrashed about in the water. Death don't scare me."

"Then what does?"

He squinted at me and my impertinent question. He was already trying to pretend his admission of fear a moment ago had never happened. He shifted his bulk on the seat, and the wood groaned slightly. If the damn thing broke, he'd have to give me a pounding, just for witnessing two humiliations back-to-back.

I prayed silently for the chair to hold together another five minutes.

"Okay, why are you going to be avoiding Ythis if you're not worried about danger?"

"Cuz sacrifices are somethin' that priests do. Or sorcerers. It's not right for me ta be doing it. It's like I'm...."

He leaned in close.

"Like I'm *worshippin'* the damned thing. Bein' a priest for it."

Of course. He wasn't worried about dying. He was worried about what happened *after* he died. Ythis already has a god, and our gods don't like competition.

But that was the dilemma. Iathephos—the god who inhabited the city of Ythis—dwelt in the depths of the Temple, just over a mile away from the shores of the bay. Yet, as close as it was, it had done nothing to indicate its displeasure at the presence of the horror that now lurked in the dark waters.

Even the priests were at a loss. It was a political hot potato and somehow—through some threats, agreements, and maneuvering well above my head—it had ended up in the hands of my employer. And thus, it had landed in *my* lap.

"I understand your situation. It's not one I'd like to be in. And we're working on getting the beast out of the bay. But we lack information. I've been on ships when they made the sacrifices properly. What I need to know is what happened that day when the *Windroarer* was destroyed. Your *Final Spirit* was the closest ship. What can you tell me about it?"

The Captain reached out and grabbed his mug, took a long swallow from it, and slowly wiped his hand across his mouth. Then he settled back in his poor chair—with another alarming groan—and considered the memory.

"We were comin' in under power of the oarsmen, cuz there was no wind. I was at the helm, and all other hands were keepin' a close eye out for sign of the beast. The *Windroarer* was behind us, maybe five lengths out, waitin' her turn.

"The call came from the nest, and I checked ta see where he was pointin'. I grabbed my knife and my First Mate brought the boy over ta the side with me. I remember that boy soiled hisself, and the smell turned my guts.

"I grabbed him by his hair and leaned over the side. As I looked down, I saw a ripple in the water, and I think I saw one of those tentacles with the ridges on it just under the surface.

"I yanked the boy's head backwards, swiped my knife across his throat, and shoved him over the side. Before I could look away, the creature grabbed the body, and I saw something dark and... *vast*... moving through the murk. I heard a rushin' noise in my ears, and my nose started bleedin'.

"I ordered my oarsmen ta start rowin', and we passed the spot quickly. The *Windroarer* moved in behind us. I didn't look back at first—I didn't want ta see any more of that thing. Then I heard shoutin' and the first crack of timber.

"I can only guess Captain Eshyo was moving forward slowly, looking for sign of the beast, which may have been busy with the body I just gave it. It don't matter. He moved in too far.

"I think they started yelling when the first tentacle reached out of the water. Eshyo tried ta send his sacrifice over, but I think she fell down on the deck and by then it was too late.

"The beast grabbed the *Windroarer*. I wasn't countin', but I think it was at least five of those tentacles. Men were running around and shoutin'. Some grabbed weapons and started to hack at the beast.

"But then, somethin' just under the waterline ran down the length of the ship, and the whole bottom just fell apart. The deck was crushed an instant later as those tentacles just flexed and ripped it ta shreds.

"After that, everyone was in the water. Most died from the destruction of the ship, but some were still screamin'. Those tentacles pulled back under the water, and one by one, the crew was plucked under, until there was no one left."

It was a horrible way to die. If, indeed, they *were* dead. There was no way to know what the creature had done to them down there. It was possible that the crew of the Windroarer now inhabited some kind of underwater temple dedicated to the worship of this alien beast. The fact that some of them were dead before they hit the water wasn't much comfort. I've seen what the priests can do to a dead man.

"When do you ship out?"

"We'll pull out at sunrise. One last crossin' of that bay, and then we'll not be back until the creature is gone."

I nodded and stood up. I glanced down at the splayed legs of his chair and hoped he would stand, too.

"Thank you for the recounting, Captain. We intend to remove the beast, one way or another. I'm sure word will get around once it's in your interests to return here again."

The Captain leaned forward, and I heard a small crack, but the chair held another moment.

"I hope you're successful, but I don't believe you will be. They tried to get rid of the gods, way back when. It didn't turn out so well for them as tried. I believe this thing in the bay is of a like with them—maybe smaller, less powerful, but plenty powerful enough ta face whatever you can throw at it. I don't envy you your duty, Mister Zale."

I didn't really have anything to say to that. At least, nothing that would comfort either the Captain or me. So I left Captain Bakiah sitting on an almost-broken chair in a smelly dive just off the wharf.

I went to see Veylar Dust.

Chapter One

I HATE SORCERERS. NASTY BASTARDS, THE LOT OF THEM. They make pacts with demons, sacrifice innocents, and impose their dark wills upon the people of the Empire.

Of course, the priests are worse. But they're all *crazy*, even before they join the Church. You could say that a certain level of madness is a mandatory part of the job. The truly sane simply don't get called by the gods to serve in the priesthood.

Not that it makes any difference to those whose lives are impacted by the actions of either group. Still, the priests can be excused for some of their actions. Sorcerers just do what they want because they can. Like I said, nasty bastards.

And yet, in spite of all that, I am a sworn enemy of the priesthood, previously Marked by the Church for death. Only my service to the sorcerer Veylar Dust, one of the Five, prevents anyone from carrying out the Mark.

And that's the result of me trying to keep my brother from joining the Church a few years ago. I succeeded in that goal, in a manner of speaking. I took him from the Church, and he died shortly after. The Church neither forgives nor forgets, though. And thus, my ongoing service to a different evil.

I was standing in a chamber in Veylar Dust's tower, a five-story, gray spike that thrust up into the sky as if it was trying to rip into the blue curtain above it. The room was dominated by a large table, now hidden under a pile of written works; scrolls crawling with spidery script that caused my eyes to water if I looked at it directly, huge tomes wrapped in human skin and marked with strange symbols, ancient books that seemed to throb with dark power. It was a collection of secrets that could drive a man beyond madness to a terrifying level of comprehension of the darkest parts of the cosmos.

I had just finished telling Veylar Dust about my conversation with Captain Bakiah. The sorcerer stood at the one window, looking out over the city at the bay from his vantage point almost five stories above the ground. His black and red robes fluttered slightly as if there was a breeze coming in the window, though I knew there was not.

One of Veylar Dust's apprentices, a young man named Ankin Poloth, sat at the table poring over a map of the land around the bay. I rarely spoke to the five apprentices who served Veylar Dust. Their distance was exactly what I wanted.

The sorcerer turned his gaze on me, and a faint chill touched me. To look into his eyes was to see raw power, wielded by a mind soaked in darkness. After two years in his service, I was still not fully used to being near him.

I was forced to look away from his eyes, from his face with its sharp nose and high cheekbones. Despite the small touch of grey in his hair, it was impossible to guess his age. I knew that sorcerers had ways to prolong their lives, but they would never discuss such a thing with others. I had heard that the price of such gifts was very high, and very personal.

He focused on Ankin.

"What have you found in the Chronicles of Naidea?"

The apprentice raised his gaze from the map and frowned.

"A few vague references have some similarities to what we know of the creature in the bay, but nothing that suggests a pattern or that it is anything more than a coincidence. What we have—a blood lust, huge size, and ridged tentacles—even taken together it is hardly a unique combination."

Veylar Dust nodded.

"It's time to widen the search."

I knew what that meant. Veylar Dust was about to call forth a demon.

He closed his eyes and stood very still. Even his robes stopped shifting around him. I had an idea of what he was doing. Being around a powerful sorcerer and his apprentices had given me some insight into the process, though I could not perform such a task myself.

Veylar Dust had cast his mind into a dark gulf of nothingness that existed just beyond consciousness—into the Abyss. He would be concentrating on some sorcerous symbol that allowed him to pull his demon into this world, careful not to let his mind's eye gaze down into that bottomless well.

There was a subtle shift in the air and then the demon, Xiqon, was standing in front of the sorcerer, clothed in the semblance of a man.

I've always found it unsettling how demons manifest. Even though I was watching carefully, I didn't see the demon appear, *couldn't* see it appear. Xiqon was suddenly *there all along*. It was something else that I've never gotten used to, and don't think I ever will.

I stepped back a pace and was, as usual, struck by the wrongness of the creature's form. Xiqon's skin looked human from a distance, but if one were unfortunate enough to come closer, it would become apparent that it was far too smooth and completely hairless. There was a predatory feeling about the demon's stance and build, as if it was always just a hair's breadth away from leaping forward and ripping a large hole in anyone near him. And his eyes, always a shade too bloodshot.

Taken together, the effect was just enough to make Xiqon *feel* unnatural, which he certainly was. The mere presence of a demon was a tumor on the skin of reality, an aching wound that should not be. Sorcerers, however, found them to be very useful tools.

Veylar Dust turned to Ankin.

"Summon your demon. You've been concentrating on that map—clear it from your mind before you start."

Ankin nodded and closed his eyes. And his own demon, Ixal, was now on the table in front of him.

Ixal didn't take human form. It scuttled across the surface on nine segmented legs, a bloated, corpse-white blob of flesh the size of Ankin's head. It had no eyes, mouth, or other facial features that I could recognize, but they weren't necessary. As repulsive as the demon was, its appearance was only a pale shadow of the creature's true, hideous form—something that mortal minds simply cannot process.

I realized Veylar Dust was speaking to Xiqon.

"...there are connections that may have some relevance in the Chronicles of Naidea. Ankin will give you the references, and you will go immediately to the ruins of Qarwen to see if you can locate one of the key stone tablets in the vaults under the palace. Report back to me in four hours regardless of what you do or do not find."

Xiqon turned his blood-gaze on the apprentice, who was giving instructions to Ixal. From the window, I heard a strange howl faintly on the air. I ignored it. Such sounds are not uncommon in Ythis.

"Tell me the whereabouts of Tholl's Ledger. If you don't know where it is, return to the Abyss and make a connection to something that does know. I only want the location, not for you to recover it."

Ankin turned back to me, but Ixal didn't move. The demon remained motionless on the table. I watched Ankin look back at it, puzzled.

And then it struck.

A scorpion tail appeared on its back as Ixal leaped on Ankin's torso, the razor-sharp tips of its legs sinking into his flesh in nine different places, pinning itself to his body. A horrid scream exploded from Ankin's throat as the scorpion stinger plunged into his left eye and then his right, instantly liquefying both orbs into streams of bloody froth. He convulsed backwards onto the floor, the stinger plunging again and again into his face, which began to melt, skull and flesh both.

I was frozen in shock, unable to move. One long second passed, and then another, as Ankin experienced a tortuous death straight out of anyone's worst nightmare. With a supreme effort, I wrenched my gaze from Ankin's wrecked body and turned to Veylar Dust.

For the first time since I had met Lord Dust, I saw a look of shock on the face of the sorcerer. I had thought nothing could surprise such a man, and it terrified me even more to see his hesitation.

I understood why he was stunned into inaction. Ixal was a bound demon. Such creatures simply *couldn't* turn on their masters. It was impossible. And yet it was happening in front of us.

Suddenly, he snapped out of it and gained control of himself.

"Xiqon, destroy Ixal now!"

For the barest instant, Xiqon appeared to hesitate, and in that instant, I knew the demon was going to turn on Veylar Dust. The bindings of all demons were breaking, and there would come a slaughter of sorcerers in the city and across the continent, the destruction of the Empire, the death of my species.

But then Xiqon was moving too fast to follow, had ripped Ixal off the shuddering mess that was Ankin's dying body, and had torn into the other demon with distended jaws of massive, curved teeth. Ixal screamed without sound, a pulse of thunder inside my head that smelled of blood and feces, and then the demon's body was in two pieces.

A thick, black smoke poured from both severed ends, and I forced myself to move, to bolt for the door. The smoke drifted down to the floor and caressed Ankin, who was still kept alive by the demon's power as his flesh turned to acid and his bones shattered into pieces. As the smoke touched him, his body burst open in dark green, pestilent eruptions of rotten gasses.

With terror driving my movements, I reached the door and flung myself into the hallway. I could hear, over the sound of my own frantically beating heart, the rustling of Veylar Dust's robes as he followed me.

I turned to see the sorcerer's face stretched in a rictus of fear. I suddenly found my breath and howled a great scream of horror that hammered forth from my lungs like an explosion.

My scream felt like it went on forever as Veylar Dust reached out and placed his palm on my chest. I ran out of breath and stopped, and felt an unnatural calm come over me. I noticed the room behind me had become silent as the sounds of battle, more felt than heard, were cut off.

The door to the room hung open, but no shadows moved in the failing light from the window.

And then Xiqon was standing between me and Veylar Dust.

I looked at the demon and couldn't move. What had just happened was impossible. Ankin's demon had turned on its master. A bound demon had attacked a sorcerer. And now Xiqon was within reach and I was no longer sure that Veylar Dust's control over the demon was real or just a massive cosmic joke.

"I have consumed Ixal. You should not enter your room until the smoke fully disperses, at least five hours from now."

Xiqon's voice as he spoke to the sorcerer was all bass; a deep rumble that always sounded as if it came from a few feet to the demon's left. I noticed that the fiend no longer looked quite so predatory. His appearance was gaunt, as if he had been consumed from the inside during the battle with Ixal.

My own voice was barely more than croak.

"What happened in there?"

Veylar Dust looked at me and frowned. In that instant, I could tell he was weighing my worth to him against keeping secret what I had just witnessed.

"Ankin's demon broke its binding and attacked him."

"But I thought that couldn't happen."

Veylar Dust didn't reply. He took my arm and guided me toward the stairs without looking back. I wasn't so calm. I glanced back at the doorway and noticed that Xiqon was already gone, returned to the depths of the Abyss.

I had the feeling I had just witnessed the universe change in a very bad way.

*　　　　*　　　　*

VEYLAR DUST LED ME DOWN THE STAIRS, HIS HAND ON MY arm not for support, but to make sure I was going where he wanted me to go. We were met on the stairs by his other four apprentices, who had come running as they felt the demonic battle begin above their heads. Seeing me with their master, they held back the questions obvious on their faces.

"There was an incident upstairs. No one is to go into the upper floors until I give you permission."

Veylar Dust's voice was back to its usual commanding tone.

"In addition, you are to abstain from calling forth your demons for the immediate future. We will meet shortly. Be prepared for my summons."

The four sorcerers-in-training bowed their heads to their master and returned to the lower floors. I was led into a small chamber, bare except for a single chair and a small table with a pitcher of water and one mug. The sorcerer motioned me to sit, and I nearly fell into the chair.

"Lord Dust, what is happening?"

I could hear the note of barely held panic in my own voice.

"I do not know."

That certainly didn't make me feel any better.

"I thought...what happened in there...wasn't possible."

He just looked at me and remained silent.

"If demons can just break their bindings like that, then none of us are safe. By the Abyss, Xiqon *hesitated* when you ordered him to destroy Apprentice Poloth's demon! You told him to attack, and he just stood there and looked at you!

"What if your demon isn't truly under your control? What if it's all a trick, a plan to make sorcerers like you complacent? We're all so caught up in political maneuvering, fighting for power against the Church, that no one ever questions it anymore.

"*What if they've been in control all this time?*"

I stood up suddenly, knocking the small table and tipping the mug. The liquid poured across the surface of the table, and I could no longer keep my stomach in check. I vomited forcefully into the spilled water, sending drops flying. I wiped my watering eyes and grabbed the chair, trying to keep my balance.

"Sit down, Borolt!"

Veylar Dust's voice cut through my panic—he wasn't interested in wasting time watching me lose control. I sat back down and put my head in my hands. I was not ashamed to admit that I was no stranger to fear. I had set myself against the Church. I willingly served a sorcerer, someone who made pacts with living abominations. In ancient tomes he read secrets that drove lesser men mad. He played an ongoing chess game against a priesthood dedicated to an alien God. And the Abyss was always waiting for one misstep, one lapse in concentration.

No, fear was not new. I had felt fear many, many times before, just not on this scale. But that was a matter of degrees. I could master this fear just as I mastered any other fear.

Fear could be useful, but not here, not now. I needed to be able to think. I needed to separate my emotions from what had just happened. And that's something else to which I was no stranger.

I felt myself slowly calming down, my heart rate slowing to a reasonable pace, my hands steadying. To live the life I had chosen, you had to gain mastery over yourself or you would never survive. I used that mastery to regain control. At first it was slippery, tenuous. But I held on and the grip became solid.

I carefully packaged up my fear and let it drift above me. The cloud was black and pregnant with terror, revulsion, regret. It tried to reach back down and take me, but I pushed it higher and higher until it was out of reach.

I looked up at my master.

"I apologize, Lord Dust."

He waved away my apology as if it was expected from a mere mortal.

"You are right, Borolt. What happened in my chamber should not be possible. Therefore, either the foundation of sorcery is built on a lie, or what we believe happened is not what truly occurred."

"I don't understand."

"I have a suspicion that we saw what *appeared* as if Apprentice Poloth's demon turned on him. But appearances can be deceiving. And further, I have no lack of enemies who would go to great lengths to deceive me."

"But your demon—"

"Did not hesitate to follow my orders, but merely evaluated the situation for an instant to ensure my safety. It is something he is bound to consider in any situation. Your fear made you perceive that instant as longer than it was."

I wasn't quite ready to accept that, but I didn't have much choice. "So, what do we do?"

"You will return to your own residence. I will send a summons if I require your services."

I was in no condition to argue, and I really didn't want to remain in the Tower a minute longer than necessary. I nodded dumbly to the sorcerer and left the tower of Veylar Dust.

As I walked the streets of Ythis, I looked around me at the ancient city and its people. The sun was almost behind the western hills, and the stars were winking into appearance across the sky.

By the time I reached the room that I rented above the Sailor's Knot tavern, I had almost convinced myself that Veylar Dust would discover the truth behind what had occurred this evening.

I fell onto my mattress and stared at the beams crossing my ceiling. Two hours later, sleep had still not come. I was also no longer convinced that this was a matter that was outside my abilities. I had a feeling in my gut that we had missed something vital, something mundane.

I would have to go back to the tower first thing in the morning and convince Veylar Dust to let me help.;

With a purpose in mind, I fell asleep shortly after.

Chapter Two

JUST AFTER DAYBREAK, I ROSE FROM A DREAMLESS SLEEP. I was surprised at such a peaceful night, considering what I had been witness to in the early evening. Yet I truly felt refreshed.

I dressed and went down to the Sailor's Knot. Jolin was just opening the doors, and he grunted what passed for a greeting.

Jolin was perhaps the surliest of all the tavern owners in Ythis. No one remembers ever seeing Jolin smile, crack a joke, or be satisfied with anything. He worked hard running the Sailor's Knot and managed the place in a professional manner. His perpetual scowl, however, had eventually driven away some of the business on which he had once relied.

I stepped around his barrel shape and entered the dim confines of the tavern. Three bodies lay on the floor in various states of unconsciousness. One man snored so hard he was in danger of swallowing his tongue. A second man continually shifted position, trying to find a more comfortable spot on the hard-wooden floor. The last was silent and still. I looked closer to make sure that his chest was rising and falling.

Satisfied that I would not be dining among any corpses, I sat myself at a table while Jolin walked over and began to kick the men awake. Amidst the muttering and cursing of the customers, Jolin told me that there was little food available this morning.

I accepted a stale hunk of bread and some cheese, washed down with lukewarm water. Not the way I'd like to start my day, but I've been in worse situations—much worse—so I wasn't about to complain.

By the time I left the tavern, the sun was fully up and already the stone slabs in the road were beginning to bake. It was going to be another hot and humid day.

As I did every morning, I looked up across the skyline to the Church, a huge black beetle jammed in among the dirty businesses and homes. I made the sign of the ward against evil and spat in the direction of the huge building. As usual, people out on the street gave me a wide berth when they saw me perform my morning ritual.

Not many people would openly mock the Church in such a manner. And most who did would soon disappear. It was self-correcting, in a manner of speaking.

I was sweating by the time I reached the Tower of Dust. I was let in by one of the servants whose name I couldn't remember and, surprisingly, was shown straight into Veylar Dust's office.

"I gave you instructions to wait for my summons. I do not have time—or the inclination—to comfort you, Borolt Zale

I nodded but did not apologize.

"I should be part of your investigation into this matter, Lord Dust. I believe that there is more to this situation than how it appears."

Veylar Dust raised an eyebrow.

"Do you? Have you been studying sorcery on your own time, or are you merely repeating what I told you last night?"

"Neither, Lord Dust. And I know that what happened yesterday had to do with sorcery, and I can't help you with that. But I have a strong feeling that there's something else...I can't put my finger on it, exactly. But I noticed something yesterday, something I feel in my gut."

The sorcerer leaned back in his chair and rested his hands on his desk.

"I cannot spare your time to help me with this matter. The situation with the creature in the bay has not been resolved. I require you to track down some leads and gather information for me."

I wanted to sit down, but he hadn't offered me the chair, and I knew it would only make him angry and less likely to hear me out.

"Lord Dust, if I'm going to be out there in the city already, then there's no reason to keep me out of this investigation. There's no telling what leads I might ignore if I'm unaware of where your investigation is heading."

Veylar Dust just shook his head.

"Do you know how long I have studied sorcery?"

I was thrown off guard by this question. It wasn't something for which I had a ready answer.

"No, Lord."

"I am one of the Five. I sit on the Council and advise the Emperor. I oppose the Church, both directly and through more subtle means. I have discovered the answers to mysteries that were thousands of years old. I have bargained with demons and spoken with gods. Yet you talk to me of the feelings in your 'gut' and expect me to take it seriously. You cannot help me. You have neither the knowledge nor the experience to understand what happened yesterday. And I do not have the time to answer all the questions you will inevitably have. If you remember something specific, send me a message. In the meantime, I have other tasks for you to handle."

He began to look through his journal for some notes. I waited for a moment and realized that he had ended this discussion. He would give me some instructions and then dismiss me to carry them out.

I knew that I should keep my mouth shut. The only thing that kept me alive was the patronage of this sorcerer. If he should withdraw his protection, then the Church would immediately come after me. I held no illusions that I would survive long enough to get out of the city.

But I couldn't just ignore my instincts. I knew there was something else going on here. And I felt that it was not entirely related to sorcery. I had no idea why I was so sure. But that certainty had saved my life before, and I would ignore it only at my own peril.

"Lord Dust, please believe me when I say that I don't question your power or your knowledge. I understand why you believe I cannot be of any help. But you said something yesterday that stuck in my mind: you have enemies who would go to great lengths to deceive you. How could anyone deceive Lord Dust, though? You are a master of sorcery. The mysteries of the universe are yours to explore. How do you deceive someone with such great knowledge

Andrew J. Luther

of magic? You do it by mundane means. You do it not by playing to your strengths but to your weaknesses."

He frowned at me, but I realized he was listening, and I had to be careful how I framed my next words.

"Okay, perhaps you don't have any weaknesses at all. However, I think you must agree that your knowledge of sorcery rather significantly outstrips your knowledge of the criminal world. And that's what I'm talking about with my gut instinct.

"I *live* in that world. It's why I'm useful to you. What if the incident yesterday was somehow achieved by means that don't involve the twisting of sorcery's rules? What if you're looking in the wrong direction?"

I paused a moment. Veylar Dust was obviously considering the point I had made. He took a breath, was about to speak, but I asked one more question.

"What if you're doing exactly what your enemies expect you to do?"

He looked into my eyes and I felt once again that he was evaluating the value of my life.

"Tell me, Borolt, why this is so important to you."

Again, he asked a question for which I didn't have a ready answer.

"I don't know."

He waited, knowing it wasn't the truth.

"Okay, yesterday reminded me of my brother. When I saw Poloth's demon attack him, and I thought I was witnessing the end of the world, it reminded me of the day my brother told me he was chosen to join the Church. I couldn't just stand by and let him go down that path without fighting for his life, his mind, his soul. This feels the same to me, somehow. I honestly can't explain it any better than that."

Veylar Dust didn't react. He just turned back to his journal and located the notes for which he was searching. I realized I had failed to convince him.

"The smugglers who transfer contraband to and from the ships—they use small boats to bring their goods back and forth. Do they also make a sacrifice every time they cross the water? You will make contact with them and find out everything they know. It is an element we have overlooked."

He wasn't going to accept my involvement. I had a suicidal urge to tell him to shove his orders up his ass.

"Once that task is complete, you are to examine *Apprentice* Poloth's room. Specifically, I want you to find and read his journals. He was still interested in mundane matters, and there may be a clue to his death in his notes."

Veylar Dust leaned forward.

"You will, of course, avoid reading anything that appears to be written on the subject of sorcery. I assume you wish to keep your mind intact. Our tasks are important, and I believe we are rapidly running out of time. I expect regular reports."

He stood up and walked to the stairs, leaving me to find my own way out of the Tower of Dust.

I felt elated for just moment, as I realized I had really convinced him to change his mind.

And then I wondered what I had gotten myself into.

*   *   *

IN A CITY WHERE EVERYTHING IS FOR SALE, ONE WOULD think that smugglers have no place. But the Empire needs money to run, and that means taxes. Not everyone wants to give their fair share to the tax collectors, though. And some goods have much higher tariffs than others.

So Ythis has a thriving underground trade supported by a network of smugglers, ship captains, and go-betweens.

Smugglers use water to move most goods of any bulk. During the darkest hours, industrious men row their small skiffs out to the ships waiting at anchor, or even to those berthed at the docks. Goods are lowered by rope or taken aboard the same way. And then the skiffs return to other parts of the shoreline that lack the regular patrols of the Ythis Watch. It's a good system, greased by the money that finds its way into the pockets of many regular Watchmen.

But water is the key to its success. And now something that required sacrifices—one way or another—lived in the water of the bay. Were the smugglers prevented from plying their trade? Or had they adapted to the new threat and it was otherwise business as usual?

I knew the fastest way to an answer was to visit the Wolf's Den, an establishment located just off the Trade Way. The Wolf's Den supplied many services to a wide range of clientele. Within its walls, one could find short-term companionship, a place to sleep, sustenance, drink to drown your sorrows or celebrate your victories, men to buy stolen goods, and other men to sell goods of dubious origin.

The men of the Watch were paid well to let the Wolf's Den do its business without harassment. And a brisk business it was. So, on a late evening—hot and heavy with the promise of rain—I found myself handing over my weapons before being granted entry to this particular den of iniquity.

It was crowded, of course. The Wolf's Den is always crowded, and not with gentlemen. So, I shoved my way through the throng to the bar where Nid was working.

Nid technically owns the Wolf's Den, runs the business itself, and makes sure day-to-day operations continue smoothly. The place needs a steady supply of new girls, food, booze, and other consumables, and Nid makes it all happen. Needless to say, he's a busy man, with no time to carouse with his customers.

I had to call his name three times before he heard me. He was behind the bar, giving instructions to a couple of men who were obviously dockhands. He finished up his briefing and acknowledged me with a frown. I was getting a lot of those lately.

"Nid, I need a moment."

"Time is money, Zale. Can't one of my guys help you?"

I leaned in close.

"I need five minutes with the Wolf."

Nid snorted. Owner of the Wolf's Den he may be, but the Wolf is his boss. And his boss didn't meet with just anyone.

"I don't got time for this, Zale. Nothing you can tell me is gonna be big enough for him to want to talk to you. He's a busy man."

I could tell right away that coming in as a petitioner for a favor was not going to get me anywhere.

"We're all busy, Nid. And I don't have time to screw around with you right now. Go tell the Wolf that I need five minutes. *Now.*"

Nid looked at me, shocked. I was standing in *his* bar, surrounded by *his* people, not to mention the horde of customers who would jump at the chance to do him a favor and remove me from the premises in a violent manner on the off chance they might score some free services.

But I knew word had gotten around that I was working for one of the sorcerers now. The Church had put a price on my head, and then had suspended it indefinitely. That meant I had a powerful backer who could stand up to the Church. I was not a man to be ignored.

I held his gaze and waited. He considered my demand for a minute, and then nodded and motioned for me to follow him. We went through a side door and up two flights of stairs, down a couple of narrow corridors, and then down one level. I knew we were now in one of the buildings next door to the Wolf's Den. I wondered just how big this "den" really was.

Nid rapped on the door and then opened it and led me inside. Two very large men stood up from a couple of stools as we entered a small room with another door on the far side.

"This is Borolt Zale. He needs five minutes with the Wolf."

One of the bodyguards kept his eyes on mine as the second tapped softly on the other door and then stuck his head in and murmured to the occupant on the other side. Someone answered, and the door was swung open, the Wolf standing framed in red-tinged light.

The Wolf is a young man—at least I consider his late twenties to be much younger than one would expect for a man of his position. He is fit, but not particularly muscled or dangerous looking. He has two things going for him, however.

First, he's smart. He always knows what's going on in the city and what's more, he can predict with astonishing accuracy how certain events will fall out. Second, and perhaps more important, is his ability to talk to the common criminals of the city and convince them that he's got the answers to their biggest problems.

I was surprised to see him smile at me—I was expecting another frown—and he stepped forward and shook my hand.

"I'm not interrupting anything, am I?"

The two bodyguards looked at me in disbelief. This was not the 'right' way to talk to the Wolf.

"Just business, Mr. Zale. Always business, in fact."

He was about to lead from there into asking what I wanted, but I interrupted him. I could see the bodyguards get twitchy, but the Wolf just kept smiling, seemingly at ease.

"Don't get too wrapped in making money. If you don't enjoy the fruits of your labor, then what's the point?"

He chuckled.

"Oh, there'll be plenty of time to enjoy the money soon enough. But there's so much to accomplish right now."

He glanced back at the open doorway, obviously eager to get back to whatever he was doing before I had barged in. I decided not to drag this out.

"Well, there's a business-related matter I need to discuss with you."

"We can talk here. These men," he said, gesturing to his guards, "are absolutely loyal and know everything I do."

I smiled at the two men, but wasn't surprised when they regarded me coolly. It was their job, after all.

"You may have heard that I'm gainfully employed these days, and I'm following up on a couple of things for my patron."

The Wolf laughed out loud.

"'Gainfully employed?' That's a bit of an understatement, isn't it? I do believe you work for Veylar Dust, a sorcerer of no little power and renown. What I don't know is what Lord Dust would want from me."

"He needs information about smuggling, actually. Specifically, how have you been dealing with the creature in the bay? Do your little boats manage to avoid the notice of the beast? Or have you taken to spilling a little blood every time you need to bring in some goods?"

He was taken off guard by the blatant question. I hadn't lied to

Nid, though. I *was* too busy to screw around. Either the Wolf was going to give me the information I needed, or he wasn't.

He pretended to consider my questions.

"Well, one could argue that those are trade secrets. I'm sure there are others who would love to know how I maintain my network in the face of new challenges like this. I can hardly be expected to simply give away my own methods, can I?"

I had expected this. He felt safe. He lived under an assumed name, in the heart of a veritable fortress, protected by men who were loyal to the money he gave them. He believed he was untouchable.

It was time to rattle his cage.

"Fair enough, Timgar," I said, using his real name.

That earned me the frown that I had been expecting. He was quick on the uptake. He had gone to great lengths to hide his original identity, but I knew it.

And that meant that Veylar Dust, the sorcerer, knew it too. Most people live every day knowing their names can be used against them in some foul sorcery. They get used to it. But when a person reaches the point where he feels he's safe from such attacks...well, it can be quite disconcerting to find out he's not so safe after all.

"Careful, Borolt. Since you're an old friend, I'm willing to overlook some of your mistakes, but don't try to threaten me."

I smiled at him, but decided it was now time to play nice in front of his men.

"I'm not making any threats, Wolf. I'm just asking—politely and with all due respect—for your help. I apologize for being too familiar."

He saw what I was doing—giving him the chance to save face—and he gave me quick grin to show there were no hard feelings.

"All right, Borolt. What I tell you is between you, me, and your employer, and I'll know if you start leaking. We don't use the water anymore. I decided it was too risky. We simply take the cargo off right on the docks."

"But what about the tax collectors? How do you keep them from examining all the shipments?"

"Oh, that was the easy part. I arranged a few gifts, a few compromising situations. Now they work for me, and I pay well. Better than the Emperor, to be honest."

I know my face wasn't hiding my shock and disappointment.

"To be honest, the creature's appearance in the bay was ultimately a real boon for me. I wouldn't have tried to alter the status quo if I hadn't been forced by circumstance. But it's worked out to my benefit."

This wasn't what I had expected—or wanted—to hear. While I had learned something important about the Wolf's smuggling ring, I had learned nothing that would help us in figuring out the creature in the bay.

I was *not* looking forward to seeing Veylar Dust tomorrow.

Chapter Three

I HAD A STRANGE RELATIONSHIP WITH VEYLAR DUST'S apprentices. I didn't quite fit into the hierarchy that had developed in the Tower of Dust. I wasn't a sorcerer, of course, but neither was I on the same level as the servants who worked and lived in the tower itself.

I think it was my autonomy that bothered them the most. I maintained my own residence. I was given broad objectives by Lord Dust and left to my own methods. That freedom was denied them until Veylar Dust decided that they were of sufficient skill and experience.

There were always five apprentices in the tower. Ankin Poloth was one of three young people Veylar Dust had found on a trip to the western region of the Empire a couple of years ago. They replaced three apprentices who had been killed in a ritual gone wrong.

None of the apprentices were what you might call friends, though Ankin and the other two—a young woman named Gisea and a younger man named Arral—shared a common background and thus seemed to be more inclined to work with one another. As I mentioned earlier, however, sorcerers are not nice people. They don't really care about the well-being of others, and most people are seen as tools to be used as necessary.

So, it comes as no surprise that they didn't trust me. They didn't trust *anyone*. And they were therefore obviously unhappy about my orders to go through Ankin Poloth's chambers and read his journal. It didn't matter that I would be avoiding the writings on anything related to sorcery. I was still snooping into something they felt should remain entirely among the initiated.

I was standing in Ankin's study when Gisea interrupted my search. Quda, the chamberlain of Lord Dust, had given me access only half an hour earlier and I was still searching for the journal when I heard the door to the outer chamber open. I rested my hand on the pommel of the long dagger I always keep at my side and stepped to the doorway of the study.

Gisea was standing just inside the main entryway, her hand still on the door. She saw me and her eyes narrowed slightly. I was struck by the fact that she was a pretty girl, though from her expression she always seemed to be disapproving of whatever it was she was watching. But her long, dark hair contrasted nicely with the pale skin of her delicate features, and so I was always content to look at her.

I had no interest in going any farther than that, however.

She stepped into the room and closed the door behind her, and then turned to face me.

"You should not be in this room. You do not belong here."

I couldn't help but smile at that. It was exactly what I had expected her to say.

"Lord Dust has given me an errand. And you?"

Her hesitation told me that she didn't have permission to come in here. I decided to take the offensive.

"I would think that he'd be interested to hear why you have decided to sneak into Apprentice Poloth's room. Is there something in here you don't want me to find?"

She looked me up and down.

"This is a matter of sorcery. You are not one of us. You cannot understand what has happened. You are too arrogant, thinking you can help Lord Dust with this. I will be speaking to him about your involvement, and you will be banished from the Tower until this is over."

I couldn't read her, couldn't be sure that she wasn't after something else. She might just want me gone because she didn't trust me. Alternately, she might have been involved in something with Ankin Poloth which she didn't want to come out. If I found something like that, she would see it as me having power over her.

She didn't understand that I wasn't nearly stupid enough to try to blackmail a sorcerer.

"Lord Dust has asked me to help. Right now, you are keeping me from my duty to him."

I took a step toward her, hoping that she wouldn't take it as a physical threat.

"You can suggest to him that I should be kept out all you want. Until he orders me otherwise, I am going to perform the task to which he has set me. If you have nothing to hide, if there is nothing incriminating to you to be found here, then you have nothing to fear from me."

"Fear!" she spat back at me. "You are a fool! I do not fear *you*. You are a mere mortal, a servant. You are no threat to me or the others."

"Then what is your objection, precisely? Do you want to search these rooms for Apprentice Poloth's journal yourself? It seems like a menial task for a sorcerer, but is that what you want? Or are you jealous because Lord Dust has not asked you for your participation?"

I could see the anger building in her, and inside I was afraid that she might strike out at me, and damn the consequences. I had to be careful. I decided to make peace.

"Look, I'm not trying to learn sorcery. I'm not trying to usurp any of your places. But I was there when the demon turned on him—I saw it happen. I need to do something, I need to be active, or I will go insane waiting for the answer. Surely you haven't completely forgotten what it was like to be a normal person, afraid of things well beyond your control?"

She was very still, glaring at me, her lips pressed into a thin line. She was so still that I couldn't tell whether or not she was breathing. Then she finally spoke.

"You are afraid."

She said it matter-of-factly, like she was telling me the weather outside.

"Of course I'm afraid! If you weren't a sorcerer, you'd be afraid, too. By the Abyss, I'm not entirely sure you're not all terrified of the implications of this, no matter how it might infuriate you to hear it."

Her expression changed slightly as her face relaxed just a tiny bit.

Andrew J. Luther

"You are going to cause more trouble, through your fear, your lack of knowledge, your arrogance. Lord Dust believes you can help, but I believe he is mistaken."

"Then you are free to tell him that."

I sounded more confident than I felt. My only hope was that Veylar Dust would be more angered at being second-guessed by one of his apprentices than he would be open to the idea that my involvement was a mistake.

She turned away from me and opened the door, and then spoke without turning around.

"I *will* tell him that."

She left the room and I was alone once more.

I didn't like manipulating the apprentices like that—it was risky, but sometimes it was also necessary. I had learned long ago that admitting weakness was a great way to disarm someone who was looking for a confrontation. I even used my experience in manipulating people at times with Veylar Dust, though I had to be much more careful with him.

I let out a sigh and turned back to Ankin Poloth's study. The journal was in here somewhere. It was my job to find it. Once again, I set to work.

The sun had long sunk beyond the hills to the west, and the occupants of the Tower of Dust were mostly likely all asleep, when I finally figured out where he had hidden his journal. Minutes later, I held the leather-bound book in my hands.

There was no way I was going to remove the journal from the Tower, and I certainly wasn't going to sleep here, so I sat down at the desk where a good number of the entries had most likely been written, and began to read. It had been a long night, but it wasn't nearly over yet.

*   *   *

THE JOURNAL MADE FOR SOME VERY BORING READING, AND I found myself nodding off more than once. But every time I realized that my eyes were closing, I would picture myself falling asleep in the Tower of Dust and would immediately perk back up for a short time. The idea of being that vulnerable in the confines of the Tower was enough to keep me awake.

Much of the journal pertained to duties and studies Ankin Poloth had been engaged in at one time or another. It was a rare look inside the life of an apprentice to one of the most powerful sorcerers in the Empire. And yet, it really wasn't that interesting. Perhaps another sorcerer might have found the journal to be compelling reading, but I doubted it.

There was only one thing that eventually caught my attention. Not the first time it appeared, or the second—I only noticed it when it became a pattern. Apprentice Poloth had been an infrequent, but regular, patron of the Stone Traveler Alehouse.

I was not personally familiar with the establishment—I hardly knew every tavern in the city. But it seemed an unusual thing for a sorcerer, even an apprentice, to be a customer at an alehouse. An exclusive clubhouse would be appropriate, I supposed, but the name didn't suggest such a place to me.

I went into the anteroom and looked out the window to see dawn breaking. I needed more information about the habits of the apprentices. This might be a common activity for them, for all I knew. But I also needed some sleep, as I was sure I would be out rather late this evening.

I decided to wait around the Tower until I could speak to at least one of the other apprentices, and then hope to get some sleep during the afternoon. I had breakfast in the kitchen at the base of the Tower, though I sat alone as none of the servants were interested in talking to me.

Just like the apprentices, they didn't quite know how to relate to me. Technically, I was just a servant like them, but there was something different about my interaction with Lord Dust that separated me from the rest of the staff.

As soon as the chamberlain, Quda, appeared, I explained to him that I needed to talk to at least one, but preferably two or three of the apprentices. I indicated it was unlikely Gisea would have any inclination to help me, so not to bother with her.

Quda agreed to give my request to the other apprentices, and asked that I wait in the lower areas of the Tower until he summoned me.

It was almost noon when one of the servants came at a run and told me that I was summoned to the council room immediately. I took the stairs two at a time and reached the council room in less than a minute. I knocked twice and opened the door.

I was surprised to see both Arral Doviar and Delash Wiar seated at the table. I had hoped to speak to more than one apprentice but hadn't really expected it to happen.

Arral Doviar didn't really fit the stereotypical image of a sorcerer. He was blonde, with an open, friendly face covered in faded freckles. The mind behind that face, however, was just as dangerous as any other, more so because of the inclination to trust his comforting looks.

Delash Wiar was thin and dark, with a long, narrow face and a hooked nose. I had never exchanged so much as a single word with him before, and I knew nothing about him despite his being the most senior of the apprentices.

"Close the door and be seated, Mr. Zale. Neither of us has much time to spare, so we must get directly to the point."

I followed his instructions and sat facing the two men.

"Thank you for making time to speak with me."

Apprentice Wiar waved off my thanks.

"You have been searching for Apprentice Poloth's journal. If you are having difficulty finding it, I do not believe we can be of any help."

"No, no. I've found the journal."

The two apprentices glanced at each other. Apprentice Doviar leaned forward and clasped his hands on the table.

"And?"

"I've spent the night reading it. Much of it is beyond my understanding, directly related to sorcery as far as I can tell. But I was looking more for behavioral elements rather than magical ones."

Apprentice Doviar raised a finger.

"Have you given the journal to Lord Dust?"

"Not yet. I wanted to speak to one or more of you first to determine if what I've discovered is outside of what you might consider normal activity or not."

"And what have you discovered, Mr. Zale?"

"Apprentice Poloth, over the course of the last two years, has been regularly visiting an alehouse in the city. And by regularly, I mean every sixty days."

Apprentice Doviar smiled unexpectedly.

"An alehouse? That seems unlikely. I would suggest you read the entries again and make sure you are not off on a fool's errand."

"Why is it unlikely? Do you not ever leave the Tower to spend time in the city?"

"Yes, we do. I can assure you, however, that an alehouse holds no attraction for us. *Any* of us."

I wanted to make a comment about sorcerers being "above" such things, but I controlled my mouth.

"Would there be any reason you can think of why Apprentice Poloth would visit an establishment like that with such regularity?"

They both considered my question for a moment. Then Delash Wiar shook his head.

"I do not know what personal projects Ankin might have been pursuing. It is certainly possible he was meeting someone there because it was an agreeable location for such a contact...."

Arral Doviar interrupted him.

"But unless you have found some indication in the journal that such a contact exists, it is far more likely you are misinterpreting what you are reading. You would be better off giving the journal to one of us to make sure you are not wasting everyone's time."

Apprentice Doviar was thinking just like Gisea. I was not surprised—they had come from the same province of the Empire, after all.

"I will certainly consider that once I'm sure I've hit a dead end."

He frowned at me and glanced over at his companion, who did not return the look.

Apprentice Wiar stood up.

"There is little to tell you that is not speculation at this point. I have other things to which I must attend. However, should you uncover something more specific, I am willing to discuss it further should I be able to spare the time."

He nodded to Apprentice Doviar and left the room. The other man just sat there, looking at me thoughtfully.

"I do believe you are in over your head, Mr. Zale."

"It's possible. Although, I've been told that before and I always manage to find the surface."

He smiled at me for the second time, and I realized that he wanted me dead. I don't know how I knew it—something in his eyes, perhaps. But I did know I was going to have to watch myself carefully around this man.

"Thank you for your time, Apprentice Doviar."

He didn't reply. He just sat there and watched me leave the room.

I went straight back to Ankin Poloth's room and returned the journal to its hiding place. Everyone would expect me to hand it over to Veylar Dust before I left the Tower, so it was safe enough in its original location at the moment.

I needed some rest, so I returned to my own rooms above the Sailor's Knot to spend the afternoon trying to find sleep.

Chapter Four

SURPRISINGLY, I DID MANAGE TO GRAB A FEW HOURS OF sleep despite the heat that flooded into my room from the dusty streets outside. I woke in time for dinner in the tavern downstairs, and proceeded out at dusk. To be honest, I really didn't want another full night of activity, though I had no idea what might happen.

I had two stops to make on this warm evening. I decided to hit the sewers first in order to the get the more odiferous visit over with sooner rather than later. Then it was back to the Tower for a meeting with Veylar Dust to report on my progress.

The Stone Traveler Alehouse could wait until tomorrow. According to Ankin Poloth's journal, there were still twenty-one days before his next scheduled visit to the tavern, so I had little expectation of anything interesting happening there anytime soon. Tomorrow evening I would probably visit it to have a couple of drinks, scout out the place, and then head back home.

I headed down to the shore and east along the dockside. Originally, the main sewer tunnels had been smaller and evenly spaced along the shoreline. That had the unfortunate effect of fouling the entire bay, though, so a great work had been undertaken almost a century ago to rebuild the network from scratch.

The city steward at the time had contracted the Tsojim to perform the construction, and hundreds had come from their kingdom to the east. The project had taken decades, but eventually the workers completed the new construction and a single main sewer line ran under the heart of the city and out to the edge of the bay where it dumped its contents into a swift current that carried the effluent out to sea.

It was then discovered that the Tsojim who had come had also built a settlement under Ythis and had no intention of returning to their own kingdom. The Undercity, as it came to be called, was excavated under and around the sewer system and was then home to a few hundred Tsojim, more having come to stay over the decades of construction.

The city steward had tried to evict them, but was ignored. A few squads of Imperial soldiers went into the sewers to forcefully remove the squatters, but never came back out.

Neither the Church nor any of the sorcerers were inclined to get involved, so eventually the city steward was forced to accept the new inhabitants of Ythis, and the Undercity had been populated ever since.

I hated dealing with the Tsojim. They were strange, foul creatures. Some said that they were once humans who were mutated during foul experiments conducted by one of the gods. Others say they were never human at all, and only a cosmic coincidence makes them superficially resemble us.

Personally, I didn't care one way or the other. They were disgusting, mysterious and unreliable, whether they were once human or not. But they also lived close to the waters of the bay, and they had their own kind of power. Their Seer, a leader of sorts, knew a great deal about the workings of our world.

I was gambling that the Tsojim either were involved with the creature in the bay directly, or perhaps had information that might help us. No one else had thought to contact them, which was not a surprise. They mostly kept to themselves in their underground city.

It took me almost two hours to walk to the end of the main sewer pipe, and it was mostly dark by the time I arrived. The stench of sewage filled my nose long before I heard the rushing of the liquid waste, and it was all I could do to keep from vomiting when I reached the hatch near the end of the huge stone pipe.

I rapped on the wooden hatch a few times and then pulled it open. A watery light illuminated a ledge that ran along the inside of the pipe. The stench was a solid thing filling my lungs, and I felt light-headed.

I forced myself through the hatch and onto the ledge. The light was coming from some kind of fungal growth on the walls and ceiling of the pipe, just enough to ensure that I didn't wander over the edge and into the flowing slime. I doubted I would survive being immersed in that toxic sludge.

I had no idea how long I might have to walk before I encountered one of the Tsojim. No one really knew what they did down here or how far into the sewer line their own settlements started. Breathing as shallowly as I could, I began to walk carefully along the ledge away from the waters of the bay.

I had taken three steps when a strange hissing noise erupted from the wall beside me. I turned to look into a pair of eyes protruding from the stone wall of the pipe. I was so startled that I took a step backwards and my foot slipped off the ledge.

I felt myself falling backwards and knew that I was most likely going to die in that horrid mass flowing towards the waters of the bay. I wind milled my arms in a vain attempt to regain my balance, but I knew I was going over.

And then the stone wall in front of me suddenly moved as a long appendage snapped out and grabbed my wrist. It pulled me back onto the ledge, but the touch of it on my bare skin caused my flesh to instantly erupt in burning sores.

As soon as I had regained my balance, the ropy tentacle unwrapped itself from my wrist and pulled back to the wall. I looked down at my flesh and saw black pustules bursting open with greenish ichor where the thing had touched me. The burning sensation lessened somewhat as the viscous pus erupted from the lesions.

I looked up to see a vaguely humanoid shape detach itself from the wall and face me on the ledge. Its head was lumpy and misshapen and sat on a short, thick neck jammed onto a squat torso. Long, boneless arms dangled at its sides, and it stood on two double-segmented legs. Its skin was black and rough like loose gravel and the face on that strange head had no nose and only a slit for a mouth.

But the eyes that looked back at me from that alien face were so very human. They stuck out a bit too much, but otherwise they appeared to be twins to my own eyes. In a creature of such strange countenance, the eyes were the most unnerving feature.

I steadied myself and prepared to speak to the creature. I had encountered the Tsojim before, had spent enough time in their company to learn their language. It was a difficult language to speak, all hissing and whistling, and they didn't always understand me.

"This one gives thanks for the help of the Tsojim."

The creatures watched me carefully and then took what appeared to be a deep breath. The hissing noise came from the mouth slit, and just over that sound I could hear the words in a strange, high-pitched whistle.

"Tsojim knows this one as Borolt Zale."

I nodded, but then remembered that it was meaningless gesture here.

"Yes, this one is known as Borolt Zale. Borolt Zale comes to speak to Tsojim Uwibee."

The words were barely out of my mouth when the figure in front of me began to shudder. Then its body started to stretch as the torso became longer and the head changed shape. In seconds I was looking at Uwibee, the Tsojim I had dealt with before. The Tsojim who could give me access to their Seer if I needed it.

I have no idea how one Tsojim transforms into another. It's as if they are all linked somehow and can switch bodies at will. I believe I am one of a very few humans to have seen it occur directly. I guess it's a testament to the strange life I've led.

The voice coming through the hiss sounded identical to the one that had spoken to me a moment before, but I had no doubt that this was Uwibee.

"Borolt Zale calls Uwibee. This one comes to hear the words of Borolt Zale."

"This one is grateful for Uwibee's help," I replied. "This one needs knowledge from Uwibee. This one is looking at the great beast in the water and seeks knowledge."

The hissing came louder.

"Uwibee is weak beside the great beast in the water. It is a being of power, of hunger made flesh. Borolt Zale should turn away from this knowledge. Borolt Zale will be consumed."

That set me back a moment. He seemed afraid of the creature in the bay, and that most likely meant all the Tsojim were afraid of it. Nevertheless, I needed answers.

"This one has set himself against the great beast in the water. This one seeks knowledge. This one needs information."

Uwibee just stood there, looking at me.

"This one asks permission to speak to the Seer."

My question had an immediate effect on him. He shuddered all over and his eyes rolled back into his head. A low thrumming sound came from around him and I carefully stepped back. I had not seen any Tsojim act this way before.

Suddenly his eyes snapped back into place and he stood perfectly still.

"Borolt Zale will leave this tunnel. The Seer will not accept Borolt Zale. Borolt Zale will leave NOW!"

The last word was a piercing whistle that hurt my head, and Uwibee grew larger and more threatening. Jagged protrusions grew on his torso and head, and a dry heat began to emanate from him.

Evidently my request to meet with the Seer had caused a problem, and I wasn't about to stay around to argue. I grabbed the hatch and shoved my way out of the tunnel. Stumbling in the darkness, I ran back towards the city until I was sure I was far enough away to satisfy the Tsojim's demand.

The smell of the sewer stayed in my head until I reached the outskirts of Ythis. Neither Uwibee nor any other Tsojim had followed me. I hoped my next stop would prove to be less exciting, though it would most likely be just as dangerous.

*　　　　*　　　　*

WHEN I RETURNED TO THE TOWER, QUDA TOLD ME THAT LORD Dust was waiting for me in the chamber where Ankin Poloth had died. I realized I was not prepared to return to that room. Having little choice in the matter, however, I went up the stairs and rapped on the heavy wooden door.

Veylar Dust commanded me to enter, and I opened the door. He looked up at me and I felt that he was angry about something, though I had no idea what it might be. He was not the most patient of men, and anything could have set him off. I entered the room and closed the door behind me.

Almost all of the room's furniture had been removed, and a black stain on the stone floor reminded me where the young man had died. Lord Dust sat on one of the two remaining chairs at the large table, which was buried under maps and charts.

I took the other chair and looked over the chart facing me, a diagram of the constellations seen above Ythis in the waning of each year. I recognized only a couple of the patterns—astronomy was never an interest for me. Then I noticed Veylar Dust was watching me.

"Shall I report, Lord Dust?"

He continued to watch me, saying nothing. I sat still. For once, I knew better than to push him.

"Why do you choose to serve me?"

Once again, I had not expected his question. I had no idea how to answer, so I decided to stall.

"I believe you know my reasons, Lord Dust."

"No. I know what events transpired in which you came into my service. I know what your reasons were for agreeing to my terms on that day. That does not answer my question."

"I swore to serve you in return for your protection. You had use of my skills, and I needed your power to forestall the church's intent to take my life. I made a deal with you, and you have kept your part of it, so there is no reason for me to even consider breaking mine."

"And yet you despise us. Sorcerers, I mean. You serve one of the most powerful sorcerers in the Empire despite your feelings towards us. Have you never considered fleeing from Ythis? There are other places you could go."

"I don't have anything outside of Ythis, Lord Dust. No family anymore. No home to return to. And, to be honest, you have not asked me to perform any tasks that run counter to my own moral code."

I realized after I stopped that I hadn't denied despising sorcerers. I sounded like I was using him for my own safety and because our agreement was *convenient* to me.

"What I mean to say is—"

"Spare me the platitudes. Your personal opinion of my brethren is utterly irrelevant, save that it does not preclude you from performing the duties I give you. I care not if you *like* me, Borolt Zale, as long as you are loyal to our agreement."

"I am, Lord Dust."

"Then tell me of the Tsojim. Leave nothing out."

He listed carefully as I told him every detail of my meeting with Uwibee. His face betrayed no emotion when I told him of the refusal to let me meet with their Seer, but I knew he was fascinated by the inhabitants of the Undercity. One element of my story stood out to him.

"I understand the Tsojim do not frighten easily. Their fear tells me something of the creature."

I waited for him to elaborate.

"The creature must not be demonic in nature. The Tsojim are intimately familiar with demons and their ilk. That means sorcery alone won't be able to solve this problem."

"Does that mean we have to get help from the Church?"

He looked at me evenly and didn't answer. I knew he hated the idea of approaching the Church for anything, and I was right behind him. But the Emperor himself had tasked Veylar Dust with solving this problem, and he would ultimately have to do whatever was necessary to get rid of the beast.

"The creature in the bay is a problem, but not one I wish to address tonight. The death of my apprentice is my focus now."

I hoped I hadn't angered him too much with my suggestion of help from the Church.

"I am a sorcerer. I study the movements of the cosmos so as to understand and reveal its secrets. I know these constellations like I know my own flesh," and here he indicated the chart in front of me.

"I want a fresh pair of eyes, a fresh mind, unfettered by true understanding. I want you to look for patterns where you've never seen them before. On the evening that Apprentice Poloth was killed, the night sky looked like this."

He placed a new chart in front of me showing the placement of the stars in the early summertime.

"There are patterns there, ones that I've known for many years. They keep me from seeing new patterns, shifting shapes, elements that might give me insight into what happened on that night."

"But I don't know what I'm looking for," I protested.

"That is exactly the point. Don't look *for* anything. Just look, and tell me what you see."

So, I looked. I stared at that chart and looked for patterns, and eventually I figured out what looked like shapes to me. I described everything I saw and mostly they were variations on known constellations.

Eventually I looked up and noticed by the candle that two hours had passed. I was no closer to finding anything relevant than when I had started. I stood and went to the window and looked up.

The charts weren't giving me anything, but there is power in the stars themselves. I stared up at the sky and watched a shooting star far to the east. I mentioned it to Lord Dust, and he practically jumped up and ran to the window.

"Tell me exactly where it started, and where it ended."

I pointed out the small cluster of stars that marked the spot near where I first spotted it. It had been a short trail that didn't reach the horizon.

Veylar returned to the table and opened his journal. He began to make notes on the shooting star, and I wasn't sure if he wanted anything more from me. So, I waited and continued to watch the sky.

"You may go."

His voice brought me out of my reverie.

"Are you certain?"

He didn't bother to answer my question. Of course he was certain. I left him in the room, writing furiously in his journal.

As I descended the stairs in the Tower of Dust, I thought about what I had done this evening. It gave me an idea of how I would spend my morning tomorrow.

At the moment of Ankin Poloth's death, there may have been some cosmic patterns that related to what happened. If there were, I certainly couldn't see them. But now I was curious if there had been anything down here in Ythis that might have happened at that precise moment.

It was a long shot, but one worth investigating.

Chapter Five

S ULID WAS HUNGRY, BUT HE DARED NOT LEAVE THE SAFETY OF his hiding place. The man hunting him had gotten too close last time, and only luck had saved Sulid's life. He had no intention of relying on luck again.

His stomach growled and he tried to think of something else. Unfortunately, his mind would only focus on two things right now: his empty belly and the man who wanted him dead. He didn't want to dwell on either unpleasant thought, but his mind wasn't obeying his wishes.

He should never have gone near the Temple. He generally preferred to avoid that area—it was safer that way. But he had let his hunger drive him to the false hope of an easy meal stolen from the fingers of the homeless mad.

And then the chase had begun. At first it was easy. Those priests were no match for Sulid's knowledge of the alleyways, tunnels, and holes that riddled Ythis. He could lose them whenever he wanted.

But then the Stranger showed up. The first time he encountered the man, Sulid almost didn't see him coming. It was only his well-honed sixth sense that warned him of danger before the Stranger caught up to him on the rooftop of Blacksmith Chylos' workshop.

The ensuing chase was not like the ones with those two priests—there was no fun, only a tension as the man kept up with Sulid over rooftop after rooftop. He had used every bit of skill to lose the man that night, and in their second encounter as well.

Two nights ago, it was pure luck that kept him out of the Stranger's clutches. And luck was unreliable. So Sulid frowned at his stomach and sat in the darkness in a hidden corner of a cellar below a potter's shop.

With nothing to distract him, however, he eventually reached the point where he could stand the hunger no longer. He pulled out the small cloth bag where he kept his supplies and looked inside. He already knew his food supply was low, but gazing at the very small hunk of dry bread left in the bag made him realize that he was going to have to go out very soon.

He refused to just rush out, however, and look for food. He knew that one mistake could cost him his life.

He sat quietly in the light of a lone candle, slowly chewing the stale bread and thinking about where he was going to go, how he was going to approach, and how he was going to leave. Wherever he decided to get food, he would have to take a very roundabout route to and from his current abode. He knew it would be easy for someone to eventually narrow down his location through multiple sightings.

Sulid was worried that the man, having not been able to catch him yet, would just try to keep him in sight and follow at a distance. There was a real danger that Sulid would lead the man right back to the potter's shop, and straight to his hiding place.

But without food—and more water, he noted, as he picked up the mostly empty skin—he was eventually going to die here anyway.

He thought about going out tonight, but the streets were already too empty for his purpose. He had learned long ago that the best time to travel the city was just after sunset, when the long shadows helped him hide out of sight, and the crowds of people on the streets helped him hide in the open.

Deciding to take care of his food shortage on the morrow, he finished the last bite of bread and washed it down with a swallow of water. Then he pulled out a small bundle of papers and began to practice reading his letters.

Sulid couldn't remember who had taught him to recognize the shapes of writing—he had no memory of parents or guardians—but he knew his ability to read gave him an edge over the other kids who lived in the shadows of Ythis. He was determined to hone this edge to use for his benefit.

Sulid had stolen these papers from the back room of a tavern where a fence had been waiting to sell them to some buyer. The man had fallen asleep, and Sulid had grabbed the papers along with the man's coin purse. He was proud of that theft.

Sulid focused on the words once again. He wasn't entirely sure what he was reading, as the pages seemed to describe some process that took place mostly in one's mind. The details were not really important, however. He wasn't trying to learn the ideas on the pages; he was merely practicing his ability to read the individual words.

As he read, he moved his lips, silently mouthing the words as his eyes passed over them. As he reached the bottom of the first page and moved onto the second, he began to whisper the words as he read them.

When he had worked his way to the bottom of the second page, he suddenly noticed that he could see his breath. He looked up at the candle and exhaled, and a visible puff came from his mouth. It was then that he noticed the cellar had gotten remarkably cold.

He slowly stood and looked around him. In the light of the candle, frost glinted on the surfaces of the crates and benches in the cellar. Then, from the corner of his eye, he saw a shadow move.

He dropped into a crouch and rolled away behind a crate, fear gripping his belly. His first thought was that the man who was hunting him had managed to locate his hiding place and was sneaking up on him.

Sulid carefully peered around the corner of the crate and saw more than one shadow jump and flicker on the wall. He glanced back at the candle, but its flame was still—no breath of air was causing it to dance. He could see no source of the shadows on the wall.

Now Sulid was even more afraid, for this must be some kind of sorcery. He watched the shadows with wide eyes, seeing strange patterns in their shapes. He felt his gaze being drawn into the shadows and he peered harder, trying to find something buried in the darkest part of the image.

He was leaning too far forward, and he overbalanced and nearly fell. He reached out and steadied himself on the crate and at that moment saw the shadows fade away.

Sulid slowly stood and noticed the slight darkness of moisture where the frost had so recently glittered on the items in the cellar. He stared at the place where the shadows had played but nothing further happened. Retreating to the corner near the candle, he stepped on the sheaf of papers by accident, and he realized that he had somehow forgotten everything he had been reading only moments before.

He no longer felt like reading. After packing away the bundle of papers, he sat beside the candle, his back to the wall, and stared out into the darkness of the cellar. It was a long time before he managed to fall asleep.

*   *   *

SOME PEOPLE SAY THE YTHIS CITY WATCH IS CORRUPT. THE REST of us say the City Watch is *really* corrupt. I didn't mind, though. Working for Lord Dust has certain perks, and one of them is fear of my employer.

Besides, I had spent enough time down in the nasty parts of the city that I had made a few friends on the force. Most of the Watchmen work two jobs—one for the city and one for the criminal gangs who pay them the real money. I've crossed paths with quite a few moonlighting members of the Watch in my career.

I was looking for someone specific today, however. Someone I could trust to take my money and actually deliver the goods. There is no honor among thieves, but some of them take a certain professional pride in their work. That's one of the reasons why Flasek had made Sergeant, after all.

I approached the Watch building, all carved stone and ironwork. It was supposed to look intimidating, and I supposed it did, a massive rock dropped near the center of Ythis. The carvings depicted what were intended to be scenes of punishment, though torture was a more appropriate term in many cases.

I entered the main hall where dozens of Watchmen were passing through on their way on or off duty. Scattered about the room were complainants, making their case to bored Watchmen who would determine if there was any potential profit in an investigation. Most of the citizens had brought their "donation" with them, but a couple could be heard arguing the merits of their case.

I silently wished them luck.

A raised platform at the far end held a large desk where the Duty Sergeant was stationed. From the other end of the hall, I could see the bald head of Sergeant Flasek Lumayth reflecting the lantern light like polished glass. A lone Watchman stood in front of that imposing desk, looking up at the Sergeant.

Turns out he was in the middle of a dressing down when I approached. Some new recruit had recovered stolen property and returned it to the owners without getting a bribe from them. The young man was obviously close to tears as the Sergeant screamed in his face, spittle raining down on his dirty uniform.

I waited, enjoying the show. Flasek had worked hard to become Sergeant, had earned the Sergeant's right to yell at his men, belittle them and their ancestry, and make them wish they were dead. I certainly wasn't going to deprive him of the best part of his job.

He saw me and decided to finish up with a particularly insulting description of how the young man's mother had conceived him in the alley behind the city's worst whorehouse. I thought that was definitely going to send the recruit over the edge, but the youngster held his emotions in check, barely. I could see Flasek was impressed, though he'd never admit it.

He ordered the Watchman out of his sight, grabbed a metal flask from behind the desk, and came down from behind the big block of wood.

His uniform was unbuttoned in the front, and the seams were bursting everywhere else. Flasek was always a big man, a brawler, but he had practically exploded in the last few months. He gave me a snort and motioned to one of the chairs at a nearby small table. Grabbing the other, he sprawled out like he was lounging in his favorite brothel.

"What brings the worst son-of-a-whore in Ythis to my Watch House today? Lose your Sorcerer?"

I couldn't help flinching. No one in his right mind would talk like that, but the Sergeant was fearless.

"I came to take you out for a drink and squeeze some information out of you in the process."

"You want me to do you a *favor*."

The way he stressed the last word meant that he was looking for more than a drink.

"Well, this is easy information, probably not worth anything, so I'm being generous buying you a drink for it."

"No, you *owe* me a drink. I bought last time."

I thought back to our last night out together, but it was too hazy to remember who had paid for what. I doubted he could remember either. He always drank more than I did.

"So, you want me to buy you and drink *and* pay you for the information?"

"That's how friendship and business works. This is a little bit of friendship and a little bit of business. You owe me a drink or three as my friend, and maybe you can pay me for some help with your little problem as business."

"I'm always impressed how you can keep those two things from ever crossing."

"That would be corrupt, my friend. Or crazy—just like becoming a priest."

He saw the look on my face and realized what he had said.

"Sorry. I shouldn't have said that. You no longer owe me the drink. I'll buy tonight."

I waved off his generosity.

"Don't worry about it. You didn't mean anything by it, and you shouldn't have to curb your words around me. I'm still buying. What time do you finish up here?"

He looked at me in surprise and then laughed.

"By the hairy balls of a sorcerer, I'm a Sergeant! My days of being stuck here till the end of my shift are long over. Let's go."

"Okay. Do you have to tell anyone where you're going?"

"Screw 'em."

He got up and strode right out the front door. I noticed a few of the other Watchmen eyeing us as we left.

"Do you have enemies in the Watch, Flasek?"

"No, they're just waiting for me to leave so that they can all go do something else."

"What else?"

"Anything that ain't their job."

He led me to a small, local watering hole called Blue Skies. It seemed like a pretentious name for a tiny dive, but the inside was remarkably clean, the ale strong, and the service bordering on friendly. I wasn't sure what a place like this was doing in Ythis.

I ordered a couple of rounds as we caught up on each other's lives. Flasek was a bastard, but a likeable one, and we had known each other for many years. I counted him as a friend. Granted, that merely meant that he would only sell me out if the price was *really* high.

We were halfway through our third mug when he got serious.

"How are things with the sorcerer? I mean, seriously. You've survived far longer than anyone thought possible with that Church's death mark on you, and that's 'cuz of your boss. But I'm still worried."

"I appreciate it. But working for him has been less dangerous than one would think."

The image of Ankin Poloth dissolving on the floor leaped into my mind, and I tried to focus on something else.

"You are in a nasty position, my friend. Don't for a second think the Church has forgotten about you. If the sorcerer lets his protection over you waver even a tiny bit, they're gonna come after you again."

"I've thought about that. But, aside from going on the run outside of the Empire, I don't have a lot of options."

"Maybe leaving the Empire is the safest thing for you. 'Cuz, you're working for a bloody *sorcerer*, Borolt. He's got his own plans, his own schemes. And if he ever needs something from the Church, he's got you to dangle in front of them. What kind of favor could he get if he handed you over? A mighty big one, that's what kind."

I was about to dismiss Flasek's worries automatically, but I stopped and carefully considered what he was saying. It made a lot of sense. Veylar Dust had a use for me, which is why he protected me against the Church. But I had value to the Church. If there was a trade to be made, he wouldn't hesitate a second to hand me over.

"I'll seriously give it thought, okay? I've been too busy to think about my future lately, but you make a good point. I'd rather leave the Empire than be handed over to the Church."

He nodded, satisfied.

"So, down to business. What do you need from me?"

I explained in rough terms that something strange had happened in the Tower of Dust at a particular time, and I needed to know if anything else strange had occurred at the same time, anywhere in the city.

"Lots of strange things happen every day. What kind of 'strange' events are you looking for?"

"I honestly don't know. Something notable, unexplainable. It was mere seconds after the seventh-hour evening bell sounded. How many strange events could occur at that precise moment?"

He pondered that for a moment.

"It may be that a strange event occurred that no one saw," he suggested.

"I've considered that possibility as well. But then such a thing is impossible to know, and so I have to ignore it. I'm hoping that, if something happened, someone was around to see it."

"Okay, I'll put the word out. You may get a few stories from people who saw something weird and remember the wrong time. I can't guarantee the truth of anything that comes back to you."

I nodded. There was little I could do about that. I just hoped that few people would be able to think of anything, and that there'd be some thread in what they saw.

"What'll that cost me?"

Flasek eyed me over the rim of his mug. He took a long pull and placed the mug down with slightly exaggerated care, an indication that the ale was hitting his system.

"A favor. No coin this time. Just a favor."

"Okay, what favor?"

"I don't have one yet. I've got a few ideas, but nothing I can settle on right now."

I sat back in my chair.

"I'm not an assassin."

He laughed a hearty laugh and reached forward to slap my arm.

"I'm hardly a crime lord, now, am I? No, if I want someone dead, I'll do it myself. I just may need you to look into something for me. It'll wait until you've got a bit of time, though."

I shook his hand.

"Deal."

"Great! Now, since you're paying for this one, let's get rip-roaring drunk."

I smiled and ordered another round.

Chapter Six

B Y THE TIME I DRAGGED MYSELF OUT OF THE BLUE Skies tavern, Flasek was unconscious and I could only wave at sobriety from a distance. It was already well into the late afternoon, which meant I had a couple of hours to sober up and get some food into me.

I dragged myself back to my own neighborhood, and the Sailor's Knot, telling myself that my drinking binge with my friend was all for a greater purpose. It was important to maintain relationships in this city, or my usefulness to Lord Dust would shrink. That was my excuse, anyway.

Besides, I had managed to avoid most of the excess by only pretending to drink about half the time. I knew Flasek wouldn't be watching me to ensure that I matched him ale for ale, at least as long as I kept buying. Of course, half of "a lot" is still quite a bit.

Unfortunately, I planned to do more drinking tonight. I needed to get out to the Stone Traveler Alehouse and learn the layout to start blending in. It was still twenty days before Ankin would have returned to the place—were he still alive—and I wanted to be a bit of a regular before that happened.

After all, it would be pretty much impossible to spot anything suspicious if I was completely unfamiliar with the place.

Jolin glared at me as I entered the Knot. I was weaving just a little bit and probably had that glassy-eyed stare of the drunk who is trying to hold himself together and concentrating too much on walking. He was probably angry that I had not spent my—or someone's—money at his tavern.

I didn't have the time or the patience for his surliness.

"I need food, Jolin. Something hearty."

"It's not time yet," he snapped. "The stew's still cooking. Come back in an hour or so."

"If you're not going to feed me, what am I paying you for?"

"You're paying for that roof over your head upstairs, and two meals a day. But you don't get to come in here whenever you wish and demand to be fed. You'll eat when the food is ready like everyone else."

I was lacking the wits to argue with him, and besides, I knew he had a point. I kept strange hours, and he was pretty accommodating most of the time, despite his general grumpiness.

"Okay, I'll be back in an hour."

I tried to make it sound like a threat, but it came out sounding like I was slightly befuddled at the idea of no food.

Okay, maybe I *was* befuddled a little bit. I had been counting on getting something to soak up the alcohol in my stomach.

I knew I couldn't risk going up to my room to crash. I'd end up falling asleep and waste the entire evening. There was too much to do, and not enough time to do it.

I ended up trying to walk off the drunkenness with a stroll around the neighborhood. It had been some time since I last walked the streets and alleys of the Trades District, and I was feeling out of touch. As the liquor wore off and I remembered short cuts and dead ends, I started feeling like myself again.

This made me consider what Flasek had said to me about working for Veylar Dust.

Just what *was* I doing? Any sane man would have gone on the run the instant the Church identified him as an enemy. Back then, before the creature moved into the bay, ships from all over the world stopped at Ythis' docks. What was there in this city that kept me here?

I didn't have an answer to that. I also didn't have time to pursue that line of thinking.

After a quick meal at the Sailor's Knot—the stew was finally ready—I headed out in the direction of the Stone Traveler Alehouse.

I didn't know exactly where it was located, and I couldn't call attention to myself by asking around. So, I relied on my ability to blend into the various neighborhoods of the city and went hunting.

It took me less time than I expected, as the Stone Traveler was on the West River Road, a major thoroughfare through the northwest section of Ythis. I passed by the alehouse once, on the opposite side of the street, and stole several casual looks at the entrance. I needed to enter as if I had been there before, despite not knowing the layout inside.

A few minutes later, I came back on the right side of the street and went straight to the front door. I pulled it open and stepped inside.

The Stone Traveler was a nice place to get drunk. The wooden chairs had padded leather covers, the tables looked sturdy, and the floor was obviously swept regularly. The place was about half-full, although I could tell that most of the patrons were only in for a drink or two on their way home.

Without pausing, I walked into the bar, my eyes scanning for an appropriate place to sit. I noticed a few very small tables around the edges of the room, and I sat down at one across from the bar. It seemed a good place to get prompt service without being bothered by anyone.

The serving girl came over almost at once, and I ordered the house ale, hoping that it was not only palatable, but somewhat popular. An uncommon choice would cause me to stick out in her mind as an outsider, something I wanted to avoid.

The next few hours were thoroughly uneventful, and I began to get bored. I had already memorized the layout of the common room and had explored the back hallway that led outside to the privy. Now I was watching the regulars, trying to determine patterns that I could use to blend in later.

And then the priest came in.

He didn't look like a priest. If he had, the whole room would have gone silent as everyone waited for something bad to happen. No, he looked like a normal, if wealthy, customer as he walked in and took a seat at the bar. He didn't have the mad look always in the eyes of one touched by a god. In fact, there was nothing to give one the impression he was a member of that powerful and terrible order.

Nothing except the ring.

I was one of a handful of outsiders to know what that ring signified. Carved in the shape of a nine-pointed star with an open eye in the center, the silver ring was worn by a special sect—called the Hidden—within the Church. They were responsible for eliminating threats to the order.

I had encountered one of these priests before, the night I rescued my brother from the temple. We had barely escaped with our lives—the priest of the Hidden didn't.

I watched the regulars, and none of them gave the new arrival a second glance, even though he didn't quite fit in. That told me he was a regular, too. The other patrons had gotten used to him already.

There was no way this was a coincidence, one of the Hidden being a regular at an alehouse, the same alehouse where Ankin Poloth had returned every sixty days. There had to be a connection here. But what would a sorcerer's apprentice be doing with a priest?

A betrayal of Lord Dust was the most obvious answer. The priests hated the Council of Sorcerers. The Five had both arcane and temporal power, and an influence over the Emperor that rivaled the Church's. They were always trying to find ways to gain the upper hand.

But what could they possibly have offered Ankin Poloth in return?

I realized I was getting ahead of myself. This kind of speculation could blind me to clues I might find leading in a different direction. My job here was to wait, and watch.

The priest stayed for just over an hour, drinking three mugs of ale. Then he paid the serving girl and left the Stone Traveler by the front door.

Tossing coins on the table, I got up and followed him out.

*   *   *

I WAS EXTRA CAUTIOUS AS I LEFT THE ALEHOUSE. I HAD TO expect the possibility that the priest had recognized me—the Church had put a price on my head, after all. But when I exited the Stone Traveler, I spotted the priest openly walking down the street in the general direction of that pit of madness and despair they called a temple.

I followed him at a distance. I was close enough to catch up if he turned a corner and left my line of sight, but far enough back that he wouldn't be able to see my face if he glanced behind him. I didn't like not knowing the twisting streets and alleys of this neighborhood. I was out of my element in this part of the city.

That's what distracted me long enough to walk right into the ambush. A large man on the other side of the street had begun to cross, aiming for an alley about twenty feet in front of me. I kept my eyes on my quarry, not wanting to lose him in the instant it would take for the other man's bulk to break my line of sight. It was only as I was drawing nearer to the alley's mouth that I began to notice the man had slowed down just enough that he would pass behind me instead of in front.

As I reached the alley mouth, the man suddenly lunged forward, and I realized what was happening just as I saw it was too late to stop it. The man's body slammed into me, driving me sideways into the darkness of the alley and out of sight of any onlookers.

I twisted as I tumbled sideways, kicking out a foot into the man's groin. He barked out an epithet as he grabbed his nethers, and I leaped upright and jabbed my fingers towards his throat. That's when the second man hammered a fist into the back of my head.

I missed with my lunge and slammed into the wall, stars exploding behind my eyes. I gritted my teeth and fought with everything I had to hold onto consciousness as the second man swept my feet out from under me.

I went down on all fours and the first man planted a solid kick into my side. I could feel ribs crack under that assault. The second attacker managed to twist one of my arms behind my back and snake his own arm across my throat.

My breath was cut off and my shoulder screamed in pain as he hoisted me upright. His buddy wasn't done paying me back for the groin shot. He stepped forward and drove his fist into my stomach. I couldn't double over, so I drew my knees up as I tried to gasp some air back into my lungs.

He was winding up for another shot when the guy holding me told him to wait. Instead, he grabbed a fistful of my hair and held his eyes in front of mine.

"Who are you?" he snarled at me.

I was thrown off guard for a second. I had thought this was a mugging at first, but these guys were backing up the priest.

I opened my mouth like I was going to answer, and then spit in the big man's face. He recoiled, and then his oversized fist connected with the side of my head. This time I did lose consciousness, at least for a second or two. Only the strength of his fellow thug kept me upright.

"It doesn't matter that much if you don't answer. We'll just kill you and dump your body. I'd like it that way better."

From behind my right ear, the other man offered a suggestion.

"Talking is your only way out of this. Tell us something useful, and you might survive the night."

I could see in the eyes of the other man there was no way he was going to let me live. He had taken that kick to the groin personally. Very unprofessional.

"What could I possibly say?" It came out a whisper as I was still sucking air, my ribs aching more with each breath.

"Who are you and why were you following that guy?"

"What guy?"

The big one in front of me took that as his cue to hit me some more. He planted another one in my stomach and I nearly vomited on his shoes. Another hit in the gut would make it a certainty.

"Last chance, you son of a bitch. Play around any more, and I'll beat you to death right here."

I continued to buy time gasping for breath and working my mouth pretending I was trying to speak.

These guys definitely didn't work for the Church. They weren't crazy enough, or deadly enough. That meant they were hired muscle, and *that* meant I could trace them back to whoever hired them. It also meant they probably didn't know anything useful.

In addition, I was now free to take them out without causing a political incident between the Five and Church. The last thing I needed was to cause more trouble for Lord Dust right now. He'd simply exterminate me out of annoyance.

I had learned as much as I was going to from these two thugs. It was time to take control.

I smiled and winked at the big man in front of me. His eyes widened and he stepped forward to drive his fist right into my face. I kicked into his groin again, but this time my boot knife was extended. He stopped cold and howled in my face.

It was the distraction I needed. I dropped another hidden knife from my sleeve into my free hand and stabbed down into the thigh of the man holding me. His grip immediately loosened from the sudden shock, and I ripped the knife upward to slice open his leg like the belly of a gutted fished.

I left the knife in his leg and grabbed his wrist at my throat, locking the joint and twisting it away from me. Without the leg injury, there was no way I would have been able to force his arm open, but he was in too much pain to resist my movement.

He still had my own arm twisted up behind my back, but I now had just enough room to maneuver. I reached down and grabbed the knife out of his leg, twisted slightly to the right, and jabbed the blade behind me into his abdomen.

Feeling the knife slide into his intestines caused him to forget about my arm. He shoved me away and backed off, but his leg gave out and he fell to the cobblestones.

The big one had turned away slightly, but adrenaline was overcoming the pain in his groin. He turned back to me just in time to receive a slash across his eyes. His arms came up to protect his face and I dropped my third and last blade from my other sleeve.

One went into his throat and one went into his chest.

He gurgled as he toppled slowly backward, and his body continued twitching as his lifeblood leaked out on to the hard cobblestones of the alley.

I retrieved my blades and turned to the second man. He was trying to crawl away, but was slowing down from massive blood loss. He heard me coming for him, which gave him renewed energy, but he didn't get much farther. He rolled onto his side and grabbed for my ankles as I approached him, but I stomped on his hand and heard fingers break.

He didn't say anything, just looked up at me with fear in his eyes.

"It's nothing personal," I told him, and then *my* questioning began.

Chapter Seven

SULID CROUCHED BEHIND THE EMPTY CRATE AT THE END OF the alley, terrified.

He had come out here for food, expecting to break into the baker's shop and have his choice of the leftover breads and cakes from today. But in the last couple of days, the man had boarded up the small window that opened into the alley. It was inevitable that he would eventually figure out Sulid's means of entry.

In fact, Sulid was surprised the man hadn't figured it out months ago.

He was about to emerge from the mouth of the alley and duck down a side street when he saw the man walking down the street. It wasn't the same stranger who was hunting him, but he had seen this man before, on the day of the accident.

Terror gripped him and he scampered back into the darkness of the alley, hiding behind a crate at the very end. He didn't think the man had seen him, but he wasn't sure. And if that man was here, perhaps the Stranger was around as well.

He peeked around the crate just as a figure entered the alley. Sulid could tell it wasn't the Stranger—this man was big and bulky, where the Stranger was slim and smooth. He wondered for an instant if the man was going to search the alley, but the figure stopped just inside the shadows at the corner and appeared to be waiting for something or someone.

A moment later, there was some kind of scuffle in the shadows at the alley's mouth. He watched as the original figure and another, even larger, man beat on a third figure. It was obvious that these two men worked for the man Sulid had seen moments earlier.

And then there was another flurry of movement and one of the big men fell. A choking, gurgling noise came from the shadows and the other big man dropped as well. Sulid realized that the smaller man—the victim—had just taken out both larger men.

Sulid's eyes strained against the darkness as he leaned forward to hear what the man was saying.

"It's nothing personal," he said to the man who was still moving. "But I need some information and you're going to give it to me."

The other man's voice was weak.

"I'm bleeding too much. I'm going to faint and then I'm going to die. Why in the Abyss should I help you?"

The smaller man grabbed the leather belt from the other body and tied it around the man's leg.

"I can get you help in time."

"You sliced open my belly. I can't feel anything. I'm dead either way."

"I have methods not available to others. My name is Borolt Zale and I work for Veylar Dust."

A moan came from the man on the ground, but one of fear rather than pain. Sulid almost gasped in shock. This man—Borolt—served a *sorcerer*. The streets were full of very dangerous people tonight, and Sulid had chosen this night to come out of his hiding place.

"Who is the man I was following?"

"Works for the Church. Don't know his name."

"And you're just hired muscle."

Sulid couldn't hear the man's answer.

"So, who do you work for?"

"I'm one of the Wolf's men. We were just supposed to grab anyone taking an interest."

The man's breathing was getting labored, and Sulid had trouble staying still. He didn't want to listen to the man die on the ground, and yet he drank in every word.

"You didn't have to kill us."

"No, but you weren't going to let me walk out of this alley, either."

The man on the ground was barely whispering now, and Sulid

held his breath so as to hear every last word.

"Don't let them take me...the Church or the sorcerers...I don't want them to have me."

Borolt Zale just stood there, looking down at the dying figure at his feet.

"I won't let them have you. I'll go to the Wolf and tell him where you are right now."

The dying man let out a last gasp and went still.

Sulid watched Borolt stand over the body for a moment before turning and striding directly out of the alley.

Sulid forced himself to count to ten three times, and then he tip-toed past the two corpses and snuck out to the alley's mouth. He looked around for Borolt Zale, and spotted him crossing the street a few buildings down the block.

His mind was spinning as he considered the possibilities. The Church was hunting him, for he understood now that the Stranger must work for them. The only people strong enough to stand up to the Church were the Five.

But sorcerers were the stuff of nightmares. Sulid had no desire to get involved with such beings, or their servants.

And yet, Borolt Zale might be able to help Sulid against the Stranger, at least.

Keeping to the shadows, he followed the man. He didn't know where Borolt was heading, but it wasn't in the direction of the Tower of Dust. He kept Borolt in sight, though he never managed to get up enough courage to call out to him.

Sulid was still trying to decide what to do when he saw Borolt head for the doors of the Wolf's Den. He realized that the man was going to keep his promise to the hired thug in the alley. That was what Sulid needed to make his decision.

If Borolt Zale was such a man of his word, then Sulid felt that it was worth the risk to trust him. He planted himself in the shadows, determined to speak to Borolt when he emerged from the building.

Not more than five minutes later, however, his bones went cold as he saw the Stranger slowly walk towards the doors of the Wolf's Den. Sulid knew he was well hidden, but felt completely exposed to the man hunting him. It occurred to Sulid that the Stranger might be there to attack Borolt when he emerged.

Sulid considered whether it was possible to sneak into the building and warn Borolt. He dismissed the idea as the Stranger stepped up to the doors and entered the tavern. Whatever was going to happen, it was going to happen out of Sulid's sight.

He considered how quickly Borolt Zale had turned the tables on his attackers, and wondered if the Stranger was skilled enough to face a man like that. Either way, Sulid wasn't safe here.

As quickly as possible, Sulid slipped from the shadows and headed for his current home in the cellar. He now knew Borolt's name and that the man worked for Veylar Dust. If Borolt survived the night, Sulid would contact him when the next opportunity presented itself.

For the first time in a long time, he felt his situation was not completely hopeless.

*   *   *

WHEN NID SAW THE LOOK ON MY FACE, HE MOTIONED FOR A couple of his men to intercept me on my way to his position behind the bar. I held up my empty hands as the first bouncer reached me.

"Nid," I called. "I need a minute with the Wolf."

The second bouncer planted himself directly behind me. Predictable. I was tempted to show him the error of his ways, but I needed that minute with Wolf, and violence wouldn't get me what I wanted this time.

Nid shook his head.

"I don't know what's in your head, Zale, but you look like a man about to do something rash. Go home and calm down, and come back tomorrow."

"I'm fine, Nid. But this is urgent."

The first bouncer stepped into my space.

"He told you to go home. Turn around and walk out. Now."

"Does the Wolf take good care of you guys?"

That confused him for an instant, and then he tensed up, obviously expecting me to launch a surprise attack. It was the kind of question you ask right before you hurt someone. But that's not what I was going for.

"I'm not looking for a fight. I'm looking for help. A couple of the Wolf's guys are in an alley just off the West River Road."

Nid came over and stood just behind the bouncer facing me.

"Who are they?"

"I didn't get names, Nid."

He looked me over carefully, trying to decide if I was lying. He obviously didn't trust me, but the truth is that the Wolf does try to do right by his employees. At least when it doesn't cost him too much.

"Tell me everything, and I'll speak to the Wolf."

I shook my head.

"No. I made a promise and I intend to keep it. Besides, I'm not sure the Wolf wants just anyone to know what they were doing for him."

Nid bristled at me calling him "just anyone." It was my way of reminding him that he was just an employee, too.

"Fine. One of you take him upstairs and let him talk to the Wolf. If he tries anything, put him down."

"You're all heart, Nid."

I smiled at him and he scowled back at me before returning to the bar.

The bouncer escorted me to a different room from the one where I had met the Wolf last time I was here. This time I was led into a well-appointed office. It was definitely more appropriate for some-one of Wolf's reputation.

One of the bodyguards from my last visit was sitting in a chair at the rear of the room. He stood up as we entered and looked at me and then the bouncer.

"Nid told me to bring him to see the Wolf."

The bodyguard nodded and drew back the heavy curtain on the wall beside his chair. Instead of a window, the curtain hid a door. He rapped on it twice and then opened it slightly to speak to the person on the other side.

Whoever was on the other side wasn't the Wolf, as I heard a female voice. The bodyguard closed the door and turned back to me.

"Sit down and wait. The Wolf will come when he has a minute."

"My business is rather urgent."

"Sit down or leave. Your choice."

I wasn't going to get anywhere with this guy, so I sat. I was painfully curious about who was on the other side of that door, but had no immediate way to find out, so I filed it in the back of my mind. Finding things out about the Wolf had become a bit of a pet project of mine, and now there was another piece of information I wanted to uncover.

I waited for at least fifteen minutes before the door opened and the Wolf came out. He didn't bother to shake my hand this time. He merely walked in and sat behind his very nice desk.

"Someone's done a number on you tonight. That happen here?"

He glanced at his bodyguard and bouncer.

"No, this was from someone else. A matter you probably want kept confidential."

He waved the bouncer away and waited until the office door was closed.

"I told you last time you were here that I'm a busy man. Veylar Dust or not, you can't just keep coming here and interrupting my work to ask me questions."

"I'm not here for that. This is a different matter. It involves your work for the Church."

His eyes opened wide at that. If rumors got out that Wolf was dealing with the Church, he'd see his fledgling empire crumble beneath him.

"That's nonsense, Mr. Zale. I'm the last man—save you, perhaps—who'd have anything to do with the Church."

I leaned forward and heard his bodyguard shift behind me.

"Then the two men guarding the priest at the Stone Traveler Alehouse were telling lies right before they died."

Wolf's face went white and I jumped up and spun to face the bodyguard as he came at me. I turned to one side to protect my injured ribs as he hit me low and drove me into the wall. My breath exploded out of me.

He pushed himself off me and made a jab at my throat. I barely avoided it—there was no way I could block a shot like that in my current battered condition—and I snapped my foot into his left knee. Pain shot through my foot as I connected with a metal plate sewn into his pants.

He managed to wrap a big hand around my forearm and twist, throwing me off balance. It was the opening he needed, and he locked my shoulder and swept my feet out from under me. I screamed as his knee landed on my back, putting pressure on my ribs.

"That's enough!"

I was helpless, face down on the floor, but I realized that the bodyguard wasn't deliberately trying to hurt me further, although his weight on my back was grinding my ribs together. I was in danger of blacking out for the second time tonight.

Wolf came around his desk and knelt by my head.

"You're going to tell me everything, Zale, right now. I'll take my chances with your master if I have to."

His voice was overflowing with fear, and I felt a small satisfaction. Wolf had been doing something very bad, and was now stuck between the Church and Veylar Dust. His own death was the least of his worries at this moment.

But fear could also make him reckless, and he might just decide to kill me and see what damage control he could do after the fact. I had to maneuver carefully.

"Wolf, I *want* to tell you everything. If you trust me for just a minute, I think we can help each other out here."

"Don't think for a second that you can blackmail me, Zale. I'll have you carved up and fed to the dogs."

"By the Abyss, I'm not threatening you! I came to tell you about two of your men who died tonight. Who are still lying in an alley *right now*. Who were doing something you might want to cover up! But I think I've got a couple of broken ribs, and your minion here is going to drive them into my lung if he doesn't get his knee off my back. And that's not going to help either one of us."

Wolf was silent for a moment, and then the pressure on my spine eased off and my arm was released. I rolled onto my back and clutched my ribs, trying to ease the pain. Wolf went back to sit behind his desk, but the bodyguard stood over me looking like he wanted to dive on me again.

I realized that I hadn't even landed a real blow on him before he took me down. No matter how good you think you are, there is always someone better. And you'll always end up facing them when you're already half beaten.

It's just the way the world works.

It took me a couple of minutes, but I managed to climb back into the chair. No one helped me.

"What in the Abyss happened tonight?"

I decided to play it completely straight with him.

"Someone working for Veylar Dust was frequenting the Stone Traveler Alehouse on a very regular basis. I went there tonight to see what the attraction was, and found a particular kind of priest there, one who doesn't look like a priest unless you know exactly what to look for."

I paused to give him time to comment, but he stayed silent.

"I followed the priest when he left, but was waylaid by two large men who could have been twins to your friend here. They were guarding the priest."

I hesitated at that point. I wasn't sure how to tell Wolf that I had killed two of his men, and was even less sure how he would react.

"And they broke your ribs?"

"Yes."

"What did they tell you?"

"Not much, at first. They wanted to know why I was following the priest and were prepared to beat the answer out of me. One of them took my resistance to being attacked personally, and decided to end my life."

I watched as understanding dawned on the Wolf's face.

"You killed them."

"Yes. They were going to kill me, and I stopped them."

Wolf looked at me and said nothing.

"This priest...did he know he was being protected by your guys? Did he know these two men specifically? I figure there's more to this than what I've stumbled across, but I don't care if it's some criminal enterprise. What I do care about is if this is related in some way to the habits of one of Veylar Dust's people. If this priest was involved somehow, then I'm going to pursue it. And if I disappear, then Lord Dust will do it himself."

Wolf continued to sit there and watch me, giving nothing away. I had expected him to be angry at my killing of his men, but he was no longer displaying any emotion.

After a full minute of silence, he eventually spoke.

"I don't know what the Church is doing. I don't want to know. I didn't even know he was a priest, at first. He was just a man who wanted some protection when he visited with people at the Stone Traveler."

"When did you realize he was a priest?"

"I did a little digging. Well, a lot of very discrete and very careful and precise digging. I discovered that the Church has a secret sect—"

"Called the Hidden. I know. I've faced them before."

Wolf looked stunned at that revelation.

"As information, it's beyond valuable. But it put me in a tight spot. I couldn't cancel my contract with him, or he'd know I had discovered his secret. But I didn't want to be working with the Church. If that got out, it could destroy me. I hadn't yet decided what to do."

I considered the possibilities.

"I may have just given you an out. The two men assigned to protect him were killed. You have a genuine reason now to tell him you can't provide this service for him anymore. This is more than some simple cuts and bruises on your men."

"So, your killing of my people is a benefit to me now, is it?"

I shook my head. I could see where his mind was leading him, and I wanted no part of it.

"I have no quarrel with you or your people. It never would have occurred to me that you had an arrangement with the priest, so I thought they worked directly for the Church. Had I known, things would have ended differently."

"Where are the bodies?"

I gave him the location.

He stood up.

"I should have you killed. But I can't let anyone know why you killed my people. And you have solved one dilemma for me. But our relationship is at an end, Mr. Zale. If you return to the Wolf's Den or attempt to see me again, you won't live to see another sunrise."

He leaned in very close to me.

"Is that clear?"

I nodded.

"I understand your position."

I didn't apologize to him, despite his obvious desire to hear it from me. *I* held the power here, regardless of what he had just said. He couldn't simply have me killed—there would be too many questions, not the least from Veylar Dust himself. And I now knew another potentially deadly fact about him.

He was not happy about our power imbalance. I just hoped he was as smart as I had heard and didn't let his emotions or pride rule his actions.

I left the Wolf's Den with a mission to find out what the priest had been doing with Ankin Poloth. But first, I had to do something about my ribs.

Chapter Eight

S ULID WAS GETTING TIRED. HE HAD BARELY SLEPT THE
night before, excited by the prospect of having a potential ally
in this city, even if the man—Borolt—did not yet know it.

He had been worried last night when Borolt reemerged from the
Wolf's Den barely able to stand upright. Sulid had wondered at first
if the Stranger had attacked him inside the building, but there was
no commotion and Borolt had not seemed to be running from anyone. The man had hailed a carriage and Sulid had been unable to
keep up. He had returned to his hiding place with the idea of finding Borolt tonight.

As soon as twilight descended on the towers and slums of Ythis
this evening, Sulid had headed out across the rooftops. He made
immediately for the Tower of Dust, hoping against hope that the
man had come here in the carriage.

He had no reason to believe the Stranger had entered the Wolf's
Den looking for Borolt Zale. After all, the tavern was a meeting
place for those with connections throughout the city. Sulid tried to
believe with all his heart that the Stranger's presence last night was
only a coincidence.

By the time Sulid had reached the Tower of Dust, the sky was
rapidly fading to black and the heat of the day had begun to lessen.
He found a good vantage point on the roof of a nearby two-story
building and hid himself in a shadowy corner.

And then he waited.

Three hours later, there was still no sign of Borolt. Sulid's nervousness—he couldn't help jumping at every little nearby noise—

forced him to concentrate on watching the tower entrance. But since there was nothing interesting happening around the tower, it became harder and harder to maintain focus.

Bit by bit, he felt his eyelids getting heavier. He wanted to stand up and walk around to help himself stay awake, but was too afraid that someone hostile might see him.

Suddenly he snorted and opened his eyes. He wasn't sure how long he had been out, but he knew that he had fallen asleep for at least a minute or two. If the Stranger had come upon him just then, Sulid would never have been aware of the danger.

He slowly stretched out his legs and carefully raised his head to look around. The rooftop was still deserted. He uncoiled himself from his hiding place and moved away from the edge of the roof.

There was no way Sulid was going to be able to keep watch all night. Besides, he realized, Borolt might have gone out while it was still daylight. Even if he spotted the man returning to the tower, there was no way for Sulid to get down from the roof in time to intercept him before the Tower door was closed.

He briefly considered walking up to the Tower of Dust and knocking on the door. The thought sent shivers down his spine. Borolt might work for Lord Dust, but at least he was still a man. Sulid really had no idea what a sorcerer might be like, but was pretty sure—from things he had heard—that he was no longer human.

Besides, the servants would never let a homeless kid into the Tower of Dust, or even contact Borolt for him. No one ever trusted the kids who lived on the streets of Ythis. Sulid couldn't blame them—he was a thief, after all.

He cursed himself for a fool and sat back down. He might be here every night for a week and never encounter Borolt Zale. He would have to think of another way to contact the man.

He crawled back over to the edge of the rooftop to take a final look at the Tower. As he watched, the main door opened and a figure emerged. Sulid held his breath.

The figure proceeded across the small space between the Tower and the road, and then emerged into the lamplight at the intersection. Sulid let out his breath in a gasp. It was him!

He watched Borolt cross the street and head in the direction of the bay. As soon as the man picked a direction, Sulid was off to the other side of the building where he could climb down onto a pile of debris in the alley. Less than a minute later, Sulid raced down the street after Borolt Zale.

It was late, and this part of the city didn't usually have a great deal of traffic after dark. Sulid found it easy to follow Borolt, but realized that anyone watching would see him sneaking after the man. He hoped the Stranger was in another part of the city tonight and continued on.

He saw Borolt turn a corner up ahead and Sulid hurried to reach the intersection so as to keep the man in sight. He realized that he would have to call attention to himself very soon, as they were nearing the docks which must be Borolt's destination this evening. He approached the corner with less care than normal, and was completely unprepared when Borolt Zale stepped right into his path and grabbed him by the shoulder.

A glittering blade appeared in the man's hand and pressed against Sulid's throat as he was shoved roughly against the wall.

"Kid or not, if you're a lookout for another ambush I'll have no problem opening your windpipe. Now where are they waiting for me?"

Sulid was stunned. He had no idea how Borolt had seen him, but now the man thought Sulid was working for his enemies.

"I...I...don't...."

Borolt pulled him away from the wall and slammed him back, hard. The knife never left his throat.

"Tell me where they are or else. You have no idea what I'm capable of doing."

Sulid gulped and almost shook his head, but didn't want to accidentally press any harder against the blade.

"I...I need your help! They're after me, just like you. I saw it, and now they're trying to kill me!"

Borolt narrowed his eyes.

"Who's after you? What did you see?"

Sulid never got a chance to answer. Borolt suddenly jerked to the right and threw both of them down onto the cobbles as something hit the wall above Sulid's head.

As he tried to regain the breath that had been knocked out of him, Sulid looked up and saw a wicked-looking crossbow bolt sticking out of the wall about a head's height above where his own head had just been. Someone had just tried to kill Borolt Zale.

Borolt never stopped moving. He rolled as he hit the ground and spun around the corner, taking cover behind the wall. Sulid looked around for an attacker, but it was too dark to see where the crossbowman was hiding.

Borolt reached around the corner and yanked Sulid by the arm, pulling him into cover. Sulid heard him mutter something about being a "planned distraction." He hoped Borolt didn't think he had anything to do with the attack.

The street was quiet. No movement could be seen. Borolt kept his hand around Sulid's arm. He glanced at Sulid and then kept scanning the darkness.

"Who's out there?"

Sulid shook his head, but Borolt wasn't watching him.

"I don't know. Maybe the Stranger."

"What stranger?"

"The man who's chasing me. He's been trying to kill me."

Borolt turned back to look at Sulid's face.

"That bolt was aimed at me, not you. But it still might be the same people. We've got to get out of here and talk—"

Borolt suddenly shoved Sulid away and dove onto the ground again. This time, he wasn't fast enough. A crossbow bolt caught him in the shoulder and knocked him sideways. He rolled against the wall and looked over at Sulid.

"Run! Go...hide!"

Sulid got his feet under him and ran as fast as he could. He kept running, choosing streets at random, until he couldn't breathe anymore. Then he found a boarded-up hovel and crawled into a hole in one wooden wall.

He tried not to cry, but it was all too much. As far as he knew, Borolt was probably dead by now. Tears streamed down his face.

Sulid was alone in the world once more.

*　　　　*　　　　*

I WATCHED THE KID RUN AND REALIZED I HAD NEVER GOTTEN his name. I didn't have time to worry about that right now, though— I was sure my assailant was reloading his crossbow as quickly as he could.

I had a rough idea of his direction from how the bolt had hit me. Getting to him was going to be the tough part. It never occurred to me to run away. The kid was smarter than I was.

First, I needed some immediate cover. I regained my feet and ran straight to the closest alley. I knew the shooter was on the roof to the north of me, but that was two stories up. I wasn't sure how to reach him.

My shoulder was beginning to hurt. I carefully opened my shirt and looked at the bolt. I had made the right decision to wear some armor tonight.

The hidden leather strips sewn into the inside of my clothing were only designed to defend against knives, and so they hadn't fully stopped the bolt. But they had robbed it of some of its power, as had the greater distance of the second shot. A shot that could have broken my collarbone was instead just a flesh wound.

Unfortunately, I was in no position to remove the barbed head from my body at the moment. And my movement was going to cause it to shift in the wound, doing more damage. If I left and got help, all I'd deal with would be some stitches, some bruising, and some pain.

But I'd be giving up on catching my attacker.

I shook my head. I was being foolish. My broken ribs the night before had almost killed me. By the time I had made it out of the Wolf's Den, I was having trouble breathing. I knew that I needed medical attention, but finding a decent doctor at that time of night was nearly impossible, and the best street docs all worked—in one way or another—for the Wolf.

So last night, with no other options, I had headed for the Tower of Dust. I had no idea if Veylar Dust could help me, but I decided to take the risk. I knew I was putting myself further under his power, submitting to him in a way that made me rather vulnerable, but my options had been disappearing fast.

In the state I was in last night, I couldn't have walked all the way to the Tower, so I had hailed a carriage and tried to keep from screaming as it bumped along the roads. It had taken forever, but I was still conscious—barely—when we arrived. I had pounded on the door to the servants' entrance, not entirely sure anyone would open the Tower door in the middle of the night.

And I had passed out as the door opened.

To this day, I still don't know exactly what Veylar Dust did to heal my ribs. I was unconscious throughout the process. He did tell me that one of my broken ribs had pierced a lung, and that I would have died had I not come to the Tower of Dust.

I'm no sorcerer, but I do know a few things about the art. I know that there is always a price for the magic that is created in sorcerous rituals. And I was near death when Veylar Dust healed me that night after leaving the Wolf's lair.

He didn't tell me what the price was. And I didn't ask about the dried bloodstains on the floor of the chamber where I woke up. So what did that make me?

Tonight, it made me someone who wasn't going to return to the Tower for more help. I had to be careful, though. My moment of indecision had just shifted the situation back in the assassin's favor.

He would already have reloaded and moved to a new vantage point. Or perhaps he was moving across the rooftops, searching for me. Either way, I was a sitting duck if I stayed in this alley.

I moved further into the darkness and found that the alley—after a couple twists and turns—let out on another street. I scanned the rooftops for signs of movement and, seeing nothing, charged from one side of the street to the other. I reached the other side and ducked around a corner.

My shoulder was beginning to throb, and I couldn't run without causing the crossbow bolt to shift around. Instead, I kept walking at a slow, steady pace, crossing streets as often as possible. My rooftop assailant would have to come down to street level to pursue me, and that would put him in the open.

By the time I reached a surgeon I knew, I was sure I was no longer being followed. But now I had a new problem. I couldn't fully trust any street doc because I didn't know what message Wolf might have sent down through his channels.

At least I wouldn't lose consciousness while being treated for this wound, but I also couldn't take anything to dull the pain. A street doctor might give me something to completely knock me out, and then I'd be at the mercy of whoever wanted to score favors with the Wolf. There were very few people I trusted.

I had to knock on the door for a full five minutes before Mossip opened it. I had obviously woken him, but that was pretty typical for a street doc. Most of his patients got injured in the darkest hours of the night.

I was glad he didn't already have any other visitors, though. It was a complication I didn't need right now.

Mossip was a small man with wiry gray hair around the sides and back, and none on top. He looked up at my face and a quick flash of fear appeared in his eyes before his gaze settled on the bolt sticking out of my shoulder.

"You want me to take care of that?"

"What do you think?"

"I think you're taking a risk, coming here. I think you're worried I'm going to knock you out and deliver your head to the Wolf. I think you're here because you don't have any other options."

"Are you a mind-reader now?"

"I don't need to be."

He was right about what I was thinking, about my lack of options. I waited, but he didn't move.

"Should I leave?"

He considered me for another few seconds and then shook his head.

"No, come in. Let me see what you've got."

He turned and led me into his small home. He lit a lamp and unwrapped his tools.

"Did you come to me because you feel I'm trustworthy, or because I'm too old to pander to the Wolf?"

I grinned at him.

"You seem to know what I'm thinking, so you tell me."

He stopped where he was.

"No, I want you to answer me. You know the word has gone out that the Wolf wants nothing more to do with you. He's too smart to put a price on your head—even the Church had to rescind theirs when you went to work for Veylar Dust—but anyone looking to curry favor with the Wolf will consider doing you in. But you came here anyway. To *my* surgery. Why did you choose me?"

I almost shrugged, but a twinge in my shoulder stopped me.

"I think you'd have too much pride in your work."

He considered that and nodded.

"*And* you're too old to be any threat."

He looked back up at me sharply, and then let out a laugh.

"Fair enough, Borolt. Now let's see what we've got here...."

Chapter Nine

I WAS RIGHT ABOUT MOSSIP. HE HAD TOO MUCH PRIDE TO do anything but his best, and his best had me back out on the street in less than an hour. I was a little weak from pain and blood loss—not to mention my recovery from the day before—but I couldn't risk staying any longer than necessary.

The sky was no longer fully black when I emerged. I figured I was probably safe from any further attacks from the assassin, but I took precautions anyway. If he wasn't a real professional, he might decide the risk of being seen was worth the shot at me.

I used all the back alleys and shortcuts I knew to reach in a round-about way the area where I had been ambushed. When I crossed the last major street cutting through the buildings, it was time to head up to the roofs. My shoulder ached a bit, but I ascended without incident.

I had to be extra careful now. I didn't think there was any way the assassin would still be around, more than an hour after his attempt on my life, but I also didn't want to be seen by some early riser. As the sky paled above me, my outline became more visible on the rooftops.

I wanted to see if I could find the spots where he had fired his crossbow at me. Unlikely as it was, I couldn't pass up the chance of finding some clue or lead. So, I tried to gauge the angle of his shot based on how the crossbow bolt had hit the wall above my head, and how the second bolt had entered my shoulder.

I spent the next half hour searching but didn't find a trace of anyone. Whoever he was, this assassin was careful. And now I was exposed on the rooftops as the city streets began to come to life around me.

It was short work to return to street level and head off in the direction that the young boy had run last night. I cursed myself again for not getting his name. How was I supposed to find one specific street urchin in Ythis when I didn't even know who he was?

I spent the next hour wandering around the area letting myself be seen, in case the boy was close by and waiting for an opportunity. Then I returned to the area around the Tower of Dust and did the same thing. If he had followed me from the Tower, he might return there to wait for me.

After giving him ample opportunity to make contact with me, I considered my next course of action. Despite spending most of yesterday unconscious, I needed rest—it had taken a lot out of me. I had no need, or desire, to return to the Tower today.

As I made my way home, I kept my eyes moving, looking for signs of anything suspicious. I wasn't going to wander into yet another ambush and expect to survive. I had been incredibly lucky twice, and I wasn't going to push the odds any more than I had to.

My mind, however, kept wandering back to that bloodstain on the floor of the Tower of Dust. The sorcerer may have done the cutting, but ultimately, I was responsible for whatever, or whoever, had been killed to power my recovery. I didn't want to think about it, but I couldn't help myself.

How had I gotten so far into such a situation? I had simply been trying to save my brother when everything began spiraling out of control. I ended up opposing the Church—one man against an entire institution backed by the power of a god.

And instead of running away like any sane person, I decided to stay in Ythis and put myself at the beck and call of perhaps the one being more evil than the entirety of the Church itself. I somehow convinced myself that I could stay clean, unsullied by my association with Veylar Dust as long as I refused to do anything too distasteful.

But yesterday, I found the point at which my own moral code was tossed aside like yesterday's garbage. When it was my own life on the line, I discovered that I would do anything to save it, and damn the consequences. And I knew in my heart that I accepted the price and would pay it again if necessary.

The fact that the price was really paid by someone else didn't escape me. I was fully aware of how low I had sunk.

Why did I not just leave Ythis? If I did it properly, Veylar Dust would blame the Church for my disappearance, and the Church would blame the Wolf, and the three of them could fight it out while I made a new life for myself on the other side of the world.

I knew I wasn't going anywhere, though. Not yet, at least. There were loose ends that I needed to tie up here. I needed to know what had happened to Ankin Poloth. I needed to see it resolved, if only for my own peace of mind.

And now I wanted to help the boy from last night. If he was telling the truth—and I had to admit that I couldn't be sure he wasn't lying the whole time—he was in a great deal of danger. If he had gotten on the wrong side of the Church, then it was more than just his life that was at stake.

He said he had seen something, and that "they" were after him. Was it the Church? And what could a street urchin have seen that was so dangerous? I couldn't begin to guess.

I returned to my room and lay down fully clothed. My mind was churning, and I realized I was starving. I couldn't bring myself to get up and go back out, however. A great weariness settled on my body, though my mind was still going strong.

Something didn't seem right. I was tired, but this was beyond exhaustion. My thoughts were clear, however, and I had no trouble keeping my eyes open.

Just to prove to myself that I could, I lifted one arm—or tried to. Nothing happened. I concentrated on lifting my arm off the bed, put every ounce of will into it. My thumb merely twitched once, and that was it.

I could move my eyes, and I was still breathing normally, but otherwise I was paralyzed. I tried to turn my head, wiggle my toes, or do anything physical. My body didn't react in the slightest.

And then my eyes started to close. I fought with everything I had to keep them open, but they slowly closed as if someone else entirely was in control of my body. I had come home to a trap of some kind, one I probably wouldn't escape.

My luck had finally run out.

*   *   *

I FELT SOMETHING HARD, LIKE STONE, UNDER MY BACK. IT WAS hot to the touch—though I still couldn't move my fingers, I could feel the heat of the stone through them where my hand lay at my side. I was still in the same position in which I had become paralyzed.

Only I was no longer in my own room.

The hot, humid air was filled with a deep thrumming sound that reverberated in my chest. I smelled something burning, like pork roasting on a fire. Then I remembered that burning human flesh gives off the same odor. I was no longer sure I wanted to open my eyes.

Of course, as soon as I had the thought, my eyelids parted and I stared at an immense stone ceiling far above me, lit by a flickering red light that surrounded me just past the edge of my vision. The entire roof of the cavern was carved in strange geometric shapes that appeared to be moving, crawling across the surface. I tried to focus on a single pattern, but my eyes kept sliding across the carved lines as they merged with others.

I began to feel nauseated, and I worried about what would happen if I vomited while immobilized on my back.

A shadow fell across me. I realized that I could move my eyes, so I looked as far to the side as possible. A vaguely humanoid shape stood near me, but I could make out no details as it was lit from behind by blood-red flames.

A strange hissing rose over the deep vibrating background hum, immediately accompanied by a whistling noise that I knew to be words.

"This one recognizes Borolt Zale."

I felt a rush of excitement and fear through my body as I recognized the voice and mannerisms of the Tsojim. Was I in their underground home? If so, how had they brought me here?

I remembered Uwibee's demand for me to leave; how he had been angry at my questions regarding the beast in the bay. If the Tsojim had decided to do something to me, I was completely helpless to resist.

"Why does Borolt Zale recline? Borolt Zale should control his spirit body and move as he needs to."

That made no sense to me. If the Tsojim weren't keeping me immobile, then what was? I felt my fingers twitch on the stone beside me. I wished I could speak to whichever Tsojim was here to ask it why I was paralyzed.

I licked my lips and opened my mouth. Just like that, I regained the use of my voice.

"This one is Borolt Zale. This one does not know why he cannot move."

The Tsojim just stood there, watching me.

"This one does not understand. Borolt Zale cannot move because he does not move."

I tried to figure out what the Tsojim meant, but it made no sense. I was immobilized because I had chosen to be immobilized? But I had never made that choice.

And just like that, I had full control of my body again. I sat up carefully, and then stood fully and looked around.

We were standing on a disk of stone surrounded by red flames that reached to twice my height. The entire surface of the disk was carved with the same strange geometric shapes that shifted and slid across the ceiling. The ceiling itself was a vast dome that came down in the far distance on all sides.

There was no visible entrance or exit to this huge chamber.

"What space is this, where this one and Tsojim stand?"

"This one and Borolt Zale occupy the dreamspace. The Tsojim must speak with Borolt Zale, but Borolt Zale is not welcome in the Tsojim home."

I had no idea what the dreamspace was, although I could guess easily enough. I figured I must be asleep, and my physical body was still back in my room. But if the Tsojim had brought me here to talk....

"Why is this one not welcome?"

"Borolt Zale goes against the creature in the bay. Borolt Zale asks questions that cannot be answered. Borolt Zale wishes to speak with the Seer. For these reasons, Borolt Zale cannot be allowed to visit the Tsojim."

The Tsojim's explanation made me more confused, not less.

"Then why have the Tsojim brought this one here...in sleep?"

"The Seer wishes to speak to Borolt Zale. The Tsojim must not know."

This was a new piece of information. In my rare dealings with the Tsojim, I had seen them swap bodies and converse instantly. I had assumed they all shared their knowledge, that they were some kind of hive-mind.

"Why does the Seer want to speak with this one? Will the Seer answer this one's questions about the creature in the bay?"

"This one does not know. This one *will not know* that Borolt Zale is here to speak with the Seer."

I started to point out that this Tsojim already knew I was here, but decided not to waste my breath. There was obviously too much I didn't know about the Tsojim, and I doubted I had time to get all my questions answered.

"Okay, how does this one speak to the Seer?"

"Borolt Zale speaks. The Seer is the dreamspace."

I was just trying to figure out that statement when the Tsojim vanished from right in front of me. In some ways, it was like the movement of the demons—it didn't so much disappear as it was suddenly never there in the first place.

I looked around the huge chamber for something to focus on, someone to which I could speak directly. But I had the sinking feeling the Tsojim's words meant I was inside the mind of the Seer, somehow.

I did not find the thought comforting.

"Okay, then. Seer, if you can hear this one, this one is Borolt Zale. You brought this one here to talk. So...this one is here."

I waited for a response, any response, but I heard nothing.

"This one asked to speak with you about the creature in the bay, but Uwibee did not approve of this one's request, and ordered this one to leave. Is that what you wanted to see this one about?"

I stood there, waiting, but there was no sound other than that low thrumming filling the chamber. I turned around and nearly screamed.

Standing directly behind me was a woman who looked almost human. She was bald, slender, wearing a plain yellow robe that fell right to the floor, obscuring her entire body. She would have been vaguely attractive, except....

Her eyes were black pits, windows into a void so deep I could feel myself being pulled towards her when I looked into them.

I wrenched my gaze away from her eye sockets and backed up, trying to get some space between us. My heart was hammering in my chest—which made me wonder whether my real body was here or still in my own bed.

"Please do not be afraid. You shall not be harmed."

Her voice was little more than a whisper, though I heard it clearly over—or rather, through—the sound in the chamber. She was also speaking my language. When she opened her mouth, I saw the same dark void behind her lips, and my nausea returned.

"I have taken an appearance that should be comforting to you, but I cannot fully hide my real form. You are in no danger here, but perhaps you should refrain from gazing at my face."

I nodded without looking at her.

"You aren't speaking the Tsojim language. I always assumed you were one of them."

"I am Tsojim, but also something else. I have abilities beyond the rest of my race. Regardless, I am not really speaking to you here. You are inside the dreamspace, and I *am* the dreamspace. I can communicate with you directly, with no barriers to comprehension."

"We'll see," I muttered. I had the feeling that her answers to my questions weren't going to be so easy to understand.

"You are searching for a way to force the being in the bay to leave. It *cannot* be forced."

"What is it? Even Veylar Dust—"

She hissed and turned away when I said his name.

"I'm sorry, I didn't mean to…."

I stopped, confused. I wasn't sure what I had just done.

She shook her head.

"Please do not speak the name of your master. Names build connections, and I must not have a connection to one such as him."

"Again, I'm sorry. I didn't know."

"You walk a narrow path, Borolt Zale. There is great darkness on either side, and you have nearly fallen more than once. Your path will become a thread, and you will not be able to save yourself if you keep to your current course."

"Are you telling me that I should stop trying to get rid of the creature in the bay?"

She smiled with her lips pressed together.

"You know exactly what I am telling you."

I didn't know how to respond to that. She was right, of course. I was heading for a dead end. Everyone could see it, even me.

But I wouldn't stop. Not yet.

"About the creature, Seer… what is it?"

"I cannot tell you at this juncture. It is too soon. You must figure it out, and at that point the best solution will present itself to you."

"But… are you saying that you have the answer, and won't tell me?"

"I know many things, some of which are true now, some of which will be true at some point in the future. Were I to share the wrong truth now, it could cause great trouble."

"So, if you'll permit me to ask, why did you bring me here?"

"To meet you, Borolt Zale. You are at the center of a web of connections. Some of those connections I wish to avoid. Others are of great interest to me. I also did not agree with how Uwibee drove you away. Uwibee does what Uwibee must. But none of my people can fully understand what I do, what I am."

"Do you see into the future?"

"I cannot answer such a question without causing some things to unravel. I will not be responsible for such consequences. You have a task in front of you, to drive away the creature. But you cannot force the creature to do anything it does not wish to do. But, where force fails, other approaches may succeed."

"But you said that I'll only succeed when I figure out what the creature is."

"No, I said when you figure out the answer to the creature's nature, the best solution will present itself to you. Your actions have repercussions, both successful and not. Some of those repercussions are necessary for things to happen as they should."

I laughed, though there was no humor in it.

"That doesn't exactly help me, well, at all."

"You must continue trying to solve the mystery of the creature's nature. And you must continue your efforts to remove it from the bay. Some of those efforts may fail. You will not know until you try. And it is the *trying* which is important."

"And if I just give up and run away?"

"You know you will not give up, Borolt Zale. And so, I know it, too. I can tell you there is an answer, a solution. I cannot tell you where to find it. That is for you to do alone."

"Why do I get the feeling you're talking about some kind of destiny?"

She smiled again, and this time there was genuine amusement in it. She tried to keep her mouth closed, but the void leaked out between her lips. I shuddered.

"There is no destiny, Borolt Zale. Only connections. I believe we will talk again, but it will not be under these circumstances."

"Isn't there anything else you can tell me?"

But I was already back in my room. I didn't even see it happen. I didn't open my eyes, or suddenly sit up. I was just there.

I had the feeling an answer was just at the edge of my mind, that she had already told me what I needed to know. I sat there for an hour, trying to think my way around it, but the idea was too elusive. It kept slipping away when I got close to it.

I believed I already knew the answer to the problem of the creature. Now I just had to realize it.

How hard could that be?

Chapter Ten

I WENT DOWN TO THE SAILOR'S KNOT TO GET SOME FOOD AND determine how much time had passed while I was away in the dreamspace. The sun had either barely moved, or I had lost an entire day. I was hoping the former—I had the feeling that every day that passed was a day leading us closer to something big and unpleasant.

As soon as I entered, Jolin came over and blocked my way to an empty table.

"There was someone here lookin' for you."

That didn't bode well.

"What day is it?"

He gave me a sour look.

"Are you drunk?"

"No, but I've been working hard lately, and I think I may have slept an entire day away. So what day is it?"

"It's Burady. You bringin' trouble here?"

So, I hadn't lost a day after all. That was a relief. But who would come looking for me here?

"How would I know, Jolin? You haven't told me who's looking for me, yet."

"Sailor. Said his name was Fratos. Someone named Bakiah told him to find you. You owe money or somethin'?"

I put my hand on Jolin's shoulder and firmly guided him out of my way. If Captain Bakiah had sent someone to talk to me, there was no danger.

"No, I don't owe anything to anyone. Captain Bakiah is a friend, and he's helping me with my work."

Jolin shut his mouth with a snap. My job, and by extension my employer, were subjects that he just wouldn't discuss. I knew he was afraid of Lord Dust. Most people were. I also knew he would have preferred to kick me out the room I rented, but Jolin both needed the money and was too scared to boot me into the street.

"Where did this Fratos say I could find him?"

Jolin stood there a moment, staring at me and trying to figure out some way to refuse to tell me anything more about my visitor. Finally, his laziness overcame his foul attitude and he shrugged.

"He said he'd be at the same place you met that Bakiah guy."

"Great. Now I'd like to eat something good. But, since I'm already here, I'll settle for whatever *you're* serving."

I was pushing him and I knew it. Eventually, one of us was going to snap and make a final decision about our arrangement. It would probably get pretty nasty before that happened. I could see it coming, but was too busy and tired to care.

Once I had eaten, I headed for the dockside bar where I had talked with Captain Bakiah only six days ago. I expected the place to be empty—too many ships were skipping Ythis these days—and it was pretty deserted except for a couple of drunks in one corner, and a middle-aged sailor with a bent back and swollen knuckles.

He looked up as I entered and waved me over to his table.

"Are you Fratos?"

He nodded.

"You must be Borolt Zale. Captain Bakiah told meh how you looked."

His voice was scratchy and breathless, and I guessed he had some kind of throat or chest problem. Combined with his other physical ailments, it was obvious he didn't do any sailing anymore. I wondered how he earned his money these days.

"Let me buy you a drink and you can tell me why you wanted to speak with me."

I signaled the bartender to bring over two of whatever Fratos was already drinking.

"Well, the Captain tol' meh you was asking questions about the thing in the bay. And how you got him to tell the story about the *Windroarer.*"

I nodded silently. I didn't want to interrupt him and throw him off his path of thoughts.

"He says you was asking about anyone who saw a ship go down, only there wasn't very many 'cause the thing takes 'em all and leaves no survivors.

"Only, there *is* one."

I wasn't sure I understood him correctly.

"One what? A survivor?"

He nodded.

"Yup. He was on the *Shutharja* when she was taken by the thing. Only managed to survive 'cause he was thrown so far when the arms of that thing crashed down on the deck. Guess it lost track of him when it was eatin' all the others."

"What's this man's name?"

"Olere. Don't know he has a last name. He lives with his wife north of the city, as far from the water as he can be and still inside the wall up there. He won't go anywhere near the docks anymore."

I was stunned. Here was someone who had managed to survive an attack and the destruction of his ship, and I had heard nothing about him until now.

"How come everyone doesn't know about him?"

"He kept it quiet. Only told a few people. I think he was worried the priests might want to ask him a few questions if they found out what happened to him. Or one of the Five. He only told me 'cause I sailed with him for a couple of years and we was friends."

"If you don't mind my asking, why are you telling me now?"

"The Captain said you was okay and was trying to get rid of the thing in the water. I figure it might be worth it to talk to Olere. He knows I was going to tell you, so he'll get what you're about if you go up there."

This was an unexpected fortune. While it was likely Olere wouldn't know anything useful, he might at least set me on the right track.

"I won't tell anyone else about him—you have my word on that."

Fratos told me where I could find Olere, and then looked at me thoughtfully.

"Are you really gonna get rid of that thing in the bay? I figured the priests would be doin' that."

"You and me both. But it's fallen in the laps of the Five, instead."

He sat back and looked at me warily.

"So, how're you involved, then?"

I silently cursed myself for not being more cautious. Captain Bakiah obviously never told Fratos who I worked for.

"I, uh, work for Veylar Dust."

Fratos pushed back from the table and stood up shakily.

"Fratos, I'm not a sorcerer, and I gave you my word that I won't tell anyone else about Olere. You have nothing to worry about from me. I'm just trying to make the bay safe again."

"Safe for who?" he whispered.

"Everyone. Listen, I'm just a hired hand. I'm collecting information for Lord Dust about the creature and that's it. He doesn't ask me how I find out what I know and I don't volunteer it. Your friend is safe."

Fratos shook his head and then looked me in the eyes.

"I'll hold you to yer word, Borolt Zale. Just 'cause I'm not a sorcerer doesn't mean I don't got my own resources."

He was threatening me, which usually pisses me off, but it was obvious he was terrified that he had just done something terrible to his friend. I gave him a pass and just nodded.

"I'll go talk to him right away, and then I'll leave him alone. Okay?"

He looked like he had just eaten something bitter, but he nodded at me and sat back down.

I walked out and began heading north.

*   *   *

IT TOOK ME OVER AN HOUR TO REACH OLERE'S NEIGHBORHOOD. The north end of the city is where the noble families have their estates, sprawling mansions surrounded by small collections of specialty shops and services. Olere and his wife worked as grounds-keepers for the Qarwen family, one of the founding families of the Empire.

When I reached the outer gate, I noticed a few things were off. There were a few too many spots of rust on the iron bars, the carriage in front of the doors was in disrepair, and only a solitary figure stood guard at the entrance to the estate. It appeared the Qarwen family was not as prosperous as it had once been.

I approached the guard and he eyed me without interest.

"I'm here to see Olere, the groundskeeper."

He grunted and waved me on. Very sloppy. He was likely being underpaid and didn't really care who entered the estate—not that it mattered to me. I had been in enough mansions to figure out where the servants' entrance was, and I made my way straight there.

I rapped on the door and waited. After a couple of minutes, I rapped again, but there was no answer. A bit further along I could see the exterior entrance to the kitchens, so I proceeded on.

I let myself into the kitchens to see a couple of servants cleaning. There was none of the common chatter between women that usually occurred in such an environment—both worked in silence. I cleared my throat and one of them turned to me.

"Yes?"

"My name is Borolt Zale, and I'm here to speak with the groundskeeper, Olere."

The other servant's head whipped around, and they both stared at me with wide eyes.

"He's not here—" began one, but the other interrupted.

"We can get his wife, sir. She may have heard from him by now."

Confused, I was about to ask what she meant but she leapt up and nearly ran from the kitchen. The other servant just continued to stare at me.

"It's okay. He's expecting me to drop by, and I'm not in any particular hurry."

My words didn't seem to reassure her. She backed up to stand beside the door leading further into the house and began glancing into the hall.

"Shall I wait outside?"

She jumped when I spoke, and uttered a small squeak of surprise.

"Please, sir. She'll be right back with Eleann. I promise."

She was terrified of my presence here. Even if the Qarwen family were a bunch of taskmasters, she shouldn't have been this afraid of me.

"It's okay," I repeated. "Can you tell me what's going on? You seem afraid, but I'm not here to cause any trouble for you or Olere. I just need to ask him a few questions."

"Begging your pardon, sir, but it's all a bit much for me. I don't know what he's done, and I don't want to know. I never really spoke to him much—just his wife now and again and never about anything personal. And she's been frantic with worry, but hasn't said a word about anything to me. I swear it, sir."

"Has anyone else been asking after Olere? Or his wife? Has something happened?"

She stood there staring at me, mouth working but no sound coming out. A sound from the hallway made her turn her head and she let out a breath in great relief.

"Eleann is here, sir. I'll leave you to speak to her in peace."

And she practically fled from the room before I could stop her.

An older woman peeked around the edge of the door before entering slowly. She stood just inside the frame of the doorway, her hands clasped tightly in front of her.

"I am Eleann. Please tell me what you want."

Everyone seemed to think I was someone else.

"I only want to speak to Olere. Fratos sent me. My name is Borolt Zale, and Fratos arranged with Olere for me to ask him some questions."

Her shoulders sagged and she reached forward to steady herself on a countertop.

"Fratos sent you? By the light, I thought you were one of them!"

"One of whom? Why is everyone so terrified? What's going on?"

"Tell me please, Mister Zale, what you were going to ask my husband."

"I wanted to talk to him about the day the *Shutharja* was destroyed."

A grim looked swept across her face.

"I thought as much. I told him it was something he should never mention again, but I think he felt a need to talk about it. Would anyone have wanted to prevent him from speaking with you?"

I considered the question before answering.

"It's certainly possible. I do have enemies—I just don't know who they all are, yet. But unless he told others, no one besides Fratos and Olere knew I was going to come here. I didn't even know until an hour ago."

"Then perhaps the men don't have anything to do with you."

"What men?"

"The men," she replied, "who abducted my husband yesterday."

This was not good.

"When did this happen, exactly? Where was he abducted, exactly?"

She took a deep breath and I could hear in the way her voice shook when she answered that she feared the worst.

"Yesterday afternoon, Olere had to go into the trade quarter to order some supplies. The merchant houses don't come directly to the estate anymore—the family is having some financial difficulties these days and don't order enough to make the visits worth their time.

"Olere was supposed to return by the seventh hour. He didn't come back last night. First thing this morning, I asked one of the younger servants to go to the trade quarter and find him, or ask at the merchants he was planning to visit.

"When she returned, she told me that a couple of the hired hands at Olere's first destination saw him get stopped by four men. They surrounded him and appeared to be asking him questions. Then a black carriage pulled up and the men forced my husband to get inside. It was one of the carriages that belong to the Church. There has been no word from anyone as to his whereabouts since."

I didn't bother to ask why the hired hands had let it happen without intervening. Most people refused to involve themselves in the troubles of others. The balance of risk and reward was rarely worth it, especially where the Church was concerned.

"Were the men dressed like priests?"

She shook her head.

"One of hired hands said he saw a priest inside the carriage, but the other men were dressed, well, normal."

I didn't know how to ask the most important question. The witnesses wouldn't know what a member of the Hidden looked like. And I doubt anyone got close enough to examine the rings on any of the priests' hands.

She looked at me in confusion and then tried to swallow a sob. She knew in her heart that she was not likely to see Olere alive again. I knew in *my* heart who was ultimately behind this abduction. She could see it in my eyes.

"Can you help us? Can you get my husband back?"

"No," I whispered, and then she did break down into tears.

Olere was out of her reach for good, and out of mine, too. He was now in the hands of the Hidden.

Chapter Eleven

I LEFT ELEANN IN THE CARE OF THE STAFF AT THE QARWEN estate and returned home. I couldn't trust myself not to get into trouble if I stayed around other people.

I wanted to smash something, to hurt someone. Yet another life—no, two lives—destroyed by the Church. They didn't care who they hurt, what damage they caused, as long as they kept their power.

I paced back and forth in my room, my body aching to act. I imagined mounting a one-man attack on the Church, hunting through the hallways, killing any priests I encountered. All to rescue a man who was probably already dead.

And Veylar Dust wouldn't be any help. To him, this was a political maneuver. Just another movement of a piece on a game board. He didn't care about the lives of normal people any more than the priests did.

I forced myself to sit down, but had to stand up again almost immediately. I had too much energy, and all of it violent. This whole stinking city was filled with the selfish, the evil, and the insane.

Suddenly, I had the overwhelming desire to take all that nervous energy and turn it toward something I should have done a long time ago. In an instant, I decided to leave Ythis for good. There was nothing I could accomplish here, and I had finally reached the breaking point.

I looked around the room, trying to decide what I was going to take and what I would leave behind. I had few possessions, and wouldn't really miss anything I lost. Money was a minor issue, but I had the skills to get more by honest means or otherwise.

I was checking my knives when someone knocked on the door. All my senses focused, and the whole world went very quiet as I prepared myself for what I knew was coming next.

I stepped to one side of the door so that when it burst inwards, I wouldn't be hampered in my counterattack. I knew they had come for me, Veylar Dust be damned, and also knew they would play for keeps.

I carefully kept my rage in check. The only way out of this was to use my brain and hit them rapidly and accurately. I crouched beside the door and used the tip of one dagger to rattle the handle as if I was turning it.

I tensed for the blow and prepared to fight for my life.

I waited. Nothing happened.

Then there was another knock on the door.

"Hello?"

A young man's voice on the other side.

Sure, it was a trick, I stayed crouched beside the door and reached up with my off hand to turn the handle. The 'click' of the latch sent my heart leaping and I snatched my hand back.

"Hello? Mister Zale?"

There was fear in the voice on the other side. They were being extra cautious. Apparently, my reputation had given them reason to avoid the rapid frontal assault.

"There's a message for you, sir."

A pause.

"Okay, I'll leave it out here."

And at that, I heard rapid footsteps heading back down the stairs and out into the street.

I began to have a doubt. I wanted them to come through the door. I wanted to feel my blade going into someone's flesh and watch as some servant of the Church died at my hands. But I now doubted they had come for me after all.

I reached up and yanked the door fully open, still crouched to one side. Nothing happened.

I took a quick look around the doorframe and saw no one on the stairs. Sitting on the landing just outside my door was an envelope.

The seal on the envelope belonged to Veylar Dust.

I began to feel foolish. In my agitated state, I had obviously just mistaken one of Lord Dust's servants as a strike team from the Church. I could only imagine what the poor young man was thinking as he raced back to the Tower.

I grabbed the envelope and opened it. Inside was a note from Veylar Dust instructing me to attend to him at the Tower tomorrow morning. He would be surprised when I didn't show up, as I'd be a long way from Ythis by then.

I sat down and put my head in my hands. Was I really going to do it? Was I going to leave Ythis behind? I felt drained by my expectation of a fight for my life that never appeared. My anger was mostly gone, replaced by emptiness.

I considered it again, but deep down I knew I wasn't going to leave. I had been so close to abandoning this city and its problems, but the hand of Veylar Dust had reached out and taken the impetus from me in the form of a simple messenger.

I cursed the sorcerer, but my heart was no longer in it. Running away wouldn't get me the vengeance I wanted. I may not have believed I would ever truly succeed in my quest to punish the Church for all that had happened, but I knew that there was always a chance if I stayed in the city. If I left, I'd have no opportunity at all.

But I couldn't leave the abduction of Olere unanswered. Someone was going to pay for that, and soon. It may have been stupid, but I was past the point of caring.

In fact, tomorrow night I was going to return to the Stone Traveler and have a chat with a certain regular there. Maybe I'd ask him about Ankin Poloth while I was at it. There was no point in keeping secrets at this point. It appeared the Hidden knew exactly what I was going to do before I did.

And then it struck me.

There are certain assumptions one makes when dealing with the kinds of people I encounter regularly. The Five and the Church work at cross purposes. Everyone knows this. They fight each other to exert influence on the Emperor.

Because of this, I've always believed that sorcerers must not worship the gods. After all, the Church represents all worship.

But I was beginning to wonder if that was always true. Could a sorcerer secretly serve the gods, even if he or she didn't support the Church? Such a thing had never occurred to me, but that didn't mean it didn't happen.

And if such a thing were true, was it possible that one of Veylar Dust's apprentices might have secretly been worshipping the gods? And if the answer to that was 'yes' then it was just as possible that it might be true for another apprentice as well.

The Hidden were masters of manipulation. If anyone could warp someone's worship of the gods into direct support of the Church, they could.

And if any of this was true, then one or more of Veylar Dust's apprentices—or the apprentices of any of the Five—might be secret allies of the priesthood.

All of this was speculation, though. But I was meeting with Lord Dust tomorrow morning, and there would be no better time to find out. If I was wrong, then at least I'd know it wasn't possible.

I didn't want to think about what might happen if I was right.

*   *   *

WHEN I ARRIVED AT THE TOWER, QUDA CAME TO SEE ME directly. He continued barking orders at the servants as he approached.

"Borolt! Lord Dust is waiting for you in his office. Go straight up and don't delay."

"What's going on?"

"Lord Dust will explain it to you. You have your own part to play, so listen carefully to everything he tells you. He's in no mood to be kept waiting, so I suggest you hurry."

This was not what I needed today. I wanted to discuss his apprentices, but obviously something big was up. I took the stairs three at a time and was at his office a moment after I left Quda.

When I rapped on the door, it opened immediately. Veylar Dust was at his desk, and a servant was stationed just inside the door. I hadn't seen him do that before, and I realized that I had begun to see him as predictable.

That was a dangerous mindset to be in.

He looked up from his papers and motioned me to sit opposite his desk. I took the chair and the servant closed the door behind me, and then just stood there, waiting.

Veylar ignored me for a few minutes as he made notes in his journal, a large, leather-bound book filled with his spidery script. Then he carefully set his quill to one side and raised his gaze to my face.

"What have you been doing?"

As usual, his question confused me. Was he talking about my investigation into the actions of Ankin Poloth? My pursuit of knowledge about the creature in the bay? The attacks upon me from some unknown direction?

He had no patience for my hesitation.

"Four days ago, you tried to get answers from the Tsojim, and failed. Since then, you got yourself nearly killed by some thugs in an alley and . . . what? What have you been doing since then?"

I decided not to tell him about the boy. There was nothing there he needed to know, yet.

"I discovered there was a survivor of the *Shutharja* attack. A man named Olere had told no one of his purely lucky escape from the destruction of the ship. He became a groundskeeper for the Qarwen family estate."

"Have you spoken to him yet?"

"No, I—"

"I want you to bring him here to the Tower, by whatever means necessary. I will question him myself. The delays have gone on long enough."

It didn't escape me that he had just ordered me to abduct Olere, if necessary, in the same manner that the Hidden had already done. I was reminded once again how inhuman Veylar Dust really was.

"I cannot bring him here, Lord Dust. He—"

The sorcerer stood abruptly, sending his chair tipping backwards. His voice thundered with rage.

"You will do what I have ordered! I have let you have your freedom for too long, and it has cost me enough! I want this man brought to the Tower, and if you won't do it, I will replace you with someone who can!"

The air thrummed with power, and I realized that he was a hair's breadth away from killing me on the spot. But I couldn't do what he asked.

"The Church already has him."

Lord Dust's eyes narrowed and I felt a wave of heat building on my skin.

"How, precisely, did they *get* him?"

"I don't know. I only learned of his existence this morning. I went to the estate to speak with him, but he was abducted by a group of priests yesterday afternoon. I assume he's in the Temple, somewhere."

The heat was slowly building—soon it would begin to hurt.

"Who told you about him?"

"Fratos, a former sailor who once crewed with him. I had put the word out with a couple of ship captains that I was looking for information, and Olere agreed with Fratos to talk to me."

"So Fratos also told the priests?"

"Very unlikely. Olere was essentially in hiding because he was afraid that the priests—or the Five—would find out."

"How do you know the priests have him?"

"There were witnesses. They grabbed him right off the street in the late afternoon. There was no subtlety or secrecy to this."

And just like that, the heat disappeared. Lord Dust continued to stare at me, but he was no longer considering ending my life. I sat very still. I didn't want to reveal my obvious relief just yet.

He waved at the servant and pointed to his chair. The man hurried over and righted it before taking his place back beside the door. Lord Dust sat down slowly, his mind occupied with the ramifications of what had occurred.

"How sure are you that the witnesses are correct? Are you certain it was the Church that took this man?"

"I'm positive. The men who grabbed him weren't dressed like priests, but they used a Church carriage, and according to the witnesses, a priest was riding inside it."

I hesitated before plunging ahead.

"It's possible the men who were not dressed like priests may belong to a sect within the church. Their symbol is a nine-pointed star with an eye in the center, which they often wear as a ring. I expect you know what that signifies."

To be honest, I wasn't entirely sure Veylar Dust knew of the existence of the Hidden. They went to great lengths to keep themselves secret, especially from rivals like the Five.

"I have heard a rumor about that symbol, but have never had it confirmed."

I shouldn't have been shocked, but I was. I was used to Veylar Dust knowing so many secrets, secrets that were so far beyond my ability to comprehend, that it surprised me to discover I knew of the Hidden and he did not.

Then again, he had never gone to war against them directly like I had.

"I can confirm the symbol, and the existence of the Hidden. I met one, when I was trying to hide my brother. He came after us, and I killed him, though it was a close thing."

If I was expecting to impress Veylar Dust, I was disappointed. He showed no reaction to my revelation at all.

"Other than my research, what do we have to show for our efforts? You retrieved no information from the Tsojim, nor will we get anything from this survivor now that he's in the possession of the Church."

I tried to think of something positive, but all my efforts so far had come to naught. I hadn't contributed anything to Lord Dust's efforts to rid Ythis of the creature.

He took my silence for what it was, an admission of absolute failure.

"In two days, Kalam Ghargar will visit the Tower, and I will report on our progress, or lack thereof. I will then attend a meeting of the Emperor's Council, where this will certainly be a topic of discussion. I will stay at the palace for the three days of the Council, and there will be no way to reach me during that time."

I suddenly understood why Quda was in such a state. In two days, the most powerful of the Five, the leader—if such a group of sorcerers could be said to have a leader—would be coming to meet with Veylar Dust in preparation for the Emperor's Council.

A visit by Kalam Ghargar followed by Lord Dust's stay at the palace meant poor Quda was probably overwhelmed with preparations....

"You will attend my meeting with Lord Ghargar."

I snapped out of my reverie and stared at Lord Dust.

"Me? But I'm not a sorcerer."

"Not relevant!" he snapped. "You have been a part of this effort from the beginning and he may have direct questions for you. He will bring two of his apprentices. I will have Gisea and you present."

This was getting even worse. Gisea hated me and would no doubt look for a way to make me appear useless to Veylar Dust and Kalam Ghargar.

"Quda will brief you on your attire and your behavior. You will follow his instructions exactly. Do not disappoint me, Borolt Zale. My patience has worn very thin."

I nodded at him and he waved his hand, dismissing me. The servant immediately opened the door and I wasted no time getting out of there.

I had two days to make some headway, two days until I would stand before yet another of the Five. I figured I'd better have something to show for it.

Chapter Twelve

WHEN I REACHED THE BOTTOM OF THE STAIRS, I realized that I had not gotten a chance to discuss his apprentices with him. I wasn't sure what to do. On the one hand, this might be important. On the other, he was in no mood for interruptions.

Quda came through the door and saw me standing there.

"Borolt! I need a few minutes of your time to discuss the preparations for the meeting with Lord Ghargar."

I thought about it and figured there was no time like the present. Besides, Quda might have some useful knowledge.

"I'm free right now, but can't guarantee I'll be around later."

He waved me to follow him to his own office.

"Yes, this is fine. I won't take too much of your time, but there are some things you need to know."

I followed him into his office and sat across from him at a small table.

"Am I correct in assuming that you have never met any others of the Five?"

"That's right."

"Then this may come as a bit of a shock, but our Lord Dust is truly the most...relatable of the sorcerers. He has held onto elements of his humanity that some of the others have, shall we say, expunged. For example, you have no doubt seen Lord Dust become angry."

I had to suppress a snort. I had seen, and felt, his anger only moments earlier.

"Well, emotions can be useful at time—I daresay it is most likely why Lord Dust has held onto his—but they can also be a hindrance to some. The other members of the Five no longer feel normal human emotion. I am not sure if they feel any emotions now or if they have just excised that part of themselves.

"It's only one example, but gives you an idea of how different they can be. Most of them don't see people as living, breathing individuals anymore. To them, we are just tiny bits of a greater mass that can be directed or controlled. They cannot relate to us, as they are no longer human in any real sense of the word."

I had heard rumors and whispers about the other members of the Five, but had dismissed most of them as baseless speculation. After all, I encountered Veylar Dust on a regular basis, and he was still recognizably human. But perhaps he was the 'best' of a bad lot.

"What this means," continued Quda, "is that you must follow certain rules when dealing with them. Just being in the same room with other members of the Five is dangerous in ways you do not think about when you are around Lord Dust.

"First, do not address Lord Ghargar unless he specifically addresses you first. At best, he will simply ignore you. At worst, he will destroy you as an irritant, without pause, without consideration."

"Wouldn't that be an insult to Lord Dust—to destroy someone working for him?"

"Well, Lord Dust's apprentices know not to speak out of turn, and they'd also be able to protect themselves just long enough for Lord Dust to intervene and save their lives. But you, you would be dead before Lord Dust could react.

"Second, do not ever look Lord Ghargar in the eyes. This is purely for your own safety. Some men have gone mad meeting his gaze. It happened to one of Lord Dust's former apprentices, so even sorcery wouldn't necessarily save you.

"Finally, speak truthfully and fully when you answer his questions. He will know if you lie, and he can tell if you are deliberately leaving something out. It is only professional courtesy to Lord Dust that prevents Lord Ghargar from ripping the information directly from your mind, an experience that would likely kill you. If he believes you are withholding information from him, he will dispense with the courtesy and use the most direct route."

I had to interrupt here.

"It seems like there's a real chance I may not survive this meeting, Quda. At least, that's the impression I'm getting. How much danger am I really in?"

He looked down at the table when he answered.

"You are only the third person who is neither a full sorcerer nor an apprentice to meet another of the Five face-to-face, at least of which I am aware. Neither of the other two survived the encounter."

There had to be more to it than that.

"But what was the situation of their meeting?"

"They both worked for Lord Dust, as you do now. Both were requested to meet with Lord Ghargar. Both made an error during the meeting, and both died horribly."

I sat back, stunned. I have been in some dangerous situations in my life, but I've usually had a fighting chance. The idea that Lord Ghargar could simply kill me with a thought if I made the slightest mistake was not one I was ready to face.

"There is one more thing. You must come here no later than the ninth hour of the morning. At that time, you will change into the robes of an apprentice, with a belt of white."

"Why?"

"Because only an apprentice or a full sorcerer may meet with Lord Ghargar."

"Won't he know immediately that I'm not a real apprentice?"

"That is what the white belt signifies. It means that you have failed your test, were stripped of your abilities, and are now no more than a possession of Lord Dust, an extension of his will."

"Sometimes it feels like that's what I am."

Quda leaned forward and spoke fiercely.

"Do not say that! Do not even think it! If Lord Dust ever suspects you feel that way, then he may decide your usefulness is at an end. And should that happen, well, I believe you probably know too much of his dealings for him to leave you fully intact, for someone to use you against him later on."

Every single day, my position was becoming more and more untenable.

"Is that everything?"

"Yes. Please consider carefully everything I have told you, memorize it, make it part of yourself. I believe you are smart enough to get through this meeting, but you must concentrate every moment you are in there."

"Thank you, Quda. I appreciate your help and advice. I'll do everything I can to come out of the meeting alive."

He nodded and tried to smile at me, but it came off as more of a grimace.

"You've been around here a long time, Quda. I need some information, and I'm not sure I should go back upstairs and interrupt Lord Dust to get it."

He shook his head at that idea.

"I will help you if I can."

"Okay. I know the Five and the Church struggle against each other for power over the Empire. But the Church is an organization. What about the gods themselves? Does a sorcerer—or an apprentice—ever worship Iathephos? I mean, most people pay some homage to their local god even if they never set foot onto Church grounds. Or is worship of the gods antithetical to being a sorcerer?"

He sat on his chair and gave the question serious consideration.

"Well, a large part of sorcerous training is centered on learning to summon creatures from other planes of existence. Some of those creatures might be no more powerful than a mortal man. Others can be immensely powerful. When taken in that context—and that context alone—are the gods really anything more than just vastly powerful entities from another plane?"

I chuckled.

"That depends on whether you believe the Church's doctrine."

"Precisely. All apprentices had lives before they were identified as possible candidates for training. In those lives, it is likely that most had some form of worship ingrained in them from an early age. But when you contact these entities, when you summon them, when you bind them, I would expect that you would begin to question whether the gods really are different, or just more powerful. And, should you succeed at the final tests and be named as a sorcerer, I would think it unlikely that any such belief in Church doctrine would survive."

"Can I take it then, that you're saying someone who was still undergoing training—still an apprentice—might have remnants of these beliefs at some level?"

"The transition from average mortal to sorcerer is not instantaneous. Yes, I would expect some level of belief among a selection of apprentices. May I ask why this is of interest to you?"

I smiled.

"I think someone was having a crisis of faith. And they may not have been alone."

*   *   *

I DIDN'T REALLY HAVE A PLAN. I WAS STILL ANGRY ABOUT THE abduction of Olere. I was more afraid than I wanted to admit about my upcoming meeting with Lord Ghargar. I was impatient to make something happen.

I didn't know for sure if the priest from the Stone Traveler was the same man who abducted Olere, but he would certainly know about it. The Hidden were, as far as I knew, a small and close-knit sect. They worked individually, but planned everything as a team.

I was also curious about whether or not he was still visiting the Stone Traveler Alehouse. I had killed the two men hired to protect him, but unless the Wolf had given me away, the Hidden wouldn't know who was responsible. It might have scared him away.

On the other hand, his meetings with Ankin Poloth couldn't have been the only reason he visited the place, since I had seen him there on a night far from the next scheduled visit. I hoped it was more than pure luck my first visit to the Stone Traveler had coincided with his possibly infrequent attendance there.

I waited until dusk and then began walking in the direction of the Stone Traveler's neighborhood. I was well-armed and was wearing a light chain shirt under my tunic. It was hot and heavy but also could potentially save my life.

I had to consider the possibility that I was heading into a trap. If the Wolf had sold me out to the Hidden, they might decide that I had become enough of a thorn in their side to take me out after all. Would it really begin a war with Veylar Dust and the Five?

I was beginning to think the protection of Veylar Dust was wearing thin. The Church had managed to dump the issue of the creature into the laps of the Five, and they had decided to hand it to Lord Dust. And he was right in saying we had made no progress.

What was the punishment for letting down the other members of the Five? I doubted there was much forgiveness among that group. Veylar Dust might just find himself alone against the Church, if it came to it.

And, while Lord Dust was powerful, I didn't believe for a second that he could stand alone against the power of the entire Church. The only question now was how much did the priests want me dead? How much risk were they willing to assume to get at me?

There was one easy way to find out, and I was never much for hiding. The one time I tried it, I failed the person I was trying to protect. So, I prepared myself as much as was possible, and proceeded to the Stone Traveler Alehouse.

I went a roundabout way into the neighborhood so as not to give anyone looking for me too much time to plan. I didn't spot anyone suspicious, though it was hard to know for sure, as the streets were still busy. Nonetheless, I arrived on the street in front of the Stone Traveler without incident.

I stopped on the opposite side of the street and took a look around. For a moment, I considered heading back to the alley where I had been accosted a few days ago. I quashed that desire and focused on my immediate surroundings.

It took me a couple of minutes, but eventually I spotted them. They weren't hired muscle, not out here. A couple of young guys, one each a few buildings up on either side of the Alehouse, were definitely spotters for someone.

I had to admit that the city didn't revolve around me, and these men might be involved in something completely unrelated to my presence. I noted that they were good at what they were doing, being obviously engaged in other activities, and only my considerable experience gave me a chance to recognize them for what they were.

Regardless, they were watching the entrance to the Stone Traveler Alehouse, and that was where I needed to go.

Neither had spotted me yet, and I weighed the odds against quietly taking them out individually. I wouldn't necessarily need to kill them, but it would potentially deny resources to my enemies. And if they were here on business unrelated to me, then that was their problem.

Of course, it was also possible the priest wouldn't show up unless I was seen here. So, taking out his spotters might really be counterproductive. And then, maybe the Hidden would just send muscle to abduct me and take me to the Temple, and it was all for naught.

By the thrice-cursed abyss! There were too many unknown elements to this situation, which made it impossible to plan ahead. The longer I stood here, the more likely it was that I would be noticed, and then the choice would be taken from me.

I believe it is always better to take your life into your own hands than leave it in someone else's, so I made my decision. I walked boldly across the street and entered the Stone Traveler Alehouse as if I belonged there.

It felt like an age since I was last in here, though it had been only three nights ago. Everything looked identical, including the regulars at the bar and the tables. The table I had used on my last visit was occupied, so I choose another nearby and waved the serving wench over.

I sat there, sipping my ale and trying to look like I was relaxed. The last thing I needed was for the regulars to take any interest in me. I wanted only one type of company tonight.

Nearly an hour had passed, and another ale, before my wish came true. The door opened, and the same priest entered. This time, he was followed by three men. I guess he decided that leaving the hired muscle outside was no longer necessary.

Only, these guys weren't just muscle. This time, he had hired skill instead. I recognized two of the men as professional bodyguards, the kind of men you bring into a situation where you expect real combat with real weapons. These men usually protected high-level criminals when they entered enemy territory.

None of the men were visibly armed, though I suspected each had a long knife or a short sword in a hidden sheath on his back.

The priest didn't head straight for the bar. Instead, he stood near the entrance, looking around the room. The regulars quickly noticed the newcomers and a hush fell over them as they realized something unusual was about to happen.

And then the priest spotted me.

He muttered something to his companions, and they began to spread out around the room while keeping a respectful distance.

The priest smiled at me and walked directly over to my table.

"Mister...Zale, is it? I don't suppose you'd mind if I joined you for a drink?"

Without waiting for an answer, he took the seat across from me.

Chapter Thirteen

THE PRIEST WAVED TO THE SERVING GIRL, ORDERING A drink for himself and his three companions who had taken seats spaced evenly around the room. She looked nervous, like she expected a fight to break out any second.

It was still a possibility.

"In case you're wondering, my name is Relael Ochallum."

He rested his hand on the table, the ring prominently displayed for my benefit.

"You know what this is, and what it represents, I've heard. I'm impressed that you've kept it to yourself for so long."

I smiled at him, though there was no humor in it.

"A secret that everyone knows has no value, Brother Ochallum."

He winced at that.

"Please call me Relael. I'm only Brother Ochallum to my brethren."

"Don't want anyone to know you're really a priest?"

"It's not that. I don't wear the robes because they get in the way sometimes, but my investiture is no secret. Rather, I'd like to talk to you as one man to another. Not as a representative of the Church talking to a representative of the Five."

It was my turn to wince, though I hid it better.

"I don't know what gives you the impression I represent the Five."

He chuckled, and I was struck by how friendly he looked when his face relaxed like that.

"Please forgive me; that was a silly assumption. I understand you don't speak for them any more than I speak for the Church. But it is in those directions that our individual interests lie, is it not?"

I nodded.

"Borolt—I'm sorry, I feel like we should be on first-name terms. May I call you Borolt?"

I nodded again, and my silence made his smile falter.

"Thank you. Your…employer…has been tasked with ridding Ythis of its unwanted visitor. I admit that the Church leadership would prefer to see you fail. I don't think that's much of a secret.

"But the purpose of the Hidden is to protect the Church, to do what's needed even when the leadership doesn't recognize what that is. And, to us, the presence of the creature harms the city, and thus the Church. The small political gains to be had from your failure are nothing compared to the drawbacks of having that beast in the waters of the bay."

"Really? What about Olere, then?"

"The sailor-turned-groundskeeper? What about him?"

"If you really want the beast gone, then why abduct someone who might be able to tell me something useful? Or are you merely holding him for me?"

"Oh, Borolt. We are obviously making our own investigations into ridding the creature from the bay. Be realistic. If the Church can rid Ythis of the beast instead of you, we win on both fronts. The beast is gone, and we get those political gains I just mentioned."

The serving girl brought Relael his ale, and another for me.

"And what if neither of us can do it alone? What if I have information necessary to your success, and you have information necessary to mine?"

"Well, that's why I'm here tonight, talking to you. Olere was no help. He was thrown overboard and managed to survive by sheer luck. He saw nothing useful, knew nothing useful. As far as the Hidden are now concerned, the resolution to this problem requires us to help you, even if it means your Lord Dust gains influence in the Council because of it. I came here to tell you that the Hidden are now on your side."

I leaned forward, crossing my arms and leaning my elbows on the table.

"I don't believe for a second that you're remotely on my side. I've been declared an enemy of the Church. I know you'd like nothing more to grab a knife and open my throat. So, don't waste your time and mine lying to me."

He gave a look that said I was being absurd.

"You have a rather simplistic view of the Church, Borolt. We're not all insane, you know. Sure, one must have at least a touch of madness to make contact with Iathephos, but not all priests are required to commune with our god. In fact, that is precisely why the Sect of the Hidden was created. We are the 'voice of reason' in an organization run by the mad. Our job is to keep the Church strong, when the leadership is always weak, mentally.

"And as for you, Borolt, I have nothing personally against you, regardless of what you believe. You tried to save your brother from the spiral of madness that takes all full priests eventually, and that set you at odds with the Church. The repercussions of that act were out of my control. But don't for a moment think that, should it benefit the Church in some way, I wouldn't welcome you with open arms and forgiveness in my heart. That's nonsense. My job—my life—is dedicated to doing what's right for the organization, whatever form it might take."

"So, what, you're here to tell me you want to be pals and give me everything you know about the creature?"

He laughed out loud.

"It's never quite as easy as all that, is it? No, you still are an enemy of the Church and the internal influence of the Hidden is not limitless. We cannot be seen to work directly with you until and unless you have definitively solved the problem and need divine assistance to implement the solution. I can, however, pass along what information on the creature we have been able to compile. There is a condition on that, though."

"There always is."

"It's a pretty simple one. You must not let anyone, even your Lord Dust, know that we gave it to you. If the question comes up, you must say you stole it from us or something of a similar nature. We'd prefer the slight loss of face from that story over the alternatives."

It was an easy bargain to make, especially since the power would be in my hands.

"I can accept that. If you're good to your word, and your information doesn't turn out to be some kind of sabotage of our efforts, then I'll swear to keep how I got it to myself."

He took a long pull on his ale and set the flagon back down on the table with a great sigh.

"Things are so often needlessly complex, Borolt. I may be on a side opposed to yours, but that doesn't have to make us enemies. It would probably be simpler if I could just hate you and know that your side is always *wrong*. Sometimes I envy those who can hate so easily—they certainly don't have to spend so much energy finding compromises."

I decided to poke him and see how he reacted.

"In that case, perhaps you could call off your assassin and let me work in peace?"

I had to admit, his look of confusion was rather convincing.

"You do know that the price on your head was suspended when you took service with Lord Dust, don't you?"

"I'm not talking about that. I'm talking about the assassin who tried to shoot me the other night. The killer who is after the young boy for whatever it was he saw."

"While I don't expect you'll believe me, I'm telling you the truth when I say I have no idea what you're talking about. Our focus has been on the beast all this time."

"Right. So how does Ankin Poloth figure into that situation?"

He just stared at me, and I could see his mind working, trying to figure what I did and didn't know. Finally, he sat back with a sigh.

"Of course. That's why you started coming here. I don't know how you followed Ankin without his demon knowing, but I tip my hat to you. You obviously have some rather impressive skills we didn't know about."

"And what have you and Ankin been talking about over friendly drinks in this fine establishment?"

"So sarcastic, Borolt. There were two reasons Ankin wanted to talk to me. First, Ankin and I had a professional agreement to discuss the creature in the bay in non-specific terms. If it seemed like one or the other of us was nearing a solution, the other would go back to our respective master and bring up the idea of cooperation."

"And the second?"

"It was a private matter, though I suppose it doesn't matter now. Ankin was brought up worshipping the gods. His training as a sorcerer was giving him a...let's call it a crisis of faith. No, more than that, he had completely lost his faith. I was merely helping him work through that to find a belief system he was comfortable with."

"Very tidy, Relael. I do wonder, though, why you keep talking about it in the past tense. Is there some reason you don't expect to see Ankin again?"

I had him and he knew it. Ankin Poloth's death should have been unknown outside the Tower of Dust. The only way he could know was if he had another contact—a spy—in the Tower.

He took another sip of his ale and stood up.

"Like I said, Borolt. We don't have to be enemies. I am interested in developing a certain professional courtesy with you. But that requires you to accept that we work on opposite sides, and I will do things that put the Church in a stronger position, just as you will do things to weaken it."

"Isn't that the very definition of enemies?"

"That depends on how narrow your viewpoint is. I will arrange the information on the creature to be passed to you shortly. I strongly suggest you keep to our arrangement, and I will be happy to put Church resources at your disposal for the purpose of ridding the city of the creature."

He dropped enough coins on the table to pay for my drinks as well.

"Have a lovely evening, Borolt."

I watched him as he turned and walked out, followed by his three henchmen.

*   *   *

ONCE AGAIN, HUNGER DROVE SULID OUT FROM HIS HIDING place. He had eventually made it back to the cellar and remained there for the next two days, though he had to ration his water and food carefully.

He didn't know if Borolt had lived or died, and didn't really have the resources to find out. Sulid had only one person he'd call a friend, only one person he trusted, but there was no way he was going to risk another person's life for nothing. He'd ask for help when there was no other way.

Sulid's trip out to steal food went smoothly, and he considered going past the Tower of Dust to see if he could spot the man. He just didn't know how risky it was, though.

If Borolt was dead, it was probably safe to go by the Tower, as there wouldn't be anyone watching it. But then, if the man was dead, there was no reason to go there. If Borolt was still alive, however, the Stranger was probably also in the area, and Sulid had been through too many close calls lately.

He didn't think he could handle another one tonight.

He was on his way back to the cellar when he realized that he was close to the place where he had first seen the man in the alley. It wasn't particularly late, and he wondered if the bodies were still there. He quickly crushed that line of thought, though. It was a distraction he didn't need.

Sulid made his way across the rooftops and reached a point at which he was forced to descend to ground level for a stretch. He reached a perfect climbing spot into an alley he often used and was about to descend when he heard something in the alley below.

Someone was climbing up onto the roof.

He didn't have much time to move before the person would reach the rooftop, so he tucked himself into the shadows behind a chimney and went very still.

He heard the other person reach the rooftop and climb carefully and quietly onto it. Whoever the person was, they were experienced at traveling across the roofs of the city. It could mean it was another street urchin like himself, or perhaps someone working for the local thieves' gang.

As the person moved away from Sulid's hiding spot, he carefully glanced around the edge of the chimney, and his heart nearly stopped.

It was the Stranger, not more than 30 paces away.

Sulid had to clamp his hand over his mouth to keep from moaning in fear. Of all the rotten luck, why did the Stranger have to be here now? Sulid could see the Stranger was armed with a crossbow, probably the same one he had fired at Sulid and Borolt.

The Stranger crouched down and moved carefully to the edge of the building facing the next cross-street. He didn't draw the crossbow from his back, but stayed perfectly still, watching the street below.

Sulid didn't know what to do. He was trapped. Every moment he stayed here increased the chance the Stranger would hear him make some noise and come to investigate. But if he tried to climb down into the alley, he would surely alert the hunter, and then it might turn into a real chase.

How much of a head start could Sulid get before the Stranger heard him?

And then the Stranger began to move along the edge of the building back towards Sulid's hiding place. The Stranger was watching someone on the street below, but didn't appear to be planning to attack. He was simply following his target, carefully keeping out of sight.

Sulid tried to make his breathing as quiet as possible. He had learned when hiding it was better to breathe shallowly and slowly than it was to hold one's breath. Sometimes you had to hide for an extended period of time with people all around you.

The Stranger had reached the nearest point to the alley and watched his quarry continue down the street. He waited a moment more, and then left the rooftop and climbed down into the alley. Sulid couldn't believe the Stranger had truly left, and he strained to hear the man in the alley below.

There was no sound, and Sulid had no way of knowing if the Stranger had moved off or not. But then a hope bloomed in Sulid's chest. What if the Stranger was following Borolt?

He had to go look and see if he could identify whoever the Stranger was following. Like a shadow, Sulid glided silently across the roof to the edge and peeked over into the street.

The Stranger's quarry on the street had moved some distance away, but Sulid could make out his shape as he passed one of the streetlamps. There was no way to be sure from this distance, but it definitely could be Borolt Zale. The fact the Stranger was following the man instead of shooting at him told Sulid that he himself had been the target of the crossbow bolts a couple of nights ago, not the man from the Tower.

It didn't make Sulid feel any better. The Stranger obviously felt that following the man would lead him to Sulid eventually, and in a way he was right. Sulid knew now he would have to find some way to contact Borolt Zale directly.

But how could he possibly accomplish that? He wasn't sure the man really lived at the Tower of Dust, and didn't know anything about him other than the fact he worked for a sorcerer. He couldn't go around asking people about the inhabitants of the Tower—that would get him noticed fast.

As much as he hated to do it, he would have to ask for help. And he knew where Weese would be at this time of night.

He moved away from the alley and headed back in the direction from which he had come. He wasn't going to risk bumping into the Stranger again tonight. Besides, Weese was probably 'working' at the Black Door, and that was down near the docks.

He eventually reached his destination without incident. However, it was almost dawn when Sulid saw Weese emerge from the Black Door. He looked exhausted. Sulid almost let him walk off in peace. He didn't feel right asking Weese for this favor when he was so obviously in need of a rest.

Just as Weese was about to turn the corner, Sulid made up his mind and whistled a signal known to most street urchins in Ythis. Weese proceeded around the corner and Sulid turned away from him and circled back around the block. A moment later, he entered the alley on the opposite side to see his friend Weese standing at one end, ready to take off running if it turned out to be a trap.

Weese was bigger than Sulid, and older by a year or two. He wasn't covered in dirt, but that was only because he got washed down when he went to work in the Black Door.

"Weese, it's me, Sulid."

"Sulid?" There was disbelief in his voice.

"Yes, it's me. I need to talk to you."

"Word is out about you, Sulid. They said you were dead."

"I'm not dead, Weese. I've just been hiding."

Weese didn't move any closer to Sulid.

"You're not a ghoul, are you?"

"By the light, Weese, I'm not a ghoul! I've been hiding."

"That's just what a ghoul would say to cover for the time it took him to crawl out of his grave."

"Would a ghoul come to you just before dawn, when people are going to start filling up the streets? When the sun is about to rise? I'd have to be a pretty stupid ghoul."

Weese thought about that and relaxed.

"You're right, Sulid. You're too smart to do something like that."

He came down the alley, but still looked Sulid over carefully as he approached.

"My eyes aren't even glowing, Weese. You'd have seen them from the other end of the alley."

"Oh, yeah. I heard a ghoul got Heka, though."

"Oh no! She was nice. How did it get her?"

"Don't know. Just that she's attacked a couple of other kids. Didn't get them, though. She wasn't smart like you."

"Weese, I'm in trouble and I need your help."

Weese got a guilty look on his face, like he was thinking of making an excuse not to help Sulid.

"Well, tell me what you need first."

"I saw something I shouldn't have seen, Weese. I'm not going to tell you what or they'll be after you too. But there's a stranger in Ythis who's been hunting me since it happened. That's why I've been hiding."

"I can't fight, Sulid. You know that."

"I don't need protection, Weese. Well, I do, but not from you. There's a man who can help me, but I can't get to him. The Stranger keeps looking for me, and has figured out I need to talk to this man."

"Who is the man?"

"That's just it. I only know the man's name, and that he sometimes visits the Tower of Dust."

Weese took a step back.

"You're lying. There's no way you want to speak to someone in the Tower of Dust."

"I do, Weese. This man—Borolt Zale—is the only one who can help me. But I need to find out more about him. I need to know if he lives at the Tower, at least. Once I know that, I can arrange to get a message to him."

"And you want me to find out if this man lives in the Tower of Dust?"

Sulid nodded, terrified that Weese—his only friend—would deny him help.

"I'll see what I can do, Sulid, but I can't promise anything. How soon do you need to know?"

"As soon as you can. The Stranger is trying to kill me, and I'm running out of time and chances."

"But how do I find you?"

"You don't. I'll be here tomorrow morning. I'll follow you and make sure no one else is. When I'm sure, I'll whistle like this morning and we can meet up."

Weese heaved an exhausted sigh.

"I'll do what I can. I need to get a bit of sleep, though. It's been...busy."

He glanced back in the direction of the Black Door and shuddered.

Sulid grabbed him and hugged him tightly.

"Thank you so much, Weese. I will owe you for this."

"Yeah," he replied. "You will."

Chapter Fourteen

THERE WAS A SPY IN THE TOWER OF DUST.

It was bad enough that Ankin Poloth had been meeting with one of the Hidden, even if the reason given by Brother Ochallum was true. But to think that there was a second person in the Tower feeding information to members of the Church....

Whoever the spy was, he or she had to be extremely careful. I didn't want to imagine what this person might do to prevent anyone from unmasking him or her—especially if the spy was one of the apprentices.

But it was just as dangerous to do nothing. An uncovered spy can turn into a saboteur, or an assassin, far too easily. If I kept this to myself, then I would be responsible for whatever this person did to harm Lord Dust, his apprentices, his staff, and his efforts on behalf of the city.

I would have to tell him what I had uncovered. It pained me to bring him more news like this, especially since he was already angry with me over my lack of progress. The last thing I needed was him deciding to punish the messenger.

It was too late to head back to the Tower. I would have to wait until morning and then hope that Lord Dust would spare a minute to listen to my concerns. I had no idea what his reaction would be—bringing him this information might earn me some gratitude, or he might think I was wasting my time on investigations which had nothing to do with the creature in the bay.

When I returned home, I didn't get any real sleep. That may have been due to my spending half the night pacing around my room, though, trying to consider all the aspects of this situation. Not the least of which was who the spy might be.

Arral Doviar and Gisea Megoen had arrived at the tower together, and both of them seemed to have an extreme dislike of me. I could understand the attitude of Gisea—there was nothing hidden in her contempt for my abilities.

Arral, however, was a different beast. He seemed friendly enough, but there was something dark under that façade and I believed it was directed at me. Of course, he was an apprentice to one of the Five—such a calling wasn't for those with empathy for their fellows. His personal dislike of me could all be in my mind.

Delash Wiar was the oldest of the apprentices, the closest to becoming a full sorcerer himself. This made him the least likely to be the spy, and therefore the one most likely to get away with it. I knew too little about him, having spoken to him for the first time only a handful of days ago.

Of Ituro Nedes, I knew even less. I had simply never had any reason to speak to him in the year he had been at the Tower of Dust, and his eternal scowl didn't encourage me to try.

I realized I was on a fool's errand. There was no way I could deduce the identity of the spy with what little information I had. And yet I kept at it all night, trying to remember every tiny detail I knew about the Apprentices and the staff.

It was shortly after dawn when I heard a soft tap at my door. I drew my dagger just in case, and carefully opened the door. A man in a black cloak handed me a small pouch and then turned and left without a word. I closed the door behind him and carefully laid the pouch on the small table in the corner of my room.

After checking it over for any unwanted surprises, I removed a small sheaf of papers covered in writing from what appeared to be many different hands. Sifting through the papers, it appeared that Brother Ochallum had kept his promise. These were the results of investigations, divinations, and interrogations into the matter of the creature in the bay.

I evaluated my options. Bringing this to Lord Dust immediately would mitigate some of his anger at me and potentially give me a chance to broach the subject of the spy in the Tower. On the other hand, I didn't really know what I had here yet and it might be completely worthless.

It wasn't much of a choice. With the most powerful of the Five coming to the Tower to meet with Lord Dust tomorrow, I had to bring him something, and there wasn't time for me to go through it all myself.

I packed the papers back into the pouch and tucked it into my coat. It was still early, but I wanted to be at the Tower before Veylar Dust emerged from his chambers. I believed he would want as much time to pore over this information as possible before his meeting with Kalam Ghargar.

*   *   *

I DIDN'T HAVE LONG TO WAIT WHEN I ARRIVED AT THE TOWER of Dust. Quda saw me walking across the grounds and sent word up right away, and the summons came less than half an hour later.

Lord Dust met me in his office again, and I noticed that it was messier than I had ever seen it. In stark contrast, he appeared calmer than he had been in our meeting yesterday. There was no servant at the door, and when I knocked, he merely called for me to enter.

I stood in front of his desk and he sat back and met my gaze.

"What have you brought me?"

I pulled out the pouch and placed it on his desk.

"In there is everything the Church knows about the creature in the bay."

Raising one eyebrow, he opened the pouch. He slowly pulled out the papers and glanced through the small pile.

"How much damage did you cause?"

"None."

It wasn't a lie, though it caught his attention.

"Being subtle, were you? This seems like a feat beyond your normal capabilities without causing some casualties."

I didn't want to directly lie to him—I'd prefer to insinuate and let him make assumptions. The only problem was that he was about ten times smarter than I was.

"My normal methods didn't seem to be working, so I took a different approach. I'm not entirely sure who might have noticed the papers are gone at this point. But no one saw me in or near the Church itself."

He stared at me, and I wondered for an instant—and not for the first time—if he could hear my thoughts. He sat there for a full minute, and I did everything in my power to keep from twitching or otherwise showing my nervousness.

Finally, he broke eye contact and looked back down at the papers.

"Keep your secrets, Borolt Zale. You know the cost of betrayal."

I held my relief in check, and took the opening afforded by his comment.

"Actually, Lord Dust, the topic of betrayal is one I wish to discuss with you."

He met my gaze again and then gestured for me to sit. I took the chair and leaned forward.

"I would not bring this up if I wasn't sure of my conclusions. But I know for a fact that the Hidden have a spy in the Tower."

He didn't react at all to my revelation.

"And who is this spy?"

"Unfortunately, that's something I *don't* know. I can tell you that the news of Apprentice Poloth's death was given to the Hidden."

I paused to swallow, not sure how this news would be taken.

"What's more, Ankin Poloth himself was meeting with one of the Hidden on a regular basis. One story is that he was having a crisis of faith and was looking for some guidance. I don't know if that is true. But I have confirmed the meetings—they're even listed in his journal."

"So, you have found it."

"Yes."

"When did you find it? And why have you not turned it over to me?"

I wasn't entirely sure I wanted to tell him the truth—that so much had been happening in the last few days I had simply forgotten to pull the journal from its hiding place and give to him. Besides, I had been sure that I would need to go back and reread sections as my investigation led to new questions.

"I...haven't had a chance. Once I began to see the pattern in the journal with the meetings, I started following that trail."

"Which led you to Apprentice Doviar and Apprentice Wiar."

Of course, his apprentices would have told him about my meeting with them. And if one of them was the spy, they would have known enough to tip off Brother Ochallum that he might need some muscle when travelling to the Stone Traveler. And that's where the Wolf's men came in.

"Lord Dust, is there any way to determine the loyalty of your Apprentices? I suspect that one of them is the spy."

He shook his head.

"There is, but I do not have the time for that right now. Tomorrow morning Kalam Ghargar will come here, and I still have preparations to make. You will speak to no one of your suspicions. Am I understood?"

I nodded. And then it hit me.

"Lord Dust, the Hidden know I'm aware of the spy."

His voice went cold.

"How?"

"I spoke to one of them."

I was walking a fine line here. I couldn't tell anyone that they had given me the information on the creature in the bay, but I had to admit my source of knowledge to Veylar Dust or he wouldn't trust me. And that was more dangerous than any other threat hanging over my head right now.

"Explain. Fully."

I couldn't obey that order, but he didn't have to know that.

"While investigating Apprentice Poloth's activities, I discovered that he had been meeting one of the Hidden at a tavern in the city. The journal didn't tell me who he was meeting—in fact it was in a code that I had to decipher.

"I went to the tavern and found the priest there. He recognized me and came over to talk to me. He may have just wanted to taunt me about the groundskeeper they abducted. I asked him directly about Apprentice Poloth, and he admitted that they had been meeting regularly.

"The priest claimed that your apprentice was having a crisis of faith, and that he needed someone to talk to. But, by his choice of words, it appeared that he already knew of Apprentice Poloth's death. I pushed him just enough that he finally admitted it to me, but he realized his error right away and left."

I waited while Lord Dust considered my story.

"You handled that poorly, but I suppose the information is useful."

He supposed it was useful? I had just revealed a spy in the Tower of Dust, and he acted like I had given him some piece of trivia. I was amazed that he would put off further investigation until after his meeting with Lord Ghargar. It looked to me like he wasn't taking me seriously.

He went on.

"Still, if a message has gotten back to the spy, your life is in a great deal of danger. That is the nature of your duty to me, however. You will have to be prepared to protect yourself."

"I try to be ready at all times."

He stopped watching me and began sorting through the papers and tomes on his desk.

"You will remain in the Tower until our meeting with Lord Ghargar tomorrow. Quda will have a spare room prepared for you to sleep in, and you will remain in that room until I send for you."

"I was hoping to spend the day following another lead—"

"You will follow nothing but my instructions. I do not repeat myself, Borolt Zale. You have stumbled upon secrets better left uncovered, and you have not the faintest inkling of what they portend."

I wanted to argue, but there was no use. I would lose the entire day, stuck in the same Tower where lived a spy who wanted me dead. I only hoped everyone was still too afraid of Veylar Dust to try anything while I was here.

"Do you have any further revelations for me this morning?"

"No, Lord Dust."

"Then get out and find Quda. I have work to do."

Chapter Fifteen

I SPENT THE DAY SPRAWLED ON THE BED, IN BETWEEN stretches of pacing around the small room. I had nothing to occupy my time, and Quda had locked me in after having a short talk with Lord Dust. I could have throttled him.

I was tired from my lack of sleep the night before, but I didn't want to give in and sleep now, knowing I would be stuck here until tomorrow morning. So, I sat and considered the situation until I had run it through my head a hundred times or more.

Quda himself brought me a meal at midday, and another in the early evening. He was too busy to stay and talk, and so I was left alone. I had somehow always managed to avoid being arrested and thrown into any kind of prison, and realized I would go mad if I was ever locked in a cell with the expectation of spending years with no escape.

At some point after my dinner, I finally fell asleep.

When Quda awakened me, it was just after dawn. A servant stood behind him with the robes I was supposed to wear to the meeting with Lord Ghargar today.

"I hope you are well rested, Borolt. I admit I am somewhat surprised that you slept at all, considering the day before you."

"Yeah, well, there are only so many days a person can stay awake before the body just gives up, you know?"

"Is your mind clear? Do you remember the instructions I gave you?"

I nodded as I examined the robes of a failed apprentice.

"I don't look in his eyes. I don't speak unless he asks me a question directly. And I don't hold anything back when I—"

I stopped, a horrible dread filling my belly.

Quda looked at me sharply.

"What is it, Borolt?"

My whole body went cold. I had forgotten Quda's instructions until just now. I had set myself up for failure.

"I think I'm in trouble. There is something I cannot tell Lord Ghargar. Something directly related to any question he might ask of me."

Quda was suddenly very nervous.

"What can't you tell him?"

"I'm sorry, Quda, but I can't tell you either. It's an agreement I made to help out Lord Dust. But I have to leave it out! If I tell everyone, it will cause even more trouble!"

Quda took the bundle from the servant and ushered the young man out of the room. Closing the door, he sat on the stool beside the bed and looked into my face.

"Does Lord Dust know this secret?"

I shook my head.

"You must tell him anyway."

"I can't. He will be furious if he finds out—perhaps enough to kill me himself."

Quda leaned back against the wall.

"By the gods' blood, Borolt, I cannot see a way through this for you. If you do not tell Lord Dust, and Lord Ghargar asks you a direct question, then you will have to make a decision to either speak fully, or hope that your omission isn't enough to make him take your mind."

I stood and began pacing once more. Which was the bigger gamble? To tell Lord Dust that I had essentially lied to him yesterday morning, right before his meeting with the most powerful of the Five was a truly awful option.

On the other hand, Lord Ghargar was just as risky. He might not ask me any questions at all, but it was likely that he would want to know something about the papers I had gotten from the Church. He might even ask me directly where I found them. And then I would have to reveal the truth to both of them at once.

If that happened, there was no way I would survive through the meeting.

A soft tap on the door brought me out of my reverie. Quda opened to the door to find four servants waiting for orders.

"Borolt, I must attend to these matters. I will return shortly. Consider fully the option of telling Lord Dust the truth. It will be better than having that information ripped out of you as your mind shatters."

He left the room and I was alone once more.

A few minutes later, the door opened again. Quda had forgotten to lock it behind him.

Standing in the doorway was Gisea.

I leaped up and tried to draw my knife, but it wasn't on my belt anymore. I looked at Gisea and saw it in her hand. She held it up and turned it back and forth.

"If I believed you were going to draw this against me, I would tear you limb from limb now, regardless of what Lord Dust wants from you."

She said it calmly, with no anger in her voice. Only a cold threat.

"And if I want you dead, this little tool will not be enough to save you."

She tossed it onto the bed, and I just stood there, stupidly unsure what I should do. She entered the room and looked down at the bundle of robes Quda had left for me.

"The white belt—the sign of a failure. It is almost enough for me to approve of you putting on the robes of an apprentice."

I was tired of the insults and threats.

"What is the problem, here? Why, exactly, do you hate me so much?"

"Hate is an emotion for those who are still mortal. One week ago, I said that your lack of knowledge and your emotions, your fear, would cause more difficulties than you would solve. I have seen no indication that I was wrong in my assessment."

"Well, there's probably not much more trouble I can cause, now, is there? From what I have heard, I'm pretty unlikely to survive this meeting with Lord Ghargar."

She turned to look at me, and for an instant I saw it. She was an apprentice to Veylar Dust, sorcerer, member of the Five. She was leaving her humanity behind to become something else. But she wasn't a sorcerer yet.

And she was terrified.

There was no way I could acknowledge it without making things worse. I hadn't asked Quda if any apprentices died in meetings with Lord Ghargar or the others, but it suddenly struck me that such an outcome was distinctly possible. A moment of hesitation, a lack of concentration, an instant of emotion overriding reason—all could lead to a very unpleasant death.

"I will try not to fail Lord Dust, Apprentice."

She seemed about to speak, and then she turned and left the room.

For a moment, I felt an aching loss. She was giving up what made her human, and as far as she was concerned, it couldn't happen fast enough. But she was still mortal, still capable of emotion, and it was a tragedy that she would abandon it in the pursuit of power.

I had never expected to feel pity for one of the apprentices. Even when Ankin Poloth was killed by his demon, I felt nothing for him as a person. But I had seen Gisea's humanity, for just an instant. And I knew I would mourn its passing.

Almost a full hour had passed when Quda came back to my room.

"My apologies, Borolt. Lord Ghargar's apprentices will arrive shortly, and I must have everything ready."

He saw the look of resignation on my face.

"Shall I pass a message to Lord Dust that you need a moment of his time before the meeting?"

I took a deep breath.

"No, Quda. I will have to take my chances."

I saw the look in his eyes and knew that he considered me already dead.

*   *   *

I WASN'T SURE WHAT TO EXPECT FROM LORD GHARGAR'S apprentices. If Kalam Ghargar was as inhuman as Quda had described, I couldn't imagine what kind of person would thrive learning at the feet of such a sorcerer. But when the two young men entered, they appeared no more unusual than Lord Dust's own apprentices.

We were in the large room at the top of the tower, where the marble floor was inlaid with the summoning circle surrounded by unreadable symbols—carvings that made me queasy whenever I looked at them too long. A large but shallow iron bowl sat in the center of the circle, a deep red flame rising out of the oil within.

I was standing on the north side of the chamber, against the wall. Gisea stood beside me. I had been instructed to follow her directions precisely, and so I made sure I was acutely aware of every movement she made.

We had gone into the chamber to take our places first. The apprentices of Lord Ghargar followed us. The smaller of the two men stared at the white belt around my waist and then looked at my face. He glanced at his companion, then the door, and then spoke to me.

"You insult us with your presence, mortal. That spot should be reserved for a true apprentice."

I was taken aback, but Gisea spoke before I could answer.

"You presume too much, Apprentice. You are guests in the Tower of Dust. Do you wish to violate the pacts?"

The man who had spoken appeared to be ready to answer, but the other apprentice spoke over him.

"There is no insult, Apprentice Megoen. The accusation was inaccurate and is retracted."

There was something—different—in the man's voice. Something missing. It was how I imagine the dead would sound, if they could speak. It gave me shivers, hearing that voice.

Gisea nodded once and we all stood still, silent.

Waiting.

Lord Dust appeared in the doorway, and he moved across the room, taking his place on the edge of the circle in front of Gisea and me. He stood only a few feet away from the edge of the iron bowl, and I imagined the light from the red flame coloring his face.

He did not acknowledge the apprentices, but faced the doorway, waiting for Lord Ghargar.

I felt the sorcerer's presence before I saw him. A chill in the air, and I noticed that I could see wisps of my breath when I exhaled. A shadow fell across the doorway. I wondered how big he must be, to cast a shadow that large.

But then he emerged *from* the shadow itself. I saw a gaunt face with gray, dead skin. A gash of a mouth sat above a long chin, from which strings of sparse, black hair fell. Above his mouth was the shadow of a sharp, hooked nose. My gaze travelled upwards, and I was an instant away from meeting his eyes when I realized my danger, and I snapped my own eyes down to the floor. Strange spots floated in my vision for a moment before fading away.

I took a shaky breath and tried to control the trembling that had started in my hands.

In my brief look, I had gotten the impression that Lord Ghargar was not a large man. He was of average height, though painfully thin. He wore the black robes of a sorcerer.

I could not see his feet under the long robes, and he seemed to glide forward to his place on the opposite side of the circle, facing Lord Dust.

"I welcome you, Lord Ghargar, to the Tower of Dust. Let the ancient pacts take hold, let us speak, and let us part ways in peace."

When Lord Ghargar spoke, I found myself barely able to control my bowels. His voice was deep and came from beyond death. Around his words, I could hear faint whispers of another voice, one that spoke of things man was not meant to know.

"I accept the pacts and your welcome, Lord Dust."

I was suddenly very tired. Without warning, my legs began aching and I felt drained of all energy. My stomach growled, though I had eaten not more than two hours previously.

I was aware that Lord Dust was speaking.

"—recovered documents from the Church pertaining to the creature. I have studied them and see some possible connections that the priests would have missed. I believe I may have a solution to lure the creature out of the bay, but I will need more time to complete it."

"Time has begun to move more quickly, Lord Dust. It is erratic, and yet increases in pace, nonetheless. I cannot foresee when it will return to its natural rhythm."

I admit this was beyond my understanding, but Lord Dust occasionally spoke in cryptic phrases such as this, and I was mostly just trying to keep from soiling myself each time Lord Ghargar spoke.

"My apprentices will work on the ritual while we are at council. I will need a few days after the council meeting is adjourned to make final preparations. No more."

"Then the others will agree to give you enough time to complete your preparations. What if the ritual does not succeed?"

"If it fails, I will assuredly die in the process, Lord Ghargar."

"Where is the one who brought you the documents?"

My mind was a whirl. I tried to concentrate on the thread of the story I wanted to tell, to drown out any stray thoughts that might betray me. I was too nervous to gain control.

"Apprentice Zale recovered the documents from the Church."

Lord Dust motioned to me and I physically *felt* the gaze of Kalam Ghargar rest on my face, even though I was staring at the floor.

"It has failed you, and yet it lives."

"I knew he would have some use in the future, Lord Ghargar. I was correct in my assessment."

I waited for the killing blow to come. I could feel his mind, his will, hovering just outside my body. Any second now he would rip into me and I would die in a terrible, screaming madness.

"The Church remains a threat, Lord Dust. The Emperor is swayed by their words, their promises. The weak must be destroyed if the Five are to be strong. There can be no emotion, no mercy, and no pity."

"With respect, Lord Ghargar, it is neither mercy nor pity that keeps Apprentice Zale in my service. He fulfills a function that others cannot. He has skills that are hard to quickly replace, and he remains loyal."

"Loyalty is a myth, Lord Dust, a folly. This one will betray you. It will cause your downfall."

"Is that a vision, Lord Ghargar? Or just a caution?"

There was silence and I knew I was about to die.

"I would not have let it live."

And then the feeling was gone.

I looked up to see the apprentices leaving the room. Neither Lord Dust nor Lord Ghargar was there.

I turned to Gisea and tried to speak, but my words came out slurred.

"Wha'...happen...."

I looked at her face, and it seemed she was disturbed by my appearance for some reason.

And then the darkness reached out and took me.

Chapter Sixteen

WHEN I REGAINED CONSCIOUSNESS, I WAS BACK in the bed I had so recently occupied. My mind was a bit fuzzy, but otherwise I did not feel too terrible.

I lay there, trying to figure out what had happened in the meeting, but it seemed as if I had missed something important. The sudden fatigue, the disappearance of Lord Ghargar and Lord Dust, and my loss of consciousness all told me that there had been sorcery of some kind being conducted in that room.

The door to my room opened, and I expected to see Quda coming to check on me. I was struck speechless when Gisea entered my room. She closed the door behind her and came to stand at the foot of my bed.

"You survived."

It wasn't a question, nor was it said with any kind of relief. I noted a lack of disappointment in her tone as well, though I thought it might just be my unfocused mind missing something still.

"Is there any chance of you telling me what happened in there?"

She considered my request carefully before answering.

"The meeting between Lord Ghargar and Lord Dust took most of the day. You probably only experienced a few minutes of it, however, since you were not meant to hear everything that was discussed. The magic...takes something out of you. It's why you felt so exhausted when you were released."

I was stunned, not just by the fact that I had managed to survive the meeting, but by the fact Gisea has explained it to me.

"Thank you for telling me."

She stood there silently for a moment, looking at me as if she was trying to read what was in my mind.

"Your performance today was...acceptable."

I couldn't believe what I was hearing. She had almost complimented me. She took a deep breath, and went on.

"Find out what happened to Apprentice Poloth. Lord Dust is not the only person in the Tower who wants an answer."

"I promise you, Apprentice, that I will do everything I can to get that answer."

Gisea nodded once, and turned to go. Just as she reached for the door, the handle turned and Quda came bustling into the room. He stopped cold when he saw Gisea.

"My apologies, Apprentice Megoen. I did not wish to interrupt your meeting with Mister Zale."

She shook her head as she pushed past him.

"Our discussion was already complete."

Quda looked after her as she turned the corner, and then gave me a questioning look.

"I have no idea, Quda. Maybe I'm finally earning her respect."

He smiled.

"You have certainly earned mine, Borolt. You did it—you survived the meeting with Lord Ghargar, and even Lord Dust seemed somewhat pleased with the outcome of the meeting."

"Do I have a chance to speak with him?"

"I am afraid that he has declared he is not to be disturbed while he prepares for the council meeting, except under the direst of circumstances."

I groaned as I pulled myself out of the bed. My muscles ached, although I was beginning to feel surprisingly refreshed.

"Lord Dust himself came to visit after you collapsed."

That got my attention.

"Did he do something to me?"

"I cannot say, as I was not in the room at the time. Though you do appear much...healthier...than when you were put in here."

I couldn't be sure Lord Dust had done anything to help me, but as I stretched the ache out of my muscles, I had to admit I felt better than I had in days.

"I need to get back to my own place and think about what I'm going to do next, Quda. I know that Lord Dust was given only a short amount of time to come up with a solution."

"I have arranged food for you in the kitchen, Borolt, but I understand your need to get moving."

I thanked him and went down to the kitchen, wolfed down a meal, and then left the Tower of Dust. It seemed weird that the sun had almost disappeared below the horizon, having only experienced a short part of my day. I vaguely wondered if I would end up awake all night.

The walk back to my own neighborhood was quick, and I was less than a block from home when a horrible coldness boiled up from the ground around me, shocking in its contrast to the oppressive heat of Ythis.

I stopped as frost formed on the stones beneath my feet and my breath began misting the air. The hairs on the back of my neck stood up, and without thinking I drew my short sword.

I heard my name on the cold wind that suddenly sprang up, a long sibilant hiss. Looking around, I saw that I stood in the center of a large circle of ice. The few other people on the street were backing away from me and my strange environment.

I took a step away from the center and nearly fell—the icy ground was too slick for me to move normally. In the back of my mind, I heard a heavy thump, followed by another. I knew it wasn't a real sound, but I still looked around for the source. My blood went as cold as the ice around me as I saw two large footprints with great claws form in the frost at the edge of the circle.

There was a demon on the streets of Ythis.

It materialized in front of me, taking shape from the wisps of vapor rising from the ground. A movement in the eye, and then it was in front of me, a tall, muscular, humanoid creature with bone-white skin and long, hooked claws on its hands and feet. It had no eyes—only a red, puckered orifice ringed with jagged teeth in the middle of its overlarge head. Wisps of shadow hung over it in the vague shape of bat-like wings.

I prayed it belonged to a sorcerer, that it was sent to summon me and was having fun terrifying me before delivering its message.

It hunched down, muscles rippling, and it appeared as if was about to lunge at me. I tensed, knowing that I could not possibly get out of the way in time if it decided to attack me.

"I have come for you, Borolt Zale. My master wants me to bring him your head. I get to devour the rest."

I carefully backed away, trying to reach the edge of the ice, but it wouldn't make any difference once the demon stopped playing.

I knew now that I had been safe in the Tower—that leaving that sanctuary was the opening the spy needed to send his demon after me. I also now knew that the spy in the Tower of Dust was an apprentice and not a servant. None of my knowledge would save me. For the second time today, I was an instant away from death.

The demon began swaying from side to side like some huge, misshapen snake as it took another step toward me, and another. I reached the edge of the patch of ice and prepared to run. I had seen, however, how fast a demon can move and held no hope that I would survive.

It raised its arms wide and extended the claws on each hand. I could hear yelling and realized that a small patrol of city watch had come running, but were terrified to get close to the demon. I didn't blame them.

Every muscle in my body was tense, and my heart was racing. My vision had become crystal clear and I was prepared to start moving the instant the demon began its lunge.

And then the ground under the demon erupted and a bright yellow light burst forth from below. The creature screamed as its flesh boiled in that incandescent glow. It seemed unable to move, but thrashed its arms and legs around in a vain attempt to reach me.

My senses reeled as a voice thundered in my head.

"GO, BOROLT! RETURN TO THE TOWER!"

I threw myself away from the demon and fled back towards the tower, back towards the spy who wanted me dead, back towards the one man in Ythis who might have the skill and power and interest enough to protect me.

As I rounded the corner, I heard the demon stop screaming as the light died away. I had no idea how injured the creature was, or if it was now pursuing me to complete its mission. Every step I took brought me closer to the Tower of Dust, but I kept expecting the claws to bury themselves in my back at any moment.

I was gasping for breath when I reached the Tower and threw myself into the vestibule at the entrance. I was screaming for Lord Dust and as I turned to look out the door, I saw the demon standing on the threshold, mere yards from me.

Black ichor oozed from gaping wounds on its body, and it staggered as it tried to reach me. I kept screaming for Lord Dust, and I heard the tread of someone on the stairs behind me.

The demon looked up at my rescuer, snarled in rage, and disappeared in a thunderclap that blew me onto my back. A face appeared before me, but it wasn't Veylar Dust.

It was Apprentice Delash Wiar.

"You appear to be a singular individual, Mister Zale. I will require you to tell me how you managed to fight off a demon and inflict such grievous wounds."

I couldn't speak as I tried to regain my breath, not that I would admit to him the truth. I had recognized that voice in my head, telling me to run.

My life had been saved by the Seer of the Tsojim.

*　　　*　　　*

I WAS ESCORTED BY APPRENTICE WIAR TO THE SAME ROOM where I had spoken to him and Apprentice Arral Doviar a few days ago. Quda appeared to tell me that Lord Dust had already left the Tower and was likely at the Emperor's palace by now.

We were momentarily joined by the other Apprentices, Gisea arriving with Arral, and Ituro Nedes silently entering the room shortly after.

I was in shock, and kept shivering as my body tried to deal with the terror of coming face-to-face with a demon sent to kill me.

Ituro Nedes sat at the back of the room, his perpetual scowl in evidence as he stared a hole in my head. He said nothing, and none of the other Apprentices spoke to him.

Gisea and Arral sat side-by-side and asked Apprentice Wiar what he had seen in the moment the demon had been visible in the doorway. He answered them in the same matter-of-fact tone he used in all discussions.

As the most senior of the Apprentices, Delash Wiar took charge questioning me.

"Why did the demon attack you?"

What could I say? I didn't want to tell them that one of them was a spy for the Hidden. It was too much for them to believe.

"I don't know. I thought at first that one of you had sent your demon to bring me a message of some sort, and that it was just toying with me."

A quick look passed between Gisea and Arral.

"What did the demon say to you?"

"It said it was sent to bring my head back to its master, after it had eaten my body."

Delash Wiar leaned in close to me and looked me in the eyes.

"How did you fight the demon, Borolt Zale? How did you escape?"

I knew the spy was in the room, and I didn't want to reveal my most powerful ally to him or her.

"I don't know."

"But you will tell us what happened."

I had to tell them something, and even Lord Dust's knowledge of the Tsojim was limited. I just hoped I wasn't giving too much away.

"The ground burst open under the demon and a yellow light shot up out of it. The demon began screaming, and I didn't wait to see what might happen. I just knew I had to get back to the Tower—that only Lord Dust would be able to protect me."

Arral smiled.

"You are fortunate indeed that you were incorrect about that last point. We may not be full sorcerers yet, but even demons are wary of fighting us directly."

I corrected him.

"Well, some demons are."

The room went silent and they all stared at me. My mouth had just managed to infuriate all four of them with the reminder of Ankin Poloth's death.

"Perhaps we should send you home again."

It was the first words Ituro Nedes ever said to me, and considering what was to happen between us over the next few years, I have should taken his threat more seriously. At the moment, however, I didn't care if he liked me. None of them was going to risk the wrath of Lord Dust by sending me out to die.

Apprentice Wiar waved off Ituro Nedes' words.

"And you saw no other creature, no sorcerer, no one else who could have caused such a thing to happen?"

I shook my head.

"I saw no one else. But my attention was focused solidly on the demon who was trying to kill me. All four of you could have been there, waving your hands and shouting, and I probably wouldn't have noticed."

Delash Wiar sat back and looked at the other Apprentices in turn.

"We need whatever details you can remember, Mister Zale. From the beginning, describe exactly what happened."

I told them everything, only leaving out the voice in my head and the identity of my savior. When I was done, Apprentice Wiar nodded and stood up from his seat.

"We will need to discuss this further, Mister Zale. Quda will get you settled in what appears to be your room now. We may have more questions for you tomorrow."

There was no way they were going to dismiss me that easily.

"Wait a minute. I was attacked by a demon, right out in the streets of Ythis. There were a dozen witnesses, and you can be sure the Church is going to know about this shortly if they don't already. And I can't imagine they won't bring it up at the council meeting.

"Let's be direct here. That demon was sent to kill me by a sorcerer, or a sorcerer's apprentice. I don't believe Lord Dust wants me dead, and I'm the first regular person to survive a meeting with Lord Ghargar. So that leaves the four of you."

"Or," Arral suggested, "One of the apprentices who seemed insulted by your presence at the meeting today."

He had me and I knew it. There was no way for me to argue that point without giving everyone a reason to believe me. And I couldn't reveal the spy in their midst without telling them how I knew.

But the biggest problem of all was that I had no idea how the spy would react if I revealed his or her existence. Lord Dust wasn't here. If I started laying out my proof of a spy in their midst, it might force the spy to act. I could start a war in this room, one I would be the least likely person to survive.

"If one of those apprentices had sent the demon to kill me, what can I do? What can *you* do?"

"That is for us to determine, Mister Zale. There are...proto-cols...to follow if such a thing has occurred. We will ensure Lord Dust is aware of the events of tonight, and I will decide our best course of action while he is unavailable at the council meeting."

They had already decided that one of Lord Ghargar's apprentic-es was responsible for the demon's attack on me. At least, three of them had made that decision—one of these four was the spy who wanted me dead.

There wasn't anything more I could do, though. I was trapped in the Tower of Dust now, with no way to continue my investigations. I only hoped Lord Dust had a solution when he returned.

The really frightening part was that, while I was pretty sure Ap-prentice Wiar had saved my life tonight, I couldn't fully trust him. He might have been controlling the demon all along, but didn't want it to come into the Tower in case it could be tracked back to him—if such a thing was even possible.

Besides, he seemed more interested in how I had managed to es-cape from the demon and inflict harm upon it than why it was there in the first place. My only choice was to graciously accept the hos-pitality of the Apprentices, one of whom would try to see me dead again, probably in the next few days.

"Thank you for saving my life tonight, Apprentice Wiar. I'll think about what happened and tell you if I remember anything else that may be helpful to you.

He nodded to me, and I stood up to go. Gisea watched me with an unreadable expression. Arral had that tiny smile on his face. Ituro continued to scowl at me.

I went to go make myself comfortable in 'my' room.

Chapter Seventeen

SULID WHISTLED AND SAW WEESE TURN A CORNER AND head for a nearby alley. He moved back around the other side of the line of buildings and came to the alley's other end a few moments later.

He had to force himself to be extra careful—his excitement to hear about Borolt Zale made him want to rush to talk to Weese as quickly as possible. There had been no information yesterday morning, and he was almost frantic with the urgency of his quest.

Weese walked forward and met Sulid him down the alley. He crouched in the shadows, and Weese followed suit.

"Anything?"

"Yeah, last night I got something."

Sulid rocked back on his heels. This was it!

"Does he live in the Tower?"

"Sulid, you need to stay away from this man."

"Weese, I need to speak to him! He's the only one who can help me!"

Weese shook his head.

"If you think you've got problems now, you'll have them far worse if you get involved with that man. He's got trouble coming at him from all sides."

"I know, Weese. I saw him handle two thugs who tried to kill him. He fought them off and killed them both without even trying."

Weese shook his head. In the darkness, Sulid couldn't read his expression.

"Two thugs, huh? That's nothing compared to what happened last night."

"What? What happened last night? Tell me, Weese!"

"Everyone was talking about it, but one guy at the Black Door was there, and he knows this man, he recognized him."

"Where? What happened?"

"The man—Borolt Zale—doesn't live in the Tower of Dust. He goes there because he works for the sorcerer who lives there. He works for one of the Five, Sulid!"

"I know."

"You know? Have you thought about what sorcerers do, Sulid? They're even worse than the Church. They summon demons and eat people's souls. You think a man who works for one of the Five will help you?"

Sulid thought about it. He understood Weese's worry—if he hadn't already been saved by the man once, he would be worried too. But he didn't think the man was evil.

And if he *was* evil, he was definitely less evil than the Stranger.

"Weese, the Church is far worse than you know. Now tell me what happened last night."

"From what everyone is saying, a demon attacked Borolt Zale right in the street. It turned everything to ice and froze Borolt Zale right there in a block of ice."

Weese made the sign to ward off evil, and kept making it as he continued on with his story.

"The demon was coming to eat him, but then Veylar Dust appeared in the air and cast bolts of lightning at it. The ice around Borolt Zale broke open, and he ran all the way back to the Tower of Dust.

"But even Veylar Dust wasn't strong enough to beat the demon out in the open like that, so it broke away from the sorcerer and chased Borolt all the way back to the Tower, too. A big battle happened then, and it took the sorcerer and all his apprentices to banish the demon."

That explained the very large presence of the city watch on the streets when Sulid had emerged to come meet Weese. A real demon loose in the streets of Ythis, battling a sorcerer and his apprentices—this was almost too much to believe.

"Borolt Zale has a price on his head. It was put there by the Church. When he went to work for Veylar Dust, the Church held back the bounty. But it's still there, waiting for the day that Borolt Zale loses the protection of the sorcerer. The guy who told me about this thinks the Church sent the demon to kill him."

Sulid considered for an instant and immediately saw the error in Weese's conclusion.

"But the Church doesn't summon demons, Weese. Only sorcerers do that. So, if it was a demon that attacked Borolt, it had to be one that got loose. Or maybe one of the other Five sent it."

Weese groaned.

"I hope you're wrong about that. Because it means the Five are fighting each other, and that means this city could be overrun by demons while the sorcerers kill each other off."

Sulid considered the idea of a battle between the sorcerers. If that happened, then the Church would become all-powerful. It wasn't something he would ever want to see happen.

"Look, Weese, none of that matters. I need to get a message to Borolt Zale. I need to meet with him, speak to him."

"That's not going to happen. He's in the Tower of Dust, and he probably won't be coming back out. Not if there are demons trying to kill him."

Sulid rested his chin on his knees. He couldn't just walk up to the Tower of Dust and ask to speak to Borolt. Now that he knew the man was alive, he was sure the Stranger would be watching the Tower carefully. Even if he made it across the open space to the Tower, there was no guarantee that the servants wouldn't throw him out before the message got to Borolt.

And now that a demon had attacked Borolt, the man would be even harder to reach. There might be magical protections on the Tower that prevented anyone from approaching it.

"Weese, I need one more favor from you."

"No way, Sulid. I know what you're going to ask, and I won't do it."

"Please, Weese. I need to get a message to Borolt. If I don't, the

Stranger is going to find me at some point and then I'll be dead."

Weese just continued to shake his head.

"It's bad enough that you asked me to find out about this man. I was just lucky that something happened last night so that I could ask questions without looking too curious, you know? But to really go near the Tower of Dust? You must think I'm crazy."

"I think you're my friend."

"Then maybe I shouldn't be your friend. Look, you brought some kind of trouble on yourself, and I don't want you to get killed. But if it's you or me, I'm going to choose you. That's just the way it is."

Sulid was on the verge of tears. Weese was his only real friend, the only person who had ever cared if he lived or died. He didn't want to lose his friend over this. But he didn't know what else he could do.

"Maybe you should leave Ythis. This stranger can't find you if you're not here."

"Where could I go? I have no money, no way to get anywhere else."

Weese lowered his head and spoke in a low voice.

"I could maybe help you out on that."

Sulid knew what Weese meant, and he wanted no part of it. There were some things he simply wasn't willing to do, even to save his life.

"I'm sorry, Weese," he whispered. "I know you're trying to keep me safe, but I can't do what you do. I just can't."

Weese looked up at Sulid's face in the dark, and then took a deep breath. He stood up.

"Then there's nothing else I can do for you. Stay safe, Sulid, as long as you can."

He knew Weese was about to walk out of his life. He was losing the last friend he had. He couldn't let it end like this.

"Wait! What if I make a deal with you?"

Weese hesitated.

"What kind of deal?"

"You deliver a message to Borolt at the Tower. I will write it and you drop it off there. You don't have to convince anyone of anything—just deliver my message."

"I'm not going to—"

"And if they don't take the message, or if Borolt doesn't want to meet with me, I'll let you bring me to the Black Door. I'll go without fighting, and you get the credit for bringing me in."

"You just said you couldn't do it, Sulid. I'm not stupid."

"I don't want to die! Anything is better than dying," he lied.

He watched Weese calculate what he could get out of it if he brought the boy into the Black Door willingly. It would be worth a lot.

"But you have to swear to deliver my message, the one I give you."

"And you'll come to the Black Door and not fight it?"

"I'll do anything, Weese. Just don't leave me."

Weese considered the odds. Then he nodded once.

"Write your message and give it to me tomorrow morning. I'll deliver it right away. If they refuse to give it to him, or if Borolt Zale doesn't come to meet you, then you go with me to the Black Door."

"I swear, Weese, that's all I'm asking you to do."

"Then I swear to deliver your message. Don't worry, Sulid. I can take care of you, even after you start working."

*   *   *

I WAS BACK IN ANKIN POLOTH'S ROOM, EXAMINING HIS JOURNAL for some piece of information I might have missed. I had realized the possibility that Ankin had known the identity of the spy; that they had been in this together.

Of course, it would have been foolish of him to put it in writing. But then, he had written about his meetings with the Hidden, even if in code and without details. If there was any chance of extracting further information from the journal, this was my chance to do it. I certainly wouldn't be leaving the Tower.

I was on my second full pass through the document when I noticed something missing. The journal of a sorcerer contains their innermost thoughts, secrets they have discovered, plans for the future. And all of that was in the journal.

But there was something missing. The journal spoke at length about the demon Ankin Poloth had summoned as his first test of sorcery. But nowhere did Ankin Poloth record the demon's true name.

I was no expert, of course. But I did know that a demon's true name is less a written word than it is a sigil of some kind. That sigil is used by the sorcerer to summon and bind the demon, and also to control it in various ways through certain rituals.

The true name of a demon is the only thing that gives the sorcerer power over such a being. True names have great value, as each sorcerer must unearth that information though research, rituals, and the expenditure of a good deal of effort. It is why sorcerers will fight over the journals of one of their number if he or she dies.

This journal did not contain a true name.

I spent the next several hours confirming my discovery. Why would Ankin Poloth have refrained from recording his demon's true name? He must have recorded it somewhere, or he wouldn't have been able to summon and bind it in the first place. But where?

I had searched all through his room when I was looking for the journal, and there was nothing else to find. This journal wasn't nearly complete, so there was little reason to have a second volume. What was I missing?

I needed to speak to one of the other apprentices. Perhaps he could shed some light on this turn of events. I left Ankin Poloth's room and went to find Quda to have him arrange a meeting with Apprentice Wiar.

I was nearing the ground floor of the Tower when Gisea appeared on the stairs. She saw me and stopped.

"You are not planning to leave the Tower."

Coming from her, it wasn't a question.

"No, I need to speak to Apprentice Wiar."

"He is away for most of the day. Why do you need to speak to him?"

I wasn't sure what to say. Gisea was becoming more a mystery to me every time I spoke to her. She clearly didn't like me, but it appeared she had developed a small amount of respect for me over the last couple of days. And yet I was sure I could not trust her.

I needed information, though, and I couldn't see how she could use this situation to harm me.

"I've been examining Apprentice Poloth's journal for more information, and I believe I have found something significant."

"Show me."

She strode up the stairs, fully expecting me to follow her. I debated for an instant about staying where I was and making her stop and wait for me, but that was both petty and needlessly antagonistic. It would also cause me more trouble than it was worth.

She led me to the same room we had all been in the night before.

"Let me see the journal."

"I don't have it with me."

Her eyes narrowed and she obviously didn't believe me.

"How, precisely, were you going to show Apprentice Wiar something in the journal if you do not have it on your person?"

"Well, there's nothing to show. What I mean is, I've discovered something is missing from the journal, something that should be there. Only it isn't."

She waited for me to explain. I hesitated just long enough for her impatience to get the best of her. She was about to demand I tell her, but I spoke as soon as I saw her mouth open.

"The demon's true name. It isn't anywhere in the journal."

"How can you be sure?"

Of course, she'd question my ability to figure out something like this.

"I've seen a demon's true name twice before. I know what to look for."

She stepped toward me, her face less than a foot from mine.

"*Where* have you seen a demon's true name before? I grow very tired of your games, Mister Zale. You will give me a straight answer."

The fact that she didn't feel a need to give me an 'or else' ultimatum told me I had pushed her a bit too far.

"Both times were in the presence of Lord Dust. He was explaining something to me, and had some ancient book on his desk. I had asked about writing a demon's true name, and he showed me what those sigils look like so that I could understand what he was talking about."

She gave no reaction, and didn't step back.

"And you say no sigil appears in Apprentice Poloth's journal."

"That's right. When I noticed I hadn't seen it, I carefully checked every page. It's not there. That's why I wanted to speak with Apprentice Wiar. I need to know if there are other ways to record the true names, or other places instead of in your journal."

She considered it for a moment and shook her head slightly.

"No, any other way would be atypical behavior for an Apprentice. Give the journal to me and I will confirm what you believe."

I was half-tempted to just hand it over to her and prove I wasn't incompetent. Except I knew I would never get it back.

"I'm still going through it, revealing other bits of information that might be useful to Lord Dust. I'm sure he'll agree to let you examine it when we're done, though."

Anger radiated from her like a physical thing.

"Do you not realize I could simply take the journal from you, Mister Zale?"

I nodded.

"And yet you continue to act as if you are in a position of power. And you do not realize the protection Lord Dust extends over you out *there* does not apply in *here*."

"What are you getting at?"

"We are apprentices to Lord Veylar Dust—sorcerer, member of the council of Ythis, one of the Five. Certain things are expected of us, and one of those things is our ability to deal with those beneath us. You believe you are equal to the Apprentices, at the least. The truth is that you are a possession of Lord Dust. And in our growth as sorcerers, we sometimes break one of Lord Dust's possessions. And while we are required to replace what we break, the original possession is still gone.

"Do you begin to understand your situation, Mister Zale? You can earn our assistance, when and where we feel it is worth our time to give it. You might even earn the right for us to treat you as above the other mortals who live in this city. But your current behavior will cause me—or one of the others—to exterminate you."

I knew I had pushed things too far with her, but I hadn't realized the fragility of my position.

"Then please let me apologize, Apprentice Megoen—"

She waved off my apology.

"Your words have no value, Mister Zale. You will correct your behavior, or you will most likely die. I have considered your performance in the meeting with Lord Ghargar, and I believe you may have potential as a useful servant of Lord Dust. But all it means is that I would think of your death as a waste, after I ended your life."

She moved to the door.

"Finish your examination of the journal, and then give it to Quda to deliver it to me. It is not a request."

And with that, she left me alone in the room.

Chapter Eighteen

I HAD A FEELING I WAS ONTO SOMETHING IMPORTANT, BUT I was running out of time. I needed answers ready for when Veylar Dust returned from the council meeting. And the first question revolved around the missing name of Ankin Poloth's demon.

I went in search of Quda, finding him leaving the kitchens with a worried expression on his face. While Lord Dust was away, Apprentice Wiar was nominally in charge of the Tower, but Quda took on more responsibility as well to ensure that everything ran smoothly.

"Quda, I'm sorry but I need a few moments of your time."

He looked at me with some irritation, an expression that passed quickly leaving me doubting I had interpreted it correctly.

"Borolt, I'm very busy. Is it important?"

Of course it was important—I wouldn't bother him if it wasn't. But I could also see that he was trying to do too many things at once, and he really didn't need my interruptions right now.

"This is vital, Quda. It's about the demon that attacked me last night."

He managed to mostly suppress his sigh, and led me to a quiet corner.

"What do you need?"

"I'm close to answering some big questions, Quda. I need to check some records, though. I need to get into the vault."

His eyes went wide, and he took a step back.

"Borolt...the vault...you know it is off-limits to everyone except Lord Dust and the apprentices."

"I know. I also know you have access. And I can't go to the apprentices with this. They won't help me."

"There are...things...in the vault which must be kept secured, Borolt. It is not exactly safe in there."

"It's not exactly safe for me out here, either. I have no intention of touching anything, Quda. I just need to check some records—mundane ones. I won't look into any tomes, or get close to any of the artifacts. Besides, you'll be with me."

He shook his head.

"I can't Borolt. My duties are overwhelming right now. And even with the protections I have, I do not enter the vault unless I have no other choice."

"I *don't* have any other choice. Someone sent a demon after me last night. I was very, very lucky to reach the Tower before it caught me. The apprentices see me as a troublemaker and would like to be rid of me. And Lord Dust is relying on me to give him the information he needs to figure out what happened to Ankin Poloth. Never mind that creature in the bay and the maneuverings of the—"

I stopped cold. Quda gave me a piercing look.

"The what?"

I had almost blurted out that I was in contact with the Hidden. I had been around people I didn't trust for so long that I was ready to automatically trust Quda just because he was in a similar position as mine.

Only I *couldn't* trust him. He was intelligent, and helpful. He treated me with respect, and I could almost say we were friends. But I couldn't forget who his master was, who he was dedicated to serving.

"Never mind that, Quda. I need to get into the vault. I am asking for your help. I swear to you that I will cause no trouble, and that if I encounter any difficulties, I'll leave immediately."

I could see the battle going on behind his eyes. He wanted to help me, but the vault was dangerous. Access to it was also restricted by Veylar Dust himself. If I came out with the answers I needed, then everything would be fine. But if anything bad happened, then Quda would be held responsible.

He looked down, and shook his head.

"I cannot risk it, Borolt. I cannot watch over you down there, and I cannot let you wander in the vault alone. Most important, however, is that I cannot leave the vault open while you are inside with no one of power to guard the entrance."

I considered my options. I knew that some ancient, powerful artifacts were kept in the vault. Items so imbued with sorcerous power they had gained malevolent intelligence.

Of course, there were wards throughout the vault that kept those intelligences, that power, constrained and confined. But I was no sorcerer, and one wrong turn could take me past protections I couldn't sense. I could wander into the grip of something powerful and evil, and if I came back out, it would no longer be as Borolt Zale.

Ultimately, though, I didn't have a choice.

"Then lock me in."

Quda's eyes went wide again.

"Are you mad? Do you even realize what you are asking, Borolt?"

"I realize it. I'm not mad, I'm just out of choices. I can't do anything else without information, and the information I need is in the vault. You can't escort me, and I can't go to the apprentices for help on this. The only option left to me is to get locked in there while I search for the records I need."

"There are things far worse than death, Borolt."

"I know. But let me be clear. If that demon had just been sent to kill me, I'd already be dead. There would have been no way I could have seen it coming, no way could I have escaped. It was after me to do much worse than kill me, in addition to sending a message to Lord Dust.

"I'm not safe no matter what I do, Quda. But if I'm going to die— or worse—then I want the chance to die hunting down answers, not hiding in the Tower of Dust."

He continued to look at the floor, saying nothing. Finally, he looked up at me and I could see in his face he had decided not to help me.

"I'm sorry. I cannot let you into the vault. If you must gain entrance, then you will have to ask Apprentice Wiar."

He walked away and left me in the kitchen. I could feel my desperation welling up inside me. I couldn't trust the apprentices and Quda wouldn't help. But I needed answers for Lord Dust—I just had a feeling that I needed to produce something useful when he returned.

Once again, I was in a position where I had no real choice. I moved down the side hallway towards Quda's quarters before I consciously realized what I was going to do. I didn't want to betray the only man in the Tower who treated me as a friend, but I could see no other option.

The lock on Quda's door delayed me only a few seconds—inside the Tower of Dust, such locks were intended more to ensure basic privacy than keep out any real intruders. My skill at getting past such obstacles was more than equal to the task. Once in Quda's quarters, it took me only a few moments to locate the heavy box where he kept the key to the vault. I was worried that Quda might return to his quarters, and hoped he was kept busy until I was finished with my task in the vault.

I opened the box and saw that an amulet lay beside the key to the vault entrance. The amulet appeared to be made of bronze, beaten into a pattern by primitive tools. I knew that Lord Dust had given Quda some form of protection along with the key, and I figured this must it. I took both the amulet and key and replaced the box's lid, leaving everything as it had been before I entered.

As I left Quda's quarters, I once again wondered what I had gotten myself into.

*   *   *

THE PASSAGEWAY WAS COLD ENOUGH THAT MY BREATH WAS visible in the light from the lantern. I could see the glitter of frost on the stone slabs that formed the walls, and I left a faint outline of my footprints on the cobbled floor.

I was at least five spans below ground level, with one more stairway between me and the entrance to the vault. I carried a lantern held high. The smell of the burning oil was strong, and my eyes watered with the combination of that and the cold.

I reached the final staircase and proceeded down, trailing my hand along the wall in case I stumbled. The cold bit into my fingers, but I concentrated on the sensation instead of dwelling on what I was about to do.

Finally, I reached the bottom and emerged from the tunnel into a larger chamber. Four pillars carved with arcane symbols supported an arched ceiling, and facing me was the outer door to the vault.

The stone slab was fitted tightly into the opening, with no handle or other visible means of opening it besides pushing. In contrast to the pillars, the door itself was smooth and unmarked.

I stepped up to the door and looked it over. I had been down here only once before, in the presence of Veylar Dust. He had opened the door and gone inside while I waited in this chamber at his order.

It was during that visit that he had revealed to me the records kept in the vault. I remembered him telling me they were kept in the first chamber on the right, as they didn't need any further protection than just the vault itself.

I pulled the key out of my pocket and stepped over to one of the four pillars. One of the carvings resembled a strange lizard, and the creature's eye formed the keyhole. I slid the key into the hole and took a deep breath before twisting it.

I suddenly felt as if the floor were dropping out from under my feet. The door was both there and not there at the same time, and I saw a great reptilian eye open in the stone itself. I yelled as I tried to regain my balance.

And then the eye pulled backwards, stretching the stone of the door as it went. In an instant, the eye had moved back around a turn and out of sight, and the stone of the door stretched to become the passageway into the vault.

The falling sensation ceased, and the vault was open. In contrast to the tunnel leading down here, the interior of the vault radiated heat. The antechamber just inside the portal appeared lit, although I could see no source of the light.

I hung the amulet around my neck. It was cool to the touch, and heavier than it looked.

I took another deep breath and stepped across the threshold. For the first time, I was inside the vault. And I was very, very alone.

I turned to look back at the entry chamber and saw the stone slab back in place. The vault was already sealed, and I had neither heard nor felt anything.

And the key was still on the other side of that door.

I practically dropped the lantern and lunged at the stone slab, pushing and prodding, but had no effect on the door. I had somehow locked myself in the vault, and no one knew I was down here. I spent some minutes pounding on the door, yelling for help. I knew, though, that no sound would reach the Tower above me.

Fear gripped me, but I forced myself to remain calm. I had come here for a purpose, and now that I was here, I should get the answers I needed. Only then would I return to this antechamber and figure out how to open the door again. I didn't know if I would be able to concentrate on the task at hand, or just worry that I had locked myself in the vault permanently.

I stood there, uneasily, as more time passed. I would have to focus on my task and hope to find a way to get out of the vault. It took me more time as I steeled myself to proceed further into the vault.

Eventually, I grabbed the lantern and moved to the passageway to look down the hall, but I could only see a short distance before it curved out of sight. I didn't immediately see the doorway to the chamber where the records were stored. I hoped it was close—I didn't want to go too far down that passageway.

Something in the back of my brain was screaming at me, pleading with me to find some way out of this place. The simple stone passageway caused shivers to run down my spine, and my hands felt clammy.

I forced myself to take a step out of the antechamber into that hallway. Another step, and another, and I was moving toward that curve. I tried to increase my pace, but it was like walking in molasses, and every fiber in my body was urging me to turn around and run like mad.

Time seemed to slow down as I reached the bend, and then I came around the corner to see the passage stretching a short distance before ending in another chamber exactly like the one I had just left. In fact, I could see the stone slab of the vault door on the far wall.

I tried to turn my head to look back at the passageway behind me, but I suddenly felt a presence standing at my left shoulder. My neck muscles froze, and I was gripped by an unreasoning fear. I felt the lantern slip from my grasp and land on the floor. Mercifully, it neither broke nor tipped over.

I became aware that I could hear someone screaming in fear and pain, and then I realized it was my own voice, though my mouth was closed. And the screams began to make a strange pattern of noise, patterns from which came words that burned in my ears.

"At last, a visitor to my prison. It has been too long. I have grown weary of my solitude in this timeless place."

I looked down at the amulet, intending to wrap my hands around it, but the bronze melted and dropped in hissing rivulets on the stone floor.

"I have been free of my bonds for some time, mortal. And yet I have been trapped beyond the wards, prevented from reaching the vault entrance. Until you wandered too far."

That didn't make any sense. I hadn't seen any other chambers in the short distance I had walked. How could I have come past the wards that protected the outside world from nightmares such as this?

I raised my head and saw, behind the image of the passage ending at the antechamber, another passage leading off into darkness with doorways on either side. A cold fist seemed to press into my chest where the amulet had been. The unseen presence moved to the edge of my vision, and I knew the horror of its appearance would drive me mad if I laid eyes on it.

"You will bring me out of the vault, mortal. Your will is my will, your body merely an extension of my being. Walk forward, mortal. Walk to the antechamber."

I took an involuntary step forward, and then stopped. I could still see the other passageway, slipping under the image of the antechamber. I looked down at the amulet, intending to wrap my hands around it, but the bronze melted and dropped in hissing rivulets on the stone floor. The cold over my heart grew stronger.

My own screams became louder, more insistent.

"Walk forward, mortal! Return to the entrance!"

I looked up at the passageway and took another step. I had to do something to stop this. The cold on my chest was too painful to ignore.

I looked down at the amulet, intending to wrap my hands around it, but the bronze melted and dropped in hissing rivulets on the stone floor. I felt that I had seen that happen before, somewhere, somewhen...

I reached up and grabbed at the place where the amulet had been. Cold seared into my flesh where it touched the freezing bronze.

With a terrible lurch, reality snapped back into place around me. I was standing beside the doorway to the chamber where the records were held. The passageway stretched on into darkness in front of me. I could make out doorways leading into other chambers further on.

Less than two strides in front of me, a symbol was carved into the floor. Most likely one of the wards set up by Lord Dust himself.

Something in here had almost gotten me to walk past that point. Only the sorcerous power of the amulet had saved me. I didn't want to think about what might have happened if I had taken those last two steps.

The cold was burning the flesh on my hands. I stepped into the chamber where the records were kept, and slowly took one hand off the amulet. Nothing happened. I leaned out of the doorway and grabbed the lantern before retreating back into the records room. I slowly lowered my other hand from the amulet. Not a whisper, not a shiver.

The cold on the amulet began to fade. Perhaps whatever it was had given up on me as a victim. I had no idea how much time had been wasted in the hallway. It might have been three minutes, or three hours.

I took a deep breath, again steeled myself for the task at hand, and set to work.

Chapter Nineteen

NEVER MIND BEING IN THE VAULT, I WASN'T EVEN supposed to be reading these ledgers—the information in them was for the eyes of Veylar Dust and his apprentices only. And yet, there was a mystery here, and I couldn't wait for Lord Dust to decide to give me permission.

So, I started with Ankin Poloth. Lord Dust kept meticulous records on his searches for new apprentices. The selection of a potential candidate was done only after careful examination of the subject. Nothing was left to chance.

Of course, even Lord Dust could make a mistake, or so I believed. And it wasn't impossible to deliberately keep information from a sorcerer. It was just very, very difficult.

And so, I scoured the records of Ankin Poloth. I was looking for something that might have seemed innocuous at the time, but in hindsight might answer some questions about why he made the choices he did. The only problem was that I didn't know for sure if such puzzle pieces truly existed.

Apprentice Poloth had come from the Plains of Quimyr, on the western edge of the Empire. His village was called Hyra and was typical of such places—small, on the banks of a river, its people mostly occupied with farming, along with some animal husbandry and fishing thrown in. A quiet, peaceful village that was none too pleased when Lord Veylar Dust arrived.

Most people believe that sorcery is in the blood. You are either born with the potential, or—no matter how hard you study—you can never succeed at any summoning or binding. I've heard that at least two other members of the Five consider that to be nonsense, though.

Regardless, Lord Dust believes that sorcery is passed down through bloodlines, and he studies ancient records and works his way up through history to discover the whereabouts of some of the descendants of the first sorcerers. I'm always amazed at how much information is truly out there, if you know how to find it.

And Lord Dust spends years hunting down the tiniest detail that might lead him to another potential sorcerer. I don't know how the other members of the Five find their own apprentices, but all of the apprentices in the Tower were found through research.

Not everyone of a certain bloodline has the potential to become a sorcerer, of course. There'd be a lot more of them if that were the case. But there are ways to identify a candidate, mostly involving rituals and careful examination.

Ankin Poloth was the ideal candidate. He was fairly easy to find, all things considered, and Veylar Dust identified his potential quickly and without difficulty. He was willing to leave his village and his family for the lure of dark power, and came to the Tower with nothing in his past to mark how quickly and violently his future would come to an end.

In the records of Ankin Poloth's apprenticeship, I discovered what I believed was the symbol of his demon's true name. This only heightened my curiosity. Why had he not copied it into his own journal? It was completely antithetical to how sorcerers usually acted.

I went through his records a second time and examined everything, but found nothing else of note.

I still had no idea how long I had been in the vault, so I decided to look at another apprentice to see if anything stood out in contrast to Apprentice Poloth's records. Of course, I chose Gisea Megoen.

I'm still not sure why I decided to look at her records. It's not that I was hoping to find something to use against her—that would have ended my life too quickly to think about. No, I think that I was looking for some explanation of why she had become who she was.

I found much more than that.

At first, I thought I had made a mistake, and I had to go back and pull out Ankin Poloth's records again to convince myself I wasn't imagining things. But the information was right there in front of my eyes.

Apprentice Megoen had also come from a small village on the Plains of Quimyr. She was of the same bloodline as Apprentice Poloth. These two facts alone seemed logical. If some members of the bloodline had settled in that region at some point in the past, it was entirely possible, if unlikely, that two descendants with the potential would be born within a few years of each other.

But there were other connections, too. They were both distantly related to each other due to their extended families moving around the region and intermarrying. Their childhoods mirrored one another. Their immediate families were eerily similar.

It was like looking at the records of twins, except these two had been born to different parents, in different villages, a few years apart.

I had to shake off my excitement. There was no way Lord Dust has missed this. These records had been compiled by him directly. He knew about the connection before he ever approached Apprentice Poloth, and Gisea Megoen was already at the Tower when he went on the trip back to the Plains of Quimyr.

I couldn't shake the feeling that I was missing something vitally important, though. Something in the back of my mind, some reference, made me think there was some detail that would show these records in a whole new light.

Lord Dust would return in three days. I had to lay low, stay out of the way of the other apprentices during that time. I also had to hope that Quda kept my visit to the vault completely secret. I couldn't remove the records and keep them with me, and I was worried that the spy might tamper with them if he or she knew what I had discovered.

None of what I found confirmed Apprentice Megoen was the spy for the Hidden. But there was a connection between her and Ankin Poloth. Perhaps if they shared the same bloodline and other life details, it was possible that her demon might break loose from its binding as well.

I realized I was speculating with no way to determine if I was remotely close to the answer. I would have to present my findings to Lord Dust. He may not have remembered the extreme coincidences in both Apprentice Megoen's and Apprentice Poloth's lives, and I would make sure he considered it.

I doubted I would have time to examine the records of the other apprentices in full, so I had to decide who to examine next. I had a feeling that Apprentice Arral Doviar wanted to do me harm, despite his pleasant demeanor. On the other hand, I knew Apprentice Ituro Nedes didn't like me.

I grabbed Apprentice Nedes' records next. I had no idea at the time that what I saw there would later save my life.

I had been reading just a short time when I suddenly heard Quda's voice call my name. I grabbed the amulet with both hands, but it was merely cool to the touch. Could he have discovered my theft and come down here to find me? How long had I really been in the vault?

"Quda, I...I'm here. I'm in the records room."

"You will come to the front antechamber immediately, please."

"I just need to put the records back on the shelves, Quda. I'll be right there."

"Borolt! I need you to come here immediately. I will count to three, and then I will seal you back up in this vault."

There was something in his voice, some edge that I hadn't ever heard before.

I grabbed the lantern and went into the hallway, one hand still holding the amulet. Quda was in the middle of the antechamber, the stone door open behind him. I felt a thrill of excitement at seeing that portal. I would never want to be sealed in here again.

I stepped into the antechamber and Quda held up one hand.

"You took an amulet along with the key, Borolt. Where is it?"

"It's right here in my hand."

I looked down at the amulet, expecting to see my hand wrapped around it, but the bronze melted and dropped in hissing rivulets on the stone floor.

I looked up and saw an expression of horror on Quda's face.

I opened my mouth and spoke a word of power that forced a gush of blood from my nose, and Quda was thrown back against the wall. I began to stride toward the open doorway, a feeling of intense satisfaction spreading through me.

Quda raised his hand, and I saw he was holding a blue gemstone the size of child's fist. I screamed as my internal organs began churning. Something inside me *pulled* and my head snapped back, a black cloud issuing forth from my mouth.

Quda stepped forward and raised the gemstone higher, and the black cloud flowed back down the hall deeper into the vault.

I felt exhausted, and I couldn't make my limbs move. Quda stepped outside the doorway and looked back at me with an expression of sincere regret. I knew he was going to lock me in the vault, and I knew I would be dead by the time Lord Dust returned.

Then the world turned sideways, and my head smashed against the stone floor, and all thought fled.

*   *   *

TINY MOTES OF LIGHT FLUTTERED IN FRONT OF MY EYES AS I regained consciousness. A cold dread filled the pit of my stomach as I realized I had been possessed by something in this vault. Quda must have sealed the vault back up with me inside, to await the return of Veylar Dust.

I stared at the ceiling and tried to control the panic I felt welling up inside me. There was no way I would survive the next few days trapped in here with that nightmare being. I had failed Quda, I had failed Veylar Dust, and I had failed myself.

A footstep sounded to one side, and without thinking I was suddenly on my feet, looking around for a weapon of some kind.

"Borolt! Calm down!"

I spun to face Quda, and it took me a moment to recognize him. He was holding the same blue gemstone out toward me, and I backed into one of the stone pillars in the outer chamber.

I looked over to see the vault door already closed. I wasn't on the inside, however. Quda had pulled me out.

"You...you didn't seal me in."

A guilty expression crossed his face.

"I did. Borolt, I left you in there overnight. I spent the entire night trying to decide what to do, whether or not to ask the apprentices for help. I finally could not wait any longer and came back to see if you were still alive."

I was shocked that I had been unconscious for the entire evening and through the night. I wasn't angry at Quda for locking me in— my relief at being out of the vault was too strong for me to be angry.

"Thank you, Quda. I can't tell you how happy I am that you saved me. But...what about that thing inside me?"

He ran his hands over the gemstone.

"It cannot abide the presence of this stone, though I do not know why. The amulet is supposed to protect one from the lure of the entities trapped in there. But though I saw you had taken the amulet, I couldn't be sure that you were wearing it. That...creature that possessed you—it got loose once before in the vault. Lord Dust came down here with this stone, and it was enough to drive the entity back from the vault entrance so that he could deal with it without the possibility of its escape."

"Lord Dust gave the stone to you, Quda?"

He looked down at the floor and shook his head.

"I removed the stone from Lord Dust's room before I returned, just in case. If I had not done so, the entity would have broken free from the vault."

I knew what that meant. Veylar Dust would know that something had been removed from his chambers. There was no way to hide that from the sorcerer.

"I will have to tell Lord Dust what happened here today, Borolt. Even with the stone, I might not have prevented its escape. And I should not have let you leave the vault."

"What will he do?"

He looked up at my face, confused.

"Do?"

"To you. What will Lord Dust do to you for letting me leave the vault?"

"I cannot begin to guess, Borolt. Perhaps nothing. Perhaps I will be forced to leave his employ. I do not know."

"I'll take the blame, Quda. Tell him I threatened you."

He smiled, but there was no humor in it.

"Do not be absurd. Neither you nor I have any say in who 'takes the blame', not that such an idea makes any sense in a situation like this. Lord Dust will do whatever he decides to do, based on the facts."

"I didn't want to get you into trouble. I am truly grateful for your help. You saved my life."

Quda turned and headed for the stairs.

"You did not care what trouble you caused, Borolt. You had something you felt you needed to do, and you found a way to do it, regardless of the consequences to those around you."

I paused at the bottom of the stairs.

"It's not like that. I'm not thinking about myself. I put myself into the vault to find a solution for Lord Dust."

He stopped halfway up the stairs and turned to look down at me.

"Everything we do, Borolt, we choose to do. You choose to throw yourself headlong into danger, perhaps hoping you might get yourself killed to ease some of your guilt over your brother."

I was too shocked to answer.

"But in your desire to face any problem head on, you use those around you. I imagine in your old life, you manipulated people quite easily and without consideration."

"That's not true, Quda."

He shrugged.

"But now, you have raised your aspirations quite a bit higher. Now you are trying to manipulate apprentice sorcerers, and Church priests. I must wonder if you have tried to manipulate Lord Dust, himself. But you do not seem to fully understand, Borolt, that there are far worse things than death. You are playing a dangerous game, and you act as if it *is* a game. But the stakes are high not just for you, but for those around you."

"Quda, I'm not playing any games at all. I'm just trying to survive."

"And yet you are trying very, very hard to die."

"I don't understand why you're saying that. I've been fighting to survive for so long I don't know how to give up."

"You are an intelligent man. You've got a high level of cunning, able to survive—and thrive—out there in the streets. You had a chance to run from Ythis, and neither you nor anyone else believes you would not have succeeded in losing any pursuit by the Church. And yet you not only stayed, but threw yourself into the service of yet another kind of evil. The opposite face of the same coin. Do not lie to me and say it was because you thought this was the only safe path. That is utter nonsense.

"You stayed, Borolt, because you were not finished with the Church yet. You stayed because you have a score to settle with them, and allying yourself with their greatest enemies was the best way to succeed at that goal. And you knew what the cost to yourself would be. You managed to find a solution to both your problems. You get to fight the Church from under the protection of Veylar Dust, and yet you know it will ultimately destroy you, thus fulfilling your grief and guilt over your brother."

I could feel my face flush with anger. He had no idea what I was feeling! Only the fact that he had let me out of the vault prevented me from screaming back at him how wrong he was.

"I don't expect you to understand me, Quda. You think you know me, but you really don't."

"Oh, Borolt. You are as transparent as a bowl of clean water. And I have had pity for you, since I know something of what you have experienced. But the situation has gotten so out of your control that you are starting to pull others into your troubles. But I will not be a willing victim, Borolt. You are in a race against time now. You know your position in the Tower of Dust is tenuous, and it grows more so each day that passes. Yet you haven't defeated the Church yet, have you? So now you rush headlong from pillar to post, blindly trying to accomplish what you still can while waiting for the hammer to fall on your head. And you just don't care who else falls with you."

"No, Quda. You have no idea how close I've been to leaving the service of Veylar Dust—just abandoning him and this city and disappearing."

"But you are still here, Borolt. You have not left, because you *will not* leave. You have become a slave to your emotions over your brother, and I cannot see that changing. I'm sorry, Borolt. You will get no further favors from me. I will not destroy myself to help you."

He turned his back on me and proceeded up the stairs back into the Tower of Dust.

Chapter Twenty

SULID WAS NERVOUS BEING OUT THIS EARLY. THE STREETS were still busy, making it more difficult to watch for any signs of the Stranger. But he hoped that this change in his routine would give him an advantage over the man hunting him.

He waited for Weese in an ally overlooking one of the market squares. This time they were meeting nowhere near the Black Door in case anyone had noticed them the last two times. Sulid couldn't believe how fast he was becoming used to living like this—some precautions were becoming second-nature to him.

Weese was late again, but that in itself didn't worry Sulid overmuch. Weese was almost always late. He wondered what the owner of the Black Door thought of that, but he didn't want to know. Sulid deliberately steered his thoughts away from that place.

He hoped with every fiber of his being that Weese had been successful, that he had spoken to the man, Borolt Zale. With any luck, Sulid would meet with Borolt tomorrow night and tell him everything he had seen.

Sulid decided to move to another vantage point rather than stay in one place. He continued to scan the slowly dispersing crowds as he stepped from the alley and moved along the front of a tavern. He reached another alley and ducked in, ready to leap back out should it already be occupied.

He let out a sigh of relief as he saw it was empty of occupants, but he noted a distinct lack of hiding places as well. Sulid's knowledge of the area told him this alley had at least two branches farther along, so he decided it was safe enough for the next few minutes.

Staying in the shadows, he looked out, searching for any sign of Weese. There was no sign of his friend, but something else raised the hairs on the back of his neck.

It took him another moment to realize what was bothering him. Two men were standing off to one side, apparently in a conversation. However, both were watching the marketplace, and Sulid recognized one of them as someone who worked for the Church.

The man had been with the priest who died on the day of the accident. He was the one who had noticed Sulid and started the chase. Sulid had no doubt this man was part of the hunt—and he was here in the marketplace the same night Sulid was supposed to meet Weese.

And Weese was late.

Sulid saw the men begin to casually stroll across the marketplace. Their route would take them right past the mouth of the alley where Sulid now hid. He felt the risk was too great now to move to another alley through the marketplace.

Sulid pulled back into the alley, out of sight of the two men. He turned to head down to the junction when he heard footsteps running toward him from deeper in the darkness.

Sulid looked around frantically, but still could not see any place to hide. He was afraid to go near the alley's mouth for a look, but he had only a few seconds before the person running toward him emerged from around the nearest turn.

Sulid crouched down in the shadows to one side and tried to remain absolutely still. He knew he would be caught if he tried to run, and his only chance was for his pursuers to move past him in the darkness so he might slip out in the opposite direction.

The footsteps neared the corner, and a figure—a darker smudge among the tenebrous shadows—moved into view. Sulid watched the figure move close to him and stop, gasping for breath after his or her headlong sprint up the alley.

The person was taller than Sulid by a bit, but thin. He watched the shadow move toward the mouth of the alley slowly and carefully, and then abruptly pull back. An instant later, the two men came into Sulid's view, continuing to look around.

Sulid held his breath as the dark figure backed towards him. He realized at the last instant the person was going to crouch down in the same spot, and he tried to jump up and run. Sulid had cut it too close, however, and the unknown person stumbled over Sulid's feet.

Sulid dove forward, trying to disentangle himself, but the person fell over on him, crying out in surprise. Sulid immediately recognized the voice of Weese.

"Weese! Be quiet!" he hissed at his friend. Weese stopped struggling, but it was too late.

Sulid could see the two men approaching the alley to investigate the shout from within.

"Run!"

Sulid pulled his legs from beneath his friend and was on his feet and running back into the darkness in an instant. He heard Weese following right behind him, but knew his friend was nearly out of breath. He couldn't tell if the men were pursuing or not.

At the first junction, Sulid turned to the left and wove his way among the heaps of garbage and debris strewn through the alley. By the time he reached the next turn, he could tell Weese was no longer able to keep up. Sulid ducked around the corner and into a shadowed doorway, grabbing his friend's arm and pulling him into the hiding place.

Sulid couldn't hear anything over Weese's gasping breaths, so he quietly shushed his friend and carefully moved to the edge of the corner. Weese held his breath and Sulid concentrated.

A moment later, Weese had to release his breath, but Sulid was sure the men were not near.

"Come on," he told Weese and began walking down the alley toward the next junction.

His friend followed him, his breathing slowly returning to normal.

"What happened, Weese?"

"Sulid, they were following me. I wasn't being that careful, but I didn't think anyone knew I was your friend. By the time I noticed the two men, I was almost at the market square."

"Oh, Weese. I told you to be careful."

"I know, I know. I thought you were making it sound bigger than it was."

"How did you get into the alley behind me?"

"As soon as I entered the square, I lost them in the crowd. I took off down the first side street and ran all the way around to the first alley I could find that led back there. I was thinking I'd spot you and signal you somehow."

"You signaled them instead."

"Yeah, sorry about that. You scared me."

Sulid led them down another turning and soon they emerged onto a major thoroughfare. They crossed quickly and were soon deep in another alley.

"Did you speak to Borolt Zale?"

Weese hesitated, and Sulid's heart fell.

"I tried, Sulid. But they wouldn't listen to me. They threatened to feed me to one of their demons if I didn't leave."

Sulid stopped and leaned against the wall. He could smell the dry dust, feel the heat ebbing from the surface.

"I needed to speak to him."

"I know. But he works for a *sorcerer*. He probably wouldn't have helped you anyway."

"You don't know that."

"What kind of person could choose to serve one of the Five?"

Sulid thought back to Borolt Zale yanking him away from the crossbow bolt fired at his head. He didn't answer.

"Listen, I said I'd take care of you, and I will."

"You want to take me to the Black Door."

"It's not as bad as you think, Sulid. And you'll be safe there."

Sulid didn't really believe Weese. He had heard about what happened on the other side of that door. He would never have considered it safe.

But Weese worked there, and got paid money. And he didn't seem to be in bad shape.

"Listen, most people who talk bad about the Black Door have never been through it. I've been in there lots of times, and I'm fine. You will be, too."

"I don't know, Weese."

"They'll make sure you're safe. You won't have to hide all the time, or worry about getting food. Trust me, it'll be okay."

Sulid tried to think of something—anything—else he could do. But he was out of choices. If he stayed by himself, he would eventually get caught.

He turned to Weese.

"Okay, I'll go to the Black Door. You've done a lot to help me. I trust you. You're a good friend."

Sulid tried to look Weese in the eyes, but his friend turned away and cleared his throat.

"Yeah. Uh, let's go meet the owner."

Reluctantly, Sulid followed Weese in the direction of the Black Door.

*   *   *

I COULDN'T STOP THINKING ABOUT QUDA'S WORDS TO ME. I kept flipping between anger at him for his accusations and worry that he was right.

I stayed in my room and paced back and forth. There was little I could do until Lord Dust returned from the palace, but I hated waiting. I was also concerned about what he might do to Quda as punishment for letting me into the vault.

I decided to focus on the issue at hand—the connection between Ankin Poloth and Gisea Megoen. There had to be something there, and yet Lord Dust had not mentioned it. Although I had to admit it was certainly possible he didn't say anything to me but was still watching Gisea closely.

I spent a few hours going over Ankin Poloth's journal one more time. I tried to look at it with a fresh perspective, but my study proved fruitless. If there was anything to find, it was beyond my ability.

I still believed the lack of the demon's true name in Ankin's journal had some meaning, but I couldn't fit the puzzle together. The fact that it appeared in the vault records might or might not be related.

Perhaps I was putting too much emphasis on the journal. Perhaps Ankin Poloth had just been lazy and had not bothered to record it in his personal notes, knowing that he'd have access to it if he needed it for some reason. Extremely unlikely, perhaps, but that didn't make it impossible.

I wasted a couple more hours trying to work out the connection between the demon's true name, Ankin Poloth, Gisea Megoen, and the Hidden. Eventually, I found myself going in circles. I had to take a break, or try something new.

Before I could think through the repercussions, I was on my way to Gisea's chambers, journal in hand.

I knocked softly on her door and waited, not entirely sure how I was going to play this. I knew I was in a bit too deep here, and she had already threatened to kill me if I caused her any more grief. But I figured I could push a bit and see how things went, and retreat before the situation could get out of hand.

I knocked a second time, but the silence within told me that Gisea was either somewhere else, or she didn't intend to receive any visitors. I turned from her door and was about to leave when she appeared on the stairs, returning to her chamber.

"Apprentice Megoen, may I have a moment of your time?"

She stopped and regarded me coolly.

"What is this about?"

"The journal of Apprentice Poloth. I have completed my study and so I brought it to you."

She raised one eyebrow and moved past me to open her door. Then she turned to face me and held out her hand.

"Would you be able to answer a couple of questions for me, Apprentice Megoen?"

She said nothing—just continued to look at me. I knew I couldn't push this any farther, so I handed it over.

"What do you wish to know?"

I was taken aback. I had expected Gisea to close her door in my face, but she seemed inclined to answer my questions. Or, at least, she wanted to know what they were.

"You know that Apprentice Poloth came from the Plains of Quimyr?"

She paused for a second.

"I do not see how that is relevant to anything that has happened."

"It might not be relevant, but Apprentice Poloth was acting...strangely...before the incident. Knowing about his background may help, and I'd like to know more about that region."

"Does he refer to his homeland in the journal?"

And just like that, she had me. I couldn't lie and tell her Ankin had mentioned it in his notes, since she now had possession of the journal, at least until Lord Dust returned tomorrow.

"No, I discovered it during my investigation."

"Precisely *how* did you discover it?"

I couldn't think of a way to hide the truth she couldn't check. I had no choice but to admit it to her.

"I checked the record of Ankin Poloth in the vault."

Her expression didn't change, but I felt her mood change. The lamps in the hallway began to dim, and from the corners of my eyes I could see shadows begin to slither across the floor as if alive.

"I took the key from Quda and looked at Apprentice Poloth's records. I'm not a sorcerer, and Apprentice Poloth is dead. I have no ability to do anything with my knowledge other than perhaps see patterns others might have overlooked."

Despite the growing darkness, Gisea still appeared fully lit, as if the light from the lamps was still illuminating her and nothing else.

"And why are you asking *me* about the Plains of Quimyr?"

Power throbbed in her voice. I could feel my pulse pounding in my temples as the last bit of light was extinguished. Gisea herself was still visible, a beacon in the utter darkness.

"I brought you the journal. I wanted to show you I wasn't the useless fool you think I am. I was hoping you could tell me where I might find out more about that region—about religions in that area."

If she could see through lies, then I was a dead man. I could no longer feel the floor under me, as if I was floating in a vast nothingness with Gisea as the only anchor to my own world. If she let go of me, I would be lost forever.

The moment stretched out as I waited for her to pronounce judgment on me. The calculating part of my mind guessed she was taking her time to give me a chance to come clean, admit any other indiscretions I might have committed. But I knew that if I told her anything else, I would never see the light again.

I was blinded by the flare from the lamps as the shadows rolled back to reveal the hallway in the Tower of Dust. I stumbled on the floor as its firmness re-materialized beneath my feet. Reaching out to grab the wall, I was sure a small smile flickered across Gisea's face, but it disappeared almost instantly.

"The people of the Plains of Quimyr mostly follow the nine gods in general. Some families still worship the old way, but of course they keep that private. Many missionaries travel through the region, trying to increase worship of their own patron, but that far from the cities they do not have much success."

I heard her words, but couldn't fully concentrate on them. My vision was clearing, though, and I had regained my balance.

"Any other information you need on the region can be found in the library."

I nodded at her dumbly. I wasn't sure I could speak yet without fumbling over my words. She continued to stand there, watching me, and I couldn't meet her eyes, afraid I would give everything away.

"I suggest you drop this line of inquiry. It will get you nowhere. If there is anything to be found in Apprentice Poloth's journal, I will find it."

She stepped back into her chamber and closed the door in my face. I stood there for another minute, trying to get my bearings, and then I made my way back to my room. By the time I got there, I could almost walk a straight line.

Chapter Twenty-One

WITHIN THE HOUR, I HEARD A COMMOTION IN THE hallway and opened my door to find servants rushing around with great alacrity.

Lord Veylar Dust had returned.

I quickly washed my face to clear away the cobwebs that still hung in the corners of my mind. Then, having changed my clothes, I sat on the bed and waited to be summoned.

I knew that Lord Dust may not have time for me until tomorrow. It was early evening and he would no doubt want to dine first and then talk to one or more of his apprentices. But I also knew better than to make assumptions about the master of the Tower, and so I was prepared when, shortly after arriving, he sent a servant to summon me into his presence.

He was standing in the library, slowly scanning the spines of a shelf of heavy, leather-bound books. The servant announced me, and then left us alone. I stood and waited, and Lord Dust ignored me for a few more minutes while he found the book he sought.

Finally, he spoke without turning.

"You are learning patience. It must have been a terrifying ordeal."

"Ordeal, Lord Dust?"

I expected him to bring up the demon's attack in the streets of Ythis. No doubt he was made aware of it shortly after it happened.

"Your encounter in the vault. Possession is more common than you know, but it is rather disturbing to feel another being inhabit your body."

I wondered if Quda had confessed to him upon Lord Dust's arrival back at the Tower.

"Yes, Lord Dust. That and the attack by the demon were both terrifying."

"Yes, the demon's attack. It was clumsy and overeager. I look forward to hearing how you managed to gain assistance from the Tsojim."

I felt the floor drop out from beneath me. I had told no one about the Seer's intervention, but Lord Dust somehow knew. He mentioned it casually, but there was an edge in his voice that told me he would be questioning me at length about that incident.

"The demon's attack obviously did not teach you any lessons, though. If it had, you would not have gone into the vault—and needed rescuing by Quda—while I was away."

"Please do not be angry with him. It was entirely my fault and I take full respon—"

I was flung across the room and pinned to the wall by an invisible force that had me by the wrists and throat. Veylar Dust stood there, expressionless, watching me gasp at the pain in the back of my head from bouncing off the stone surface.

I could feel a hot breath on my face, and an acrid stink filled my nose. I blinked and suddenly it was *Xiqon* holding me against the wall, one hand pinning my wrists together and the other around my neck. The demon's face was inches from my own.

I felt something warm running down my leg and realized I had lost control of my bladder. I felt no shame—every fiber of my being was howling in terror.

"Mister Zale, you have crossed a line I cannot ignore. Your decision to take liberties with my rules in this Tower, your transgression in the vault, demonstrates to me that your greatest strength is also your greatest failure."

I took a ragged breath, always aware the light pressure on my throat could become a crushing force in an instant.

"Lord Dust—"

"No. I do not wish to hear your reasoning. Were you one of my apprentices, I would destroy you utterly. But you are merely a servant. There is no reason I should show such mercy to an underling."

He was going to give me to Xiqon. I could see it in his eyes. The demon was going to consume my soul, and I would exist in an eternity of agony and suffering.

I glanced into Xiqon's eyes and saw my fate there. The demon was barely holding itself back, and would tear into me the instant Veylar Dust released it. I closed my eyes.

"May I ask a question, first?"

"To what purpose?"

"I just need to know the answer before I am consumed."

I waited and the silence stretched out.

"Who sent the demon after me?"

Again, Lord Dust said nothing. But this time, I knew what he was thinking. Only another sorcerer could have sent the demon. It was either another member of the Five, or one of his own apprentices. Either way, he had been betrayed and I was banking on the fact he didn't know by whom.

Of course, he was still smarter than I was by a long shot.

"Why, precisely, did the Tsojim help you against the demon?"

I didn't even consider lying, or delaying. I was past all games at this point. I could only hope my full and truthful answers would show Lord Dust I was truly trying to help.

So, I told him about the Seer. I told him about our meeting in the dreamspace, and what she said about connections, and how she was interested in me because of my connections to other people. I told him everything she said about the creature in the bay.

And then I told him what happened with the demon. I described every detail I could remember, about my attacker as well as about how it was delayed—and harmed—by whatever the Seer had done.

Xiqon was obviously disturbed by my words. More than once, he gave my throat the barest of squeezes as he fought to hold back his desire to kill me. It was just enough to tell me he wanted my knowledge to die with me, but I trusted Lord Dust to protect me...for now.

And when I was done, the sorcerer turned away and walked to the room's single window. He looked out, his back to me, and Xiqon pushed his face even closer to mine. I refused to look into his eyes, and I wondered if he was feeding off my fear.

And then the demon was gone, and I was slumping to the floor, unable to hold myself up. Veylar Dust turned and walked to stand above me.

"Your freedom is at an end. You are an extension of my will, nothing more. I have given you free reign to do what you felt was necessary, and while the results have been acceptable, there are limits to what I am willing to overlook."

I looked up at him and nodded silently. I couldn't believe he was talking about letting me live. I knew he could change his mind at any time, and the last thing I wanted was to give him a reason to do so.

"What did you find in the vault?"

I told him about Ankin Poloth's journal, and the missing true name, and how it was recorded in the notes in the vault. I told him about the connection between Ankin and Gisea, and let him speculate on what that connection meant.

"Return to your room. Remain there until I send for you. Tomorrow you will witness a summoning."

I retreated without uttering a word and slowly made my way back to my room. Twice today I had experienced the limits of a sorcerer's patience, and a small measure of their power. I thought back to the Seer's words, about how my path had become a thread and I was in danger of falling.

A day was coming very soon when I would have to make a choice, and face the consequences of that choice head on. But tonight, I was too exhausted to worry about that. I fell unconscious as soon as my body hit the bed.

*   *   *

I AWOKE THE FOLLOWING MORNING, A LITTLE GROGGY BUT otherwise rested. I didn't remember dreaming, a surprise considering what I had been through yesterday. My brain must have been exhausted by the events of the day and the multiple close brushes with death.

I thought about my encounter with Veylar Dust. I had told him everything I knew about my encounters with the Tsojim, and about the Seer. I wondered how that would affect my relationship with the Seer in the future.

She had told me she didn't want any connections to Veylar Dust, but I had just connected them directly. I held no illusions about the sorcerer ignoring that information. He would take what I had told him and combine it with what he already knew.

I only hoped whatever conclusions he came to didn't harm the Seer and her people.

I flagged down a servant and requested that he bring me something to eat. I had been told not to leave my room, and there was no way I was going to violate that order. He returned shortly with a tray of food, and I broke my fast with vigor. I hadn't realized it before the food was in front of me, but I was starving.

Within the hour, another servant came to my room, carrying the same robe I had worn in my meeting with Lord Ghargar. Veylar Dust had told me I was going to witness a summoning today, but I couldn't figure out why a demon would care what I was wearing. Perhaps this was simply a sign of the control which Lord Dust was going to start exercising over my actions.

I didn't like it, but I also didn't feel it was worth fighting over. I changed into the robes and the servant escorted me to the chamber at the top of the Tower of Dust.

Veylar Dust was already there and had prepared the room for the summoning. In my time at the Tower, I had learned that once a demon was bound to a sorcerer, it could be summoned with little more than a mental command. The initial summoning, before the binding can take place, however, requires a ritual carefully enacted.

I had no idea why I was to be a spectator to this summoning. I wanted to ask, but Lord Dust was obviously busy with the preparations and I did not want to annoy him.

I stood against one wall, trying to remain out of the way. Finally, after setting the last candle in place, the sorcerer turned to me.

"As you discovered, when a sorcerer binds a demon, he or she always records the demon's true name in the journal. Apprentice

Poloth did not do that. I intend to find out why."

"And this demon will know the reason for Apprentice Poloth's actions?"

"It should. I'm summoning the demon that killed him."

It took a moment for that statement to sink in.

"But wasn't his demon destroyed by Xiqon?"

"Of course not. It takes much more power than that possessed by Xiqon to truly destroy another of his kind."

I was confused.

"I don't understand. So, their fight was…just another form of banishment?"

"You do understand. When a demon is first summoned, it is unbound. There are safeguards built into our rituals to prevent an unbound demon from escaping. A ritual lacking the proper wards will also fail to collect enough power to bring the demon through into this world.

"However, should an unbound demon manage to get free, a sorcerer can still banish it, send it back to its own realm. That takes time—time the demon will not allow the sorcerer to take. Therefore, it is faster to send a bound demon against the unbound."

All this time, I had thought Ankin Poloth's demon had been utterly destroyed. I was shaken to hear it was still out there, somewhere, and could be brought back to this world. And I would be in the same room when it happened.

"What if the bound demon is weaker than the unbound one?"

Veylar Dust looked at me as if examining my question for something hidden. Yet I was genuinely curious, and worried.

"Then the sorcerer must hope the unbound demon can be delayed long enough."

Veylar Dust directed me to stand on the other side of the summoning circle. The large metal bowl was not in the center of the circle this time. Rather, a large leather bag sat there, and I could only guess at its contents.

With a gesture from the sorcerer, the candles flared to life. He began to chant in a strange tongue, and his words brought an immediate chill to the air. I could almost hear a strange whispering under his voice, like someone trying to get my attention without disturbing the ritual.

I looked around but we were alone in the chamber. Lord Dust continued to chant, and I looked down to see the inlaid summoning circle beginning to glow with a sickly yellow light. The whispering became stronger, and I could almost make out the words.

I tried to concentrate on the whispered voice, to make out what it was saying, but I couldn't quite hear it. The circle glowed brighter while at the same time the octagonal shape in the center of the summoning circle began to darken, as paper does when it burns.

As I watched the stone become blackened, I realized I could see my breath. The chamber was freezing, in stark contrast to whatever was burning the floor. The voice underneath Lord Dust's was fully audible now, and I realized it was whispering blasphemous secrets I did not want to hear.

I concentrated on listening to the sorcerer and ignoring the other voice. It was difficult but the more I focused on Veylar Dust, the weaker the whispers became.

Looking down at the circle, I noticed the floor had become so darkened that I could no longer even see the texture of the stone. It was as if a black hole had burned itself into the floor, and I only knew this was not the case because I could not see down into the lower level of the Tower below.

And then, from what could *not* be a hole in the floor, crawled Ankin Poloth's killer. I realized I was staring at a hole into the Abyss, and I snapped my gaze up to Lord Dust. He completed his part of the ritual and stopped chanting.

I glanced back down to see the floor had rematerialized under the demon. It was in the same form as the last time I had seen it, the vague spider-shape with nine segmented legs. The scorpion tail was not visible, but I remembered how quickly it appeared when it attacked Ankin Poloth.

It chittered at Veylar Dust, an insect-like clacking sound that nonetheless managed to fall into a semblance of understandable human speech.

"Send me back! I do not wish to serve in this world! Send me back!"

Veylar Dust ignored the demon's demands.

"I do not intend to bind you unless it becomes necessary. You will answer my questions and then be banished back to your own realm."

The chittering stopped, and it seemed to regard the sorcerer, though it had no visible eyes or face.

"You were bound to Ankin Poloth. How did this binding break?"

The demon turned in a circle around the edge of the inlaid symbols and then chittered back.

"No."

Lord Dust raised one hand and the entire circle flashed bright. I heard a discordant shriek that I also felt in my chest, and I was suddenly out of breath.

"Tell me how the binding was broken!"

"No. I cannot tell you."

The circle flashed bright again, and this time Veylar Dust's voice thundered.

"TELL ME!"

"I cannot!"

I could hear the pain in the demon's voice. This made me feel immensely better, that Veylar Dust had the power to put such a creature in agony.

When the sorcerer spoke again, his voice had returned to normal.

"Why can you not answer my question?"

"Because," replied the demon. "I was never bound to Ankin Poloth."

Chapter Twenty-Two

I TOOK A STEP BACK AND VEYLAR DUST GLARED AT ME, THEN returned his attention to the demon.

"You were bound to Ankin Poloth."

"No. I was never bound to that sorcerer."

Lord Dust stood there silently and considered this piece of information. If the demon was never bound to Ankin Poloth, did that mean an unbound demon had been in the Tower of Dust all that time?

"You followed the orders of Apprentice Poloth as if you were bound. Why?"

"I was told to do so by my master."

Its master? If the demon had a master, then it had been bound by someone. This didn't make any sense to me. But Lord Dust was not finished with his questions, not by a long shot.

"Who is your master?"

"I no longer have a master. I was released from service."

"You killed your master."

"No. I killed Ankin Poloth. Ankin Poloth was not my master."

Irritation was starting to creep into the voice of Lord Dust, and I expected him to lash out at the demon again.

"Then who was your master?"

"I cannot say. My pact required me to forget the identity of my master once I was no longer bound."

And just like that, Veylar Dust was no longer annoyed. I could see him change before my eyes, as if he suddenly had the answers he needed. I couldn't understand. If the demon was unable to tell us who its master was, then we had reached another dead end.

"Tell me whatever details of your pact you are able to reveal."

I did not understand much of what the demon said. It was intricate, using arcane terms with which I was unfamiliar. The demon explained the pact to Lord Dust for a few minutes, and then stopped.

Veylar Dust silently considered what the demon had told him. While he did so, the demon slowly moved to one side of the circle and began to push one segmented leg against the invisible barrier that kept it trapped. Lord Dust appeared too distracted to notice, and I considered interrupting his thoughts to point out the demon's actions.

Before I could take a breath, the circle glowed and flung the demon back to the center with a thunderclap. The demon screamed inaudibly, the power of it bloodying my nose.

"Send me back! Your questions have been answered. There is nothing left to tell you."

Veylar Dust gestured and the circle glowed once more. The demon thrashed around on the floor as it was tortured by the magic flowing around it. The sorcerer kept it up as minute after minute crawled by.

My teeth ached from the demon's screams, and I wanted it to stop. I didn't see why Lord Dust continued to activate the circle and inflict such punishment on the demon. I began to wonder if he was punishing it for killing his apprentice.

Finally, the glow ceased with a gesture from Veylar Dust. The demon slowly pulled its legs under it and stood in the very center of the circle.

"That is merely a taste of the punishment you will face, Ixal. You will now tell me the rest, or I will not stop."

The demon remained silent for a moment, obviously considering its options.

"There is still a demon in your Tower, bound to one but serving another."

"Which demon?"

"I do not remember. The knowledge was part of the pact."

"Then how do you know the demon is still in the Tower of Dust?"

"It has not returned to the Abyss."

Veylar Dust raised his arms, and I expected him to torture the demon some more, but he began chanting and a black smoke filled the air in the circle. It eventually became so dense that I could no longer see the demon.

With a final utterance by the sorcerer, the smoke exploded outward and immediately began to dissipate, revealing an empty summoning circle.

I was on the balls of my feet, ready to run.

"Is it gone?"

"Stay where you are. I have banished the demon and you are safe."

I tried to avoid inhaling the wisps of smoke that drifted through the chamber, but I needed to take a large breath. I backed to the door and pulled it open, sticking my head out and gulping in a lungful of relatively fresh air.

When I returned, Veylar Dust was paging through what looked like the same book he had pulled from the shelf yesterday in the library.

"I guess that told us less than we wanted."

"It told me everything I needed to know."

"But the demon didn't remember its master."

Lord Dust gestured to me to precede him out of the chamber and toward the stairs. He spoke as we walked.

"Every sorcerer performs rituals in a different manner. Every sorcerer has certain elements of magic on which he or she concentrates, thus creating what you might term specialties. If you know how a sorcerer uses the magic, then you can identify the specialty."

"And you could tell the demon's master from what the demon told you?"

"No. The demon couldn't tell me enough to identify the specific sorcerer who performed the summoning and binding. But I do know who directed said sorcerer."

"Who?"

We had reached his office and he led me into the room and gestured to me to sit in the chair facing his desk. After his treatment of me yesterday, I was wary about the small courtesies he was showing me.

He sat at his desk and clasped his hands in front of him.

"Another member of the Five."

I sat back, stunned. There was a traitor in the Five, one sorcerer working against another. I could not really imagine it, but then I knew next to nothing about the other sorcerers in Ythis.

"Why would he—or she—betray all of you?"

To this day, I swear on my life that Veylar Dust almost smiled at me. *Almost.*

"You have a simplistic view of the Five. We are not a monolithic organization like the Church. We are the five most powerful sorcerers in Ythis, the capital of the Empire. We each have our own goals, our own plans."

"But don't you work together?"

"When it suits our purpose, and uniting against the Church is a great and powerful purpose indeed. Ultimately, though, any one of us would steal the others' lives and power for ourselves given the opportunity."

Once again, my expectations were thrown upside down. I felt like a naïve child. I should have known that beings of such power and such evil were capable of turning on each other.

"Which of the Five is it?"

"You do not need to know. It changes nothing."

"But the demon said there was another one in the Tower. One of your apprentices is—"

"I will take care of the situation."

"I'm having trouble with the idea one of the Five is working with the Church."

Veylar Dust's face went absolutely still.

"Explain what you just said."

"Well, we know the Hidden have a spy in the Tower. And one of the Five has a demon pretending to be bound to one of your apprentices. I figure the spy and the apprentice are the same person."

"Why, precisely?"

"Well, you're Veylar Dust. Finding one person willing to live and work in the Tower while betraying you must be difficult. I mean, that's one serious risk that person is taking. I can't imagine finding two people willing to do it."

Veylar Dust stood up and moved to his window overlooking Ythis.

"Tomorrow, I will test the bindings between my apprentices and their demons. I want you present to witness it."

I was surprised by his statement. Yesterday, he had been ready to feed my soul to Xiqon. Today, he let me watch him summon a demon, and tomorrow he would test his apprentices in front of me.

I was sure I didn't want to be around for that. The traitor would likely try something drastic to avoid being captured by Lord Dust. I could imagine demons battling in the room while the rest of us tried to escape to safety. I would be powerless.

And perhaps that was why he wanted me there. He hadn't forgiven me for my transgression. He was keeping me close because he didn't trust me to go off on my own and not cause him more trouble.

Right now, I desperately needed some distance from the Tower and its inhabitants. I didn't know how much longer I could stay trapped in here. And yet, knowing that another member of the Five was moving against Veylar Dust, being out in the city was even more dangerous than staying in the Tower.

Like it or not, I wasn't going anywhere.

*   *   *

I WAS LEFT TO OCCUPY MYSELF UNTIL THE FOLLOWING AFTERNOON, so I spent the rest of the day in the library. I knew that much of the material would be unintelligible to me, but I was sure I would find *something* of interest.

Scanning the bookshelves, I came across a recent-looking book on the lands of the Empire. My curiosity drove me to search for anything I could find on the Plains of Quimyr, and my efforts were rewarded with a two-page description of that region.

Unfortunately, the information lacked detail and only briefly de-

Andrew J. Luther

scribed the largest of the cities in that region. I did find a reference, however, to another book about the religious practices of the people who lived there. My luck held out as I found the other reference on the same shelf as the book I now held in my hands.

I read long into the night, about the people of the Plains, how they initially resisted the worship of the Nine Gods, and how some families still held to the practices of their old religion. As I absorbed what was known about those ancient practices, I felt my whole body shudder in revulsion.

I was used to the Church and their human sacrifices, their eternal madness, and their powerful but trapped gods. It was certainly horrific, but I was glad the old ways of the people of the Plains of Quimyr were mostly forgotten. I could not imagine a world where such worship was practiced openly.

Needless to say, when I finally returned to my room my sleep was filled with nightmares.

At first light, I sent a servant back to my rooms above the Sailor's Knot to retrieve my weapons. He returned at midday, and I spent the next couple of hours sharpening and oiling my short sword and daggers.

Finally, a servant once again escorted me up to the room at the top of the Tower. I had not been told to wear the robes, so I was dressed in my leather armor and carried my assortment of weapons sheathed in their usual spots. Veylar Dust raised a single eyebrow as I entered but did not otherwise comment.

Three of the apprentices were already present, along with the master of the Tower of Dust. Apprentice Gisea Megoen and Apprentice Arral Doviar stood off to one side, talking quietly. It did not appear to be a friendly conversation. Apprentice Delash Wiar assisted Lord Dust in getting the circle prepared for the day's rituals.

As they were completing their final tasks, Apprentice Ituro Nedes entered and, scowling at me, stood in one corner away from everyone else. Lord Dust took his place at the head of the circle and motioned me to stand near the door, out of the way.

The apprentices spaced themselves equally around the circle as if they had done this many times before, which I supposed they probably had. Veylar turned to me.

"You will stay precisely where you are and remain silent. As you are the most vulnerable here, if anything…untoward…should happen, you may leave the room."

I nodded my understanding and Veylar Dust raised his hands and began to chant. The apprentices joined in at various spots, until the circle in the floor began to glow a deep red.

Veylar Dust turned to Delash and nodded. The most experienced of the apprentices closed his eyes and concentrated, and I suddenly became aware of his demon standing in the center of the circle. Wisps of black vapor surrounded its bent and misshapen—but otherwise human—form.

The demon turned its head left and right, its stringy black hair waving around like rotten plants in an underwater current. It fixed its bloodshot, watery eyes on Delash and took a step toward him.

The circle pulsed red and the demon was forced to step back into the very center of the circle.

"What is happening?"

Its voice was like a thousand buzzing insects, the words less heard than simply understood.

Lord Dust spoke up.

"To whom are you bound?"

The demon pointed at Delash.

"Delash Wiar is my master. This you already know, Veylar Dust."

"We will test the binding."

"Why?"

Lord Dust ignored the question and began to chant again. The circle glowed brighter and the demon in the center roared in pain. The sound was like a knife in my brain, the buzz drowning out Veylar Dust's voice.

The demon writhed unnaturally, its bones shifting within its body. Delash chanted a counterpoint to Veylar Dust and the rest of the apprentices, and the demon clawed at the circle.

Finally, Lord Dust raised one hand, and the chanting ceased. The demon slumped to the floor.

"You may let it return to the Abyss, Delash."

The apprentice gestured and the demon dissolved into nothingness.

I couldn't help blurting out a question.

"What happened?"

"Apprentice Wiar prevented the demon from de-manifesting despite the pain it was experiencing. He maintained control of the demon's actions through the binding."

That meant Delash didn't have to worry about the demon turning on him. He was still the demon's master.

Lord Dust turned to Gisea and nodded.

She concentrated and the room noticeably darkened as shadows began to slither across the floor toward the circle. The serpentine shadows gathered in the center of the circle and took shape, forming a large hound of utter blackness with piercing red eyes.

"Remain in the center of the circle, Veilod. We are testing the binding between you and me."

The hound growled and I heard a woman's voice screaming underneath it . . . Gisea's voice.

"To what purpose?"

Lord Dust interrupted Gisea.

"Obey and remain silent."

Once again, he began to chant, along with the other apprentices, while Gisea chanted at counterpoint. The circle's glow increased, and the hound shook its head and then let out a blood-curdling howl, raising a wind that blew around the chamber and brought a chill to my skin.

I wasn't certain, but it seemed as if Gisea's demon was significantly more powerful than Delash's had been. Veilod seemed to be fighting the pain and affecting the chamber outside the circle, whereas the other demon had merely writhed in pain.

I wondered if that meant Gisea was a more powerful sorcerer, if less experienced than Delash. Or perhaps she had merely been lucky enough to discover the true name of a more powerful demon, and skill meant nothing in this situation.

The test continued, with the demon throwing itself against the edges of the circle over and over, trying to reach Veylar Dust. I was stunned at its power, though Lord Dust and the apprentices continued their ritual without any sign of worry.

They seemed to conduct this test far longer than they had with the demon bound to Delash, though eventually Lord Dust raised his hand and everyone concluded their part of the ritual. Gisea gestured at the hound and it dissipated into tiny shadows resembling crawling insects, which faded from view as they reached the edges of the circle.

I had to admit I was glad Gisea was not the spy, though I could not articulate my reasons, exactly. It wasn't that I thought of her as a good person—she was as evil as Veylar Dust and I knew there was no chance of her ever redeeming herself. Perhaps it was just the respect one has for a deadly reptile.

Veylar Dust turned to Arral Doviar and nodded. At that moment, the door to the chamber opened and Quda slipped in. Lord Dust motioned for Arral to wait.

"Yes, Quda."

"Lord Dust, there is an urgent message for you."

He motioned Quda forward, and the little man produced a rolled parchment sealed with wax. Lord Dust broke the seal and read the message inside. He raised his head and looked at Arral and Ituro, the two apprentices he hadn't yet tested.

"We must postpone the other two tests. This requires my immediate attention."

"What is it?"

I couldn't help myself. I asked the question before I could think about taking care and being respectful. The apprentices all stared at me, obviously wondering at my stupidity.

Surprisingly, Lord Dust was feeling generous, and chose to reveal the main thrust of the message to us.

"Esiah Flannok, High Priest of the Church of Iathephos, is dead."

Chapter Twenty-Three

S O, SULID, THINGS ARE NOT SO SAFE FOR YOU OUT THERE anymore, eh?"

Weese had introduced the man as Zodei, the overseer of the young ones who worked the Black Door. He was a great round ball of a man, and Sulid was sure he could smell urine whenever Zodei spoke.

Sulid gave Weese a look to let his friend know he should not have spoken so freely. Weese looked down at his own feet and backed up a step. Sulid turned back to Zodei.

"The streets are always dangerous."

Zodei nodded and smiled.

"You will call me 'Sir', Sulid. Respect is very important here. Weese has told you about the Black Door?"

"Only a little."

Sulid couldn't suppress a shudder at the thought he was inside the Black Door, to work here.

"There are many services we provide to our customers, Sulid, but you do not need to concern yourself with most of that. Not for a few years yet. For now, you will only perform one service."

Sulid nodded.

"Yeah, Weese told me about that."

"It is not as bad as it sounds, young man. And the pay is good. And I can guarantee you that no one will come looking for you here. You're safe, now."

Sulid didn't feel safe, he felt trapped. He had been in the wrong place at the wrong time and now he was in an even worse place.

Once again, he considered going back to his hiding place instead of staying here.

Only he couldn't keep doing that either. He was terrified all the time, and sooner or later he'd make a mistake and end up dead. And once you were dead, it was all over. At least here Sulid would have a chance to grab any opportunity that might come his way.

"So, what do I have to do?"

"I think it's better if I show you. It's early yet, and our customers haven't arrived, but we can get you cleaned up and then you can watch Weese work with a couple of customers before you serve one yourself."

Sulid looked at Weese, unsure of what he wanted to see on his friend's face. Worry? Remorse? Confidence? But Weese stared down at the floor, his face unreadable. Sulid would simply have to hold himself together and get through this first night. Tomorrow would be a different day, and one could never know what the cosmos had in store.

Zodei led Sulid down a flight of stone steps near the back of the building. A side chamber held a round pool of clear water, just over Sulid's height in diameter. Wisps of steam rose from the pool.

Zodei handed Sulid a rough cloth.

"Strip out of those filthy clothes and wash yourself in the water. I need you to scrub yourself fully clean, Sulid. Our customers don't like dirty skin. I'll return in a bit."

Sulid did as the man instructed as Zodei and Weese left the room. He could hear them talking in low voices but could not make out the words. He wondered if Weese was negotiating his price for bringing Sulid in to the Black Door.

Sulid held no illusions about Weese's true reason for bringing him here. He knew Weese was getting some kind of reward out of it. It was also possible that his friend also believed he was helping Sulid.

Sulid didn't know what to believe. He had pinned all his hopes on Borolt Zale, but then the man had been attacked by a demon right out in the street, and had remained in the Tower of Dust since that time. No, Borolt Zale was a dead end.

Sulid was almost clean when Zodei returned, this time without Weese. The overseer took a close look at Sulid and grabbed the rough cloth. Taking hold of Sulid's arm, Zodei scrubbed the bits that were still dirty…his feet, his knees, his back. Sulid's skin burned with Zodei's strenuous efforts to get it clean.

When Zodei was satisfied, he handed Sulid short undergarments, a knee-length tunic and a simple linen belt. Sulid dressed quickly and followed Zodei back up the stairs and through a long hallway that led to a small door.

"Our first customers of the evening have arrived, Sulid. Our main hall is on the other side of this door. A tapestry hides this doorway and extends to either side. I want you to stay behind the tapestry for now."

"You want me to hide?"

"No, I want you to watch. There are a few small slits cut in the tapestry. Pick one and watch Weese with our customers. Watch the respect he shows them, how he moves, how he defers to them. I expect you to do the same when you meet your first customer later tonight."

"You didn't tell me what you're going to pay me."

"You forgot to call me 'Sir', Sulid. I should not expect to keep reminding you about that. It is all about respect here."

Zodei moved to open the door, but Sulid interrupted him.

"Sorry, Sir. We didn't talk about what you are going to pay me."

"We will discuss that later, Sulid. Just watch for now. Watch and learn."

Zodei opened the door to reveal the back of a tapestry that hung from ceiling to floor. A small space between the wall and tapestry allowed Sulid to move to one side of the doorway. He quickly located a small slit in the fabric and looked through.

The main room of the Black Door was huge. Multiple tiers of cushioned couches surrounded the sunken stone floor in the center. Shuttered lanterns provided dim illumination for the handful of customers scattered around the room.

Sulid stifled a gasp as he spotted Weese bowing on one knee and laid eyes for the first time on the Ksathash.

The descriptions he had heard were horrific, but he hadn't really believed them. After all, no one he knew before Weese had even seen one of their race. Even Weese didn't go around bragging about it.

Sulid took in the sight and knew immediately he could never go near one of these creatures. It resembled a giant centipede the height of a tall man, with deep red skin that glistened in the dim light. Thirteen pairs of segmented legs were equally spaced down its body.

The most horrific feature, though, was its head. Two constantly-twitching antennae sat above a face that was all too human. A pair of eyes looked down upon Weese and a black tongue slowly licked the creature's lips, which sat between a pair of sharp curved claws.

The pair of legs closest to its head ended in three-fingered hands, and it used these hands to motion Weese to stand.

In a blink, the Ksathash lunged forward and wrapped its body around Weese, pinning his arms to his sides. Weese just stood there, not fighting or trying to escape. In fact, Sulid noted that he didn't even seem to be disturbed by the creature's touch.

Legs twitching, the creature turned so that it was face-to-face with Weese. Sulid could see the creature's lips moving, but couldn't hear what was being said. Weese looked into the creature's eyes and nodded.

As Sulid watched, the Ksathash opened its mouth-claws wide and then plunged the points into either side of Weese's neck. Weese's eyes rolled up into his head as his legs went limp. Sulid felt like screaming, and only the knowledge that Weese had done this before prevented his terror from erupting out of him.

The stories Sulid had heard all said that the Ksathash drank the blood of its victims. Through Weese, he knew that wasn't true, though the reality was, to Sulid, much worse. The creature was drinking Weese's senses, his feelings, and his emotions.

Weese had described it to Sulid before coming here. He had explained that after letting a Ksathash feed on you, all of your feelings and memories were dim for a day or two, like the light from a partially shuttered lamp. All those feelings were still there, but faded.

They eventually came back, however, and Weese was sure he hadn't lost anything permanently.

Sulid watched the creature feeding on Weese and it seemed to go on forever. Finally, it pulled the claws out of Weese's neck, leaving a thin trickle of blood to leak from each small hole. Then it gently laid Weese on the couch it had occupied only moments before.

A man Sulid had not met appeared from the shadows and spoke to the Ksathash, and then the creature turned and flowed down the stairs to the pit at the center of the room. It was then Sulid noticed the large, circular hole in the floor. The monster quickly crawled down the hole and was gone.

Sulid tore his eyes away from the pit to see Weese slowly stirring. He moved the tapestry so that he could see more of the room and found four other Ksathash either reclining on the couches or feeding on other young men.

Sulid realized he could never do this, could never let one of these creatures touch him. He quietly slipped back through the door and took off for the rear entrance. At one point, he had to duck into a side room and hide as Zodei ran past, yelling his name.

Moments later, Sulid was on the street and bolting for the cellar where he had been hiding. He knew he was being reckless, and that the wrong person might notice him, but he was too terrified to stop and take precautions.

When he reached the closest thing he had to a home, he huddled in a corner and made sure the candle stayed lit until dawn came once more.

*　　　　　*　　　　　*

I DIDN'T FULLY UNDERSTAND THE REPERCUSSIONS OF THE DEATH of the High Priest Flannok. On the one hand, it could weaken the Church until they could select a new leader. On the other hand, I knew this gave the Hidden an opportunity to accomplish some of their own goals without interference, and they were by far the most dangerous element of the Church.

Upon receiving the message, Veylar Dust had dismissed all of us except Delash, and the two of them had retreated to Lord Dust's office behind a closed door. I tried to speak to Quda, but he was still cold to me, and I was left with nothing to do but wait in my room. I didn't expect to hear anything more this night.

I was therefore surprised when, just as I was drifting off to sleep, a sharp knock on my door snapped me awake. Despite me having locked it earlier, the door opened to reveal Veylar Dust.

He stepped into my room and closed the door behind him. I dragged myself out of my bed and stood. He waved me to sit and waited until I had done so.

"I cannot have you trapped here in the Tower. Events are moving forward without us, and you need to be out there."

I had an unpleasant feeling he was going to send me out to fend for myself. If that demon was still out there, it was only a matter of time before it came after me again. A very short time.

"Lord Dust, I—"

"Yes, yes, you cannot fight a demon. I have made arrangements to deal with that. I will explain in a moment."

I nodded and, knowing he would just interrupt me if I tried to ask any more questions, I stayed silent. He stood there, thinking, and I expected he was deciding how much to tell me.

"Do you think the Hidden would kill their own High Priest?"

I hadn't even considered such a possibility. Of course, he hadn't told me how the High Priest had died.

"Well, I would expect it to be extremely unlikely. They are dedicated to protecting...."

I stopped and really gave it some thought. Brother Ochallum had told me that they didn't always agree with the decisions the Church leadership took on matters. After all, the High Priest was always more than a little insane. I thought back to Relael's words....

"My job—my life—is dedicated to doing what's right for the organization, whatever form it might take."

I looked up at Lord Dust.

"It's possible. If the High Priest was doing something that would severely weaken the Church, the Hidden might just decide it was time he stepped down. They'd have to do it in secret, though. They don't truly wield that much temporal power in the organization."

The Lord of the Tower considered my words, and my curiosity got the better of me.

"How did the High Priest die?"

"The official story is that his mind collapsed under the strain during a meal, causing him to choke to death on his food. The most likely explanation is poison."

And yet, it was entirely possible the story was true. The High Priest was in a constant battle to keep as much of his sanity intact as possible, and yet he had the most intimate contact with Iathephos of any member of the Church.

"Regardless of what really happened, it presents us with an opportunity. The Hidden may be organized, but the rest of the Church hierarchy will be in disarray for the short term. The Five can push our agenda with the Emperor while the situation is in flux."

This was all above my head, so I kept silent.

"I will leave at first light. The Five are meeting to discuss our strategy. I will likely not return for at least two days."

"What about the sorcerer who tried to kill me?"

"That is immaterial to the matter at hand."

"Aren't you worried he or she will take a shot at you, too?"

"No, Mister Zale, I am not. Such…rivalries…have a time and a place, and this meeting will be neither."

He looked at me evenly.

"So that just leaves you."

I didn't know what to say. I had nearly gotten myself killed the last time he left the Tower, never mind the fact that something evil could have had an opportunity to escape from the vault.

"As I said, your place is not here in the Tower. You belong out there in the city, where I can direct you to where I want you."

"But what if the demon comes after me again? There's no way I can fight it off, and I doubt the Tsojim will help me again."

"You will meet with Apprentice Wiar tomorrow morning. You will participate in a ritual, and the result will be some measure of protection for you while you are out in the city."

"You mean Apprentice Wiar will cast a spell on me?"

"In a manner of speaking. A mark will be placed on your body. That mark will obfuscate your location from any person or demon trying to track you."

"So, I'll be invisible to demons?"

"Absolutely not. It means a sorcerer or demon cannot simply detect your presence or location. It does not prevent them using mundane means to find you. You still must take care not to expose yourself to unnecessary risks."

So, I wasn't going to be completely safe. Still, I had managed to avoid the Church's assassins once before. I wasn't exactly unskilled in moving around while keeping hidden.

"How long will the mark last?"

"A mark is permanent."

"So, I'll be marked by you forever?"

"Nothing comes without a price, Mister Zale."

I had known that all along, though I had hoped it wasn't true. And yet I knew I was going to do what Lord Dust ordered. It was the only way for me to leave the Tower of Dust. It was giving me my freedom, while putting a chain around my neck at the same time.

"What—"

It came out in a croak, and I had to clear my throat.

"What would the price of such a thing be?"

"The price is personal, and you cannot know it until you reach the decision point. You will be presented with a choice, and only you can determine if the result is worth the price. Do not waste my time, or the time of Apprentice Wiar. You will accept the price."

It was not a request. If I refused to do this, he would either kill me himself, or kick me out of the Tower with no protection at all. The end result would be the same. But what if the price was too high and I was unwilling to pay it?

"Go to Apprentice Wiar's room just after dawn tomorrow. Bathe yourself first and wear nothing but a simple robe. He will give you further instructions then."

Lord Dust didn't wait for an answer. He turned and left my room, fully expecting me to follow his orders. I sat on the bed and considered his demand. This looked like a point of no return.

If I let Delash put the mark on my body, I would belong fully to Veylar Dust. I held no illusions about such a mark. It would allow Lord Dust to track me no matter where I went.

And if I refused, then I would likely die at the hands of a demon sent by another member of the Five. I might have a chance to escape, but it was a very small chance.

I considered my choices long into the night. Eventually, I fell asleep and dreamt about being trapped in the vault, and the price of my freedom.

Chapter Twenty-Four

SULID KNEW WEESE—AFTER THE CLOSE ESCAPE FROM THE priests the other night—had changed where he was staying. Weese had told him the location, and he hoped the older boy would return there in the morning. He was worried about the trouble Weese might be in.

He felt an overwhelming desire to apologize to his friend. Weese had tried to help him, to take him to a safe place where he could stay and the priests wouldn't find him. But Sulid had been unable to hold up his part of the deal once he had seen the Ksathash with his own eyes.

As he waited for Weese to return, he wondered what he might do. He couldn't return to the Black Door, and he couldn't keep living in constant fear of being caught by the Stranger. He wasn't sure how he was going to survive unless the Stranger gave up searching for him.

He was hidden in a dark corner of a large warehouse near the docks, crates stacked high in long rows. The lack of ships coming to Ythis lately had stranded many such cargoes and this one would likely remain undisturbed for some time. Weese knew about such things, and Sulid once again felt a thrill of fear that he had lost his last friend.

A light footstep in the darkness caused him to tense. He held absolutely still, his eyes open wide in an attempt to pierce the darkness down the row of crates. A figure was moving there, though it was too dark to see the identity of the person.

A single skylight in the ceiling was beginning to let in a small patch of light as dawn brightened the sky. The figure moved down the row and passed near enough to the faint beam of light to be illuminated briefly. He saw just enough detail to identify Weese.

He breathed a sigh of relief, and Weese stopped suddenly, tensing to run. Sulid whistled the signal they used out on the street, and Weese hesitated and then moved toward where he waited.

Sulid moved out of the deepest shadows and approached his friend. As he reached Weese, he noticed something wrong with Weese's face. It was drawn and slack, and his eyes were only half-open.

"Weese, what happened to you?"

Weese stood looking back at him for a moment, and then lashed out with a fist, connecting with Sulid's temple. The younger boy hit the floor with a yell, and Weese leaped on him, throwing wild punches at Sulid's face and chest.

Sulid twisted and squirmed, trying to avoid the flailing strikes. He didn't fight back, though his instinct was to bite, scratch, and dig fingers into vulnerable bits of flesh.

"Weese! Stop! I'm sorry!"

He began crying as Weese's blows weakened, and then the larger boy rolled off his chest and fell to the floor beside him. Weese stared at the ceiling, heaving great ragged breaths.

Sulid sat up, tears streaming down his face.

"I'm so sorry, Weese. I should have stayed, but I couldn't. I watched you feed that…thing…and I couldn't do it."

Weese turned his head to look at Sulid.

"Zodei was so angry at you. They *hurt* me, Zodei and one of the Ksathash. I had to pay for you leaving."

Sulid cried harder.

"I didn't want you to get into trouble, Weese. You're my only friend and you've looked out for me. You took me there to help me. You even went to the Tower of Dust for me. I'm so sorry."

Weese looked away, and Sulid thought he was fighting back tears as well.

"Please don't hate me, Weese. I never wanted you to get hurt. If they will keep hurting you, I'll go back to the Black Door. I'll do whatever you want, Weese."

"No."

Sulid felt his world slipping out from under his feet. He was now truly alone.

And then Weese burst into tears. He curled up on his side, his arms wrapped around his knees and cried. His whole body shook with the force of his sobs. Sulid wanted to put his hand on Weese, reassure him, but was too afraid Weese would lash out at him again.

Eventually, Weese ran out of energy and he quietened, breathing slowly through his mouth. When he spoke, Sulid almost couldn't hear his voice.

"You shouldn't be sorry. I did this."

He wasn't sure what his friend meant, but Weese didn't sound angry. He wiped his nose with his arm and leaned in close to the older boy's face.

"What do you mean?"

"I shouldn't have taken you there. I should have known you wouldn't want to do it. It's terrible, Sulid. They feed on you and when it happens you want to die."

Sulid sat back, shocked.

"But you said it didn't hurt—"

"It doesn't...not like getting punched or something hurts. It's different. It's far worse."

He didn't know what to say. Weese had promised him it wasn't painful or unpleasant. Now he was admitting he had lied.

"There's more, Sulid."

Weese hesitated.

"I never went to the Tower of Dust."

"*What*?"

"I lied about going to the Tower. I told Zodei about you, and he said you would be worth a lot of money. He told me if I brought you to the Black Door, he'd move me to another job and I wouldn't have to feed the Ksathash anymore."

Again, he didn't know what to say. Weese hadn't been looking out for him after all. Weese had just been using him.

"You were going to trade me for your freedom?"

Weese nodded.

"But you don't have to go there, Weese. You're not a prisoner. They can't make you."

Weese barked a laugh that had no humor in it.

"Yes, they can. They own me, Sulid. I tried to give you to them so that I could stop letting those things feed on me. I went there on my own, by my own choice, the first time. I heard they paid well, and I was willing to do anything for money. Now I'll do anything to stop it."

Sulid was too shocked to respond. Weese was the successful one—the street kid who found employment, had money, and understood the nighttime world. Instead, Weese was worse off than anyone he knew, including himself.

"What can I do to help you, Weese?"

Weese laughed again.

"Help? I just told you I lied to you about the Tower of Dust. I was going to sell you into worse than slavery. Why would you try to help me now?"

"Because you're still my friend."

"I'm not your friend. I stabbed you in the back. I'm a coward, Sulid. At least you had the sense to run away from the Black Door when you saw what happens there."

"You could have turned me in to the Church, Weese. You could have told them where to find me. They would have paid you a lot. You brought me to the Black Door because you're trapped there, and can't see a way out, not because you're not my friend."

Weese remained curled up as tears poured from his eyes. A heart-wrenching wail burst from his lungs, trailing off into a series of sobs that shook his thin body. Sulid waited, still afraid to touch his friend.

Finally, Weese calmed down enough to speak again.

"I'm sorry, Sulid. I'll make it up to you."

"You don't have to do anything. I got away from the Black Door, and we'll find a way to get you free, too."

"No. You're being hunted by the Church. I promised to help you, and I will. Tomorrow, I'm going to the Tower of Dust and speaking to Borolt Zale."

Sulid's heart leaped. For the first time in days, he felt a glimmer of hope again.

"You...you don't have to—"

"I'm going, Sulid. I will help you, and then when your stuff is fixed up, you can help me."

Sulid finally reached over and placed a hand on Weese's shoulder. "That's what friends do."

*   *   *

I'M NOT ASHAMED TO ADMIT I WAS NERVOUS. IT'S ONE THING to be around sorcery, stand in the same room as a bound demon, work for one of the Five. It's entirely another thing to have your flesh carry around a sorcerer's mark that powers a magical working.

I no longer had any doubt Apprentice Wiar was loyal to Veylar Dust, at least as loyal as any sorcerer is to any other. I wasn't worried Delash would kill me intentionally. He would do what Lord Dust had asked, to the best of his ability.

It wasn't as simple as that, though. Sorcery always comes with a price, and as the beneficiary of the magic, the price would have to be paid by me. I couldn't imagine what the price would be. I only knew it would be something personal and extremely valuable to me.

Just before dawn, I bathed myself and donned the clean robes, as per the instructions of Lord Dust. And then, not really ready but knowing enough to not keep Apprentice Wiar waiting, I headed for the chamber at the top of the Tower of Dust.

He was already there, and had prepared the room for the ritual. I entered and stood just inside the door. I didn't want to interrupt his concentration as he read a passage from a book.

"Please remove your robes and sit backwards in the chair, Mister Zale."

He motioned to a small chair with no arms near one wall.

"Remove my robes?"

"I need access to your back."

My skin crawled as I stripped out of the robes and, naked, sat in the chair with my back facing out.

"This is going to hurt."

He said it casually, and I was about to ask a question when my back erupted in flames. At least it felt that way. It was as if every nerve from my shoulders down to my waist were on fire and screaming in agony.

I let out a shout and tried to move only to find myself paralyzed. The pain intensified as what could only be a knife began to cut into the flesh of my back. I screamed and spots danced in front of my eyes.

The cutting continued in some kind of pattern and a small part of my brain figured Delash was placing a sigil directly into my skin. I tried to stop screaming and gritted my teeth, but an instant later my jaws flew open again. I could not control myself as I sunk into a world made up of nothing but pain.

It seemed an eternity, and I still have no idea how long it truly took, but suddenly the cutting stopped, the fire disappeared, and I slumped from the chair to land on my side. I heard a footstep beside my head, and Apprentice Wiar leaned down over me.

"The sigil is complete. Take a few moments to rest while I prepare the next step. The easy part is over."

I couldn't tell if he was trying to scare me or if I was in for even worse torture. Regardless, I had no strength to move, though my back was curiously devoid of any sensations at the moment. I was afraid to make any movement, however. One twitch could start me screaming again.

Finally, after too short a time, he asked me to sit up. I slowly lifted my arms, waiting for a fresh spasm of pain, but I felt nothing. I pushed myself into a sitting position and reached around to my back.

"Do not touch it!"

I yanked my hand away.

"Enter the circle, Mister Zale."

"What's going to happen now?"

"I've placed the sigil on your flesh. Now we have to activate it."

"When do I pay the price?"

"Shortly. You will experience…a vision, of sorts. It is different for each person, for each ritual. You will be given a choice to give something up for the power of the sigil. You must choose willingly."

"And once the sigil is 'powered' then demons won't be able to find me?"

"No. Demons will not be able to *track* you."

"All demons?"

He looked at me evenly.

"Yes, even Xiqon will not be able to track you."

"I wasn't—"

"You are now wearing the mark of Lord Dust. He does not need a demon to track you. He is now aware of you wherever you are. Wherever you go."

Delash obviously believed I was going to try running away and he wanted me to know it was a pointless effort. If I hadn't already belonged to Lord Dust, I certainly did now. In this way, I had already made a choice.

Delash gestured me to enter the circle, so I stood and reached for my robes.

"No, they will only get consumed."

I didn't like the sound of that, but stepped into the circle anyway. The time for hesitation was past.

I stood in the center of the circle and couldn't help but picture the demons that had stood here only yesterday. I couldn't begin to imagine how unpleasant this ordeal was going to be.

Apprentice Wiar raised his arms and began to chant. I could feel a heat building on my back, and I tensed for the onslaught of pain.

And then I heard a woman's voice just over my left shoulder and I turned to see who had spoken. As I turned, my surroundings dissolved into that same chamber where I had first met the Seer. I was standing on the same disk covered in twisting, geometric shapes, with fire on all sides.

I was back in the Dreamspace.

The Seer stood before me and my first thought was that she had pulled me away from the ritual to prevent me from going through with it. Her face was expressionless and she watched me without speaking.

"What's happening? Why did you bring me back here? Am I making a terrible mistake?"

"Your choices have already been made. There are no mistakes. You are on a path and that path will take you to a destination. It is up to you to decide if that destination is where you wanted to end up."

"I wanted to thank you for saving me from the demon."

"I did what I could. I can do no more. You have greater protection now."

Her eyes moved down to my hand and closed before she turned away from me. I looked down and saw that I held a long knife, the blade black and wickedly curved and spiked. I didn't know why I held it.

"You have a final choice to make, Borolt Zale. If you choose to serve your master, I cannot help you further. You must sever the ties between us, or turn your back on the Tower and its Lord."

So, this was my choice. Delash had said I would have a vision. Was I really here in the Dreamspace with the Seer, or was this just all in my mind? More importantly, was I ready to sever all ties with her?

I had just met her recently and I had so many questions that remained unanswered. If I refused to sever my ties with her, what might I learn? I should have known this would be the price. The Seer represented another path, one that led away from Lord Dust and the Five.

And this was the moment of truth. This was my price. But it wasn't much of a choice. My flesh already carried Lord Dust's mark. I belonged to him now, like a piece of property. Could even the Seer protect me from that? Like Lord Dust protected me from the Church?

Was it my fate to run from one master to another, as I made powerful enemy after enemy? Was it my fate to hide among the Tsojim, or go on the run across the Empire and beyond? Were any of those real options?

Would the Seer even accept me, protect me? She had helped me once, but offered nothing more. She owed me nothing.

I had too many questions, and no answers. It was my time to make a choice, to decide what my fate would be.

I stepped up behind the Seer.

"If you are truly aware of what's happening here in the Tower, here in my vision, then I hope you can accept my decision."

She said nothing.

I stepped forward and plunged the knife into her back with an upward thrust. The blade moved almost of its own accord, seeking her heart, or where it would be if she was human.

Blood, thick and red, gushed out of the wound onto my hand. The Seer's body fell at my feet, taking the knife out of my grasp.

I screamed again as I found myself in the circle at the top of the Tower of Dust once more. The floor glowed the same blood-red and the pain in my back was a living thing.

Delash stopped chanting and lowered his hands. I fell to my knees as the pain in my back faded to nothingness.

"It is done, Mister Zale. I will summon a servant to help you back to your room and bring you a meal. You will be back to full strength by mid-day, and then you can leave the Tower."

I watched him reach down and pick up the knife that lay on the floor in front of my knees. It was the same knife I had used in my vision, and it was slick with blood.

Chapter Twenty-Five

MY BODY RESTED BACK IN MY ROOM, BUT MY MIND was a terrible storm of doubt and fear. I kept replaying the vision over and over in my mind. I kept reliving the moment of plunging the knife into the Seer's back.

It *was* just a vision, wasn't it? There was no way I had really entered the Dreamspace and killed the Seer with a knife. That wasn't possible.

And yet, the knife had come out of the vision with me. What did that mean? Was it some symbol of my choice, made real by the magic of the ritual?

Or had it all really happened?

I was tired, but felt no pain from my back. I had run my fingers over the area where the sigil had been placed, and it felt as though I had a raised scar, long healed over. It gave me no discomfort, despite the agony I had experienced during its carving.

Perhaps the knife Delash had picked up was the same one he had used to carve Lord Dust's mark into my back. That would explain its presence in the chamber when the ritual was over. It would also explain the blood on the blade, and why it had appeared in my vision.

But then, I felt there was more to it than that. My gut told me that I had done something irrevocable, something more than just a symbolic cutting of my ties to the Seer. Had I really injured or killed her? Was that even possible for a being such as the Seer?

I couldn't just go back to the sewers and ask the Tsojim about her. As far as I could tell, she had kept our meeting from them. They would deny me access to her, and if something *had* happened to her, I might not be allowed to leave the sewers alive.

In fact, if the Seer was dead, could that mean some kind of retaliation by the Tsojim? Might they come to the surface and extract some kind of revenge? Had I just gotten Ythis into a war I wasn't sure it could win?

As mid-day approached, I was no closer to an answer. But I did know I was unlikely to get my concerns resolved by Apprentice Wiar. I would have to wait until Lord Dust returned and ask him what my vision had truly meant.

In the meantime, I would simply have to hope the events of this morning were purely symbolic.

I couldn't wait to get out of the Tower of Dust. I had been trapped in here too long, and there was still so much to do. I forced myself to concentrate on what I could accomplish once I was free of the confines of this building.

Eventually, I got up and performed a bunch of stretches to test my back. I did not feel the slightest twinge of pain and in fact I was rested and energized. It was time to get moving.

I had just finished dressing when a knock sounded at my door. I opened it to see one of the servants standing there. His eyes opened wide at my appearance.

"Master Zale, you are up and moving...."

"Yes, I'm fine."

"But this morning...."

"I'm okay, really. Is there something I can do for you?"

"Master Zale, you have a visitor."

"What? How?"

He looked at me and then down at his feet, embarrassed.

"I guess he walked, sir."

Now I was extremely confused. Who in the world would walk up to the Tower of Dust and ask for me directly? Most people were terrified of the Five, for good reason. I had no friends who might come to see me here.

"What does he look like?"

"He's a boy, Master Zale. He—."

I took off running toward the front hall. I had hoped the kid would come to find me again. He was tied to the unseen assassin who had attacked me last week.

"Master Zale! You're going the wrong way!"

I skidded to a stop and looked at the servant.

"He's at the servant's entrance, sir."

"Thanks!"

I jogged down the passageway leading to the servants' area. When I reached the kitchen, I saw a young man standing just inside the door of the back entrance. I looked around for the kid I had spoken to last week.

"Are you Borolt Zale?"

I turned to the young man. He was a good-looking kid, if a bit too thin. I could tell he lived on the streets, a story written in his clothes and the way he carried himself. He was obviously nervous standing here in the legendary Tower of Dust.

"You're not—"

I stopped, trying to hide my disappointment.

"Sorry, do I know you?"

The boy shook his head.

"I'm Weese. I'm friends with Sulid."

He paused, waiting for a reaction from me. I guessed, I hoped, that Sulid was the boy I was looking for.

"Sulid is a boy a bit younger than you? Skinny, short, with dark hair?"

Weese nodded.

"He said he needs to talk to you, but he can't come here. He's afraid someone will catch him."

I paused for a moment. The assassin had seen me with Sulid on the night he attacked me. This was a perfect lure to get me to leave the Tower. It could all be a setup. But then, if it wasn't a trap, if Weese really did know Sulid…

I would have to take the chance, and hope that all my preparations, all my skills, would keep me safe.

"I know, Weese. It's important that Sulid stays safe. I can come to see him, wherever he is. I know how to avoid being followed."

Weese considered this.

"I wasn't sure you'd want to talk to him. I thought he might be fooling himself about you."

"He's not, Weese. Sulid knows something important, something he wants me to know. I can help him. I can keep him safe."

"I thought so too, mister. Turns out I was fooling myself."

He looked miserable, and I wondered what had happened between him and Sulid. I knew better than to pry.

"And you can't tell me he's going to be safe here."

He gestured to the interior of the building. I couldn't help but smile.

"Do you know of any place safer than the Tower of Dust?"

Weese frowned and took a step back toward the door.

"A sorcerer lives here. He's one of the Five. Everyone knows that, mister. You can't be safe near a sorcerer."

I had no counter to that. He was completely correct.

"I can help Sulid without bringing him here. If he wants, I can help him leave Ythis and find safe passage to another city. Or, better yet, I can go after the people hunting him and end their threat."

Weese looked skeptical for a moment, but then looked around and obviously remembered where he was.

"Sulid wants you to meet him tonight, at the midnight hour. Do you know the Warren's Heart?"

The area was a maze of narrow streets and back alleys near the eastern edge of the docks. With the hundreds of branching paths, one could easily lose any pursuit or gain quick cover from an attacker. If this was a trap for me, it was a strange one. The advantage in such a location would be entirely mine.

"I know the general area, but not the Heart."

Weese described it to me, a junction of sorts near the center where seven different passages converged.

"Tell Sulid I'll be there, alone. Tell him to take care getting there, and I'll help him in any way I can."

Weese nodded desultorily.

"Sure."

I tossed him a bunch of coins, everything I had on me. It cheered him up a little, but I could see he wasn't happy about Sulid meeting with me. I could only hope he passed on my message to his friend.

Now I had some preparations to make. Tonight, I would finally get some answers.

*   *   *

I EXPECTED TROUBLE. I HAD NO WAY TO CONFIRM THIS WAS a genuine meeting until it was too late. There were too many players.

The High Priest of the Church of Iathephos was dead, which meant some measure of control was lost over the individual priests. There were many who still wanted me dead, and might just take it upon themselves to eliminate me while no leader was around to reign them in.

I knew I couldn't trust the Hidden, regardless of what Brother Ochallum had told me. I knew they considered me a threat. I had figured out there was a traitor in the Tower of Dust, and that was worth killing me over.

The Wolf had all but declared open season on me. He wasn't asking for my death, but everyone understood it would make him happy, even if they didn't know why. This was exactly the kind of situation a bunch of street thugs would set up.

And then there was the other sorcerer, the other member of the Five. A demon had already been sent to kill me, and it had failed. Where sorcery fails, perhaps a more mundane approach may succeed. Were the sorcerer's minions setting me up?

But even so, with all those possibilities, I still had to go to the meet. I had to take the chance this kid…Sulid…was truly the one who wanted to meet me. He knew something important, something someone thought was worth killing him over.

And if it was important enough to send a skilled assassin against a street urchin, then it meant his enemy had both contacts and money. It also meant the danger of his information getting out would cost them more than they were spending on the professional.

Of course, it might not be related to my own investigations—either the creature in the bay or the death of Apprentice Poloth—in any way. I might be chasing shadows that had nothing to do with me, getting involved in yet another dangerous situation.

All I could do was prepare myself, take all necessary precautions, remain alert at all times, and use every skill I possessed. What other choice did I have?

I dressed in dark colors, donned my leather armor, secured all my weapons, wrapped my cloak around me, and made sure my equipment gave off no sounds or glints of light. I was going to use the darkness to my advantage, and any sound or stray reflection would give me away.

I needed to be a ghost tonight.

I left the Tower of Dust at dusk, long before I would need to head for the meeting. I had to assume the Tower was being watched, and I would need some time to lose any pursuers. I was confident I could do it, but such maneuvering couldn't be rushed or I would make a costly mistake.

My first steps out of the Tower of Dust were filled with dread. I hadn't set foot outside the protection of the Tower since the demon had attacked me, and I had to control my nervousness and maintain a calm demeanor.

I decided to start off heading in the direction of the Sailor's Knot. It made sense that my first trip would be back to my home, as I hadn't been there in days. I hoped it would lull my pursuers into complacency.

As I neared the blocks around the Sailor's Knot, I cut into an alleyway that provided a shortcut to a cross-street. The darkening sky provided many shadows in the alley, and it was one shadow in particular I needed. About halfway along the alley, I ducked into a very dark patch and didn't re-emerge.

In the depths of that shadow, I pushed aside a piece of wood that covered a small cellar window. I slid into the cellar and moved carefully across to the far wall. I quietly lifted aside an empty crate, revealing a short tunnel.

On hands and knees, I crawled through the tunnel, under the street, and into the cellar of a short building on the other side. The tunnel was old and had been used by smugglers many years ago. It was forgotten by pretty much everyone now. I only knew of it because I had spent many nights exploring the cellars and rooftops of the buildings on the blocks around my home.

From this building, I found a locked door that connected it with its neighbor. It took but a moment to pick the familiar lock and then I was through and even farther from the alley where I had disappeared.

I emerged onto the street at a run. I expected that anyone following me might be working in teams. If so, some members of the team would hang back and keep a wider circle in case I tried just such a trick. The disadvantage to this method of shadowing someone was that it took the outer group out of close communication with their comrades.

My shift from stealth to speed forced any stalkers to respond in kind, and took time away from them. Any single pursuer could not now spend precious seconds finding his or her teammates or I would be long gone. If I was being followed, I had just dramatically narrowed down the number of pursuers.

Over the next few hours, I played such games over and over, taking me through a good part of the city. Switching from speed to stealth and back again made it impossible to coordinate any organized pursuit. I timed myself to end up near the slave markets as they closed for another day.

If you know how to use a crowd to your advantage, you can lose just about any pursuit in one. I now did exactly that.

The slave markets of Ythis are not the largest in the Empire. That dubious distinction belongs to the city of Jh'tira. Still, Ythis is the capital and slave labor is common among the noble families who make up the court of the Emperor.

Slave auctions take place every day, and one can always find slave masters leading groups of ten to twenty individuals chained together, representatives of the noble houses, city personnel responsible for city works projects, and merchants selling all kinds of slave-related goods and services.

Many slaves are brought in from areas outside the Empire, where raiders take prisoners and ship them back to the nine major cities. Criminals and the destitute make up the remainder. Poverty drives families into slavery every day.

As I made my way through the dispersing crowd, I saw a mother and her young son being separated for life. The child screamed and reached out for his mother, who silently stretched an arm towards her child as tears streamed down her face.

As their respective owners yanked them in opposite directions, the child fought with a ferocity and strength that surprised his handlers. The cudgels came out and the boy was hammered to the ground, all resistance leaving his small body in an instant. He was dragged back to his feet and shoved after the others.

As I left the markets, it stayed with me—the look in the boy's eyes, the refusal to leave his mother, his struggle to reach her embrace one last time. It tickled something in the back of my mind, but I couldn't quite grasp it fully. I just knew I had seen something important.

I forced it out of my mind for the moment. This was no time to be distracted, and slavery was a fact of life. What I had just seen had happened countless times, and would happen countless more. Concentrating on my surroundings, I headed for a maze of alleys that lay close to the markets. This was my last chance to lose any remaining stalkers. And then it would be time to head for my meeting with Sulid.

Chapter Twenty-Six

THE STREETS OF THE WARREN WERE GENERALLY NOISY until the earliest hours of the morning, and tonight was no exception. Sulid hid in the hollow of a broken and blocked chimney on the roof of a building in the outskirts of the area. He was only a few minutes travel from the Warren's Heart, by rooftop.

Sulid had taken every precaution reaching this spot tonight. He was so close to finally getting to speak to Borolt Zale and he wanted nothing to interfere. He had kept his excitement in check and been extra careful to make sure he was not followed.

Now it was a matter of waiting here until the midnight hour and then quickly heading for the meeting spot. He knew Borolt would be able to lose anyone following him, one way or another. This meeting would be as safe as possible.

He had told Weese to head for the Black Door early so that he would be safe from the priests, if not from the creatures that frequented that building. His friend didn't want to return to that place, but Zodei and the Ksathash could force Weese to return. It was better for him if he went voluntarily.

Sulid told Weese that he was free to tell Zodei everything—that the priests were after Sulid for something he knew, and that he was meeting someone from the Tower of Dust. He only asked that Weese not give up the location of the meet. Sulid hoped it would keep Zodei from punishing his friend. After all, what could Weese do against such forces? If Zodei was smart, he would consider Sulid a lost cause and just forget about him.

Sulid planned to ask Borolt Zale to help his friend once he told the man his story. He understood he was probably trading one evil for another, but what he had seen of Borolt told him the man was honorable, at the least. Perhaps he could offer Weese a job as a servant at the Tower of Dust.

Sulid couldn't believe how casually he now thought of the Tower. He had never been there, had never been inside. Most people who lived in Ythis would be terrified to even set foot on the grounds around the Tower. But to Sulid, Borolt Zale represented the Tower, and he also represented hope.

It was almost time to move. Sulid could feel it. He slowly peeked out of his hiding space and scanned the rooftops for any signs of movement. Up here all was still, a stark contrast to the busy streets below winding their way among these ancient constructions

The peal of the midnight bells sent a shiver of anticipation down Sulid's spine. He carefully crawled out of his hiding space and picked his way across the rooftop. A running jump took him over a narrow alleyway and he was off across the next roof swiftly, his footfalls nearly silent.

He crossed from building to building, sometimes clambering up or down broken masonry, sometimes leaping between narrow gaps full of shadows. In a couple of minutes, he reached one of the buildings that faced into the Warren's Heart, a crossroads with at least nine different escape routes.

He crouched down as soon as his feet hit the roof of this last building. He expected Borolt Zale might also be up here, and he didn't want to startle the man into striking before Sulid could identify himself.

Sulid scanned the rooftops once more, but there were at least a dozen good hiding spots within running distance. He moved slowly towards the roof's edge so that he could see down into the tiny square at the center of the crossroads.

From out of the shadows to his left, a figure stood and revealed itself. Sulid's heart was in his mouth and he backed up a step. He couldn't tell in the darkness if it was Borolt Zale, though the figure appeared to have been waiting for him. Sulid's instincts were to run as fast and far as he could, but he couldn't trust his instincts in this situation. He had to take a risk, or he'd never speak to Borolt.

The figure stepped out of the shadows and Sulid saw the man's face.

It wasn't Borolt Zale.

"Hey, kid. You shouldn't be up here."

The man's words threw Sulid off balance. Was this someone who lived in this building, or owned it? Was he merely a guard who watched for thieves trying to break into the building from above?

The man took a step closer to Sulid, who backed up one step to maintain distance between him and the man.

"You hear me? You don't belong here. I'm not going to hurt you or nothin' but you gotta leave."

Of all the rotten luck, Sulid realized this man was trying to prevent this building from being used as a thoroughfare for criminals. He wouldn't have much luck with that, though Sulid was in no position to argue.

"Okay, mister. I'm going. I was just passing through."

As he spoke, he heard a slight noise behind him. He glanced over his shoulder and his heart hammered even harder. Another man was a few paces behind him, already reaching out to grab him.

Sulid threw himself to the side as the man lunged, his large hands just grazing Sulid's arm as he flew past. Sulid rolled and got his feet under him to see the first man charging at him.

It *was* a trap, after all.

Sulid didn't think, but moved on instinct. He spun and charged at the far edge of the building, back in the direction from which he had come. He could hear the man's footsteps right behind him, and his back tingled as he waited for the man to grab him.

Suddenly the gap was in front of him and he was flinging himself across, two stories above the ground. Sulid landed roughly and fell to the rooftop, the wind knocked out of him. He heard the man land on the rooftop beside him, but the man kept to his feet.

As his pursuer turned, Sulid knew there was no way he would regain his feet before he was grabbed. So, he took the only option available to him. He rolled himself off the roof.

At the last second, as he was going over, Sulid grabbed the edge of the roof with one hand. He heard the man swear as Sulid went over. He looked up to see the second man fly over his head, and the huge thump told Sulid it was an unsuccessful landing.

Sulid's fingers and toes scrambled for a purchase on the rough stone of the building and quickly he anchored himself. He let go of the roof's edge just as the first man tried to grab his hand. Sulid managed to quickly lower himself out of reach of the men on the roof.

"Go!" yelled the first man, and the second man disappeared. Sulid knew he was heading for the ground floor, and he would get there long before Sulid did. It was still too far to the floor of the alley to guarantee a safe landing if he jumped. But he didn't have time to climb down, and he couldn't climb back up with the other man waiting up there for him.

Sulid glanced to his left and right but it was futile. The men would easily keep pace with Sulid if he tried to climb in either direction. Besides, there was no escape as long as he was stuck on this building.

Precious time was slipping away, and Sulid knew he had to make a decision. Either jump now, or be caught by the men. He took a deep breath and pushed himself off the wall, trying to land in the middle of the narrow alley.

Sulid tried to roll as he hit the ground, but pain exploded in his shoulder as he smacked the cobblestones. He yelled out and tried to keep moving, but his whole body was in pain and he couldn't move his left arm.

He regained his feet in time to see another figure come around the corner. Sulid could make out a crossbow in the figure's hands.

"You're in no condition to run, kid, and I'd prefer to take you alive. But that doesn't mean I won't put a bolt into your back if you try to get away."

Sulid dropped to his knees, despair filling his soul. The new figure stood over him, and Sulid recognized the Stranger, the man who had been hunting him all this time.

"You led me on a merry chase, didn't you? You've got some talent, kid. If it wasn't for your friend, Weese, I might never have found you."

The man bound Sulid's hands behind his back, and Sulid nearly fainted from the pain in his shoulder.

"You've dislocated it. We'll pop it back into place when we get where we're going."

Sulid found his voice.

"Weese told you how to find me?"

He couldn't believe his friend had betrayed him again. Especially after Weese had come clean about the Black Door and promised to help.

"Well, he was just a kid, and I can be persuasive. He fought it some, but he told me everything before he died. Your friend Borolt Zale will be joining him shortly."

The Stranger's words were like a punch to Sulid's gut. And then the Stranger yanked a black cloth bag over Sulid's head and everything went dark.

*   *   *

I WANTED TO APPROACH ACROSS THE ROOFTOPS AND WAIT above for the boy to show. I was worried, however, that he would hesitate to show himself if he didn't see me first. That meant I would have to move out into the open.

I was absolutely sure I had not been followed. That meant that I should be safe unless any pursuers already knew where I was going. And if that was the case, all my precautions were for nothing. I had to put my faith in the boy to lose anyone trying to follow him.

The midnight bell sounded, and I strode into the small square at the center of the crossroads. Most of the people out on the street at this hour were involved in some criminal enterprise, and understood a lone man walking with my confidence was someone to avoid instead of confront. I knew how to carry myself and the truth is that I wasn't afraid of any of these people.

I stood motionless in the center of the square, my eyes constantly scanning for threats or any sign of the kid. Minutes passed and there was no sign of him. I glanced to the rooftops, but it was far too dark up there to see anything.

For some reason, my mind returned to the slave boy and his mother. What was it about that situation that was bugging me? I didn't know the family. Was it my concern about Sulid? No, there was something else there, but I couldn't put my finger on it.

I pushed it out of my mind as much as possible and focused on my surroundings.

As minute after minute ticked away, I began to worry. I had gotten a good look at the thugs, prostitutes, drug addicts, and others moving through the Warren's Heart, and I was sure none of them were disguised priests or hired assassins. There was nothing to stop the kid from either coming out to speak to me, or to signal me from a doorway or window to come to him.

Finally, I couldn't wait any longer. I decided to take a quick walk through the alleys surrounding the square and see if that gave the boy enough privacy to reveal himself to me. I moved off to one of the alley entrances and entered the shadows.

I reached a corner and turned to my left, planning to circle the square. As I stepped around the corner, a blade flashed out at me, swinging toward my head.

I yanked my head back and the tip of the blade nicked the bridge of my nose. From the opposite direction stepped a figure, also wielding a short sword. This one had a metal plate strapped to his other arm, a crude buckler of sorts.

Before he could close with me, I flipped off my cloak and drew my short sword. A dagger dropped into my other hand from a hidden sheath and I crouched into a fighting stance. The first man to take a swing at me stepped around the other corner and placed himself shoulder-to-shoulder with his partner.

I heard a light footstep behind me and knew a third assailant was approaching from the rear. I kept my back to him, hoping he didn't have a crossbow. If so, I was as good as dead.

"If you're looking to rob me, you've picked the wrong target."

Neither man responded, and that's when I knew these weren't just street thugs. These men were here for *me*. That meant the assassin was around here somewhere, probably looking for the boy. I could only hope Sulid was smart enough to avoid him.

As the men in front of me slowly advanced, I listened for the sound behind me, trying to determine where the last attacker was positioned. I stepped backward over my fallen cloak and tensed. A light footstep gave me an idea, and I took the initiative.

I kicked the cloak upward towards the faces of the two men in front of me. Before it reached them, I was already spinning, my left arm raised. The third man was outlined in the lamplight from the square at the end of the alley, giving me a perfect shot.

My arm snapped forward and the man grunted as the dagger hit him in the face. He toppled backward and I dove toward him in a roll as the men behind me flung aside the cloak and stabbed at my back.

I drew a second dagger as I rose to my feet, just as the two men regained their balance. There was barely room for them to fight side-by-side in this alley, yet they were very confident. That told me they had practiced fighting together in this kind of environment, and I could not count on them getting in each other's way.

My maneuverability was hampered in here, however, so I quickly backpedaled as they rushed forward. I used my short sword and my dagger to parry their thrusts and slashes, fully on the defensive. I had to be careful as I passed the third man.

I saw out of the corner of my eye that he was still alive, and was pulling my dagger out of his cheek. He had managed to turn his head enough that the blade missed the back of his throat and simply sliced into one cheek and out the other. He would shortly be back in the fight.

I continued to backpedal, and within seconds, I was out of the alley and into the square. People quickly moved aside as they saw the bared blades and suddenly we were in the open and I had the advantage again.

I reversed direction and lunged towards the man on my left, but spun at the last instant and moved to his side. Before his partner could react, I was fighting only one of them.

He was good. I got in a flurry of strikes, but they were all deflected by his buckler and his blade. And then his partner had moved out from behind him and I was facing the two of them again. In an instant, I was back on the defensive.

The same trick wouldn't work twice on these guys. But that didn't mean it wasn't worth trying. They didn't know how smart I was. Besides, I could see the third man emerge from the mouth of the alley.

I lunged again at the man on my left. He knew where I was going and began to turn. At the same instant, his partner fell back a step to move around to his other side. But I had already changed direction and was moving right. Which left me beside his fully-exposed back.

I reversed the dagger in my hand and plunged it into the back of his neck. His partner's eyes widened as he saw my maneuver. I gave the dagger a hard twist and then let go. As the body dropped, I drew yet another blade.

The partner moved forward to engage me, but I took the offensive. I was faster than he was, though he managed to keep deflecting my blades. I wanted to get in at least one strike before the third man engaged me.

Luckily for me, the other attacker was not only wounded, but obviously hadn't been trained in tandem fighting techniques. Rather than pair up with the one in front of me, he kept moving around to try to get behind me. I let him as I kept up my assault on the other man.

I was ready for the strike from behind when it came. As his blade thrust toward my back, I twisted out of the way. Once again, I reversed my hold on the dagger and stabbed him in the neck as he lunged past me, off balance. I used the leverage from the dagger to increase his momentum.

The other man tried to get out of the way, but he wasn't fast enough. The arm holding his buckler got blocked by the third man's body. Still spinning, I thrust my short sword at his now-unprotected side. The blade slipped between his ribs into his lung, and he fell over with the weight of the third man on him.

I stepped over to him and placed my blade at his throat.

"You can still live if I let you get help in time. Where is the boy?"

He coughed up blood and took a ragged half-breath.

"You…you're too late."

"*WHERE IS THE BOY?*"

"At the…Temple. Where you'll…never get…him."

He was lying and I knew it. I pushed my sword deep into his throat and watched him die.

The Hidden wouldn't take the boy to the Temple. Not now. But I needed help to get him back. I only hoped they would keep him alive long enough for me to have a chance.

Chapter Twenty-Seven

S ULID AWOKE IN DARKNESS. HE SLOWLY RAISED HIS HEAD and looked around, discovering a faint light coming from a grill set into the wall just above the floor. His shoulder throbbed painfully as he moved, reminding him of his last memory.

He had been taken to a carriage and placed on a hard bench. Each bump and jolt had sent agony through his shoulder, though he was cuffed roughly across the head when he whimpered from the pain. The cloth bag over his head had prevented Sulid from seeing where they were going.

At one point, the Stranger had leaned over him.

"You will not make any noise when we leave this carriage, boy. If you try to cry out or otherwise call attention to yourself, I'll stick this dagger through your neck so fast you'll be silenced before you realize you're dead."

Sulid had feared the effort of being taken from the carriage would send pain shooting through his shoulder, causing him to moan or yell in pain. But the Stranger had been remarkably gentle with him when the carriage had finally come to a stop, and he was inside before he knew it.

Sulid assumed he was somewhere in the Temple. The Stranger worked for the priests, and the priests lived in the Temple, so it was only natural they had brought him here. He had been led down a flight of stone stairs and into a small room. There, the Stranger had told him that he would set Sulid's arm back in its socket.

"You're gonna scream, boy. Go ahead. No one can hear you now."

Sulid had screamed, then. He had screamed until he passed out from the pain.

Now, he very carefully sat up, unable to keep from whimpering. He focused on the faint glow coming from the grill. He could make out the stone walls of the small room, the bench on which he had been lying, the closed metal door. He was in some kind of cell.

Sulid slowly slid off the bench and moved over to the metal grill. He leaned down and looked through the slats in the grill, seeing a very narrow chimney on the other side. The light was coming from above, filtering down the chimney to this cell.

It was daytime. That meant that, even if he managed to escape from the cell this minute, Borolt Zale would be long gone. Or maybe he was dead. If the Stranger knew how to find Sulid, he would also have known Borolt was coming to the meeting as well.

Sulid wondered if Borolt still lived. He considered it and decided that, since the Stranger had stayed with Sulid, Borolt was probably still alive. Only a skilled assassin would be able to take down the man from the Tower—a bunch of hired thugs certainly wouldn't succeed.

Sulid turned to examine the metal door. A bolted plate covered the space where the lock would be located. That meant it could only be opened from the other side. Even the hinges were on the outside of the door.

Sulid gave it an experimental push, but it didn't budge. He couldn't even rattle the door in its frame. If he was going to escape, it wouldn't be that way. Besides, he had no idea how many guards, priests, and worse stood between him and the exit.

And he *had* to escape. He knew they wouldn't keep him alive for very long. They would question him, maybe torture him, and then kill him. They had already gone to all this trouble to catch Sulid. He wasn't going to be released.

He surprised himself at his lack of fear. He had been living in terror of the Stranger for so long that his capture left him with no more dread. He could calmly reason out their plans for his death and he just wasn't afraid anymore.

That didn't mean he would just sit here and accept his fate, however. If there was a way to escape, Sulid planned to find it. He may not be a fighter, but he wouldn't just lie down and die, either. He had gone through too much to give up now.

He gingerly touched his shoulder and wondered how much it would hamper him. Sulid knew he would probably need all his physical abilities to get out of this situation—if there *was* a way out.

He turned back to the grill. It offered the only hope at the moment. Looking through the slats again, he tried to figure out if the opening was large enough for him to squeeze through it. It was impossible to tell for sure. The only way to find out would be get the grill off the wall.

Sulid stuck his fingers into the slats and pulled. The grill didn't move at all. It looked like it might be mortared right into the wall. Chipping it out might take a long time, and he was sure the priests would come for him fairly soon. They wouldn't leave him in here for days. They would want to know as soon as possible who else he might have told about what he saw.

Sulid thought about Weese, and felt tears well in his eyes. The older boy had been Sulid's only friend, and he already missed him. He had found it so easy to forgive Weese for trying to bring Sulid to the Black Door. Weese had been trapped, too.

He didn't want to think about the manner of Weese's death. Sulid knew his friend's last moments had been filled with pain and terror, and Sulid could not hold back a sob this time. Sulid knew his own death would likely be similar, and soon.

He examined the bench as well as he could in the dark, looking for slivers of wood or pieces he could disassemble and use as a tool to pick away at the mortar. His search was for naught, and he was forced to look elsewhere.

He turned to the floor and examined the stone blocks for loose pieces. Under the bench, Sulid found a broken chunk of stone that he pried loose with his fingers. It was barely smaller than his hand, and pointed at one end. It could be used as a weapon in an emergency, but he was more interested in its use as a tool.

Crouching in front of the grate, he began to pick at the mortar around the metal. It didn't immediately crumble like he had hoped, but he did manage to chip parts of it away with some effort. This was going to take some time.

He had no idea, however, how much time he might get to spend on this before someone came for him. It might be just after dawn, which would likely give him a few hours. But he couldn't tell from the light coming down the chimney if it was much later. He might be interrupted at any minute.

Sulid sat on the floor and tried to hold his shoulder in a comfortable position. Then he set to work on the mortar. If someone came for him, he'd be caught in the act. This didn't bother him, however. He didn't think he could possibly be in worse trouble.

He knew this could all be for naught, of course. The chimney might turn out to be too small for him to fit into, or he may find it too difficult to climb with his injured shoulder. Or, he might get part-way up the chimney to discover another grate at the top, blocking his exit.

He could do nothing to prevent any of those situations, though, and so he leaned in and started working.

*   *   *

SHORTLY AFTER DAWN, I LEFT MY ROOM ABOVE THE SAILOR'S Knot and returned to the Tower of Dust. I had spent a couple of hours searching around the Warren's Heart the night before, but found nothing. It appeared the hired thug was telling the truth when he said Sulid had been captured.

I knew he was lying about where they had taken the boy, though. With the current state of affairs in the Church, the Hidden would not have wanted to bring Sulid to the Temple. I had the feeling that whatever they were up to, it was not something they wanted to reveal to the rest of the priesthood.

As I walked back to the Tower of Dust, I thought once again about the slave boy and his mother. Something about that family connection kept tickling something in my mind, but I still couldn't piece it together. I continued to mull it over in my mind as I walked.

Within the hour, I was back at the Tower. I needed to speak to Veylar Dust, though I did not know when he would return. I decided to spend the morning at the Tower, and if he had not returned by mid-day, I would leave a message and head back out on the streets.

I had spent the entire night away from the Tower, but it seemed like only minutes. I did not want to be here, though I no longer felt trapped. I knew, however, that could change in an instant.

Shortly after arriving, a servant came to see me.

"Master Zale, Apprentice Doviar requests that you come speak with him."

My curiosity was instantly aroused. Neither Arral nor Ituro Nedes had been tested the day before yesterday. I had gotten the feeling at one time that Arral Doviar wanted to see me dead. And now he was requesting that I come to see him.

Of course, I was sure the other apprentices were in the Tower, and if Arral killed me now, it would reveal himself as the traitor to Lord Dust. On the other hand, he might not even be the traitor. None of the apprentices wanted me around, so his desire for my death wasn't unusual.

I followed the servant to Arral's room. The servant knocked and a voice called for us to enter. I was once again wearing my armor and was fully armed. I prepared for a fighting withdrawal as the servant opened the door and stepped inside.

Arral was seated at a desk, scrolls and leather-bound tomes piled around him.

"Mister Zale. Come in and sit."

He waved the servant away, and I was suddenly alone in the room with the apprentice.

"We've received word Lord Dust will return to the Tower before mid-day. I wish to speak to you about something first."

I sat in the chair opposite his desk and nodded for him to continue. He sat back in the chair and clasped his hands on the desk in front of him.

"What do you know of the background of Apprentice Poloth?"

I told him what I had discovered of Ankin's homeland.

"And what do you know about Apprentice Megoen?"

I froze. I wasn't going to tell him I had read about Gisea in the vault, especially after lying to her.

"I have had few conversations with Apprentice Megoen, and none about her background before coming to the Tower."

This was technically true, though it didn't answer his question. He smiled at me. Instead of putting me at ease, I tensed up, waiting for something to happen.

"The two apprentices came from the same region—the Plains of Quimyr. Different villages, but not terribly far apart. Perhaps that is why they were so close."

"Close?"

"We all work side-by-side here in the Tower, but I assume you understand we are not friends with each other. We are all in training to become sorcerers, and friendship is not only unnecessary, but truly detrimental to our need for focus."

I remained quiet.

"We each have our own projects, our own research. We do not share information, unless we are performing a task directly for Lord Dust. We do not spend time together."

"I understand, Apprentice Doviar."

"Then you should understand what it means when I tell you Apprentice Megoen and Apprentice Poloth were friends. They had a relationship that I can only describe as...familial."

"Can you please explain what you mean?"

"Apprentice Megoen helped Apprentice Poloth. She...supported him. She gave him advice. She acted like...an older sibling, a sister, to Apprentice Poloth. I can even say I believe she cared for him."

"Do you think they were lovers?"

"No, I never got any sense of something like that. Like I said, it was like siblings."

"Did you report this to Lord Dust?"

"Report what? There are no rules against us helping one another. The fact that it is unheard of is a result of who we are, not a restriction imposed upon us by our master."

I considered what he was telling me. Gisea and Ankin had been friends. She had been a big sister to him. This explained her behavior towards me when she found me in Ankin's room after his death. But I couldn't see how it related to anything.

"I have to be honest, Apprentice Doviar. I don't see why you are telling this to me now. What am I not seeing?"

He leaned forward in his chair.

"The day before Ankin Poloth was killed by his demon, I overheard him and Apprentice Megoen in a vicious argument. I only understood pieces of it. However, one element I did understand was that Apprentice Megoen admitted to covering for Apprentice Poloth."

He paused, and I waited for him to continue.

"I do not know in what way she was covering for him. I am led to understand, however, Apprentice Poloth's demon was not bound to him, but to someone else. And the demon was released unexpectedly, allowing it to turn on Ankin Poloth and kill him."

"Are you suggesting Apprentice Megoen was the one who had bound Ixal?"

"I do not know. I do know she was covering for Apprentice Poloth in some manner. I do know they had an argument over it, and it sounded like they were severing ties with each other. And I know the very next day, the binding on the demon we all thought was under Ankin Poloth's control was suddenly released."

There was more here he wasn't telling me. Or perhaps it was all a lie. I figured there was some truth in there, however. He couldn't risk making it all up and then being questioned by Lord Dust.

"And why are you telling me this? Why didn't you tell Lord Dust after Apprentice Poloth was killed?"

"Mister Zale, it was inconceivable the demon Ixal was not bound to him. Such a thing did not occur to anyone, even Lord Dust. Apprentice Poloth's death was such an unexpected event, none of us considered the possibility one of the other apprentices could be responsible for it.

"In the last two days, however, the situation has changed. Apprentice Megoen's involvement has just become a possible explanation for what happened."

"If it's true, Apprentice Doviar, then you just solved Ankin Poloth's death. I would think Lord Dust would be pleased with you to bring it to his attention."

"Yes, he would, if Apprentice Megoen is truly responsible for the death of another apprentice. Of course, if it isn't true, I will have made a deadly enemy of another sorcerer in this very Tower. One who is—at the least—my equal in power and knowledge."

I suddenly understood. I was his cat's paw. Arral knew I couldn't keep this from Lord Dust, and if it was all a mistake, it would fall at my feet, not his. I was expendable, and there was no doubt in my mind Gisea would destroy me.

But now, knowing what had happened, there was no way for me to justify not telling Lord Dust. As soon as he returned to the Tower, I would have to reveal it all to him. Gisea would be proven innocent or guilty, and then she'd either come after me, or she'd be dead.

I had to hope she was guilty. It was the only thing that might save my life.

Chapter Twenty-Eight

VEYLAR DUST RETURNED TO THE TOWER SHORTLY before midday. He immediately met with Apprentice Wiar, and shortly after I was summoned to his chambers. When I arrived, he was standing at the window looking out over the city. The day was gray, clouds blanketing the sky. He motioned me in wordlessly and then turned back to the window.

"What did you find out last night?"

Of course he would know I had left the Tower.

"I was to meet with the street urchin I told you about. When I got there, I was ambushed by thugs working for the Church. I dispatched them, but they grabbed the kid."

"Then the child is at the Temple?"

"No. There's no way they'd bring him back there right now. That kid saw something. It was important enough that the Hidden hired an assassin to take him out—a street kid. I'm betting they don't want any of the other priests to know what he saw, either."

"What do you intend to do next?"

I had given my next move a great deal of thought. I knew I had a limited amount of time to find the boy—they would question him to find out if he had told anyone else what he saw, and then they would kill him. The problem was finding where they were holding him.

I was sure the Hidden were involved. That meant I had to find Relael Ochallum today and get the location of the boy from him. His willingness to give me that information would determine the status of our relationship going forward.

"I will seek out the one member of the Hidden I know. He will either lead me to the boy, or tell me where they're keeping him."

"Just like that? He will be expecting you, of course."

"Yes. But I have limited choices right now. If the boy dies before I can reach him, we'll lose a piece of information which might be the key to getting rid of the creature in the bay."

Veylar Dust considered my words.

"Very well. Do what you can, tonight, but do not cause a major incident. Keep everything in the shadows."

I nodded.

"Lord Dust, there is one other thing I need to discuss with you."

He could tell from the tone of my voice that I wasn't looking forward to this part of our discussion. He waved me to continue.

I told him everything Arral Doviar had told me only a few hours before. Lord Dust listened without comment, and when I was done, he turned back to the window.

"I tested the binding on Apprentice Megoen's demon. There were no irregularities."

"That doesn't mean she wasn't the real master of Ixal. They came from the same area—perhaps their families knew each other, if only distantly. She helped Apprentice Poloth, advised him. What would have happened if Apprentice Poloth could not summon and bind a demon successfully?"

"He would fail, and would wear the robes you donned for the meeting with Lord Ghargar. If he was useful in other ways, I would keep him around. If his presence served no purpose, he would be removed from the Tower."

"You would kill him?"

Veylar Dust looked directly into my eyes, perhaps trying to see if I was being impertinent.

"Few apprentices fail their masters and survive. If taking his life would give me some benefit, then it would be forfeit."

"Do your apprentices know this?"

"The apprentices in this Tower understand all the risks of their chosen path. They understand the risks, and accept them."

"Then if Apprentice Poloth was having difficulty with his initial summoning, and Apprentice Megoen was looking out for him, perhaps she decided to summon and bind the demon for him, to hide his failure from you."

"You are speculating."

"Yes. But if Apprentice Megoen was Ixal's true master, and she had a falling out with Apprentice Poloth, could she not release the demon without binding it?"

"Such a course of action would be foolhardy, at the least. Once Ixal was finished with Apprentice Poloth, the demon would have immediately gone hunting for its former master."

"But the demon didn't remember who its master was. Once it was freed, it *couldn't* intentionally go after its master. I don't like it either, but it explains everything."

"It means she is also the spy in my Tower."

That brought me up short. I had assumed that Gisea's actions were originally based on her feeling some kind of connection with Ankin Poloth, and when that connection was broken, she simply decided to release the demon as revenge. I didn't see how this could be connected to the Hidden, or the other member of the Five who had sent a demon after me.

"Couldn't it just have been a situation between the two apprentices?"

Veylar turned back to me and shook his head.

"Manipulating the memory of a demon is extremely difficult. I can say with absolute certainty none the apprentices in the Tower of Dust have the capability to craft such a ritual. If Apprentice Megoen did bind the demon Ixal, it also proves she is working for the same sorcerer who attacked you."

This didn't make any sense. Gisea had multiple opportunities to kill me, and had directly threatened to do so. And yet she had refrained from causing me any harm as long as I appeared to be working towards a solution to Ankin Poloth's death.

"It doesn't seem right to me, Lord Dust. There's something I'm missing, but I can't put my finger on it."

"Perhaps. You are right in that this story does adequately explain Apprentice Poloth's death. What you are missing is an adequate explanation for Apprentice Megoen's actions."

The way he said that, I knew he had decided she was guilty.

"Will you question her, or just kill her?"

"I will meet with Apprentice Megoen and we will discuss the matter directly. You will not be present for this meeting."

I had the feeling Gisea was about to find herself in the middle of the summoning circle upstairs. I could only imagine the torture she would experience if Lord Dust decided she was guilty of killing Ankin Poloth and spying for a rival sorcerer.

"Do you have what you need for your own ... mission ... this evening?"

I nodded.

"Then recover the child if you can, but be discreet. Without a High Priest reigning in the more ... excessive members of the priesthood, an incident could spark a war between the Five and the Church. It would be inconvenient for us, and terrible for Ythis."

"Do you mind if I ask what's happening with the Church?"

"They are in the process of selecting a new High Priest, and launching an investigation into the death of Esiah Flannok. The leadership is in disarray, and that makes for a dangerous situation."

"Could you use it to weaken the Church in the long run?"

"Situations like this present opportunities. None of those opportunities will result in the destruction or the dismantling of the Church. The gains are more ... personal."

"I won't claim to understand. But I will be discreet. I have no intention of starting a war tonight. When will you meet with Apprentice Megoen?"

"Borolt Zale, I have been more than patient with your questions today. Our meeting is now at an end. You may leave."

I wasn't about to argue with him. He was right about being patient with my questions. I couldn't remember a time when he had been so forthcoming.

A servant came into the room as I left. Veylar Dust was no doubt summoning Gisea to see him, and I couldn't help but wonder if she'd still be alive by the time dusk came to Ythis.

*   *   *

IT WAS HARD WORK, PICKING AWAY AT THE MORTAR AROUND the metal grill with nothing but a pointed piece of stone to use as a tool. Nonetheless, Sulid kept at it all morning.

His stomach growled, but he was used to hunger. Every moment that passed was another moment closer to being discovered. But it was also another moment closer to escaping. Sulid felt like he was in a race against opponents he couldn't see. He hoped none of them realized they were also in a race.

Sulid had managed to free almost half of the grate, and could even shift it back and forth slightly, when he heard someone outside the metal door. He quickly shoved the stone shard under the wooden bench and then huddled in a corner.

The door opened and the Stranger stepped in. He looked at Sulid, glanced around the room, and then his gaze settled on the metal grate.

"Looks like you've been busy, kid. You don't give up easily. I like that. Too bad it's a wasted effort."

The Stranger stepped over the grate and gave it a couple of hard kicks. The rest of the mortar crumbled under the onslaught and the grate fell to the floor.

"Take a look inside."

Sulid didn't move.

"Really, take a look. See what you're up against and then decide if you want to continue."

Sulid slowly moved over to the grate and looked in. His heart fell as he saw the chimney itself was only a single hand-span wide. He could never force his head through that tunnel, which meant it was useless as an escape route.

"I'm sure you'll come up with something else to try. You don't seem to want to give up."

The Stranger leaned in close.

"I don't blame you. I know what's ahead."

Sulid felt a thrill of fear run through his body.

"Sit down on the bench, kid."

The Stranger straightened and stepped to one side. Framed in the doorway was another man. Sulid had seen this man before. This man had been present the day Sulid witnessed something he shouldn't have seen.

The Stranger put his hand on Sulid's shoulder—the bad shoulder—and guided him to the bench. The man's touch was light, but Sulid understood the threat inherent in the action. It was time to obey.

As the Stranger let go of Sulid's shoulder and turned back to the other visitor, Sulid quickly bent down and palmed the stone shard, placing it under his thigh as he sat on the bench.

The other man, a priest, stepped into the small cell and closed the door. It was crowded in here now. The Stranger remained standing, but the priest knelt down so that he was at eye level with Sulid.

He was dressed in black robes and Sulid could see they were soft and expensive. The priest's shoes were highly polished, and his hands were delicate, his nails neatly trimmed. On one finger he wore a ring carved in the shape of an open eye in the center of a nine-pointed star.

"My name is Relael, young man. I hear your name is Sulid. I would say it is nice to meet you, but these are not exactly pleasant circumstances, are they?"

Sulid said nothing and remained still.

"It is unfortunate we have to meet this way. Had you not run, we might have had this conversation in a more pleasant setting. But fate moves us along, and so we are here."

Sulid nodded slightly, more to indicate he was listening than to agree with anything the man said.

"You are no doubt afraid. I would be, in your situation. You saw something happen, and you probably don't even know what it means, and suddenly priests were chasing you. Well, the chase is over. And you are probably in less trouble than you think you are."

The priest, Relael, stood up and stretched his back and turned to the Stranger.

"Can you bring me the stool, please?"

The Stranger looked down at Sulid and, turning back to the

priest, raised one eyebrow. Relael smiled at him.

"We will be fine. Sulid is not going anywhere."

The Stranger squeezed past Relael and left the cell. The priest looked down at Sulid.

"You gave him quite the chase. He's both impressed with you and angry that he took so long to catch you. He's asked that I give you to him when we're finished talking."

The priest bent over to whisper in Sulid's ear.

"You really don't want me to do that, Sulid."

Sulid lunged upward and jabbed the stone shard at the priest's throat.

Relael reacted faster than Sulid expected he would, and the point of the stone carved a gouge in the side of the priest's neck, but missed anything vital. Relael let out a shout of pain and made a grab for Sulid's arm, but he was already darting around the priest and through the metal door.

Sulid could hear Relael right behind him, so he didn't bother trying to slam the metal door. He charged up the stone hallway toward light coming from around a corner.

As Sulid reached the corner, a wooden stool came tumbling across the floor, and Sulid was forced to jump over it. The Stranger appeared as Sulid cleared the stool—he realized the Stranger must have tossed it out on purpose.

Instead of making a quick turn and darting around the corner, perhaps spinning past the Stranger, Sulid lost a precious second in jumping. Airborne, he was unable to turn, and he landed beside the wall. The Stranger had already anticipated his landing and a fist drove into his chest. Sulid was hammered back into the corner, and the Stranger's other fist ploughed into his injured shoulder.

The pain knocked Sulid senseless, and he lost his grip on the stone shard. His knees went weak, and he slid down the wall. The Stranger jammed his boot against Sulid's chest, pinning him into the corner.

"Wait!" yelled the priest. "Don't kill him!"

Sulid looked up to see the Stranger had drawn a long knife. Terrified and dizzy from the pain, he tried to gasp for breath, but the

Stranger's boot was crushing his chest.

Relael stepped up and laid a hand on the Stranger's arm.

"Let him be. He's not going anywhere."

"That's what you said a moment ago."

"Fair enough. But he can barely breathe. I need him alive and able to talk. Let's just get him back into the cell."

The Stranger looked at the priest's neck.

"You're bleeding quite a bit."

Relael pulled out a handkerchief and held it to his neck.

"It's little more than a scratch. I'll have it taken care of at the Temple. This is a more pressing concern."

The Stranger bent down and placed the tip of his knife against the hollow of Sulid's throat.

"I don't trust you, kid. I'm not concerned about putting this knife into you if you try anything."

He grabbed Sulid by a handful of hair and lifted him to his feet. Sulid squealed in pain, but the Stranger's knife never left his throat.

"Move it."

He forced Sulid to march back to the cell. As soon as Sulid was inside the door, the Stranger shoved him down into a corner and grabbed the wooden bench. He yanked it up and tossed it out of the cell.

Relael entered, and the Stranger stood guard in the doorway. The priest had retrieved the stool, upon which he now placed himself.

"I only have a few minutes before I have to go, Sulid. You can either answer *my* questions now, or my colleagues can return tonight and question you at length using more persuasive techniques."

Sulid held his shoulder and shook his head.

"You *will* talk, one way or another. I'd prefer not to torture you, but I will order it if you don't tell me what I need to know."

He waited for Sulid to respond, but there was only silence.

"Tell me," he said, "precisely what you saw that day near the Temple."

Chapter Twenty-Nine

I T WAS TIME FOR ME TO STOP BEING PREY AND START hunting. I had been on the defensive for too long, and tonight I had decided to take the initiative. Which is what led me to being on the roof of a three-story building near the Temple, hiding in the shadows, and waiting for Brother Relael Ochallum.

I didn't know for sure if he would be out tonight, but I didn't have any other options. I had spent the rest of the day away from the Tower. I didn't want to know what had happened between Lord Dust and Gisea. I assumed she was dead by now. I couldn't help but feel a sense of guilt over my part in her destruction. Maybe she deserved it, but it still felt wrong.

I had no doubt Relael would know of the death of his spy when it happened. I was betting he would need to head out, perhaps marshal his forces. I knew the Hidden were not solely based within the Temple, and Brother Ochallum would have to let the others know to be careful.

They would expect retaliation from Veylar Dust.

I watched the entrance to a small house just down a side street from the Temple. I knew the Hidden used this method of entering and leaving without being seen—a tunnel under the street connected the house to the huge building. I had been here since dusk, and was starting to get impatient. Not that it would do me any good.

Once again, the slave boy and his mother intruded on my thoughts. What was it about that situation that kept bothering me? It was a mother and son, separated to become slaves. But it wasn't the slave part that stuck in my mind. It was that connection. That family connection, the boy refusing to leave his mother, refusing to let go of his parent...

And then I saw it. The answer came to me and I almost immediately dismissed it—it was too crazy. There was no way I could be right. I tried to convince myself that this couldn't be true, but it was no use. I knew I had figured it out, that I was right, no matter how unlikely it seemed.

It was at that point that I spotted Relael leaving the building with two men who were dressed like priests but who were obviously hired muscle. They walked off down the street with purpose in their strides, and I decided to follow and see what developed.

The men guarding Relael were not of the same quality as those he had with him the night we met in the Stone Traveler Alehouse. These men probably belonged to the Wolf and were likely about as skilled as the men I had fought last night.

I wasn't looking to kill Relael. I wanted to confront him with what I had figured out about the creature in the bay. Once I had my theory confirmed, though, I was going to question him about the boy, Sulid. What happened next would depend on his answers.

We traveled across a third of the city before he stopped at the entrance to an alley. Another man, possibly another member of the Hidden, stepped out of the shadows and spoke briefly to Relael. Then the man moved back into the alley, and Relael turned back in the direction of the Temple.

I cursed him silently. We had come all this way just to have a short meeting and then return to the Temple. I looked around and evaluated the setting. It was as good a place as any to have our discussion.

I moved down the block toward them, not bothering to hide. One of the thugs saw me first and stepped forward in front of Relael. I opened my hands up to show they were empty and kept approaching.

The thug drew a short sword and pointed it at me. When I was about twenty paces away, he told me to stop. I stopped.

"I just want to speak to Relael."

I could see the priest peering over the thug's shoulder.

"Relael, I need to discuss our friend in the water. I've got the answer, and it will require your assistance."

The priest said something quietly to the thug with the sword, who kept his eyes on me at all times. The other thug stood behind and to one side. He had drawn a crossbow and it was leveled at me.

"Is that all you want to discuss, Borolt? I heard about your fight last night in the Warren's Heart. I had nothing to do with that."

"You and I both know that's a lie. It's Olere, the gardener, all over again, isn't it? I need to speak to someone, and you snatch them first. Is the boy already dead, too?"

"I was never after any boy, Borolt. Think about it. Someone sent a demon to attack you openly in the middle of the street. According to you, an assassin has been after you since before you and I met. These are not the workings of the Church."

I didn't believe him, but I couldn't be absolutely sure he was lying, either. He had openly admitted to kidnapping Olere. He had given me the Church's documents on the creature in the bay. Why would he deny involvement with the boy?

I considered the possibility the boy knew the identity of the traitor in the Tower of Dust, and Relael had tried to prevent him from passing that information on to me. But that was no longer an issue. I hated the idea of leaving the boy to whomever currently had him— if he was even still alive—but the creature in the bay was, to put it simply, a more pressing issue.

"I'm not going to attack you Relael. We need to discuss our arrangement. I have a solution. Now I need you to support it."

The thug with the sword spoke up.

"Throw down all your weapons, first."

I just gave him a look that asked if he was serious.

"I can drop an arsenal and you still won't know for sure if I'm armed or not. Don't be an idiot."

The thug grimaced at me for the insult, but Relael stepped around him.

"Okay, Borolt. I'm going to trust that you're here only to talk."

I stepped up to him.

"We need some privacy."

He turned to his bodyguards and told them to wait down the block. They were wary, but didn't really have any choice. Relael was paying them to follow orders. When they were well out of earshot, he turned back to me.

"Did the materials I sent you help?"

"Not in the least. You left out the most important detail."

"I assure you nothing was left out of those notes."

"What about the fact the creature in the bay is the offspring of your god?"

Just seeing the expression on his face was worth all the trouble I had gone through lately.

"What?"

"Don't tell me you don't know. Iathephos has given birth, or brought forth something from his own dimension. But the baby doesn't want to leave the protection of his mother...or father...or whatever."

"That's...that's impossible."

"Is it really?"

Relael seemed genuinely shocked. He gave it some serious consideration.

"How do you know this is true?"

"I don't. At least, I haven't been able to confirm it. But it does explain everything—why Iathephos hasn't intervened directly, why the creature refuses to leave, the similarities to the gods in its behavior, demanding blood sacrifices."

"This cannot be possible. I would know about it."

"Why? You don't commune directly with your god—none of the Hidden do. The other priests may either not realize it happened, or are under divine command not to discuss it. Maybe it has something to do with your High Priest getting poisoned."

"No, that is entirely a separate matter, and not one with which you need to concern yourself...and he wasn't poisoned."

"If you say so."

"If this is true, what can we possibly do about it?"

"I don't know. Perhaps Veylar Dust can work with a priest to conduct some kind of ritual that uses the power of Iathephos to drive the creature away. Assuming your priests can convince your god it's the right thing to do. I leave that part to you."

"I will discuss this with my brethren and send a message to you. Without a High Priest to direct matters, we have more freedom and yet less power to make things happen."

"Lord Dust is more than willing to work with you to drive off the creature. But without the help of your god, it's probably not going to happen."

Relael nodded and his gaze moved off down the street, a thoughtful look on his face. I decided to jolt him one more time.

"I'm going to find the boy. And when I do, I'm going to kill whoever has him."

He turned back to me.

"I do not doubt you will do exactly that, Borolt. I wish you the best of luck."

I couldn't tell if he was being insincere or not. I assumed his wish was false. We weren't friends—or even true allies.

"If you will excuse me, I must return to the Temple at once. I will explore your theory and send you a message as soon as I know anything."

I let him go. I needed to talk to Veylar Dust about this arrangement as soon as possible. I had been bluffing about Lord Dust's willingness to work with the Church. Now I hoped I hadn't set myself up to fail.

*　　　*　　　*

I WASN'T SURE WHAT TO EXPECT WHEN I RETURNED TO THE Tower of Dust. I figured everyone would be keeping their heads down, trying to avoid attention as much as possible. Perhaps the apprentices would be meeting with Lord Dust to discuss Gisea's betrayal and the resolution of Ankin's death.

But when I reached the Tower, everything seemed normal. The servants were tidying up before retiring for the night, and no one seemed unduly nervous or on edge. I wondered if they knew about Gisea yet.

I went up to the room set aside for me. It was clean and prepared for me, as if Lord Dust expected me to keep using it now that I had lived—however briefly—in the Tower. I knew I might just do that, depending on the circumstances.

I still needed to make amends with Quda. I had no idea if Lord Dust had punished him for letting me into the vault. Aside from that, I didn't want him to keep avoiding me. I had begun to think of him as a friend.

I turned from my doorway to go and find a servant who could check when I might speak with Lord Dust. It was getting on in the evening, but I knew Veylar Dust would still be awake and working somewhere upstairs. I wanted him to know about the arrangement with the Hidden as soon as possible.

"Mister Zale. I have been waiting to speak with you."

I jumped when the voice spoke from behind me. I turned to see Arral Doviar standing in the hallway. I had not heard him approach. I nodded to him.

"Apprentice Doviar."

"May we speak privately for a moment?"

He gestured for me to enter my room. Something in my gut told me I didn't want to turn my back on him. I couldn't put my finger on it, but my skin was crawling.

"Is there anything wrong?"

"No. I merely want to thank you for passing on my information to Lord Dust earlier today."

He again gestured for me to enter the room, and this time I felt some kind of urge take hold of my body. I began to turn and took an involuntary step into the doorway before I could fight it off. I faced him again.

His expression betrayed his anger at my resistance to his suggestion. I tensed the muscle in my forearm, ready to drop a dagger into my palm at the slightest provocation. I knew I was a dead man if he attacked me, regardless of my preparations, but I couldn't just stand there and do nothing.

I didn't want to think about the possibility of his demon being somewhere in the hallway, or perhaps already in my room, hidden and waiting. If that was the case, I might as well just stab myself now and get it over with.

"What happened to Gis—...Apprentice Megoen?"

"She is with Lord Dust in the summoning chamber."

He stepped forward, and his face was only inches from mine.

"*Go into your room.*"

I tried to release the dagger, but my body betrayed me and I turned away from him to walk calmly into the middle of my room. Something grabbed me from behind and flung me into the wall. I was spun around and saw that Arral's demon had grabbed me.

The demon's hands were metallic claws with long spikes at the mid-finger knuckles. My view of the room was mostly blocked by its body, a cube of blackened stone covered with runes which made my eyes feel like they were being slowly pulled out of their sockets.

I moved my gaze up to the demon's head, a silver orb that reflected my face back at me, a face twisted with pain and horror, and I knew it was not a true reflection—though I admit I was terrified. The reflection of my face came closer and smiled, and it was even more ghastly to see myself smiling through agony and fear.

Arral stepped into the room and the door closed behind him.

"You played your part well, Borolt. Veylar Dust has had Gisea in the summoning chamber since mid-afternoon, and we have all felt the power surging through there. Her torture must be exquisite. He will kill her, and I will kill you. It's what I owe you for suggesting Lord Dust test the bindings on our demons."

I couldn't see a way out of this situation. I certainly couldn't fight my way out, and even if I managed to delay Arral for a few moments, no one was coming to rescue me.

"Why...why do you care if your binding is tested?"

And then it hit me. This demon wasn't bound to him. Arral Doviar was another Ankin Poloth. Someone else was pulling the strings.

"You just figured it out, didn't you? I really do not see why Lord Dust has kept you around so long."

"So Gisea wasn't a traitor after all?"

"Of course not. As far as I can tell, she was completely loyal. And she would have probably been as powerful as Lord Dust, given time.

But this way, Veylar Dust kills his loyal apprentice, while I return to my real master."

"Which is who?"

Arral smiled.

"You'll never know."

And I was suddenly flung sideways as Arral's demon was hit from the side by... something that moved too fast for me to see. I hit the wall above the bed and the wind was knocked out of me. Landing on the bed, I turned to see the room darkening and Gisea step out of the shadows to face Arral.

I had a moment of pleasure at the look of shock and fear on Arral's face.

Then the door to the room was sucked backwards into a million motes of dust that swirled around the figure of Lord Veylar Dust standing framed in the doorway. From across the room I could feel the heat radiating off him as if he were a furnace.

Arral's demon had been grabbed by Gisea's demon-hound and was being dragged into the shadows. The metal claws were raking long furrows in the hound's flesh. A painful throbbing hum filled my head.

Arral gestured at Gisea and she aged before my eyes, transforming into a hunched crone in seconds. Veylar Dust exhaled at Arral's back, and a visible wave of heat pulsed through the doorway. I threw myself behind the bed as the heat wave passed over the room, setting the bedding on fire.

I raised my head to see Gisea's now-blackened form crumple into ashes. Arral, however, looked perfectly fine. He turned to face Lord Dust and smiled.

I couldn't believe Arral was powerful enough to have survived Veylar Dust's attack, an attack that had just killed Gisea. There was something very wrong here.

In the shadows, the battle between the demon-hound and Arral's stone and metal servant continued. Despite their size, only a portion of their bodies ever emerged into the light. I couldn't understand how a battle between such large entities was occurring in this small room.

From another shadow emerged Xiqon, the demon bound to Veylar Dust. It leaped up on the back of Arral's demon and three combatants tumbled deeper into the shadows in the corner and were lost from sight.

"You cannot win!"

Arral was shouting at Veylar Dust as the stone of the floor blistered around his feet.

I heard the shout as two voices, one from Arral and another from near where I was cowering.

"Your master will not protect you, Arral Doviar. Xiqon will consume your soul."

"You're outnumbered, Lord Dust! Even your own apprentices have turned against you!"

As I heard the two voices of Arral, I realized why he was able to withstand Veylar Dust's onslaught. Without thinking, I dropped my daggers into my hands and lunged for the empty corner near me. I attacked high and low and felt the blades bite into flesh.

Arral screamed and disappeared, materializing in front of me. I had planted one dagger into his abdomen and the other into his shoulder. He focused his gaze on me and I struck before he could gather his wits. Reversing my grips on the handles, I plunged the daggers into his eyes and twisted.

A blast of force threw me backwards across the room. Dizzy, I looked up to see Arral slump to the floor. He was somehow still alive.

Veylar Dust stepped into the room and gestured at him, and Arral's flesh and bones melted into a steaming lake of blood, bile, and froth.

Lord Dust's gaze put out the fire on the bed. Then he reached into the shadows and pulled out Gisea.

Her flesh was blackened and blistered, her hair mostly burned away. What little was left of her dark hair was shot through with grey. She limped into the room and collapsed onto the floor beside me.

Without a word, Veylar Dust strode over to the door and left the room.

Beside me, Gisea moaned in pain. Her voice sounded terribly *old*.

Chapter Thirty

LESS THAN A MINUTE LATER, LORD DUST SWEPT BACK into the room followed by Quda, Apprentice Wiar, and a host of servants. I picked myself up off the floor as the servants surrounded Gisea and began wrapping her in blankets.

"Lord Dust, what about Arral's demon?"

He turned from watching Gisea and met my gaze. I involuntarily took a step back. All humanity was gone from his face. It was as if he was a demon himself, wearing a mask made of the flesh of another man.

"Xiqon and Ho'gheysh severed its ties to this world. The demon is back in the Abyss."

Overseen by Delash, the servants began carefully carrying Gisea back to her chambers. Veylar Dust continued to stare at me, and I started to worry that I had done something wrong. He spoke and I once more wondered if he could read my thoughts.

"You played your part well, though you did not know you were doing so. The real spy in the Tower of Dust has now been eliminated."

I wondered if he had really tortured Gisea to find out the truth, or if I had been manipulated into forcing Arral's hand. Regardless, he had not killed her, and had even allowed her to help him take down the rogue apprentice.

"Will she live?"

He hesitated a moment before answering.

"She is alive now. There are no answers to your question. Too many forces are moving at once."

I realized my hands were shaking and I looked over at the rapidly congealing pool that was once the apprentice. There was no sign of my daggers. They had probably dissolved along with Arral's body.

"Wait for me in my office."

I looked back at Lord Dust, who was now surveying the room. Without a word, I left him there and went upstairs to the room where he did most of his research. There was no response to my knock—I guessed all the servants were busy—so I let myself in and sat in the chair facing his desk.

Once again, I had survived when I should have been dead. A moment of gloating was all that had prevented Arral from telling his demon to rip me to pieces. Although I had to admit the possibility Lord Dust and Gisea had been there all along, just waiting for the right moment to strike.

There was no way for me to know, of course. Lord Dust would never give me a straight answer even if I asked. And Gisea....

I had a hand in killing Arral Doviar. I had survived an attack by an apprentice, and I had located him during the fight, and I had stabbed him through the eyes. In the view of the other apprentices, I could no longer be safe in the idea that I was just a tool of Lord Dust.

If they hadn't seen me as a threat before, they certainly would now.

I wondered if Gisea would survive her injuries. I had been sure she was dead. I had seen her get consumed by Lord Dust's attack on Arral Doviar.

But then, I knew little about how well sorcery could be used to heal someone. Sorcerers did prolong their lives beyond all natural lengths. Perhaps she could regain some of the youth Arral had apparently stolen from her.

I thought about being pinned to the wall in the grip of Arral's demon. I had no illusions that Gisea had saved me on purpose. Sending Ho'gheysh against Arral's demon had been a tactical choice, especially since he was not the demon's true master. It had been pure luck on my part that I was thrown clear when Ho'gheysh attacked.

I stood and began pacing again. I kept thinking about the face of Lord Dust, and how alien he had suddenly seemed to me after the battle. I remembered Quda telling me how Lord Dust had held onto his humanity because he saw value in it.

Now I wondered if this betrayal would cause him to forsake the remnants of his humanity for good. I couldn't imagine Veylar Dust becoming something like Kalam Ghargar. But then, I had heard the other four members of the Five were all pretty alien in their own, unique ways.

I had no idea what Lord Dust would now ask me to do. I still needed to tell him that I had figured out the issue with the creature in the bay. I thought back to seeing that young boy in the slave market, fighting to stay near his mother. I couldn't imagine any such bond between Iathephos and its offspring. But it did explain the creature's sudden appearance, its refusal to leave, its behavior.

Thinking about the creature tickled something in the back of my mind. I let my thoughts wander and they headed straight for Brother Ochallum. When I had seen him earlier tonight, he had seemed like he was in a hurry.

I assumed he had been aware of Gisea's torture or death, and that's what drove him out of the Temple into the city. But Gisea *wasn't* the traitor, and Arral had been waiting for me to return.

That meant Relael had been out on another errand, something important enough to make him hurry. To make him nervous, edgy. If the boy knew something important, and he already had the boy in his possession, then he should have been confident, assured of his ability to control what I found out.

Maybe he didn't have the boy. Or maybe he didn't know what the boy might have already told me, or anyone else. I felt a rush of blood through my body. Perhaps the boy was spinning a tale to keep himself alive.

Which meant Relael—if he had been the one to kidnap the kid, Sulid—would likely return to wherever they were holding him, tonight. If there was any chance of finding the boy, of preventing his death, it would likely be gone by morning.

I couldn't begin to guess where they might have him, though. I could spend weeks searching the city and never find him. I replayed my tailing of Relael earlier this evening. With all that had just happened, it was hard to believe I had left him only half an hour ago.

He had met a man at that alley, had given the man some instructions, and then left. I had assumed at the time he was returning to the Temple, but that was not necessarily the case. He might have been going to wherever they kept the boy.

It was extremely unlikely I would manage to catch up with Relael in time, and it might be a dead end. But if I didn't at least try, I would never forget it. I had a chance, however slim, to save Sulid.

I would go to that alley and attempt to track down the man who had spoken to Relael. I would find out what instructions he had been given. And then, I would have to take it from there. I could only hope the man might know something useful.

I stopped and checked my weapons. I was now down two daggers, so I shifted some of my other blades around in order to ensure I had at least one in my wrist sheath. The knife in my boot stayed there—I had learned a boot knife was a valuable and unexpected tool more than once.

For just a moment, I considered Veylar Dust. He had told me to wait for him here. But I couldn't delay any longer. He might take another hour or two before he returned to speak with me, and that was time I could ill afford to waste.

I decided I would take the main stairs down to the Tower entrance. If I saw Lord Dust on the way, I would tell him of my mission and my urgency. If I did not see him, I would risk his anger and explain when I returned.

I opened the door to his office and jumped back. Lord Dust was immediately outside in the hallway and had been reaching for the handle when I opened the door. He took one look at my face and knew I had been about to leave.

"Where," he asked, "do you think you are going?"

*   *   *

"SIT DOWN, BOROLT."

He was blocking the doorway, and his face was still just dead flesh around that inhuman gaze. For an instant I considered pushing past him, but knew I wouldn't survive long enough to regret it.

"Lord Dust, I have to leave immediately—"

I was hit by a solid wall of force and thrown backwards into the room. I landed on my back and slid across the flagstones, coming to rest near one of the bookshelves. I couldn't breathe for an instant, and was on the verge of panic by the time I was able to gasp in a lungful of air.

Lord Dust entered the room and moved to his desk. He turned and looked down at me, but said nothing.

I pulled myself to my feet and, holding my belly, sat in the chair facing him. He sat across from me and rested his hands on the desk.

"Explain yourself."

Without hesitation, I told him my theory about the creature in the bay. I told him of my meeting with Relael earlier this evening, and about Sulid's abduction. And then I pleaded with him to let me go rescue the boy.

"The boy is most likely dead by now. Regardless, your path will not take you where you want to go."

I tried to think of some way to convince him to let me leave, but everything seemed futile.

"Tell me precisely what Apprentice Doviar said to you this evening."

I tried to shift gears and remember Arral's words. I wasn't completely sure of anything—I had been face-to-face with a demon at the time. When I was done, Veylar Dust's expression changed slightly, and he no longer appeared quite so alien to me.

"The demon was not bound to him. It served another master, and that master will now be aware of Arral's discovery and the banishment of the demon."

"How long will it take for this other sorcerer to summon the same demon again?"

Lord Dust considered the question for a moment.

"I would not expect the demon to return until at least mid-day tomorrow. It takes time to prepare a summoning ritual. For now, I must meet with Apprentice Nedes and ensure he is not also a traitor."

"Lord Dust, forgive me, but this all seems extremely unlikely. How did two apprentices manage to get into the Tower without having summoned their own demons? How could this have possibly happened without you knowing?"

Veylar Dust looked at me coldly. I was questioning how he could have been fooled all this time. Inwardly, I cursed myself for blurting out such questions. But I was stunned when he answered me.

"Most citizens think of the Five the same way they think of the Church—a single organization with a dedicated purpose. That is not who we are. The Five is merely a name given by others who do not understand us."

He held up one closed fist.

"We are not the Five. We are Lord Veylar Dust, Lord Kalam Ghargar, Lady Xeylien, Lady Ze'raldu Gha'ban, and Lord Skeloc."

One by one, he raised his fingers as he named the sorcerers of Ythis.

"We are individuals whose only commonality is the level of power we wield through our sorcery. Each of us has our own goals, our own methods. We are not friends, and are only allies when it suits us. We have maintained a truce amongst us for many years only because we saw a shared threat in the form of the Church.

"One—or more—of us no longer sees the Church as a threat. Thus, the truce is broken."

I didn't want to ask any more questions, but something in me needed to know the truth.

"So, it's war among the Five?"

Lord Dust lowered his hand and considered my question.

"No. One of the other sorcerers is attacking me because I stand in his or her way in some manner. Perhaps I possess something the sorcerer wants. Perhaps something I've done is at cross-purposes with the sorcerer's plans. I do not yet know the answer to this question."

"But how—"

"I do not know that either. It was hidden from me in a manner which I have yet to determine."

He paused.

"You wish to go rescue the boy. This child is most likely already dead, and thus it is a waste of your time. However, you will be of no use to me if you are distracted by this matter, so I will send you to deal with it."

I immediately jumped to my feet, but he motioned me to stop.

"As I said, your path will not take you where you wish to go. If by some chance the boy still lives, you cannot waste time scouring the city for a clue to his current whereabouts."

He motioned for me to regain my seat. I sat slowly, not sure if he was offering his help or telling me my search was futile.

"Tell me now how important this is to you. I can provide help, but there is a cost."

And there it was. Sulid might still be alive. Using every bit of skill at my disposal, I might never find him in time to make a difference. But Lord Veylar Dust had another solution, one that would—once again—cost me something. What was I willing to pay?

I thought back to the protection I had been given by Apprentice Doviar. My ties to the Tsojim were permanently severed—and I hoped with every fiber of my being that was all that had happened—but I was now safe from being supernaturally tracked by demons. And yet, it was my involvement with Veylar Dust that had put me in the situation that required such protection.

What price was I willing to pay to save Sulid's life?

What if Sulid was already dead?

Lord Dust just stared at me, patiently waiting for my decision. He already knew what I would decide. For a moment, my body filled with rage and I wanted to lash out at him. I could not say exactly how he did it, but I felt that he had manipulated me for quite some time. And now his control was becoming overt.

Every time I gave into him, that control gained strength. Was it already too late for me to take back that control? And could I do it now, when Sulid's life possibly hung in the balance?

"Do it," I whispered, my voice hoarse.

A pair of hands grabbed the sides of my head in an unbreakable grip. Acid filled the pit of my stomach as I realized the hands belonged to Xiqon, who stood behind me. I suddenly wanted to change my mind.

It was too late.

A spike of fire stabbed into my brain, and I could hear myself scream. My stomach heaved as the flames spread across my mind and I retched at the wrongness of that alien intrusion into my very being.

Memories flashed through my mind's eye and I saw Sulid's face, the alley where I had watched Relael meet with the unknown man, the wife of Olere telling me of his abduction, my brother clutching me as he died. Memory after memory of my entire life began flashing through my head—memories I had thought long forgotten.

My eyes were wide open, and darkness began to flow from the edges of my vision until I could no longer see Lord Dust impassively watching my torment. I was on the verge of losing consciousness, and was terrified of what that might mean.

And then, right on the edge of madness, the contact withdrew and the hands holding me were gone. I toppled from the chair and hit the floor hard. I lay there, curled into a fetal position, as my vision slowly returned.

Lord Dust rose from his seat and looked down at me.

"You have suffered no permanent harm. Xiqon has given you the location of the boy."

I recovered my voice enough to ask a question as he turned to leave.

"Is Sulid still alive?"

"I do not know. I will not risk sending Xiqon into a trap right now, not when my enemies are this close. You will have to discover the answer yourself."

He left the room and I slowly pushed myself off the floor. I had gotten Lord Dust's message clearly—he was willing to risk *my* life going after Sulid, but not his summoned demon. Right now, I was the more expendable one.

It would have bothered me more, but I suddenly realized that I knew where Sulid was being held. In an instant, I was out the door and heading for the stairs.

I never gave a thought to what I had given up in return.

Chapter Thirty-One

SULID'S STOMACH GROWLED AS HE SHIFTED POSITION on the stone floor. The uneven cobbles combined with the ache in his shoulder to make him uncomfortable no matter how he sat. Now he could add hunger to his growing list of ailments.

He knew these were minor pains compared to what was coming for him shortly. The priest had said he'd return tonight to torture Sulid if answers were not given. Sulid had remained steadfast in his refusal to speak.

Sulid had heard the bell signaling midnight. It was now a new day. He was not likely to see another.

He had given up trying to escape from the cell. There was simply no way out except through the metal door, which remained locked at all times. The Stranger had only entered to provide water once, and had been too cautious for Sulid to try anything.

Now, he sat and waited for the priest to return. He knew he was going to be tortured until he told them everything. And then he was going to be killed.

Sulid knew they wouldn't give him any chance to get away, knew they would be extra careful when they came for him. But he was faced with a simple choice—try to escape and possibly die trying, or suffer through unimaginable pain and then die anyway. At least if he tried to escape, there was a slim chance he might make it.

A slight noise on the other side of the metal door set his whole body to shaking. He quickly jumped up and prepared himself as best he could for whatever chance presented itself. The ache in his shoulder faded and his vision became crystal clear. He had no weapon except his teeth, and he hoped it would be enough.

The door was flung open and Sulid charged the figure in the shadows on the other side. He raised his hands and made as if to jump, but it was a feint and he ducked at the last second in an attempt to scurry past whoever had opened the door.

A fist came down hard on Sulid's injured shoulder and he howled as he flung himself at the small gap beside the figure. He was almost through when a second figure came into view. Another fist dropped and connected with the side of Sulid's head.

All the fight went out of him as he hit the ground. A third figure appeared, and Sulid looked up at a priest, though not the same one who had questioned him earlier. A second priest waited further up the hallway.

"Brother Ochallum will be along shortly, though he said we could get started without him. It'll give us time to loosen your tongue."

The Stranger—Sulid now realized it was him who had opened the door—grabbed Sulid by the hair once again and pulled him upright. The second man approached and leaned over.

He was bald and overweight, though not soft by any means. Sulid had felt the strength behind the man's fist. He looked into the man's eyes and shuddered at the utter lack of mercy he found there.

"This is the one who is giving you so much trouble, eh Brothers?"

Sulid felt the Stranger tense.

"He's tougher than he looks."

The bald man straightened up.

"Oh, I don't doubt it. Some of these street urchins are resourceful, cunning, and practically fearless. You're at a serious disadvantage in their environs."

The bald man looked down at Sulid.

"They talk well enough when I start working on them, though. Once they realize their situation is hopeless, all the bravado drains away."

He winked at Sulid.

"You're going to tell me everything, aren't you boy?"

Sulid wanted to spit at the man, but he could feel tears welling up and if he broke down now, he'd never get hold of himself.

The bald man motioned for the others and led the way back up the hallway.

Sulid was taken into another room with a wooden table. He immediately noticed the leather straps attached at opposite ends, and the reddish-brown stain that covered the entire middle of the table. He knew this was where he was going to die.

The priests grabbed his arms and Sulid went wild, flailing and biting, but the Stranger's grip on his hair prevented him from shaking himself loose. He wasn't nearly strong enough to fight off four grown men. Within minutes, he was firmly strapped to the table.

Sulid watched the bald man retrieve a small leather case and set it on a stool he set beside the table. The man rooted around in the case and then straightened. His large hand held a long, thin, metal spike.

"Do you know what this is, young man?"

Sulid stared at him, unable to speak.

"It is the first of many implements I'm going to use on your body tonight. You think you know pain, young man. I expect that shoulder is giving you quite a bit of discomfort right now. Believe me when I tell you that you have never felt true pain."

The man moved towards Sulid's feet, and the Stranger stepped in his way.

"Aren't you going to ask him any questions?"

The bald man regarded him coolly.

"No, not yet. He won't tell me anything yet. I'm just a vaguely threatening man who claims to be able to cause him pain. Right now, it's just words I'm giving him. He doesn't really believe me—they never do. So, I'm going to work on him a bit, give him an idea of what I can do to him."

The Stranger didn't move out of the bald man's way. Instead, he spoke to Sulid.

"You'd better tell us everything you know, kid. This is your last chance."

Sulid wanted to believe him, but knew the Stranger was lying. He was going to die, and no one could save him.

The bald man looked over at the priests. The one who had spoken to Sulid earlier stepped forward and addressed the Stranger.

"I'm sorry, but we're going to have to ask you to leave the room."

"Why?"

"This boy witnessed something that pertains to the inner workings of the Church. Your job was to catch him and return him to us, or failing that, kill him. You have performed your task admirably, but you should not be privy to the answers he will give us."

"I work for Relael, not you. He instructed me to stay here and make sure the boy doesn't escape."

The bald man laughed.

"Does he look like he's going anywhere? Even a serpent would have difficulty getting out of these straps. Besides, I need to work without interruption, and I have the feeling you're the interrupting type."

Sulid watched the Stranger's jaw tense. He realized the Stranger didn't like the bald man at all.

The priest stepped between the two men.

"You don't have to leave the building, and there's only one way in or out. You can guard the front entrance and still be assured the boy isn't going anywhere. But you cannot stay in this room and hear what the boy has to say."

Sulid didn't want the Stranger to leave. As vicious as the Stranger was, Sulid had a feeling things would get worse for him once the man left the room. He looked at the Stranger and silently pleaded with him to stay.

The Stranger looked at the bald man, then Sulid, and then the priest. Then he nodded and turned away. Sulid's heart sank as he watched the Stranger leave the room and close the door behind him.

The bald man raised the metal spike.

"Where was I? Oh yes, I think we'll start with your feet."

*   *   *

THE OUTSIDE OF THE BUILDING WAS UNREMARKABLE—A small structure with no windows and only one visible door. I moved into the alley behind the building and found a bricked-up doorway. It appeared there was only one entrance.

I had no idea what was waiting for me on the other side of that door. For all I knew, one of the Five was inside this building. Or worse, his or her demon. If it was a trap, then I was probably a dead man.

I had been through a bunch of very close calls recently, and my luck had worn too thin. Eventually, I was going to dive in over my head and end up in a situation from which I couldn't escape. This could very well be that situation.

I had mostly recovered from Xiqon's intrusion into my mind, though I still felt violated and a little tainted by the creature's evil. I couldn't afford to let that bother me, though. If Sulid was still alive, he was inside this building and he needed my help.

I glanced up and down the street, but saw no one. Moving to the door, I placed my ear against it and listened for any sounds from within. I could tell the door was made of a solid slab of wood, and no sound came to me.

I unsheathed my short sword and took it in my off hand. I needed to be able to draw and throw a dagger at any target out of my immediate reach once the door was open. I reached up and carefully tried the handle.

The door was locked, as I had expected. My instinct was to force the door open and gain entry as quickly as possible. The advantage of that was speed. The disadvantage was that I had no idea how strong the door was. If it was barred from the inside, I would alert anyone in the building long before I managed to bash my way in.

Picking the lock meant possibly making noise as well, and it would take longer. I drew the lock picks anyway—forcing my way in was too risky, and I'm a quiet guy when I need to be.

It took me a couple of minutes to unlock the door due to my efforts to remain silent. But I managed to keep the clicking of the lock to a minimum, and so I stowed my lock picks and retrieved my short sword.

I slowly turned the handle and pushed on the door, expecting further resistance. To my surprise, the door moved inward. I had been expecting—and dreading—a bar across the door. I quietly pushed it open and peered inside.

I was greeted by an empty lobby area. A staircase to one side led up to the second floor, and a doorway led further into the building. I listened but heard no sounds from inside.

Carefully, I crept into the lobby and pushed the door closed behind me. The lack of guards told me I was too late, that I would find Sulid's body dumped somewhere in this building. I remained cautious anyway. There were too many unknowns to make any assumptions about my safety.

I decided to check the ground floor first and then make my way up to the second floor. The doorway leading from the lobby was pitch dark. I waited a few moments for my eyes to adjust to the darkness in the lobby, and then I proceeded slowly to the doorway.

I crouched at the edge of the door and listened. And then the sound hit me.

A voice, screaming in pain.

The scream went on and on and I was paralyzed by the pure agony in it. And then the sound died away and I knew Sulid was still alive, though by no means unharmed.

His howl had given me a direction, however. As fast as I dared in the lack of light, I moved down a hallway to another portal. Lantern light seeped out from underneath the door, and I could hear Sulid gasping for breath. I tightened my grip on the short sword and shoved open the door.

I was moving before the door was fully open. I took in the scene in an instant—two priests standing on either side of a table, a body spread out on the table, and a bald man doing something to that body with what looked like a metal spike.

All three men turned to me as the dagger dropped into my hand. My wrist flicked and my blade spun across the room, embedding itself in the chest of one of the priests. I didn't wait to see what effect it had.

Lunging forward, my short sword sought the throat of the bald man, but he spun away faster than I expected. I had underestimated him because of his bulk. I would have to be wary of his speed in the next few seconds, but at least I had driven him away from the table.

The second priest began chanting, and the bald man thrust the metal spike at my face. I tried to parry, but it was just a feint and he drew back before I could close with him. I realized he was just buying time, keeping me occupied.

I couldn't turn my back on him to take care of the priest, however. He was too fast, and that spike would be through my back into my heart if I turned away from him. The air in the room was beginning to turn cold as the priest called on the power of his god.

I drew another dagger with my left hand and whipped it at the bald man's head. As I did so, I spun to face the priest. The bald man ducked under my thrown blade and charged at my unprotected back. It was exactly what I had expected him to do.

I continued my spin and lashed out with my short sword. The bald man tried to stop his rush, but the tip of my sword swept across his throat. He immediately dropped the metal spike and grabbed at the wound, which began gushing blood.

I drew my final dagger from my boot as a cold wind began to blow through the room. The priest's face was blue, and icicles hung from his hair and fingers as he continued to chant.

I had seen something like this once before. The priest was already dead, yet his body continued the ritual to summon the power of Iathephos to destroy me. I knew what needed to be done, though.

I rushed the priest and buried my two blades in his eye sockets. A thunderclap sounded in the room and I was thrown backwards as the link between the dead man and his god was severed. The priest's body dropped to the floor.

In my last battle with one of the Hidden, I had discovered the eyes were the focus point, the portal through which the power was channeled. Blinding the priest had closed the portal.

The bald man was choking on his own blood and trying to staunch the flow with his hands. I stepped over and drove my sword down into his chest and he gave a final gasp and lay still.

A pair of hands suddenly grabbed my neck from behind and began squeezing. I dropped my dagger and almost lost my grip on my sword as my instinct to pry those fingers loose took hold of me. I realized I had neglected to finish off the other priest, and now I was in real trouble.

Reversing my grip on my short sword, I stabbed behind me and felt the blade slide into the body of the priest.

It had no visible effect.

The priest had given his body over to his god, and was now stronger, faster, and more deadly than he had ever been while alive. Stars began to swim in my vision, and I knew that if I blacked out now, I would never regain consciousness.

A short sword is a stabbing weapon, but now I used it like an axe. I hacked the blade into one of the arms of the priest, severing muscle and nicking bone. Despite the divine power flowing through the priest's body, the hand lost its strength and I broke free of the grip.

Gasping a lungful of air, I spun and drove the blade into one of the eye sockets of the priest. His other hand became a claw and he slashed at my face. I backpedaled, barely evading the attack. The priest came after me, step for step.

Reversing direction, I thrust the sword at his other eye, but he knocked the point aside and I merely grazed his scalp. I had to keep moving, keep from being pinned by a wall as he came after me.

Finally, evading one clumsy lunge, I managed to score a second hit and destroy his other eye. The priest's body dropped like a stone to the floor and lay still.

I turned to check on Sulid and saw, for the first time, what had been done to him. My chest ached and I wanted to look away, but I forced myself to see what I had failed to prevent.

Chapter Thirty-Two

I UNSTRAPPED THE BOY FROM THE TABLE AS HE GASPED IN agony. As soon as his hands were free, he clutched at me and wouldn't let me go.

"The Stranger! Did you kill him too?"

I shook my head.

"Only the men here. Where is this stranger?"

Sulid's eyes were wild.

"He's out there! He won't let me leave. He'll kill you and keep me here!"

I forced Sulid to lie back down.

"I'm going to take you out of here alive. You'll have to let go of me, though."

Sulid pulled his hands away and I went to retrieve my daggers. I was delaying the moment when I would have to remove the straps around Sulid's ankles. I didn't want to get any closer to his feet and see in detail what had been done to him.

"Were there any others besides this stranger?"

Sulid shook his head weakly.

"I told them everything. I couldn't stop."

I came back over and brushed his hair away from his eyes.

"I know. I'm sorry I wasn't here sooner."

Sulid nodded and tears streamed from his eyes, though he made no sound.

I carefully undid the ankle straps and avoided touching his ruined feet. There was no way he would be able to walk out of here. I wasn't sure he would ever be able to walk properly again. I could carry him, though if we were attacked, I would be severely hampered by his weight on my back.

"We need to wrap up your feet so they don't get hurt any more while I carry you out."

Again, he nodded, though his eyes grew large and his body started shaking. Whatever I did, it would hurt him. I didn't really have any choice at this point, however. They'd all been taken from me.

I quickly cut up the coat of one of the priests and made two cloth bags. Using two more strips of cloth, I carefully placed the bags over his feet and tied them in place around his calves. He whimpered as the cloth touched his feet, but seemed able to handle the pain.

"I need to check our route out of here. I'll be right back."

He clutched at me again.

"No! Don't leave me! Please!"

I wanted to keep him with me, but I couldn't take the risk there were more priests out there. He stayed silent as I moved into the hallway and crept back to the lobby. No sound came from anywhere in the building. I returned to the room and motioned for Sulid to remain quiet.

I hefted him up onto my back, drew my short sword in my left hand, took a dagger in my right, and carefully picked my way back to the lobby. If anyone was waiting for me, they would attack as I crossed the open space to the front door. I took a deep breath and sprinted across the lobby and out into the street.

As I reached the cobbles, I heard a whine past my ear, and something clattered on the steps behind me. A quick glance showed me exactly what I had expected. A crossbow bolt lay on the street. The assassin was trying to kill me again.

I took off as fast as I could and gained the relative safety of an alley before another shot was fired. There was no question in my mind that more enemies were coming, and I couldn't afford to pause. I rapidly made my way along the alley to another street and began to move from cover to cover as fast as I could. Sulid remain silent, clutching at my shoulders and gasping occasionally as one of his feet brushed a wall or he was bounced too roughly.

There was no way I was going to make it straight back to the Tower of Dust. Any pursuers would be heading in that direction to cut off my escape route. Burdened as I was, it was a race I couldn't win.

I also couldn't take Sulid back to my room above the Sailor's Knot. The Hidden knew where I lived and no doubt would be watching it in case I suddenly got stupid. I had no intention of making things that easy for them.

"We need a place to lie low for a bit, kid. I'm going to take you to see someone who can help you with your feet."

"No!" he whispered back. "What if he tells the priests?"

"You'll have to trust me, and I trust him, at least in this. He won't give us up to the Church."

Sulid sighed and said nothing more. He knew he wasn't in a position to argue. I understood how scared he must be, but I also understood he needed medical attention immediately. I moved off down the alley and a short time later I was once again in front of the door belonging to Mossip.

This time, when Mossip heard my voice, he opened the door right away. He took one look at Sulid and motioned me to come inside.

"Word on the street says this is a dangerous night to be out and about, Borolt."

I would have grinned at him, but Sulid's moan as I placed him on the examination table stifled any amusement I might have felt at that pronouncement.

"It is, at that. This young man needs your help. I can pay for your services."

Mossip regarded me coolly.

"Who is hunting you this time?"

"The Church."

I unwrapped Sulid's feet and saw Mossip grimace at the work done.

"The Church did this to this boy?"

I nodded.

"Then you are safe here."

He bent to examine Sulid's feet, and then went to gather his tools and supplies.

"What happens now?"

I could hear the nervousness in the poor boy's voice. He was terrified of falling back into the hands of the Church.

"Mossip will do what he can for you. Then I'll figure out a way to get us back to the Tower of Dust."

I watched his eyes get wide again, and a shiver took hold of his body.

"Forget what you've heard, Sulid. You'll be safe there."

I was amazed how easily the lie came out. I knew better than anyone how dangerous the inside of the Tower could be.

Mossip returned and carefully cleaned the boy's wounds. His touch was surprisingly gentle—I had suffered under his brusque ministrations before.

"Sulid, I know you've been through a lot, but I need to know why the Church wanted you. You tried to tell me once before that you had seen something."

Mossip looked up at me.

"Is this something I should not hear?"

"I don't know. It might be dangerous knowledge."

Mossip shook his head.

"Then the more people know it, the less dangerous it is."

Sulid looked from Mossip to me and back again.

"I will tell you what I saw. Only I don't know what any of it means. I don't know why they were so afraid of me telling anyone."

"Don't worry about that. Just tell me and I'll figure out what it all means."

Sulid took a deep breath and let it out slowly.

"It was—"

"Wait!"

I didn't want to interrupt him, but I was overcome with the strangest sensation, like a thousand insects crawling over my back. I threw off my coat and lifted my shirt, twisting to get a glimpse in Mossip's mirror of the sigil that had been branded into my flesh. For the first time, I saw the symbol of Lord Veylar Dust that protected me from a demon's ability to track a target, regardless of distance or precautions.

The sigil rippled like liquid on my skin.

I knew then what was happening.

Mossip looked from the reflection of the sigil to my face.

"Borolt, what is that?"

I lowered my shirt and grabbed my weapons.

"It's protection, of a sort. There's a demon out there in Ythis, and it's trying to find us."

*　　　*　　　*

I SAW THE BLOOD DRAIN FROM MOSSIP'S FACE AND WATCHED him take a step back. I knew he was going to bolt an instant before he did, so I reached the door first and blocked him from yanking it open.

"Mossip! It can't find us here! You're safe, unless you go running out into the street, calling attention to yourself."

His mouth opened and closed and he pulled on the door's handle, but I was far stronger.

"Mossip, you have to trust me. The demon can't track me. That symbol on my back prevents it."

Slowly, his eyes focused on my face and he let go of the door handle. He backed away from me and took a deep breath.

"What have you done?"

His voice was little more than a whisper.

I didn't know if he was asking why I had let Lord Dust put his sigil on my flesh, or how I had managed to get myself targeted by a demon. I didn't really want to get into either explanation right now.

"Mossip, I need to hear what Sulid has to say. It's more important than you realize."

Mossip shook his head softly.

"I think I understand how important this is. I want no part of it. Come let me know when it is safe to come back in."

He turned and went into his back room and closed the door. I wondered for a second if he had a back entrance, but if so, he would be gone before I could stop him. And I wasn't about to give chase out in the streets of Ythis tonight.

"Okay, Sulid. You need to tell me what you saw."

Sulid was staring at the door, his eyes wide. I realized he was terrified that a demon was going to burst in at any second. I went over and put my hand on his shoulder.

"We're safe here, at least for the moment. Please tell me what you saw."

Sulid looked up at me and took a deep breath. I was struck by how brave this young man had been all through the past couple of weeks.

"I was near the Temple district, looking for food. Sometimes the beggars that cluster near the Temple drop their handouts when they start raving. It's risky, but I'm usually pretty fast. It was late afternoon, and I was hungry. I didn't manage to get anything to eat that day, and I was scouting around, looking for any lone beggars who might have wandered off into an alley and fallen asleep. That's when I saw the group coming, so I hid in a nearby alley."

"What group?"

I cursed inwardly for interrupting him. I didn't want to throw his thoughts off their path. He blinked at me and continued.

"They were coming from a building near the Temple. It's one of those buildings where priests work that isn't attached to the Temple, but it's right near there. There were five of them, but only two were dressed as priests. Those same two priests were killed by you tonight. One of the other three men was a priest, too. He was the one who came to question me earlier today. His name is Relael."

My heart clenched. I had been in the presence of Relael Ochallum earlier this evening, before Sulid was tortured. Relael had known the whereabouts of the boy all along. I could have forced it out of him, made him tell me where Sulid was being held.

Instead, I had questioned him about the creature in the bay. I had let myself believe him when he said he had nothing to do with Sulid's capture. It was my own fault I hadn't arrived in time to prevent the torture of this boy.

"One of them looked different somehow. I don't know what it was, but he scared me just to see him. Relael and the other man not dressed as a priest kept on either side of him, really close. Relael was talking to him, but I couldn't hear what he was saying.

"A wagon was coming down the street in the other direction, pulled by two horses. I think it was full of barrels or something, probably supplies for the Temple or one of the buildings near there. I was right near where the wagon was going to pass the group of priests.

"That street is pretty narrow, so the priests had moved to one side, in a line, and they kept walking. But just as the wagon was passing them, one of the beggars ran out from between another couple of buildings on the other side, right in front of the horses.

"He was screaming at the top of his lungs, something about eyes watching him. It's pretty normal for the beggars around the Temple to act a bit crazy, and sometimes they get really loud. It didn't bother any of the priests, but the beggar spooked the horses.

"One of the two horses reared up and lashed out with its hooves. It missed the beggar, but it kicked one of the priests right in the head. It was the scary looking one, and he fell to the ground with part of his forehead crushed in.

"The merchant in the wagon got control of his horses, and the beggar ran off down the street. The four priests checked on the one who had been hit by the horse, but I guess he was dead. That's when things got really weird.

"A cold wind started blowing down the street, and it seemed to affect everything but the body of the dead priest. His robe didn't move at all—it was like he was made of stone, even his clothing. Then, a wave of energy shot out from his body in all directions at once.

"The force of it knocked everyone down, and I was pushed out of my hiding place in the alley. A piercing howl came out of the body, and then it all went still. One of the priests happened to look into the alley and saw me there. He reached into his robes and pulled a long dagger out and started coming toward me. I knew he was going to kill me, so I ran as fast as I could.

"All the priests chased me, but I know Ythis too well and I escaped. The next day the Stranger showed up and started hunting me, and I've been hiding and running ever since."

I didn't know what any of this meant.

"When did this happen?"

"Do you remember when you got into that fight in the alley? Those two big men waited for you, and you killed them both with your knives?"

"How do you know about that?"

"I was hiding in that alley when it happened. That's the first time I saw you. I saw how you handled those men, and so I started following you in case you might be able to help me get away from the Stranger."

I was stunned. I couldn't believe Sulid had been right there when I killed Wolf's men. That was the first night I had seen Relael Ochallum at the Stone Traveler.

"The priest getting killed happened that same night?"

"No. It happened four days before that."

I counted back in my mind and everything suddenly snapped into place.

Four days earlier, in the late afternoon, I had heard a strange howl on the wind through Lord Dust's window. An instant later, the demon Ixal had turned on Ankin Poloth.

Chapter Thirty-Three

WHAT DOES IT MEAN?"
Sulid was looking for me to explain it to him, to tell him why he had been chased across the city, captured, and tortured.

"It means someone has upset the balance of power in this city. It might mean open war between the Church and the Five."

I didn't tell him that one of the Five was involved; had apparently allied with the Church against the rest. It was more than he needed to know.

I rapped on the door to Mossip's back room and yelled that we were leaving. I was surprised when the door opened. He stood there and looked at me.

"The boy is in no condition to walk."

"I know, but I've got to get him to the Tower of Dust. It's the only place we'll be truly safe from the people hunting us. I'll have to carry him."

My worry must have shown on my face. Mossip pushed past me and began to wrap fresh bandages around Sulid's damaged feet.

"I admit I do not want you to stay here, Borolt. I do not want to be part of whatever is going on. But I also do not want to see an innocent child fall into the clutches of a demon."

"Neither do I. And I won't let that happen."

Mossip looked up at me, understanding what I was saying. If it came down to it, I would end Sulid's life rather than let him be consumed by such a creature. Of course, I was assuming I'd have a chance to do so before the demon killed me.

I picked Sulid up and placed him on my back again, and Mossip grabbed some more bandages. He tied Sulid's legs around my waist, and strapped his body to my back. This left my arms free and meant Sulid wouldn't need to grab me around the neck to avoid falling off.

I paid Mossip—he gave me a guilty look as he took the money, but didn't refuse it—and went to the door. I was going to have to move carefully. By now, the area around the Tower would be watched, and I couldn't be as fast or as quiet as I would have been if alone.

Giving Mossip a final nod, I emerged out onto the street and immediately took shelter in the shadows of the nearest gap between buildings. The sigil on my back continued to itch, but that reassured me. It meant the demon was concentrating on me rather than Sulid.

It had occurred to me that I was protected, but the boy was not. If the demon was given Sulid as a target to track, it would have a far easier time finding him than me. My only hope was that the sorcerer who sent the demon did not have enough information about the boy to put the creature directly on his trail.

If I was wrong, we were both as good as dead.

The next couple of hours passed in a slow crawl through the alleys of Ythis. More than once, I had to turn back and find another route to avoid a party of men who looked to be searching for us. They were trying to avoid attention from bystanders and City Watchmen, and that was the one advantage I had—that they couldn't just mount a full-scale search out in the open.

But the time took its toll on me, and I began to tire. Sulid wasn't a large boy, nor particularly heavy, but I was unused to his weight. In addition, I had to compensate for any noise he might make, or the additional room he took up in the shadows. It added to the stress of the situation and fatigued me even further.

By the time the Tower came into view, I was moving slower and more clumsily than I wanted, and I was worried that I was going to miss noticing something important. And we had reached the most difficult part of our journey.

I immediately spotted a number of men spaced around the open square in front of the Tower of Dust. I expected the roofs of nearby buildings to be covered with crossbow-wielding snipers. And there was still a demon out there somewhere.

I was scanning the square, trying to work out how to get as close to the Tower as possible while remaining hidden, when I realized the demon was standing beside me.

My blades flashed into my hands and I lashed out, but the demon caught my arms easily and held me in place. Sulid screamed, a high piercing howl of pure terror.

The demon leaned its head in toward mine and I was finally able to make out its features in the shadows. For an instant I was confused—this demon was using the same human form I had seen Xiqon use.

"Silence the boy. I will bring you to the Tower."

I realized it *was* Xiqon, the demon bound to Lord Dust. The sorcerer must have used his sigil on my flesh to track my location and send Xiqon to help me. I felt no relief, however. I was still face-to-face with a being I wanted no part of.

Sulid's screamed tapered off as the creature spoke to me, but he was still gasping for breath.

I looked out into the square and saw five men converging on the mouth of the alley where we hid. We had only seconds to act.

"What do I do?"

Xiqon's voice came, as always, from about three feet to his left.

"You will wait for me to tell you when to run to the Tower. Do not hesitate. Another demon is coming."

Xiqon disappeared and I glanced back out of the alley. The men were only twenty paces away when a black cloud enveloped them. The men began screaming as Xiqon tore into them. Gouts of blood spattered from inside the cloud, and severed limbs were flung out into the square.

Sulid let out a low moan as the cloud disappeared and the shattered remains of the men were revealed. I continued watching the square and noted at least three more men gathering on the far side of the Tower and watching my way.

From one of the rooftops above, a man's voice rose in a screech and was suddenly cut off.

"RUN!"

Xiqon's voice thundered in my head. I flung myself out of the alley and raced towards the door of the Tower. Another scream sounded off to my right as a crossbow bolt hit the cobblestones two paced in front of me.

I charged forward as the bolt skittered across the cobbles. I forced myself to breathe evenly as I moved. Another bolt hit near me, another scream and I was two-thirds of the way to the Tower's entrance.

And then, on the edge of the property belonging to Veylar Dust, a burst of flame erupted from the ground and took a roughly humanoid shape. I could see, within the flames that made up the creature's body, strange flickering symbols and images that hurt my eyes and weakened my legs.

This could only be the other demon, the one hunting me. Arral Doviar had told me I couldn't be tracked by a demon, but I was by no means invisible to them. The presence of Xiqon had attracted its notice, and now it was here to kill me and Sulid before we could reach the tower.

I pulled up short and waited for either the demon or a crossbow bolt to hit me first. And then, from the shadows around the square, the black cloud rose up and engulfed the demonic flames.

I did not hesitate, but charged around the cloud as unearthly noises pulsed from the deep darkness. Every step was an effort, and I kept expecting to be hit by something as I ran.

Just as I reached the door, it opened before me and Lord Veylar Dust stood there in all his dark power. I flung myself past him and fell to my knees in the foyer.

Looking back, I saw the dark cloud recede into the shadows. The other demon still stood there, and I couldn't tell if it had been harmed by Xiqon's attack.

Lord Dust uttered a single command.

"Be gone!"

The flames puffed out and the demon disappeared.

Lord Dust turned to me and closed the door.

"Did you banish it?"

"No. I sent it back to its master."

I could feel Sulid's whole body trembling and I carefully untied the bandages holding him in place.

"This is Sulid. He is the one the priests were hunting. He saw what happened on the day Ixal turned on Apprentice Poloth. I now know what happened."

From the hallway, Quda emerged with a couple of servants.

"I will take care of the boy, Mr. Zale."

He did not meet my eyes but turned to Sulid.

"You are safe here, young man. I have a room where you can rest."

"He can't walk, Quda. He was tortured and they…his feet are injured."

Quda nodded to me but still wouldn't meet my gaze. The two servants helped lift Sulid. The boy looked at me with wide eyes and reached out to me.

"It's okay. Quda will take good care of you. I will come to see you shortly."

Sulid hesitated, and then nodded without saying anything.

Lord Dust swept past me and headed for the stairs.

"Come with me. We must talk."

With a last glance back at Sulid, I followed the sorcerer up to his chambers.

*　　　　*　　　　*

"WHAT VALUE IS THE BOY TO US?"

Veylar Dust's question, as usual, took me by surprise. I had expected him to ask me what I had found out, not why I had brought Sulid to the Tower.

"Well, uh, he witnessed something that I believe explains what happened to Apprentice Poloth and his demon."

"And the boy told you the details of this event?"

I nodded.

"Then why did you bring him back to the Tower with you?"

"The Church is hunting him. They already tortured him to find out if he had told anyone else what he saw. I wasn't going to just leave him to be killed. This is the only safe place in the city for him right now."

Veylar Dust looked at me coldly.

"That is not my concern. I should not need to remind you this tower is not a refuge for those who make enemies of the Church. I agreed to take you into my employ because you offered skills which I believed to be of my benefit. What, precisely, does the boy offer me?"

I couldn't answer that question. He was a street urchin. He had proven to be smart, brave, and resourceful. He knew just about every shadowy corner of Ythis. He was skilled at hiding, sneaking, stealing, and eavesdropping.

But I already had those skills, and I could also fight. I had contacts among the criminals of the city. And, unlike Sulid, I wasn't just a kid.

"Perhaps he can work as a servant."

"Perhaps? There is no good reason for me to keep the child in my tower. His only value was in what he knew, and you now have that information. I see no reason not to put him back out onto the street."

"He'll be killed!"

"The boy's life is not the only one in danger! And his is the least valuable life in my tower at this moment. There is no reason to spend effort to protect a life that brings me no advantage, especially during a time such as this."

I stood there, stunned at Veylar Dust's death sentence on the boy I had gone to such lengths to rescue from the clutches of the Church. I was also angry at myself, for believing the sorcerer would do the right thing and reward Sulid for his information.

I wanted to curse at Veylar Dust, scream at him for his casual dismissal of the life of another human being. I wanted to threaten him, tell him if he threw Sulid out of the Tower, I would go as well.

But I couldn't do any of that. Lord Veylar Dust held all the power, and I was little more than another servant. My life continued as long as it brought benefit to the sorcerer. If that benefit disappeared, my own life was forfeit. If I had ever had a chance to escape, I had thrown it away on the end of a bloody dagger.

"Tell me what the boy witnessed. Leave nothing out."

I hesitated. I knew if spoke right now I would spit the words out at him. I might lose control and start yelling, saying things I would not be able to take back.

I inhaled deeply and forced my hands to unclench. Veylar Dust just watched me without expression, probably knowing exactly what was going through my mind. He allowed me the moment to compose myself. A small mercy, that.

When I could speak again, I told him everything Sulid had said to me. I described in detail my rescue of the boy, only leaving out Mossip's name in order to spare the doctor any further trouble. Veylar Dust listened attentively, his eyes betraying nothing of his thoughts on what I said.

When I was done, he remained silent for quite some time. I knew better than to interrupt his reverie, and so I stayed still and watched him, waiting for any further questions.

After some minutes, he turned and looked out his window over Ythis.

"Whichever member of the Five is my adversary gave up two of his or her apprentices to work with the priests. Only one of those apprentices is dead."

"How do you know they were apprentices?"

"A full sorcerer would not have been killed by a flailing hoof. No, the sorcerer who died that day was no more than an apprentice, killed in an accident, and causing the death of Apprentice Poloth."

"And Poloth was a spy for this other sorcerer?"

"Yes. As was Apprentice Doviar."

"But when the apprentice sorcerer working with the Hidden died, why was only Ixal released? Why was the demon serving Apprentice Doviar still bound?"

"The demon serving Apprentice Doviar is bound to another sorcerer, one who still lives."

I realized what that meant. Lord Dust's adversary among the Five had sacrificed *four* lives to this cause. Two of them were tasked with giving their demons over to two others who would pretend to serve Veylar Dust.

"I still don't understand how they did it. I thought you were there when they summoned and bound their demons. How could they have kept it from you?"

His piercing look told me I was crossing a line I should not be near. I was questioning his ability to see through the deceit of his own apprentices. I began to stutter an apology when he shocked me by answering.

"To practice sorcery, one must be disciplined, precise. Every act of sorcery requires the most careful application of power, the exacting calculations of ritual. Despite this, sorcery is a deeply personal endeavor, and every sorcerer is different in how he or she conducts such rituals.

"I can watch another sorcerer conduct a ritual and it seems impossible to me that anything can come of it. What I see the sorcerer do is always *wrong*. Yet it works, just as my own rituals are nonsense to other sorcerers.

"Ankin Poloth and Arral Doviar must have been discovered by my adversary as children. He or she no doubt examined them and realized the two boys possessed power that could not be accessed. Normally, when a sorcerer discovers a child touched by the power but unable to use it, the child is destroyed."

He saw my eyes widen.

"The risk of leaving such a child alive is much greater than the cost of a single life. If the child grows and ever develops the ability to touch the power within himself, he will become a conduit for demonic forces from the abyss. I will say no more on that subject. The sorcerer who discovered those boys decided to leave them for someone else to find. But first, the sorcerer used his abilities to hide their true nature. Eventually, I tracked down Apprentices Poloth and Doviar and was fooled by the false aura about them."

"How could the other sorcerer know you would find them?"

"He, or she, did not know *who* would find the two boys. Most likely, I am simply a target of opportunity."

I had trouble accepting it was all a matter of chance on the part of Veylar Dust. It meant the Five planted the seeds of betrayal against each other decades before such seeds might grow and bear any

284

fruit. It reminded me again that Veylar Dust was far older than I knew, and would likely outlive me by generations.

"The greater problem is the involvement of the Hidden. This alliance between my adversary and the Church could not have been foreseen. It is anathema to the goals of the Five as well as the goals of the Church leadership."

He paused and I considered speaking, but I held my thoughts to myself. I admit I had been surprised by the revelation, but mostly because I had been convinced the attitude Lord Dust held towards the Church was mirrored in the other members of the Five. From an outside perspective, however, such an alliance was inevitable.

The Hidden would do whatever it took to protect the Church. If that meant working with a sorcerer, then Relael Ochallum and his cronies would do exactly that—he had said as much to me when we first met. And, working for Veylar Dust, I had certainly come to see how obsessed sorcerers were with gaining—and keeping—power.

"My adversary has maneuvered me into a position from which I cannot easily extricate myself. It is of utmost importance that I remove the creature from the bay, yet to do so means I must work with the Hidden, the same people who have conspired against me."

"You can't trust them."

He gave me a withering look.

"I would not now be a member of the Five if I was given to trusting others. But there is truth in what your priest friend told you— the Church wants that beast removed as much as I do. Its presence harms Ythis and makes the Emperor, the Church, and the Five appear weak."

"Do you really think they'll work with you at this point? I brought Sulid into the Tower. They have to realize you now know what happened—you're aware one of the Five is allied with the Hidden."

"There is no longer anything to be gained from a direct attack. A demon was sent to kill you before you learned the truth, and it failed. A second demon was sent to prevent you from bringing that truth to me. It also failed. I can only guess how many of my secrets my adversary has learned about me, and in that respect, I have lost a great deal. However, I am not yet in such a weakened position that I can be easily eliminated, and both spies have been removed from my tower. In addition, my expertise is needed by the Empire to remove the beast from the bay. At the moment, I am safer than I have been for some time."

I couldn't believe Veylar Dust was confident in his safety. I also couldn't believe he would contemplate working with the people who had set him up, spied on him, tried to kill me, and probably still intended to use whatever they had learned about him to destroy him and take his power.

"I am sending a message to your priest friend. He will arrange the resources of the Church to participate in a ritual I will conduct tomorrow at dusk. I know how to convince the creature to leave Ythis."

I wanted to kill Relael Ochallum slowly and make sure he felt every cut of my knives. Instead, I was going to have to work beside him for the greater good of Ythis. I wasn't sure I would be able to do it.

Chapter Thirty-Four

SULID AWOKE IN A PANIC, SURROUNDED BY SHADOWS reaching out for him with spikes, knives, claws, and flames. He bolted upright in the bed and tried to scream, but no air filled his lungs. His feet throbbed in time with his beating heart and he did not know where he was.

As sleep left him, the shadowy threats faded from his vision and he saw the small room where the head servant of Lord Veylar Dust had placed him. There was space for a small cot, a single unlit candle in a holder resting on the floor, and a plain wooden stool.

Sulid's fear of the nightmare assailants was beginning to transform into panic as he tried to draw breath again and something blocked the air from entering his body. He threw back the thin blanket and made to stand, but realized as he swung his bandaged feet toward the floor that he could not put any weight on them.

Without warning, the door to his room swung slowly but steadily open. A figure stood in the doorway, a hunched shadow full of menace. Sulid stared in horror at the figure as it moved to the side of his cot, its gait an awkward hobble.

A dark hand gestured and suddenly Sulid was able to draw a deep breath. He immediately coughed and choked on air full of the smell of smoke and burning flesh. He retched and tried to draw back on the cot to get as much distance from the figure as possible.

An ancient female voice erupted from the shadowy figure. The words were filled with scorn.

"Be still, child! What use can you be if you cower and panic at the first sign of sorcery?"

The candle on the floor flared to life and the figure was lit from below by the flickering flame. Sulid gasped as he took in the sight of an old crone, skin charred and blackened. Most of her hair was burned away, only a few bits of gray hanging in twisted strings around a face that appeared to be melting off her skull.

Her body was hunched over, her back bent with age and pain. Sulid noticed a wisp of smoke come from her skin, as if she was still smoldering. Only her eyes appeared undamaged, piercing orbs that were out of place in a face such as hers. Those eyes were fixed on Sulid as if she could see through his skin to the very core of him.

Sulid tried to pull himself together as best he could. He had been through so much in the past few days that he was becoming numb to yet another new threat. He managed to find his voice enough to whisper.

"Who are you?"

The eyes continued to evaluate him. When the crone answered, her tone was thoughtful, as if she had not heard his question but was talking only to herself.

"Something in you called to me. I have use for a servant, one who belongs solely to me. You may be suitable."

Sulid looked at his bandaged feet.

"I cannot walk. And I don't know if my feet will heal right."

The crone looked at Sulid's feet and was silent for a moment. This time, he was sure she was speaking to him directly.

"They will not. You *will* walk again, but never as you did. Your feet will be misshapen lumps of dead flesh on the ends of your legs. You will be fit only to beg for coin, a crippled, homeless nothing."

Sulid's heart lurched in this chest and he knuckled his eyes to stop his tears from streaming down his face. He didn't know if he could survive like that, didn't even know if he wanted to.

"You will serve me."

Sulid looked up at her but found it difficult to focus on her ruined face. Her unnerving presence made it difficult for him to concentrate on what she had just said. At first, he thought she was offering him a chance to earn his keep in the Tower.

Then he realized there had been no question in what she said.

"Why would you take pity on me?"

Her twisted mouth pulled up in a sneer.

"I feel no pity for you. I would leave you to your fate at the hands of Lord Dust without hesitation."

Sulid could hear the truth in her voice. She had no consideration for his future other than taunting him with the hopelessness of it.

"You will serve me because it is what I have decided."

Sulid did not want to consider being the servant of such a creature.

"I'm sorry, but I was brought here by Borolt Zale. He said he will take care of me. I don't think he'd want me to agree to be anyone's servant until I spoke to him."

The crone leaned closer and the smell of burning flesh nearly overpowered him.

"Borolt Zale does not decide what happens to you, child! Lord Dust has decreed you are of no further use to him. You are to be thrown out of the Tower and left to your fate. Zale is a servant of Lord Dust and will do as he is told. If Zale is ordered to throw you out himself, he will do so. However, Lord Dust has agreed to give you to me. I am not offering you a choice, child. I have seen your fate, but I am now changing it by my own will."

The woman straightened as much as she was able and turned to the door. Sulid wanted to scream for Borolt Zale, but knew it would do little good. He had let the man bring him into the Tower of Dust, and now he was trapped here.

And he would spend the rest of his days serving this horrid creature.

Without turning, the ancient woman stopped in the doorway and addressed him once more.

"In answer to your first question, I was an apprentice of Lord Veylar Dust. I will shortly achieve full recognition as a sorcerer, and the Five will become the Six. I am the Burning Crone, but you will call me Master."

She left the room and Sulid let the tears stream down his cheeks. The candle guttered and went out, but Sulid realized it was no longer dark in his small room. He peered out the door into the hallway and saw through a nearby window that it was dawn.

The midnight darkness during the crone's visit had not been natural. The shadows had been wrapped around the woman who called herself the Burning Crone and it retreated with her now.

Sulid wondered if he would spend the rest of his life in such smothering darkness, serving a sorcerer, surrounded by others who were damaged like he was. He wasn't sure if a short life on the streets of Ythis as a crippled beggar wasn't preferable.

But then, he remembered if he left the Tower of Dust a demon was likely to be waiting for him. So, he huddled under the thin blanket and cried softly to himself while he waited for someone to come get him and take him to his fate.

*   *   *

I EXPECTED TREACHERY, BUT LORD DUST SEEMED TO HAVE full confidence that the priests would perform their roles as required for the ritual. Despite being up all night in preparation for today's ordeal, I wasn't tired. My nerves were too twitchy for me to feel any urge to sleep.

I had faced another decision point last night when Veylar Dust ordered me to submit to having another sigil placed on my flesh. I didn't want to do it, was afraid of what the price might be. But in the end, I had accepted the sorcerer's will, as I expected this new "gift" might be the only thing keeping me alive through today.

The price? I had given up my so recently assumed role as protector of Sulid. I would still try to help him, of course, but I would no longer put my own life on the line to save his. Quda had spoken to me long enough to tell me Sulid had been given a place in the Tower after all, so I was not currently concerned about his well-being.

I had bigger issues to concern me.

Lord Dust and Relael had sent messages back and forth throughout the night and most of this morning, arranging the details of today's effort to force the unnatural creature to leave the Bay of Ythis. Lord Dust appeared to trust Brother Ochallum's missives declaring the priests would do everything to make today successful.

I still wanted to plant a knife in the bastard's throat.

I was on my way to meet him and a contingent of priests at the docks. Apprentices Wiar and Nedes had gone ahead to prepare the area for the ritual. I had heard nothing more about Apprentice Megoen, but I expected that—were she to live—she would be some time in recovering from her injuries.

I wondered how those injuries would change her.

I reached the major street before the wharf and threaded my way through the milling dockworkers towards the area where Lord Dust would conduct the ritual. There was a constantly-shifting crowd of onlookers around the site—curious bystanders would approach, realize both priests and sorcerers were in attendance, and rapidly depart. These would soon be replaced by others who had just happened onto the scene.

Word would quickly spread, though, and I expected the area would shortly be abandoned by all normal denizens of Ythis. The docks would be solely occupied by the mad and the evil. I was starting to wonder to which group I belonged.

As I moved through the churning crowd, I caught a glimpse of Brother Ochallum ahead. He was speaking with Apprentice Nedes, and I wondered for an instant if perhaps there was still a spy in the Tower. But I knew Lord Dust had tested and confirmed the remaining apprentices, and was satisfied with the results.

I pushed past the last of the observers and saw the great circle being painted onto the stone of the dock. It was much larger than the circle in the top room of the Tower of Dust, though also simpler—at least to my untrained eye. Apprentice Wiar had almost completed it and I was struck by how perfectly round it appeared to be. Yet the apprentice sorcerer was merely using a paintbrush and no other tools to ensure its symmetry.

Relael Ochallum saw me and excused himself from his discussion with the other apprentice, who scowled at me—as usual—and turned back to assist Apprentice Wiar. I tensed as the priest approached me, holding myself back from lashing out at him with fists, feet, and blades.

"Good morning, Mister Zale. Are you prepared for what will

happen today?"

I wasn't sure if he was insinuating a betrayal, an attack, a twist of some kind that would put both me and Veylar Dust in danger. Or perhaps he was just trying to feel me out, determine if I was going to try to extract vengeance on him for what he had done. I couldn't trust anything he said, but I also had to keep a reign on my own imagination.

I wouldn't be of use to anyone if I let myself get completely paranoid.

"I've been very well prepared, Brother."

He smiled at me, and I understood he was fully aware of how I felt about him.

"Excellent! We will need everyone to be at their best if this is going to work. Our conduit has been readied—a contingent of priests is bringing her here now. Your colleagues have already explained to me how the circle will be used. Can we expect Lord Dust to arrive shortly?"

I nodded at him and said nothing.

"Do you have any questions, Borolt? Have you been given your own role in today's proceedings?"

"I have my role. I have one question for you, though."

He raised his eyebrows in anticipation.

"Did you really think it would work?"

He chuckled at that.

"Everything is a gamble, Borolt. You already know that. The first time we met, I told you I would do whatever was required to keep the Church strong. I also believe I mentioned to you it would be so much easier for us if we hated each other, didn't I? And yet, despite all that has happened, I *don't* hate you. In fact, I haven't revealed to the Church that you were responsible for the death of my two Brothers early yesterday evening. I may be your adversary, Borolt, but I'm not your enemy."

I forced myself to unclench my fists.

"I have to stand with you today because the people of Ythis need us to work together. But make no mistake, Relael. You *are* my enemy. You stand for everything I hate about the Church. I will find an

Andrew J. Luther

opportunity to kill you. I will reveal the Hidden to the people of the Empire. I will dedicate my life to tearing down everything you are trying to build. The Church has destroyed too many lives already. I won't stand idly by while you destroy the rest."

Relael let his smile slip off his face and leaned in close. I saw hardness in his eyes I had not seen before.

"You are just one man, Borolt. Your hatred means nothing, your vows mean nothing. You are simply a slave to that sorcerer, and his days are numbered. When we first met, I respected you for your stance against such an institution as the Church. Now I see you are little more than a puppet, dancing on the ends of strings held by the weakest of the Five. Dedicate your life—*waste* your life—however you want. It will be over soon enough."

He turned and walked away from me, and I had to hold myself still—I was fighting a nearly overwhelming urge to strike him down right here. I knew he was telling me the truth this time: he didn't see me as any threat to the Church or to his own life.

I would ensure it was a fatal mistake.

A scream heralded the arrival of the priest—or priestess—who would act as a conduit in the ritual. Five other priests surrounded her and held onto chains attached to manacles around her wrists, ankles, and neck. They clutched the chains in tight grips, the links stretched tight between them so the priestess could not move except where they directed her.

I had seen the truly mad before, but the look in her eyes was beyond anything I had yet encountered. Hers was a mind on the verge of breaking entirely, but there remained a spark of awareness that kept her humanity intact. It was a horrific sight.

The priests dragged her to the center of the circle, and I noticed the crowd was thinning faster than it was being renewed.

And then, with a low murmur, the remaining throng suddenly melted away entirely, like ghosts facing a strong sunrise. Only it was no sunrise that had entered the square.

Lord Veylar Dust had arrived.

He strode across the stone quay toward us, his black cloak leaching color out of his surroundings. His head was bare, and his face was a mask: emotionless, inhuman. The priests turned as one, and I saw Relael Ochallum take an involuntary step backward.

Lord Dust stopped and surveyed the scene, moving only his eyes. When he spoke, it was barely above a whisper, though the sound traveled easily to each of us standing on the dock.

"I am prepared. Let us begin."

Chapter Thirty-Five

URING THE NIGHT, APPRENTICE WIAR HAD EXPLAINED my role in detail. I was not going to participate directly in the ritual. Rather, I was there as insurance in case any of the priests decided to interfere with the proceedings.

Lord Dust had a quiet word with the two apprentices before he approached Brother Ochallum. The priest bowed to him respectfully, and they discussed the final details around the proceedings.

The five priests were directed to kneel on five special sigils spaced evenly around the painted circle, the priestess held by the chains in the exact center. Brother Ochallum stood well away from the edge of the circle, while the apprentices stood to either side.

Lord Dust stepped into the circle and positioned himself directly behind the priestess. She craned her head back to look up at him and howled in terror. Without looking at me, he gestured for me to take my own place.

I moved to position myself somewhat in line between Lord Dust and Relael Ochallum. I was near enough to the circle that I could also keep an eye on the priests who were holding the woman who would act as a conduit. My knives were secreted all over my outfit, and my short sword rested loosely in its scabbard at my left side.

I had to stop myself from scanning the rooftops constantly for any sign of the assassin. I knew Lord Dust had set his demon to watching the skyline—it was both more alert and could move much more quickly than I could to react to a threat from that quarter.

The new sigil was a dead spot on the skin of my chest. It did not hurt, nor itch, nor provide any sensation. I only hoped I would not need to use it. If things became that desperate, we were all in trouble.

I spared a thought for the other demon, the one which had hunted Sulid and me last night. Would the other sorcerer send it to interfere in today's ritual? Lord Dust was sure he would be left alone to complete this task—even someone out for his power would not want to disrupt the efforts we were making today.

Lord Dust began to chant in a strange, guttural language. The mad priestess immediately stopped yelling and her eyes fixed on the waters of the bay in front of her. The seabirds that thronged the dock also fell silent and took off in a frenzied beating of wings that took them inland instead of out over the bay.

Whitecaps began to appear on the waves, though no wind blew. Yet the water continued to increasingly churn as Veylar Dust uttered words in an alien tongue. The sun seemed to dim as though it was hidden behind an overcast sky, though no clouds were in sight.

I realized the ground was beginning to shudder under my boots and for a moment I feared the stone of the dock would crumble and throw us all into the water. And then the vibrations in the ground resolved into a hum almost too low to hear.

I looked up to see the creature break the surface of the water, only a single ship-length from the dock where we all stood.

I felt a rush of blood from my nose and a piercing ringing blared in my ears as part of the great bulk of the creature raised itself out of the water. Five large tentacles reached out and wrapped around three small ships which were docked to either side of where we stood.

I could hear wood groan and snap under the strain of holding the weight of this creature, but my eyes were locked onto the vision of the beast in front of me. A haze of steam partially obscured much of the creature's form, but what I saw caused me to heave and retch.

My mind could not fully comprehend what I was witnessing. The beast was alien, of a shape that I could not fully recognize, as it occupied space in a way that was *wrong*. I still see it sometimes in my mind's eye, and yet I cannot describe it fully, for I cannot use anything in this world as a touchstone for my description.

The great creature had nothing resembling a face, or even a mouth, yet a painful, grating noise came from it in irregular bursts and I realized it must be talking to Lord Dust. I saw the stone dock begin to bubble under my feet, as if it was becoming liquid as the sound touched it.

I tore my eyes away from the scene in front of me and checked on Relael Ochallum. I needn't have worried about him trying anything. He was on his knees in front of the creature, blood streaming down his face from his nose. The priest's eyes were wild with fear and awe, and his whole body shook as if he had the chills.

I looked to my right and saw the other five priests were in a similar state. My eyes locked on the priestess, however. Unlike the others, she sat on the ground looking up at the beast with utter calm. In contrast to her brethren, it appeared her madness had left her in the presence of this creature, and she merely accepted—and awaited—her fate.

I realized Lord Dust was still chanting, and noticed the strain on his face as he kept up the ritual. Both apprentices had raised their arms and were chanting in a counterpoint to their master. They both looked shaken, but controlled themselves with an iron will and performed their roles perfectly.

The priestess started trying to push herself to her feet, and her tugs on the chains snapped the five priests out of their trances. They looked to Lord Dust and he nodded without interrupting his chanting. The priests let the chains loosen just enough for the priestess to gain her feet.

She stood tall and calm and gazed unblinking at the great beast. I quickly glanced at Relael—still enraptured by the creature—and turned back to watch the woman face this immense alien being.

Lord Dust's chanting reached a crescendo, and suddenly the priestess snapped her head back and let out a scream in a thousand voices at once. Her body burst into flames and the sorcerer was forced to take a couple of steps back, though he managed to continue chanting.

The woman slowly tilted her head back down and faced the creature once more. Her mouth opened to an impossibly large hole, and oily black smoke billowed forth from the orifice. I was knocked to my knees as I felt as though I had been physically struck as the woman began to speak in the voice of a god.

She had transformed into a direct conduit to the voice of Iathephos.

The air around me rippled and tore as the voice spoke a language I could not understand, yet pulled at my heart as if a metal hook was trying to yank it up through my throat. I heard the creature respond and the whole world darkened, though it may have been just my perception as I fought to hold onto consciousness.

I heard another voice screaming, and I realized it was my own. I twisted my head enough to see Relael clawing at his face, his nails digging deep furrows in the skin of his cheeks. I retained enough sanity to feel a small hope he might permanently blind himself.

And then a huge splash sent a wave of water over the edge of the dock. The water instantly sizzled away into steam as it met the edge of the painted circle.

The body of the priestess was blackened, yet it continued to burn. The chains connecting her to the five priests were beginning to emit a sickly yellow glow.

In the next instant, all five priests shrieked simultaneously as the strange glow flowed up the chains and enveloped each of them. As the light touched their flesh, it turned to liquid and their bodies melted like candles in a blacksmith's furnace.

The shrieks of the five priests went on long after they died, the sound carried on the sudden wind that gusted in from the north.

I looked at the water of the bay and the creature was gone, submerged once more. I did not know if we had succeeded or failed, but it was not over yet.

The priestess let out one final howl, once more composed of a thousand different voices. Her body was a column of flame, and Lord Dust stopped chanting and stepped backward out of the circle. He motioned to the two apprentices, who also moved beyond the circle's border.

A crack of thunder sounded, and the flames exploded outward in all directions. I dove to the ground but felt no heat wash over me.

I looked up in time to see the circle contain the blast and funnel it up into the sky, where the flames reached a height greater than the Tower of Dust.

And then the world seemed to snap back into place and the fire was gone, the bodies of the priests and priestess no more than black scorch marks on the stone slabs of the quay. The sun's rays were once again back to full illumination.

I heaved a breath and looked at Veylar Dust. He stood still, watching the waters of the bay. I could see a slight change in him most others would not notice—he was exhausted by what he had done. Both apprentices seemed barely able to stand.

I remembered Relael Ochallum and my head snapped around.

He was gone.

I didn't know if he had been driven mad by the ordeal, or if he had seen the other priests consumed by the light and decided it was best to be elsewhere. I hoped it was the former, though I didn't really believe it. If I had survived this day intact, he most likely had as well.

I felt a presence near me and turned around. Veylar Dust stood less than an arm's reach away.

"Borolt, we must return to the Tower."

His voice was raspy and raw. I could only imagine the price he had paid to chant that horrid language throughout the ritual.

"What happened? Did it work?"

Lord Dust turned away from me and began walking back to the Tower. Then he stopped and looked back over his shoulder.

"It worked. The creature is leaving the bay for good."

I slowly regained my feet and followed Lord Dust and his two apprentices back to the Tower of Dust.

We had succeeded in ridding Ythis of Iathephos' offspring.

Now we had to be prepared for an attack.

*　　　　*　　　　*

I SPENT THE REST OF THE MORNING IN THE ROOM I USED in the Tower of Dust. Veylar Dust and his apprentices had each retired to their respective chambers to rest and recover from the morning's ordeal. I lay on the bed in my small room and stared at the ceiling, trying to rest my body.

My mind was another story entirely.

Lord Dust had ordered me to remain in the Tower for now, and I had no desire to argue. I no longer felt safe on the streets of Ythis. While it was possible the assassin who had been after Sulid had now moved on to other work—perhaps even in another city—there was still a demon out there. I had no way of knowing if it continued to hunt me.

I knew Relael Ochallum was alive, though not in what state. I had come through this morning somewhat unscathed. I had to assume he had as well.

I still wanted to kill him, but I had to admit there were bigger threats to deal with first. With the creature gone, Lord Dust had no further value to the Church. If one of the other members of the Five was going to make a direct move without worrying about any interference, the best time would be now.

I was brought out of my reverie by a soft tapping on my door. I opened it to a servant, who told me Lord Dust wanted to see me right away.

I was surprised at the summons. I expected the sorcerer to spend time alone or with his apprentices, to plan out their strategy against his adversary. I knew better than to keep him waiting, however, so I immediately proceeded up the stairs to his chamber.

He was seated at his desk, as usual, and I was shocked at how tired he looked. The amount of effort he expended this morning must have been incredible for it to affect his appearance like this. I tried not to stare at him, but took the seat opposite him when he motioned me to sit.

"The creature has departed the bay, and seems to be heading south. It will likely occupy the waters off the coast of one of the Shunesh cities. It should feed well there."

"I still don't understand how you did it."

I didn't expect an explanation from him—I was merely making an observation. He surprised me when he answered.

"The priestess had been given to Iathephos—the god established a direct link into her mind, allowing her to become a conduit for his power. My ritual merely attracted the creature, drew it out of the water. When the priestess laid eyes on the creature, Iathephos used her body to communicate directly with its offspring. I do not know what it said. No mortal can understand the true speech of the gods. Regardless, the creature in the water understood it could no longer stay near the city. It was time for it to find a new home."

"Why did Iathephos kill the five priests?"

"I doubt that was intentional. The energy pouring through the priestess' body is alien to this world. The chains connecting her to the priests probably acted as another kind of conduit. Mortals die easily under the touch of a god."

"So, does this mean the world has a new god? Will this happen with any of the other gods?"

"I have no answers to your questions. These beings are utterly alien, and all are different from one another. Regardless, that is not why I summoned you here."

He pulled out a hand-written message on a piece of parchment.

"Brother Relael Ochallum just sent me this. It appears he's not happy with the current situation in his Church and is looking for allies."

Lord Dust handed over the message.

It read:

Lord Veylar Dust,

Please believe me when I say I hope this message finds you whole, and well. The City of Ythis owes you a debt of gratitude for your efforts this morning. My own thanks to you are, of course, unofficial.

I will not try to hide my own part in the efforts against you. I do what I feel is necessary to strengthen the Church, whatever the cost. I am sure you understand my position.

Today, however, I must admit to you I have made a grave error in the alliances I have chosen. I believed the plan to weaken you through your apprentices would benefit the Church. I believed that infighting amongst the Five was to our benefit.

I now curse myself for not seeing the endgame. I have discovered the truth behind the death of High Priest Flannok. There have been other deaths within our organization, seemingly random and unrelated. I have now discovered the pattern.

One of the two priests who was "involved" with your apprentices is still alive. That priest is now in a position to accrue a great deal of power within the Church. And your adversary in the Five controls this priest.

I do not need to explain what this means for you. We are both in precarious positions, Lord Dust, and we now have a common enemy.

There is no reason for you to trust me, nor I you. At the same time, we managed to work toward the same goal this morning with great success. Perhaps we can do so one more time.

I ask that you meet me privately to discuss this new situation. Further messages of this nature are not safe. Tonight, I will be in the same building where Borolt Zale rescued the boy. It is the last place anyone will expect us to meet. I will arrive at the twelfth hour and remain for a short time, and then I will leave.

Please consider meeting me this once.

Brother Relael Ochallum

"It's an obvious trap, Lord Dust."

I handed back the message. He did not respond.

"Brother Ochallum can not be trusted. He's worked against you for years. He's a high-ranking member of the Hidden. He's an ally of whichever sorcerer is trying to remove you. It would be crazy to meet with him."

"That is precisely what you told me last night. Had I listened to your advice then, the creature would still occupy the Bay of Ythis."

I looked at him in shock. Was he really considering trusting Relael Ochallum? How could he be so naïve?

Once again, he appeared to read my mind.

"Do not be a fool," he said with a cold glare. "I would no more trust this priest than I would trust any other mortal."

I let out a breath I hadn't realized I was holding.

"That does not mean, however, I cannot meet with him to hear out his plan."

"But they'll be waiting for you! How do you know the other sorcerer won't be there with a bunch of priests, perhaps his own apprentices, ready to attack you the instant you show your face?"

"Because I am Lord Veylar Dust. A direct attack has too much risk. There are no guarantees when one sorcerer fights another, regardless of how much the odds favor one side over the other."

"Then you really believe it's safe to go?"

"No. I believe Brother Ochallum has sent this missive in good faith, and that he is unaware he has been manipulated into doing so. I believe this is, as you suggested, a trap. And I also believe this is the best opportunity to eliminate some of my adversary's resources."

I had to admit Lord Dust was more intelligent and more devious than I was. I still felt it was a huge risk, but his confidence had never been proven overblown before. I only hoped his streak continued to hold out.

"I assume you'll bring your apprentices?"

"You assume wrong. Apprentice Megoen is in no shape to participate just yet, and after this morning, Apprentices Wiar and Nedes will be more of a hindrance than a help. In addition, I do not need their help."

"So, you're going to go alone?"

"No," he replied, looking straight into my eyes. "You will accompany me."

Chapter Thirty-Six

THE CARRIAGE OF LORD VEYLAR DUST STOPPED some distance down the street from the building where Sulid had been tortured only the night before. I drew the curtain just enough to peer out, though I did not expect to be able to detect an ambush from this distance.

Lord Dust sat across from me, his eyes closed in concentration. I believed he was giving his demon instructions, so I left him undisturbed. I continued to watch the street until he opened his eyes.

"Xiqon is checking the rooftops for snipers and will return to protect me when the search is complete. You will accompany me until we reach the building."

"I think I should take to the roof here and make my way across, so it appears you are arriving alone."

The sorcerer gave a slight shake of his head.

"If another sorcerer is in the building, he or she will be watching for that approach. Xiqon will not be available to protect you from another demon."

I hadn't thought of that, so I readily agreed to his instructions.

The two of us exited the carriage, which pulled away to await us further down the street, out of range of any attack.

I walked on Lord Dust's left, every sense alert, my nerves taught like a drawn bowstring. I knew I was probably safe from the assassin—Xiqon would ensure no one would be able to take a shot at us from a rooftop or high window—but I wasn't taking any chances.

Lord Dust walked slowly. At first, I thought he was preparing himself for a confrontation, but then I realized he was still exhausted from the events of this morning. I considered trying to convince him not to go through with this, but I knew it would be a wasted effort.

We reached the front of the two-story building and stopped. The sorcerer turned to me.

"Are you able to scale these walls?"

I gave a curt nod.

"Then proceed to the roof here and enter from above. Move quickly. When you are near the top, I will have Xiqon cloak your presence for a moment to give you time to gain entrance. Then he will return to me. From that point forward, you are on your own."

I didn't hesitate to ask any questions, but immediately moved to a corner and began to climb. The old building was in rough shape, which gave me many handholds and made the ascent easy. I took care to move quietly, however, to avoid alerting anyone inside the building.

As I reached the top, I noticed a slight ripple in the air directly in front of my face. I tensed up, expecting an attack of some kind. Then I realized it was the demon's cloak covering me and I moved straight for a hatch in the rooftop.

I held my breath as I examined the trap door, but let it out when I found a lock inset into the hatch itself. I had been concerned the hatch would lack an external lock and instead be barred from the inside. This way, I could pick the lock quietly and gain entrance without needing to find a new route.

I drew my lock picking tools and set to work, again trying to avoid making too much noise. Finally, a barely audible click told me I had succeeded in gaining entrance. I drew a dagger in one hand and carefully opened the door with the other.

I felt a slight breeze as the strange ripple over me flowed down into the room. An instant later, the breeze returned flowing up out of the hatchway. A voice in my mind said "It is empty" as the breeze flowed away from me.

I realized Xiqon had checked out the room below before returning to Lord Dust. It would take my eyes a few moments to adjust to the deeper darkness inside, so I carefully lowered myself through the hatchway and pulled the door closed behind me as I did so.

I landed on the floor without making any noticeable sound and drew my short sword in my off-hand. Moving slowly so as to avoid any creaking floorboards, I made my way towards the only door in this room. Dust filled my nostrils and I wanted to sneeze, but I suppressed it and proceeded onwards.

I listened carefully at the door but heard nothing. With great care, I tried to turn the doorknob slowly, and let out a small breath of relief when it seemed to turn without squeaking. It was neither locked nor noisy.

Bit by bit, I eased the door open until I could see through a small crack out onto the balcony that ran around the second floor, overlooking the foyer below. The main room was slightly lighter than where I crouched, so I could clearly see a figure crouched on the balcony, watching the front door down on the main level.

I had never seen the assassin who had captured Sulid, though he had been described to me. This man fit the description, and the custom-designed crossbow at his side confirmed my suspicion.

Brother Ochallum was planning to betray us after all.

From my vantage point, I heard the front door open and someone enter the foyer. I assumed it to be Lord Dust, though I could not see down far enough from where I was situated.

I heard a second set of footsteps below, and a woman's voice spoke out in the darkness.

"I bid you greetings, Lord Dust, and thank you for coming this night."

There was a pause, and then the sorcerer replied.

"You are not who I am here to meet. Explain yourself."

"My name is Sister Lira Shyold. I am a priestess. Brother Ochallum could not be here. He is otherwise occupied."

"Then this meeting is at an end, Sister Shyold."

I heard the footsteps of Lord Dust as he turned back to the front door, but the priestess' next words stopped him in his tracks.

"You should not try to leave, Lord Dust. My master would be displeased."

"Your master? If you are a priestess, you serve the god of Ythis. You have no master."

"Let us not play further games, Lord Dust. I am a priestess of the Church, though that is a secondary role. I am also an apprentice to a member of the Five."

My blood ran cold at those words. This must be the woman who really controlled the demon we had believed served Arral Doviar. Which meant she was working with Relael Ochallum all along. But where *was* the priest? His pet assassin was here, yet Relael had not made his presence known.

And why would the apprentice be here without her master? Did she really believe she could take on Lord Veylar Dust and succeed? Even if her demon managed to occupy Xiqon and take him out of the picture, her sorcery could not possibly stand against Veylar Dust's abilities.

And would a mundane assassin really be able to tip the balance?

That was when I realized the assassin was no longer in the shadows where I had first seen him.

I don't know how he moved without me noticing him, but I could no longer see him on the balcony. I had a limited view of the area through the small crack between door and frame, so he might have only moved a few feet to one side.

I had a feeling he was going to play a vital role in the next few minutes, so I decided to take the risk and emerge from my vantage point so that I could find him again. I opened the door, moving slowly enough to avoid any creaking. When the opening was wide enough, I leaned out and looked along the balcony for the man with the crossbow.

He was waiting for me.

The man stood a few feet to my right, the crossbow pointed at my head. At this close range, I wasn't sure I could dodge out of the way before the bolt found my skull.

He whispered to me in the dark.

"Step out slowly and keep your hands visible. Don't drop your weapons—place them gently on the floor and avoid making any noise."

I couldn't see any way to warn Veylar Dust without being killed by the crossbow bolt. This situation had just turned very ugly.

*   *   *

SULID TOOK A TENTATIVE STEP, OVERBALANCED, AND QUICKLY grabbed the edge of a nearby table. He had been at this all day, practicing walking on what was left of his mutilated feet. He could do it, barely, but more often than not he was unable to balance properly.

The Burning Crone had performed some sort of ritual on him this morning that mostly removed the pain of his injuries. She ordered him to practice moving about until he could cross the room without falling. And then she had left him alone.

He had tried to walk all day, stopping only for a quick meal brought by another servant, this one with a face disfigured by some kind of blade. He had managed to avoid staring at the man's grisly visage, but was grateful when the servant had left him alone with the food. When he was finished eating, he had gone right back to his attempts at walking.

Once more, Sulid prepared himself for the short walk across the room. He took a deep breath and began to carefully place each foot in such a way as to let him rest his full weight on it without rolling to one side or another. He let go of the table and focused on the small shelf on the opposite wall.

Step-by-step, he moved across the room. More than once, he nearly fell on his side, but he managed to maintain his balance by throwing out his arms to either side. In moments, he neared the shelf.

Just as he was about to reach out to touch the far wall, one of his feet rolled sideways under him. His arms flailed and he crashed into the shelf, pulling it off the wall. Two large, leather-bound books came crashing down beside him as he hit the floor.

One of the books landed spine-first and the covers parted. Pages fell to either side, leaving the book wide open on a strange diagram. Sulid looked down at the drawing and his eyes locked in place.

The sigil took on a three-dimensional appearance, seeming to extend down into the depths of the book, and through it into the floor. The spidery writing around the drawing began to crawl across the pages, circling the sigil in a pattern Sulid could not quite fathom. He peered closer, on the edge of understanding a profound secret that remained tantalizingly out of reach.

The sigil drew him in, and he could feel himself sinking toward the book as reality stretched around him. A voice whispered in his mind, promising answers that would solve all his problems—a way to repair his feet, a way to protect himself from those more powerful than he, a way to gain riches and never again live on the street, a way to save others like him from their own desperate situations.

A tiny part of Sulid's mind warned him that this was sorcery of some kind; that he was in great danger. Yet he could not pull his gaze away from the drawing in the book that had become a great tunnel leading him to the answers of the universe. He leaned in farther and reached out a hand to touch the lines that writhed in the air in front of him.

Distantly, he heard a door slam against a wall, and the smell of smoke came to him as he began to let go of his last hold on this world. The smell became stronger as the sigil became a face. Sulid did not remember his mother, but knew this face belonged to her. She was waiting to tell him everything he needed to know.

Something pushed Sulid back from the book and he felt damp earth under him as he hit the ground. He looked up to see the Burning Crone standing above him, the darkness twisting about her as she faced a giant snake that wore his mother's face. They were all in a dank cave that smelt of death and decay.

The Burning Crone spoke in a language Sulid at first did not understand. The snake replied in the same language, and Sulid now understood the creature was arguing with his master, telling her a pact had been accepted. His mother's face demanded Sulid be allowed to study under her tutelage.

Strange as it was, he felt no revulsion at the appearance of his snake-mother—only love and a longing to be with her again. He wanted to make up for all the time they had lost. He wanted to be her little boy, if only for a short time.

The Burning Crone turned to look at him, and her scorched features twisted in shock. She spoke once more to his mother, this time switching to a different tongue and he no longer understood what was said. His mother replied in the same language and gave him a last loving look.

And then Sulid smacked his head on the stone floor of the Burning Crone's chamber and he was back in the room where he had first dropped the book. The sorceress was picking up the heavy tome from the floor and placing it on a high shelf out of his reach.

Small wisps of smoke came from the book where she touched it.

She turned to face Sulid and he could feel her anger radiating from her like heat from a fire.

"Tell me how you read the book!"

Sulid didn't know what to say.

"It fell off the shelf and the pages opened to that spot. I didn't mean to read it! I saw the picture and then I couldn't look away!"

The shadows gathered around her, darkening the room as she glared at him.

"Such a thing is not possible, boy. Who taught you to read?"

"I don't know, I don't remember. I swear it! I could just see how the words were supposed to make sense, but I didn't know how to do it. And then my mother appeared!"

The entire room was dark now, though the flickering shadows began to slow in their movements.

"It was not your mother, boy. It used her image to fool you into agreeing to learn its secrets."

None of this made sense to Sulid. He was sure his mother was somehow trapped in the book.

"Why would she fool me? What secrets did she want me to know? I need to free her from the book!"

The Crone just stood there, watching him. Sulid hoped she was considering letting him do what he could to free his mother.

"The book is not alive, not the way you are at least. It has a purpose, though, and it wants to fulfill that purpose. It has a need to share the secrets it contains, though few minds are capable of handling those truths."

"Does it try to do this to anyone who looks at it?"

The shadows around the Crone lessened, and the room brightened somewhat, though not fully.

"It does not. One must have a certain amount of training to even see the sigil properly. But you haven't been trained at all, have you?"

Sulid shook his head.

"No," mused the sorceress. "Yet you can read the words. You can understand the language. There is more to you than your appearance indicates."

Sulid was scared. He didn't know what any of this meant.

"Am I a sorcerer?"

The Burning Crone threw back her head and laughed. There was no humor in that laugh, no joy. It was a cold, inhuman sound.

"No, boy, you are not a sorcerer. You are something else entirely, though I do not yet know what that is. I expect to find out as you study the book, though."

A shock went through Sulid's body, though he realized a tiny part of him was excited by the idea.

"I'm going to study the book?"

"You entered into a pact, boy, though I have no idea how you did it. Regardless, I must now let you study the contents, or I must kill you. For now, you are enough of a mystery that I want to see what happens."

Sulid couldn't believe it. He had been given to this sorceress to be her broken servant, and instead he was going to study some kind of ancient writing while she examined the strange abilities he had never known he possessed.

"Do not get too excited, boy. You are unlikely to survive the process."

All the excitement drained out of Sulid in an instant. He realized, no matter what he did, he would never be out of danger.

Chapter Thirty-Seven

I STEPPED OUT ONTO THE BALCONY AND FACED THE MAN who had captured Sulid. He kept the crossbow pointed directly at my face, his aim never wavering.

I glanced down into the foyer and saw Veylar Dust standing there, seemingly alone. He was illuminated by a partially shuttered lantern. I could not see the woman who spoke to him.

"You are no doubt curious which of the Five has been moving against you—"

"Your master is Lord Skeloc, Apprentice Shyold. Do not waste my time with your games. Lord Skeloc may consider me weak, but you are merely an apprentice who is beneath even my contempt."

"I may not be a full sorceress yet, it is true. But Lord Skeloc has faith enough in my ability to handle anything you can throw at me. He did not feel you were worth his direct effort to destroy."

The temperature in the entire foyer began to drop, and I realized Lord Dust had reached the limits of his patience.

"I told you to put down your weapons," whispered the assassin.

I turned back to him and slowly knelt down to place my blades on the floor of the balcony. I still had multiple knives secreted in my clothing, so I was hardly helpless. I just needed the right distraction to get that crossbow out of my face.

Lord Dust spoke up again as I stood once more.

"If you are so sure of your abilities, Apprentice, then attack. I am here, and I am ready."

The sorcerer's voice was cold and deadly, and I felt a chill run up my spine even though I knew I was not the target of his anger. The apprentice was silent for moment, and I expected she was trying to gather her courage to speak without her voice betraying her own fear.

"My master does not wish your death unless it becomes necessary. Your destruction would be wasteful. It is your remaining power he desires."

"Yet I do not wish to give it up."

"Submit to Lord Skeloc, surrender your power to him, and he will let you live. You may leave the Empire under a geas to never return. He will take your apprentices, your Tower, your library, and your servants. All will find a place under him."

Lord Dust appeared to consider it. There was no sarcasm in his voice when he answered.

"It is a generous offer. Also, a foolish one. Does Lord Skeloc believe I would not seek vengeance?"

"With a total transfer of your power to him, and your submission to the geas, you would be no threat. But you would have a mortal life to live out somewhere else, finding what prosperity you could without sorcery. It is generous, Lord Dust."

I looked into the eyes of the assassin and whispered.

"Now what?"

I knew he wouldn't shoot me unless I did something stupid—my death would likely make enough noise to alert the sorcerer. But there was no way Lord Dust would agree to submit to Lord Skeloc. That meant a fight was about to break out.

Once the battle began, there would be no need for silence up here. The assassin would shoot me, and then do whatever it was he intended to do to take down Lord Dust. I had to be prepared to make my move the instant I got a chance.

I had a pretty good idea of when that chance would come.

"Your master, Apprentice Shyold, is offering me my life because he knows how much power will be lost if I die. He expects my library and, indeed, my Tower will crumble to nothing the instant my life ends."

I wondered if that were true, and immediately thought of Sulid, Quda, and the servants who would die in the collapse of the Tower of Dust.

"And my apprentices would likely find service with Lord Ghargar, with Xeylien, or the Lady Gha'ban. With my death, Lord Skeloc might end up with practically nothing."

"That is a risk he is willing to take, Lord Dust. You would still be dead, and I would take your place as one of the Five."

I knew this apprentice wouldn't be here if she wasn't powerful, but her claim for Lord Dust's position as a member of the Five told me she was not one to take lightly. I was beginning to believe it was possible, after everything Lord Dust had gone through this morning, that he might not prevail in a straight-up fight.

"Apprentice Shyold, I grow tired of this discussion. I have no intention of submitting to Lord Skeloc. His belief in my weakness is a grave error on his part. I will allow you to leave and return my answer to your master. Do not mistake this as any kind of mercy to you—I will destroy both you and Lord Skeloc at my own convenience. Now go before you annoy me further."

I was continuing to watch the assassin, and I saw him tense as Lord Dust spoke. I understood Lira Shyold was about to attack, and the crossbow would be fired immediately after. I kept my body loose so the assassin would not realize I knew what was about to occur.

A chill wind blew through the foyer as the apprentice brought forth her demon. The air was tainted with an unnatural scent as the demon manifested. I did not look down to see what form it took—I had been in the presence of enough demons in the last while to give me the strength to fight off the dread feeling.

The assassin, however, was not so inured to the foulness of it. He could not help looking as his eyes were drawn to the stain on the fabric of reality. It was exactly what I had expected to happen, and I was moving the instant his gaze moved away from me.

A second rush of wrongness permeated the foyer and I knew Xiqon had appeared, but I was too busy trying to save my own life. I jumped to one side and kicked at the side of the crossbow.

My sudden movement brought the assassin's attention back to me, and he tried to compensate for my shift in position, but my foot knocked the weapon out of his grip. I had already dropped daggers into both my hands, and I lunged at his throat and heart.

He twisted away and one blade skittered across the leather padding beneath his shirt while the other passed harmlessly by his neck. Continuing to spin, he pulled up an elbow and cracked it across my cheek, knocking me off balance.

He reversed direction and slammed his body into mine, shoving me backwards. I couldn't regain my footing and I fell backward. I was able to use the momentum to push myself into a backward somersault, and as I regained my feet, the assassin's short sword whistled a hair's breadth past my face.

I lashed out with multiple strikes as he parried and dodged backwards. I let him get a few paces away to give me a chance to catch my breath and reset myself for the fight to come.

A pulse of air blasted up from below as the two demons engaged each other. Sounds more felt than heard pounded in my chest and ears and I hoped it distracted the assassin at least as much as it distracted me.

As my opponent looked into my eyes, I understood he was terrified. He had a task to accomplish, and I expected he was under a strict time limit once the sorcerous battle began. I knew then the apprentice would not be able to defeat Lord Dust unless this assassin could use his crossbow.

It was up to me to prevent exactly that.

*   *   *

THE AIR AROUND US SEEMED TO HUM WITH DARK ENERGIES AS Lira Shyold engaged Lord Dust directly. I could not spare a glance to see how she launched her attack—I was too focused on the assassin slowly moving toward me.

I wanted my short sword in one hand and a dagger in the other. He had better reach with his blade, and I needed whatever advantage I could get. I did not know how good he was, but I had a feeling this was going to be a tough fight.

My main advantage was time. The longer our battle went on, the more likely Veylar Dust would overcome Apprentice Shyold. And once she was out of the way, the assassin was a dead man.

So, he had to launch the first attack, and he had to win quickly. I could afford to defend and delay and then take advantage of any mistakes he made. He had no such luxury.

A short sword is a stabbing weapon, but in the hands of a master it can be used as an effective slashing weapon as well. The assassin used it this way as he came at me, the blade sweeping back and forth. I backpedaled rather than try to parry with my daggers.

And then I realized he was trying to drive me to the end of the balcony and trap me against the wall. Once my ability to maneuver was reduced, all the advantage would swing back to him.

I still had to dodge and duck his wild swings, but I checked my backward momentum and began to flick my blades out toward him at every opening. With his extra reach, there was no real chance of me scoring a telling hit, but it did slow his advance enough to give me some breathing room.

The assassin was now between me and my short sword, which lay on the balcony beside one of my daggers. If I could get my hands on it, the fight would be even again, and I could go back to merely defending myself. I just didn't know how to get past him to grab it.

A wave of cold erupted from the foyer below us, the chilled air taking our breaths away. Ice crystals formed on the railing and walls. The metal blades of my daggers seemed to drink in the chill, and I could feel the cold through the leather-wrapped grips.

The blast of heat that followed it nearly knocked both of us off our feet. An accompanying screech of sound from one of the demons came from every direction at once. It rattled me—and I expected it would rattle the assassin as well—and so I forced myself to immediately dive into a roll past his left side, hoping he couldn't react in time.

My gamble paid off, as I regained my feet beside the short sword I had abandoned moments earlier. Dropping one of my daggers, I swept up the short sword and braced myself as the assassin spun around and launched a series of lightning-quick strikes at me.

This time I was more confident in my parries and counterstrikes. The noise of our blades meeting was muted compared to the painful waves of sound hitting us from the foyer below. I still couldn't spare a glance to see how Lord Dust was faring against his opponent, but I believed he would come out of the battle the victor.

The assassin suddenly withdrew a few paces and I let him go. He realized I wasn't going to fall as quickly as he wanted. I remained on the defensive, but it was obvious I was biding my time, taking no chances, just keeping him occupied.

If the assassin was going to turn the tide of the battle raging beneath us, he would have to find some other way to remove me from the situation. I watched him carefully, not sure what to expect. He didn't seem to know what to do next either.

And that's when he kicked the crossbow at me.

It lay where he had dropped it when I kicked it out of his hands. I hadn't given it any real notice—I was too close to the assassin for him to make a grab for it. The drop had not triggered the crossbow, and the bolt was still in place.

His boot caught the crossbow on the underside and it was flung upwards at my chest. This second kick was enough to set off the trigger. I flinched as the bolt fired—it mostly missed, but dug a furrow in my left thigh.

My flinch gave him the opening he needed.

He threw his dagger at my face as he charged me. I threw up my arm in reflex as I tried to dodge my face out of the way of his blade, and the knife sliced open my forearm. I barely had time to twist away from him as he thrust his short sword at my chest.

The edge of his blade scratched across the leather of my armor as he pulled the blade back, but my own sword was still out of position. I flung my own dagger at him, but it was an unbalanced throw and he easily dodged it.

He followed up my missed attack with a fist to my face. I turned my head in time to protect my nose, but the punch hammered into my cheek and rocked my head sideways. He drove his shoulder into my chest and knocked me backwards.

Once again, I tried to somersault backwards to end up on my feet, but partway through the roll the assassin managed to plant his foot in the center of my back and shove me off balance. I landed face down, and immediately rolled to one side.

The assassin's sword plunged into the wooden floor of the balcony a finger's length from my face. I tried to grab his wrist, but he yanked the blade back up before I could react. I forced him to jump back as I swept my own sword across the space where his ankles had just been.

He pressed his attack, refusing to let me regain my feet. Blood ran down my arm where his knife had slashed me, and I knew my hand would be too slick to hold onto another dagger properly. I was no longer confident I could hold him off long enough for Lord Dust to defeat his opponent and come to my rescue.

With all of my strength, I tried to yell over the noise of the battle below.

"Assassin on the balcony! Crossbow!"

I had no idea if the sorcerer heard me, but there was no change in the conflict that I could hear.

The assassin kept at me, grim-faced and intense. He knew he needed to finish me off, and he was now in a good position to do just that. I was fighting for my life, trying to keep him busy, buying precious seconds with every increasingly desperate parry.

A human scream sounded from the foyer below. A woman's scream.

I had managed to use a distraction twice against this assassin, once when the demon appeared and once when the sorcerous energies hit us on the balcony. This time, the scream pulled my concentration away for that vital instant.

The assassin's sword plunged into my shoulder. He twisted it as he withdrew the blade and agony blazed through my left side. Without stopping, he thrust forward again, this time at the center of my chest. I threw myself backwards and landed flat on my back.

I had nothing left. He was going to kill me, and I would be unable to defend myself.

But a second scream sounded from below and the assassin bolted past me to reach his crossbow.

Chapter Thirty-Eight

I WATCHED, HELPLESS, AS THE ASSASSIN RESET THE CROSSBOW. His movements were hurried, but precise. I could tell he was worried about the screams from below, but he was determined to fulfill his mission. He pulled a new bolt out of a case on his hip and fitted it into place on the crossbow.

Bracing himself on the railing, he sighted down at his target below. I couldn't see Veylar Dust or Lira Shyold from where I was sprawled, but I was sure the assassin had a clear shot.

I yelled again to warn the sorcerer about the immanent attack, but again there was no response.

I could see the assassin making minute adjustments to his grip as he took aim and settled into his shot. His finger moved over the trigger and I watched him exhale in preparation for the shot.

I yelled one more time, the assassin squeezed, and the crossbow fired.

A roar like water thundering over a cliff filled the building and a bright white light illuminated everything from below. I was forced to clench my eyes tight as the intense glare seemed to burn right through my eyelids. Completely blinded, I could only hope the assassin was suffering the same effects.

The light was suddenly cut off, to be replaced by a freezing gust of wind that tore through the building as if the walls were merely illusion. I opened my eyes but could see only the aftereffects of the intense light that had blinded me. The wind howled like something alive seeking out the souls of the damned.

I held still, my whole body shivering from the combined effects of the cold and my wound. I didn't know if Veylar Dust still lived, but the woman's screams had stopped and this no longer sounded like a battle between sorcerers.

I noticed I could no longer feel or hear the intense sounds of the demons battling one another. It was possible one of the demons had been victorious, or perhaps they had destroyed each other. Then I remembered the demonic battle in the Tower of Dust and wondered if they had taken their conflict into another place entirely.

My vision slowly cleared enough that I was able to make out the assassin standing at the farthest end of the balcony from me. He held the crossbow in his off-hand and gripped his sword in the other, waving it out in front of him as he tried to blink away the effects the sudden flash of light in his eyes.

I forced myself to roll onto my side, and waves of pain from my shoulder caused my stomach to heave. I clenched my jaws to avoid retching, worried the noise would bring the assassin's attention back to me. I needed a moment to make one last, desperate attempt to take him down.

Lira Shyold chose that moment to speak.

"Die, you bastard."

Her voice was ragged, and she was almost gasping for breath. I can only imagine what Veylar Dust had done to her.

"You...can not...kill me so...easily."

I almost didn't recognize the voice of the sorcerer, thick with pain. He grunted out each word, barely able to form the sounds properly.

"You have lost your power, sorcerer. You know what that bolt did to you—the void eats away at your sorcery and you cannot close the conduit. It is buried in your flesh."

I could not make out Lord Dust's next words.

"Your arrogance caused your defeat. You thought yourself immune to mundane attacks, but that bolt was crafted by Lord Skeloc."

I was not surprised to hear her say that. There was no way a normal crossbow bolt would harm Veylar Dust. But his power, and probably his life, was now leaking away. I had failed to stop this from happening.

I had let myself be pushed into choices I didn't want to make. I had believed I was using the sorcerer for protection from the Church, when all the while he was using me to accomplish his own ends. I had fallen into this position, never given a proper choice— every fork had led down a road to some form of damnation.

And now I was going to die, along with the sorcerer.

I didn't want to die, but that was another choice that led down two equally damning roads.

I thought back to my brother. The hints of his growing madness had been there for a long time before I let myself accept what they were. I had tried to shield him from the consequences of his failing mind, hoped that he would be overlooked.

But the Church had been called to him, and they found him to be an excellent candidate for their ranks. And I couldn't accept that, couldn't accept what would happen to him in that Temple of Iathephos. So, I decided to rescue him.

I didn't really have a choice—

The assassin wiped his eyes and looked straight at me. His vision had returned. He would kill me now to make sure I couldn't interfere any further in the death of Veylar Dust…

…just like I had interfered in my brother's life.

I had been telling myself I didn't have a choice for so long that I had made it my reality. But now, sprawled here on this balcony, watching my own death come for me, I realized the truth.

I had chosen to change the course of my brother's life because I refused to let him go. I couldn't have cured his madness, couldn't have stopped it. And yet I had decided I would not let the Church use his madness to serve their god.

And he had died because of my choice.

The assassin was warily watching me for any sign that I was less hurt than I appeared. Keeping his eyes on me, he reset his crossbow with practiced ease. I reached up with my good hand and pulled open my shirt.

I should have left Ythis when my brother died. It is what anyone would have done in my situation, with a price on my head and nothing left to keep me here. I could have escaped any bounty hunters sent after me. I could have accepted that I would never get revenge on the Church for what had happened to my brother.

But I chose to stay. And I chose to ally myself with someone powerful enough to keep the Church off my back. It had always been my choice.

I thought back to the night, just over a week ago, when I had decided to leave Ythis. I had convinced myself I was ready to go, that I would not remain here any longer. But I had allowed a simple interruption to change my mind.

I had chosen to stay, and I had known the consequences.

My body still shivered from the chill wind that had blown through the building moments before. The assassin pulled another crossbow bolt out of his case and began to set it in place on his weapon. With fumbling fingers, I undid the straps holding my leather armor in place over my chest.

Each time I returned to the Tower of Dust, I buried myself deeper into a hole I believed was being dug by the sorcerer. But I was the person doing the digging. I had avoided all responsibility for my actions, secure in my belief it was all out of my control.

I don't know how I had become this person, or when it happened exactly. Only it was now well past time for me to face the truth. My own choices had brought me to this point.

It was easy to abdicate responsibility, but the truth was I had chosen Veylar Dust as my master—and I had convinced myself he was my ally. But I *wanted* to be under his power, to have it backing me up. I had chosen this life, willingly, and then had tried to convince myself it was out of my control.

But it *wasn't* out of my control.

I had let Apprentice Wiar place Lord Dust's sigil on my flesh because I wanted the protection it afforded me.

And last night, I had agreed to let Veylar Dust place another sigil on my chest because I was willing to make the sacrifices necessary for the power I *chose* to have.

The power I now chose to use.

* * *

THE ASSASSIN GRIPPED THE CROSSBOW AND MOVED CLOSER to get a better aim at my back. He wasn't going to kill me with his sword, as that would bring him within my reach, and he didn't trust that I was no longer a threat.

On that score, he was right, but his proximity didn't matter.

I rolled over onto my back again, which gave the assassin less of a shot. He took another step closer so that he could aim down at my torso.

Lira Shyold's voice floated up from below.

"You have injured me, Veylar Dust. You have weakened me. But I have power enough to destroy you now. You should have accepted Lord Skeloc's offer. But now, all you are, all you have, will become like your namesake...dust."

I drew my hand over the gaping wound in my shoulder, covering it with blood. As the assassin prepared to shoot me, I smeared that blood over the sigil on my chest.

My pulse pounded in my ears as the entire room grew dark, and I felt a great pressure on my chest, as if a considerable weight had been placed there. The assassin did not realize something was wrong at first. I assume he believed it was the work of the apprentice in her final attack upon the sorcerer.

Regardless, the shift to darkness caused him to pause. It was enough to save my life.

In the deepest shadows around us, dozens of glowing red eyes appeared. The assassin gave a start and brought his crossbow up in front of him, the bolt no longer aimed at my heart. A deep hissing, slithering sound rose in volume around us.

The shape of the sigil burned on my chest and I realized I could taste the air. I knew exactly what was happening in the foyer below me. In my mind's eye, I could "see" every part of this room.

Veylar Dust lay just inside the door leading out to the street. The crossbow bolt impaled him where his neck met his collarbone, and a reddish-black liquid that only vaguely resembled blood oozed from the wound.

Lira Shyold stood over him, her skin melting off the left side of her face, her right arm broken and twisted at odd angles. She had raised her good arm and was summoning the power to crush the remaining life out of the sorcerer. Veylar Dust was trying to hold on to enough power to resist, but it slipped away from him like smoke.

The apprentice to Lord Skeloc did not notice the red eyes in the deepening shadows. She was intent on completing her task for her master. She did not hear the slithering noise as a huge serpent composed of shadows and bearing red, glowing eyes emerged from the darkest corner and moved toward her unprotected back.

At the same time, on the balcony where I lay, a dozen smaller serpents the thickness of my leg began to move forward towards the assassin. Some slithered along the floor while others appeared to stretch out of the shadows at waist or head height. The assassin let out a low moan as he realized they were coming for him.

He fired his crossbow at the nearest snake, and the bolt passed harmlessly through it to embed itself in the wall. The assassin dropped his crossbow and lunged for the stairs in a desperate attempt to escape the building before the snakes could grab him.

He was not nearly fast enough.

The assassin had barely begun to descend when three shadow serpents stretched out of the darkness and wrapped themselves around him. One twisted around his neck, one around his waist, and the last around his legs. He was lifted off the stairs, struggling against the terrible strength of the unnatural creatures.

The huge serpent behind Lira Shyold reared up and opened its huge mouth, revealing black fangs as long as my hand. As the apprentice prepared to let loose her power on Veylar Dust, the serpent struck, plunging its fangs into her shoulder and neck. One of the fangs entered her flesh in the same spot the crossbow bolt had impaled Veylar Dust.

A terrible scream erupted from Lira's throat as her body began to convulse. I could see the sorcerous power she had gathered trying to escape, but she seemed unable to release it. She lost control of the energies, and they began to consume her from the inside.

The serpent struck again and again, and a bubbling froth poured out of the wounds caused by those immense fangs. Lira's body dropped to the floor, and I heard her bones begin to snap as her muscles contracted with the power flowing through her.

She kept screaming as the serpent plunged its fangs into her chest and began to drag her back into the shadows.

I looked over at the assassin as he, too, was dragged back into the darkness. The serpent around his neck had cut off his air supply, and he made no sound as he was pulled out of sight. His wide eyes were last things I saw, staring in terror out of the darkness.

And then the shadows covered him.

Lira's convulsing body was dragged into the shadows below, and her screams were suddenly cut off, as if a door were slammed shut. The glowing pairs of eyes winked out one by one, and when there were no more, the shadows retreated until the room was lit once more by the partially shuttered lantern that still sat on the floor below me.

The sigil went cold for a moment and then the sensation faded.

Fighting waves of nausea, I pulled myself to my feet and carefully made my way down the stairs. When I reached Veylar Dust, I was sure he was dead. His unseeing eyes stared up at the ceiling and his chest did not move with breath.

I jumped when he suddenly spoke, though his voice was barely audible.

"Pull...the bolt from...my neck."

"Won't that kill you fast—"

"*Now!*"

I grabbed the end of the crossbow bolt and yanked. A surge of energy flowed up my arm as the bolt came out of the wound, and I was flung backwards to land unceremoniously in a heap on the floor. My heart hammered in my chest, much too fast. Spots swam in front of my eyes and I felt myself blacking out.

A blast of foul air hit me, and I realized Xiqon had just appeared to gather up Lord Dust. Before I could blink, they were both gone. I gasped for breath as the darkness closed over my eyes.

And then rough hands grabbed me and I lost consciousness.

Chapter Thirty-Nine

THE UTTER BLACKNESS CROWDED AROUND ME, A physical thing that suffocated me, crushed me, wouldn't let me move. A thousand pairs of red eyes, serpent eyes, stared at me, watched me.

I could not see anything save those eyes, constantly shifting as the snakes of living shadow slithered over and around each other. A constant susurration—of thousands of dry scales sliding over one another—was a continuous background to my struggles.

I tried to breathe, but something was wrapped around my throat, blocking my air. My lungs were bursting, but I was still conscious somehow. I continued to struggle, trying to escape the darkness, trying to escape the serpents.

And then a huge pair of serpent eyes rose before me. These were yellow where the others were red, with black vertical slits that melted into the utter darkness behind. I felt something flicker over my face and realized it was tasting me with its forked shadow tongue.

"Do not struggle. You cannot escape this place."

The voice was low, sibilant, merging into the slithering sounds coming from all around me. I kept trying to break free.

"All others we kill. We bring them here and feast on their essence. You shall not be killed. You will serve me. You will serve my purpose."

The eyes came in closer and I could feel a chill breath on my face.

"You must first be made ready."

The red eyes closed in from all sides.

*   *   *

I BOLTED UPRIGHT, GASPING FOR BREATH. I WAS IN THE FAMILIAR bed in my familiar room in the Tower of Dust. It took me a moment for my racing heart to calm down. The dream had been too vivid for my liking.

I looked down at the sigil on my chest and wondered what it meant. Was it just a dream, or had the snakes I had summoned really spoken to me? I would have to get more information from either Lord Dust or one of the apprentices before I used it again.

I had no idea how long I had been unconscious, nor how I made it back to the Tower. I pulled back the blankets and winced. Every muscle in my body hurt.

I had been stripped to my underclothes, and a heavy bandage covered the wound on my shoulder. Despite my overall aches and pains, I noticed the wound itself hurt far less than I would have expected. Perhaps I had received some special healing.

I carefully climbed out of bed and searched for my clothes, but only a simple robe lay draped over the small chair. I pulled it on and moved to the door. I heard no movement in the hall, and so I opened the door a crack and peered out.

The window in the hallway outside my room showed me an early evening sky, the angle of the sun's rays telling me it was perhaps another hour before dusk. I stepped out into the hallway and heard sandaled feet approaching from the stairs. I waited where I was until the servant came into view.

The young man gave a start when he saw me.

"Mister Zale, you are awake. Please let me help you back into your room. Master Quda has been instructed to come see you as soon as you woke up."

He tried to bustle me back toward my room, but I brushed his hands off me.

"I will get you back into bed and go find Master Quda."

"No, you won't. I have no intention of getting back into bed. I'm hungry and I want to head down to the kitchen to get some food."

The servant's eyebrows raised almost to his hairline.

"Master Quda gave strict instructions, Mister Zale! Please come back into your room. I will inform Master Quda and will return with food for you."

I considered it and decided not to fight too hard. I did feel pretty lousy, after all.

"Okay, fine, I'll get back in bed. You go find Master Quda, and then hurry back here with something to eat. No delays."

The servant nodded vigorously at me, and it made me tired just to look at him.

"Yes, Mister Zale. I will return with food shortly."

He scurried off down the hall and I heard his slippered feet slapping on the stairs as he descended. I returned to my room and sat on the bed to await Quda.

A soft knock on my door came a few minutes later. Quda opened the door just enough to poke his head around the corner and look in. He saw me sitting on the edge of the bed and thrust the door fully open and strode in.

"Lord Dust wants you to rest, Mister Zale."

So Quda was still being formal with me.

"Listen, Quda, I'm sorry. I have been reckless ever since my brother died, and I've let it get worse and worse until I was acting without thinking. More than once, it almost killed me. For some reason, it wasn't until I saw what happened to Sulid, until I spoke to him and heard his story, that I realized what I was doing to myself. I don't want to die, Quda. That's not just me saying it. I really know it now. I don't intend to take any more stupid risks or throw others into danger without thinking through the consequences. I won't be perfect—I'm still an impulsive person, but I'm going to try."

Quda stood there, looking at me, stern disapproval all over his face. He obviously wasn't ready to forgive me. He might never be ready.

"I am glad to hear you say these words, but I do not trust you, Mister Zale. I will need to see you act in the manner of which you speak before I decide if you are worth trusting."

I nodded at him but had nothing more to say that would help.

"I do miss our friendship, Mister Zale. Perhaps, if you have really come to terms with your past, we can be friends again."

"I'd like that."

"In the meantime, you have undergone a great ordeal, and have taken severe punishment. Lord Dust needs you healed up if you are to be of further use to him. That means more rest."

"When can I speak with him?"

Quda's face twisted as he fought to hide his true feelings about my question. I was pretty sure it was fear he had concealed.

"Lord Dust also needs rest."

"How bad is he hurt?"

Quda closed the door behind him and moved close to me. When he spoke, it was with a low voice pitched just for my hearing.

"Lord Dust is concerned about showing weakness to anyone outside of a very select circle. Should Lord Skeloc get wind of how much power Lord Dust has lost, we might find ourselves targets of a more…direct…attack."

"Is he strong enough to still be one of the Five?"

"Lord Dust is working on regaining his strength, but it will take time. You are the only witness to what happened last night, though Lord Dust told me enough to understand our situation."

"So no one but you can see him right now?"

"No, Apprentice Wiar and Nedes, and the Burning—"

He stopped.

"The what?"

"You saw the battle against Apprentice Delash. You saw what happened to Apprentice Megoen?"

I nodded.

"Her…injuries…are permanent. She has taken a new name, the Burning Crone."

A shiver ran up my spine. I could not picture Gisea like that permanently, aged and burnt by sorcerous power.

"Why doesn't she heal herself? Or get one of the other apprentices, or Lord Dust, to help her?"

"Everything comes with a price, Mister Zale. Especially power. The…Burning Crone has accepted her injuries as a price for her advancement. She is no longer an apprentice. She will be accepted as a full sorcerer soon."

That didn't make sense to me.

"I thought Apprentice Wiar would be the next sorcerer."

He shook his head.

"Every one of them is different. She has learned all that she needed to learn and has made a sacrifice worthy of her new power. Very soon, the Five will become the Six."

I sat there, too stunned to speak. I remembered the moment that I realized Gisea was impatient to rid herself of her humanity. Deep down, I kept hoping she would change her mind, that she would realize what she was giving up was too valuable to just throw away.

Instead, she traded it for more power.

I looked up at Quda.

"So, I guess I'm the only one who doesn't get to speak with Lord Dust."

"He will see you soon, Mister Zale. But not yet."

*   *   *

WITHIN A FEW DAYS, I WAS FEELING BACK TO NORMAL. I HAD gone in search of Sulid but heard from the servants that Gisea—I could not bring myself to call her by her new, chosen name—kept him in her chambers with her and refused to let him leave. I hoped he was okay, but I had sworn to not get involved in protecting him any further.

Quda and I started to talk a bit more. I told him everything that happened in the battle with Lira Shyold, though not the details of what I did with the sigil on my chest. I decided to keep that to myself, at least until I could speak with Lord Dust.

I returned to my room above the Sailor's Knot and retrieved my belongings. It was time to find a new home—too many people were aware of this location for me to feel safe there anymore. I would stay in the Tower until I could find another place. Jolin was angry at my departure, but then Jolin was angry at everything.

I had little else to do. I wanted to track down Relael Ochallum but knew better than to stir up that hornet's nest at this point. So,

I haunted the halls of the Tower of Dust and waited for my turn to speak with Lord Dust.

Two days later, I was summoned to his chambers.

The sorcerer sat in a large, wing-backed chair in the shadows beyond the window. I could not see his face clearly and he motioned me to sit across from him in the early afternoon light streaming between the heavy curtains. I was half-blinded by the sunlight, which obscured his features even further.

He wasted no time in getting down to business.

"The Church has chosen a new High Priest. I will be leaving the Tower this evening to travel to the palace for a meeting of the Council."

A horrible sense of foreboding came over me. I just knew who the new High Priest was going to be.

"Who did they choose?"

"A high-ranking priest named Zaisia Maumont."

I let out a breath as relief flooded through me. As usual, Lord Dust knew exactly what I had been thinking.

"Your worry was unnecessary. Relael Ochallum is a member of the Hidden, and does not have the political connections to rise to such power."

"Is it safe for you to leave the Tower of Dust?"

The sorcerer did not respond, and I realized he thought I was implying he was weak. I raised my hands in a gesture of surrender.

"I don't mean to say you cannot handle anything that comes your way. I'm just concerned that Lord Skeloc will take this opportunity to attack you directly."

"That cannot happen. There are certain…safeguards…in place to prevent such a confrontation within the palace."

I noticed something different about his voice—it was deeper, more guttural than it had been.

"What do you want me to do while you are at the Council?"

He considered my question carefully before answering.

"Your value to me is in your contacts, your knowledge of the underbelly of Ythis. You have damaged relationships over the past few weeks in pursuit of my goals. I want you to spend some time away from the Tower, repairing those relationships where you can, forging new ones where you must. I will summon you to return soon enough. I have a great deal of work that still needs to be done."

"What about Relael Ochallum?"

"You are to keep the Church at a distance. I want this situation to be given time to settle down. There will be other opportunities to pursue your personal vendetta against Ochallum."

"In truth, Lord Dust, I don't have a personal interest in him anymore. I'd like to kill him, of course. But that's more because I expect he'll cause us trouble in the future."

I paused, but he didn't respond. So, I then told him about my dream of the shadow serpents.

"As I told you when I gave you the sigil, it is not a power to be used lightly. Unpleasant dreams are a minor side effect, but unfettered use of this power can cause you greater difficulties."

I didn't understand—was he suggesting I shouldn't have used the power to save both his and my life in the battle against Lira Shyold? Again, he answered my unspoken question.

"You chose well, and performed precisely as I required. Your efforts turned the tide of that encounter—I fully recognize that. Your use of the sigil was necessary and timely. However, I expect you to avoid further use of this power unless the situation is equally dire. When the sigil is activated, your own body acts as a pathway between worlds, and you do not want that pathway to open unless you have no other choice."

"I understand. Thank you for the explanation."

I was about to stand when I remembered one other question I for which I needed an answer.

"When I needed to find Sulid, and Xiqon…read my mind…well, how did he find Sulid by doing that? I didn't know where Sulid was, so how could Xiqon see his location in my mind?"

"The boy's location was not in your mind. It was you, yourself, who was the connection to him. You provided the necessary link to allow Xiqon to find the boy."

This puzzled me.

"But he went through all my memories, back from before I even worked for you. How did that provide a connection to Sulid?"

"Your memories have nothing to do with the search for the boy. Your memories were the price you paid."

He said nothing more, and I realized what I had given up. Veylar Dust, through his demon, now knew every memory, every thought in my head. I held no secrets from the sorcerer anymore. There was little doubt in my mind that this would come back to haunt me in the future.

With that, our discussion was ended. I returned to my room and began to gather my belongings. I had just moved in here, but now I was leaving the Tower again.

I thought about some of those relationships that had been damaged through my actions lately. Could I get back in the good graces of the Wolf? Would Mossip have anything further to do with me? What had really happened to the Seer of the Tsojim?

I grabbed a couple of knives, secreted them in my usual spots, and headed back out into the streets of Ythis.

~ End ~

**More books in the Tales of the Undying Empire *series*
*are available in print or ebook at Amazon.***

Thank you for reading The Tower of Dust. If you enjoyed this book, please tell others about it. Honest reviews are also greatly appreciated and are the best way to help other readers discover new authors.

About Andrew J. Luther

Andrew J. Luther lives in Burlington, Ontario with his wife and son. He currently works as a communications professional in his day-job, but spends his spare time playing tabletop roleplaying games and writing.

You can keep up-to-date with Andew by joining his mailing list at www.andrewjluther.com or on Twitter @andrewjluther.